Marie Tierney lives in The Fens with her husband, son and two cats.

MARIE TIERNEY

Deadly Animals

ZAFFRE

First published in the UK in 2024
This edition published in 2024 by
ZAFFRE
An imprint of Zaffre Publishing Group
A Bonnier Books UK Company
4th Floor, Victoria House, Bloomsbury Square, London, WC1B 4DA
Owned by Bonnier Books
Sveavägen 56, Stockholm, Sweden

A CIP catalogue record for this book is
available from the British Library.

ISBN: 978-1-80418-190-4

Also available as an ebook and an audiobook

1 3 5 7 9 10 8 6 4 2

Typeset by IDSUK (Data Connection) Ltd
Printed and bound in Great Britain by Clays Ltd, Elcograf S.p.A.

MIX
Paper | Supporting
responsible forestry
FSC
www.fsc.org
FSC® C018072

Zaffre is an imprint of Zaffre Publishing Group
A Bonnier Books UK company
www.bonnierbooks.co.uk

To my husband, Steve, and my son, Joe

There is never only one, of anyone.

Margaret Atwood
Cat's Eye

PART ONE

Chapter One

Mid-May 1981, Rubery, South Birmingham

WHEN EVERYTHING WAS DRENCHED IN sleep, Ava knew it was time. She eased out of bed and, when her feet touched the floor, she became still. No stirring from her younger sisters in their bunks – only soft snores. The trick at night was to banish all thoughts and let instincts govern. She must be stealthy and quick: the Small Hours were called small with good reason – especially as dawn approached. The dark was not absolute, only monochrome, though the night was her ally, and never harmed her.

Her pupils were matt black and massive in the gloom. She cocked her head to one side and listened. Only the tick-tock of the clock. Her mother was sound asleep in her room at the end of the hall. Ava was the only thing awake.

She padded to the front door. She reached for her coat but did not put it on: the polyester lining rustled too much. No shoes: shoes were inflexible, rowdy. She tucked her pyjama trousers into her sock tops. Thick socks lent silence to movement. After thumbing the latch off, she gradually pulled open the door.

Cold air nuzzled without bite as she stepped out onto the communal gallery. She tucked a wad of tissue paper between the door and the frame. Although the latch was on, Ava couldn't risk either being discovered or being locked out. No moon, no mist: the ground dry as burned bone. Somewhere far away, a dog barked its warning to an unseen intruder. Ava's nose twitched – petrol, earth, stone. Her skin prickled and her belly quivered with anticipation and the excitement of being out alone in the dark.

The apartment block hunkered in its trench, and faced the looming bulk of the Quarry. She scurried along to the central stairwell, which stank of ciggies and chip fat as concrete steps ascended and descended into blackness. She didn't consider the noisy elevator. Ava swung her coat on, felt in her pocket for her blue pencil sharpened at both ends, retrieved her Red Book from behind the huge metal bin and exited the open foyer. She swept into the laburnum bushes that hugged the low wall of the property then stepped forward into the gap with a view of the street, silent as an abandoned film set. The street lights tipped everything in a pallid glow, and a strange peace wavered in it.

Ava surveyed the realm: no people, no animals. She straddled the wall, crouched, then ran for the sanctuary of the red telephone box on the corner of the next street. She pulled her hood over her face. She was darkness against darkness, therefore invisible.

Ava scampered to the dun maisonettes, to the last building in the row, which was a burned-out shell after a major fire the year before. It was supposed to be demolished but it still stood, its scorched walls buttressed by scaffolding, its immediate perimeter protected by a high wooden fence. Kids avoided it because they thought it was haunted and grown-ups avoided it because it was unsafe. There was a gap in the fence closest to where the communal front door used to be, and Ava squeezed through. She dashed through its hollow bulk to the backyard, which smelled of mulch and a milder version of the stink that had been permeating the district over the last week. There was a tiny patch of balding lawn framed by untidy heaps of rubble and swept ash. The orange lights from the A38 metres away illuminated the garden in sepia tones.

In the earth, she could make out a crescent shape made of twigs, widely spaced, some aligned with an object: a small cardboard box, a piece of wood, a metal bowl. Each thing covered or partially covered the remains of dead animals. Those carcasses, uncovered, were left open to the whim of the elements. A few years ago, Ava had created a secret roadkill body farm to feed her curiosity about dead things. It was both cemetery and laboratory and this patch of it was the only site enclosed, because if local children crunched through bones suspiciously batched in one small area with lollypop-stick tags then there would be an uproar. Therefore it was sprawled across the estate, arranged as if the dead animals had died in their places naturally and Ava would visit each subject once a week then record her findings in her Red Book. She noted how flesh decomposed in water, how much faster it decomposed in air, how much slower in earth; if temperature slowed it down or exacerbated the process; if corpses decomposed quicker beneath concrete slabs, in boxes; the effect of weathering and what time insect activity took place, the roles insects played in breaking down the corpses to skeletons. At the end of each study: she said The Rabbit's Prayer from *Watership Down* because she believed it was the only invocation good enough. She thanked them then buried them properly so they could rest in peace.

Here, her experiments were more concentrated and in total privacy. She flitted to each twig, like a moth collecting macabre nectar, lifted each object to study what lay beneath and record its progress. She had never observed how death behaved at night, and she was taking this opportunity to do just that, in the quiet stillness, while the occasional car zoomed past on the road nearby, her back to the light so she could quickly note her findings with her blue pencil in her Red Book.

A few weeks before, she'd found a dead adder on the Quarry. She'd never had a reptile specimen for her observations before so she'd placed it in her strange laboratory. In open air, and over the weeks, the snake's skin had flaked and blown away, and its form had eventually skeletonised. It glowed like a barbed Möbius strip carved in ivory.

Having completed the task in the garden, knowing she would have to return to bury her subjects properly in daylight, Ava decided to view her prize specimen and it was only a few feet away. She darted into bramble bushes, whose thorns tore skinny spite lines on her hands. She peeked out at the dip and rise of the embankment on which the big road bellowed. She could smell exhaust, and the malodour of rotting meat. She was close to the hidden place she'd found last autumn, situated in a place no kids went because why would they? It was in the corner of the embankment that met the fence of the maisonette's abandoned garden and concealed by a snarl of brambles beneath the roar of the road. It was a good place to conceal things and was the reason why she'd risked so much to see her latest find.

She was alert to subtle pressure changes; a reminder to beware. She reached into her pocket for the sharp blue pencil, and it reassured her. The cluster of psychiatric hospitals around had mythical maniacs escaping all the time. Just because there were no people around didn't mean there were no people around. She didn't feel watched, however: there was no familiar weight of judgement on her back.

And Ava wasn't afraid, as it was impossible for her subjects to harm her. Because they were, after all, dead.

The Flyover murdered animals every day as did its feeder road, the Bristol Road South. Pets and wildlife alike were victims of the ceaseless, grinding traffic: metal monsters spat furry corpses either side, much too fast to eat them properly. Some of them died right before the horrified eyes of pedestrians, others more out than in. Ava used to cry when she came across the mangled remains but now her natural inquisitiveness trumped any childish sentiment left.

Over the past few months, the kills were fewer. Ava doubted it was because the road ran less traffic – if anything it had increased. Sometimes, there'd be evidence of a little death here and there – bloodstains or fur swatches – but the bodies were missing. It was why her latest find had become so important.

She'd discovered it two weeks ago, and it was her largest so far: a male fox (*vulpes vulpes* – 170 bones, 42 teeth), flung intact over the embankment, and hadn't been dead long by the time Ava found it.

She bolted for the corner, kept her head down, careful not to show her pale face under the florid lights. She ducked beneath the natural arch created by branches and found the fox just where she'd left him; stretched out on the hard-packed earth as if lazing in sunshine. The stench was solid, almost touchable. She frowned. There'd been warmer days the previous week but not enough heat

DEADLY ANIMALS

to generate such explosive ferocity. The fox was the largest creature she'd ever found but the smell was too *immense* to emanate from its sunken shell.

Ava observed that brown cocoons left by maggots after each moult littered the earth like bullet shells. There was desiccation around its head and limbs, and hide moths and beetles paraded in the split seams. There were too many green bottle flies: the cold made them slow but they were too numerous for night or for a cadaver this advanced with decay. Gem-bright *Lucilia caesar* weren't interested in mummified remains, and preferred juicier feasts for their babies. *Something wasn't right.*

Ava adjusted her position to avoid cramp in her legs, and it was then she was accosted by the full wave of putrescence. Her eyes, now accustomed to the gloom, followed the sordid march of sexton and rove beetles towards their manna from heaven. Her gaze crept further on, and then she saw him.

Mickey Grant.

Fourteen-year-old Mickey Grant had been missing for a fortnight. His school photograph had been on every news programme every day, local and nationwide. He'd vanished so utterly it was as if he'd popped out of existence. He might have run away because sometimes teenage boys ran away. It was possible he might be with family in a foreign land. After all, grown-ups said, it was rare for *boys* to be abducted: it was girls who were usually fiend's fare but nobody had seen Mickey since Deelands Hall disco two Fridays ago. Ava knew him as an unpleasant boy, a bully you couldn't walk past without him saying something spiteful. When he went missing, Ava hadn't cared.

But Mickey wasn't running and he wasn't safe with a far-off relative. He was dead. Slumped like a thrown scarecrow: a writhing slope of maggots that undulated in blubbery waves as they rose to breathe before plunging down into the stinking recesses. Viscous juice oozed into the drip-zone beneath. The once blond hair was patchy with despicable fluids.

Ava wasn't scared. She wasn't a girl who screamed even when hit, yet she sought inside for panic, terror or disgust and found

7

nothing but useless pity. She took mental photographs, recorded the entire scene for her Red Book. He *hadn't* been in this space two weeks ago. This wasn't the kill-site, this was recent waste disposal.

Putrefaction had advanced, though Ava judged him to have been kept in a relatively cool place for a while before, but she'd no experience with such big furless animals. She wished she had a torch. Ava shifted position, out of the stench corridor: rotting flesh was a heavy scent that could be carried home on clothes and hair. She wouldn't be able to disguise it with a spray of Mom's Tweed.

She could just make out familiar circular wounds etched along his forearm: human bite marks. Murder stained below and tainted above. Mickey Grant was carrion, as much so as the fox lying a few feet away, and all three shared a grim tableau. His parents would be devastated, and they seemed such nice people on telly. He'd been dumped here on purpose, as if whoever had murdered him had known the den was there, as if tipped as an ideal hiding place for the worst of secrets. Dead things were heavy and unhelpful when it came to changing their location. Ava scanned her surroundings: there was nowhere for a killer to hide on the grassy embankment.

Even though her common sense told her that the killer was long gone and not likely to be watching a girl out in the night on her own when she shouldn't be, it was time to go.

Quickly, Ava said The Rabbit's Prayer over the animal and to Mickey's ruined face. She remembered good things about him: how he used to stroke every cat in the street, and smiling when he walked his dog, Starsky. She backed out of the hollow.

Ava scuffed her footprints with a twig. Footprints were bad news even if her feet were small for a thirteen-year-old, and there were a great many thirteen-year-olds in the world. She fled the den, and adrenaline ensured she thought of nothing else until she took a breath behind the telephone box. Nine-nine-nine calls were free, and if she disguised her voice nobody would ever know a girl had found the missing boy. Ava didn't *have* to call the police but she *did* have to: it was only right. The kiosk was brightly lit and she risked being seen, but it faced away from the road so, if she was quick, she could be back in bed in minutes. Ava swung the heavy door open on its leather hinges, grabbed the clunky receiver and rang 999 before she changed her mind. She'd no idea which Voice would arrive out of her mouth but when the operator at the other end said, 'Emergency Services. How can I help?' it was Mrs Poshy-Snob who spoke up.

'Hello? Yes! The police please – *immediately*. Mickey Grant, the *missing* boy, is lying in bushes on the embankment of *Rubery Flyover*.' Mrs Poshy-Snob was a woman with a low voice, flawless diction, and took no nonsense. 'At the rear of the *abandoned* garden off *Homemead Grove*.'

There was a pause then the controller said, 'Do you need an ambulance as well, Mrs ... ?'

'An *ambulance*? No, dearie! He's *dead*.'

'Er ... Who are you?'

'*Please* be quick. His poor *mother* needs to know where he *is*.'

'Is this a joke call, Mrs ... ?'

'Really? *Do* I *sound* as if I am joking? *Do I*? At two o'clock in the *morning*? You *sound* like a clever chap so *do* get on. *I* was out walking my dog and I found Mickey Grant.' People were always finding dead bodies whilst walking their dogs: it was like a rule. People were always walking their dogs at stupid times of the night. It was always so on *Police 5*.

Strange, though, how no dogs – or any other opportunistic scavenger – had tugged at Mickey, and those bite marks were human. Ava hung up. Outside her front door, she composed herself, tried to halt the heavy panting so that she could ease back inside and quietly close the door. She'd seen her first dead human body and she was fine; she hadn't vomited or cried. Her heartbeat ticked in time with the hall clock. She removed her socks and rolled them into a ball. She would wash then hide them as if tonight's adventure had never been but they smelled of mud and nothing more. She sniffed the skin on her arms and the ends of her hair: just her, not Mickey. She washed her hands quickly in the sink. She couldn't hear sirens and her hope sank. The police weren't coming: they hadn't believed Mrs Poshy-Snob. She was too tired to think about it and she couldn't do anything except crawl into bed and sleep.

Ava had just settled beneath the blankets when Veronica slurred from her cave bunk, 'You smell of winter, Avie.' She rolled over to face the wall.

Ava immediately dropped into slumber, as if from a great height into a woolly void, her body curled around her damp hands, the balled socks at her feet, her breathing regular: her dreams untainted – if she dreamed at all.

Chapter Two

SETH DELAHAYE RESENTED DAYS OFF. It was difficult for him to sit still, to be simply Seth and not detective sergeant. He stood at the window and looked out at the street at night.

His flat was on Wheeley Road. The street had a dark history: in 1959, a young woman, Stephanie Baird, had been mutilated and murdered by Patrick Byrne at a local YWCA hostel, a mansion converted for short-stay accommodation. The murder had shocked the city – not only due to the killer's blasé, bloodstained escape on a bus but because Stephanie had been decapitated, and a cryptic little note had been found at the scene:

This was the thing I thought would never come.

Byrne was detained eventually, and imprisoned. The building was demolished, and a bland apartment block took its place, with horror now clawed into its foundations. Delahaye doubted its residents were even aware they lived on contaminated ground.

Delahaye loved Birmingham – even its Brutalist city architecture which jostled amongst the great Georgian and Victorian soot-stained buildings. He loved its proud industrial history, and its gruff, honest people with their off-kilter, ironic sense of humour. It was as different from London as London was from Lancaster, his hometown.

In Delahaye's own tale of three cities, the only one he couldn't bear to return to was London. Murder was as constant as the flow of the Thames in London, but in Birmingham murder was a staccato event. And somehow more savage when it occurred.

Delahaye sipped a tumbler of Scotch as the Small Faces on the stereo soundtracked his thoughts. Family photographs sat foremost on the mantelpiece, his old boxing trophies tucked behind. On a shelf, among his books, stood his framed graduation certificate from Hendon, alongside a photograph of him and his classmates in their parade uniforms, unsmiling. He'd no idea where most of those faces were now.

He was home but his mind was elsewhere. Being a police officer was a calling and being a detective meant he was an eternal student, always learning on the job in the college of life, where people were tutors who always changed the lesson plan.

It was then his telephone rang.

Chapter Three

SATURDAY WAS *TISWAS* DAY!

It was also Daddy Day. In a brief flash of happy, Ava forgot. When she heard her mother's voice in the kitchen she remembered, as Mickey Grant's decaying face appeared behind her eyes.

Her mother's boyfriend, Trevor, wasn't around. If Trevor had been around last night, Ava would never have dared go out and certainly would never have discovered Mickey. She supposed she should've thought *Poor Mickey* but she didn't. Nor did she think he *deserved* it. After all, Mickey had been fourteen not forty, and would now never get the chance to become a better human.

When Ava walked into the kitchen, her mother said, 'Ava, they've found the missing boy. It's all over the news it is, poor sod.'

Before Ava could respond, the letter box clanked. Half frowning, half smiling (Mom hoped it was Trevor – Ava saw her mother's mind as clearly as a large print Mr Men book), she answered the door. It was one of their neighbours, Susan Shaw, with ciggie in hand, in a dressing gown. Colleen Bonney nattered with Susan about Mickey Grant, and Ava heard men's voices in fore and background, the shutting of doors, the sudden fall to a whisper as Susan said, 'I haven't seen this many police round here since Gail was killed last year, poor babby.' Pregnant teenaged Gail Kinchin had been accidentally shot dead by police as her boyfriend used her as a human shield. It had happened in the next street.

Veronica stood beside Ava and held her hand as Rita ran down the hall, pushed past her sisters, eager to charm whoever was at the door.

'They found him then,' murmured Veronica.

'Hmm,' said Ava. The Passions sang about German film stars from her mother's radio. Next door's doorbell buzzed. Susan stood back, flicked ash, took another drag, and said to someone out of sight, 'Edna's gone out, sweetheart.'

'Thanks.' Ava's ears pricked: a man's voice with a Northern accent. 'I'm Detective Sergeant Seth Delahaye – West Midlands Police.'

He stepped into view and showed them his warrant card. The detective was sinewy, as tall as Dad, taller than Trevor: immaculate in a tailored navy suit under a brown leather jacket but the hems of his trousers legs were muddied. There was a walkie-talkie at his hip. Ava sidled closer to pick up his scent and there it was – night-flesh under faded cologne, and not the cheap stuff. He had short thick hair, a prominent Nigel Havers nose, and a well-trimmed moustache. His gaze was direct and not for sale. He was a little older than Colleen, and attractive in a severe, old-fashioned way, out of step with the modern suit. Still, his presence turned Colleen fleetingly pleasant even though attractive evidently wasn't her type, judging by her infatuation for pug-ugly Trevor.

'I'd like to ask you a few questions, please, Mrs—?'

'Bonney,' said Colleen. She moved her hands so the wedding ring she still wore was visible.

'And . . . ?'

'Mrs Shaw,' said Susan, aware she was in her dressing gown whilst Colleen obliterated in her new sweater and tight jeans.

'Is this about the Grant lad?' asked Colleen; all dazzling eye contact, pecking for fresh admiration.

'Yes,' said Delahaye.

'I wouldn't want to break the news to his mother,' said Susan.

'Nor me! You'd have to be hard as nails. You get me?' Colleen folded her arms. Ava could see that the detective already disliked her mother because Colleen made it seem as if everyone was somehow beneath her.

'Was he murdered then?' Susan asked.

'Ooh, I don't want to know,' said Colleen with a fake shudder. Or a real shudder – it was hard to tell.

'We don't know at the moment,' said the detective sergeant. Ava knew there would be a post-mortem. There hadn't been much left to post-mortem.

'Who found him then?' asked Colleen.

'Somebody out walking their dog,' said the detective sergeant.

'It's always "somebody out walking their dog", ay?' said Susan.

Very few people in this area walked their dogs on a lead as most people let their dogs out to foul and fight in the streets. It was why there was so much dog poo around. The detective sergeant asked if the women had known Mickey and both said no. Ava was almost to the open door, Veronica's hand in hers, shy but not as shy as they used to be.

The policeman's gaze settled on Ava and Veronica standing behind their mother; and Ava blushed but didn't look away. She was aware of her faded, baggy pyjamas, her index finger keeping place in *The Plague Dogs* novel at her side. Veronica squeezed the fingers of her other hand, and Ava squeezed right back. The detective didn't bend to condescend but flipped over a page in his notebook and then said, 'Did you know Mickey Grant, young ladies?'

Startled, Ava froze. Veronica tightened her grip on her sister's hand. Her mother performed a fake startle then a withering look. There was no need for her scorn but she had a male audience so maybe she felt she had to prove something. Though what that was Ava had no idea.

'Oh! I swear Ava's like bloody creepin' Jesus!' Colleen's hand flew to her chest as if to quell a heart attack. Colleen deeply irritated Ava because she was always trying to act 'classy' but she was little more than a vain doll with a thuggish temper – sort of like Marchpane from Rumer Godden's *The Dolls' House*.

'Yes, Detective Sergeant,' said Ava. 'He smelled of Zest soap and Orbit chewing gum.' She knew her voice was surprisingly low for a girl, people had always told her. 'He liked animals, especially cats.' Veronica nodded in agreement. The policeman stepped forward so that the mother had to stand aside in the door jamb.

'What's your name please, Miss . . . ?' the sergeant asked as he wrote her response down, as if it was something important for him to record.

'Ava Bonney,' said Ava. She squeezed her sister's hand. 'This is my sister Veronica.'

'Thank you, Ava and Veronica,' said Delahaye.

Ava's youngest sister barged forward and declared to the detective, 'I'm Rita!'

'Good for you!' said Delahaye. His gaze switched back to Ava. 'What was Mickey like, Miss Bonney?'

'He was horrible. He spat at us,' said Ava, without hesitation. 'He threw gravel at Veronica's eyes . . . and he said disgusting things.' Veronica nodded. Mickey had been a troglodyte, a *trog* – a bully.

'Don't speak bad of the dead!' snapped Colleen, and both girls flinched, expecting a cuff across the face.

Delahaye's tone was sharp. 'He spat at your daughters, Mrs Bonney. He threw stones and said awful things. I'd consider such behaviour towards them intolerable.'

Ava and Veronica hadn't told their mother about Mickey Grant's behaviour because she wasn't a mother to defend her own children. Colleen Bonney rarely indulged in self-reflection so his comments were met with silence.

'The emergency call was made from the telephone box on the corner of Rubery Farm Grove at twelve past two this morning,' he added.

Ava gulped: they could trace the telephone numbers of public telephone boxes to their exact locations.

'Weird time to be walking a dog, ay?' said Susan. 'Dodgy as you like, that is.'

Ava rolled her eyes and she noticed the detective saw her do it. He almost smiled.

'The recording of the call will be on the news tonight,' he said.

'Will they be in trouble?' asked Veronica.

The detective smiled. 'No, they won't be in trouble. We just want to talk to them, ask them about what they saw, and thank them for finding Mickey.'

'I hope we don't have one of them mass murderers,' Susan mused.

'Well, if he kills boys he won't show interest in my girls, will he, ay?' said Colleen.

'The Moors Murderers,' said Ava.

'Trust *her* to bring that up,' said Colleen to the policeman.

Why her mother had said that was beyond Ava: she never talked to her mother about such things if she talked to her mother about anything at all. Good question: what *did* she ever talk to her mother about? Not much.

He closed his notebook, his gaze only on Ava. His eyes were dirty blue, large and piercing and they smiled before his mouth smiled, which created a deep dimple in his cheek. 'Go on, please, will you, Ava.'

'The Moors Murderers killed girls *and* boys,' she said, then stopped. She could mention Peter Kurten, who had murdered *everything* from the age of nine but self-preservation silenced her in time. If she bit down on her lip any harder it would bleed, and this was not the time to enjoy it.

'That's true, Ava, they did,' said Delahaye. 'Excellent point well made.' In the background, a theme tune caught the girls' attention.

Veronica and Rita said, *'Tiswas!'* and fled as if summoned. Delahaye extended his hand and Ava shook it with solemn regard.

'Thank you very much, Miss Bonney,' he said. 'You've been very helpful indeed.'

Ava nodded; then joined her sisters where she stared at the TV without actually watching it. Her mother entered the room, crossed her arms and leaned against the jamb. She glared at her eldest daughter, her desire to strike palpable in the air. Ava watched sexy Sally James strut in long boots amongst the audience but she used peripheral vision to note her mother's position; her back braced and her jaw tense. But Colleen only turned away.

Chapter Four

'**D**ADDY!'
They were going to visit the Birmingham Museum and Art Gallery, one of their regular haunts, and Ava couldn't wait. Mike Bonney was accosted by his daughters, who sought through his pockets with the thoroughness of macaques, and he handed them each a tube of sweets. They tore off the wrapping, and devoured them rapidly, as if they'd never had sweets before.

'Like gannets, they are,' said Colleen even though she didn't know what a 'gannet' was. She let them go with Mike without further comment, still feeling sore from Detective Sergeant Delahaye's mordacity.

They took the flats' gloomy stairwell instead of the lift, their voices echoing as if in caves. Ava had had to move her Red Book from the alcove behind the bin because the police might search everywhere for clues so she'd had to tuck it behind the large heavy wardrobe in the girls' bedroom.

Outside the block of flats, there was no sign of Trevor: his recent car, an Austin Princess, wasn't parked outside his flat. There was no sign of anyone, and no traffic going up or down Cock Hill Lane.

Mike tutted. 'Come on! We've a bit of a walk.' He shook his head. 'Police have blocked off everywhere.'

'Did they ask you questions, Dad?' Ava asked in a cheerful voice. She was getting good at this impersonation of Normal Girl. It was even better than Mrs Poshy-Snob, Northern Lad and even Tennessee Tara.

'Yes, but I couldn't help them, though. I didn't know the poor kid,' said Dad.

They walked past Deelands Hall, the last place Mickey had been seen alive, past the local shops outside which the two self-employed delivery boys, Nathaniel Marlowe and Karl Jones, sat chatting on their bikes with large trailers at the rear. Karl ignored them but Nathaniel tipped an imaginary hat at the girls.

Dad switched the radio on as he drove the Ford Anglia along Callow Bridge then through the Village. As they neared the scene, Ava fell silent.

The Flyover loomed alongside them like a concrete behemoth, and the car turned in below it then out the other side. Ava craned her neck to see. There was a white tent in that far corner with people in overalls pointing out things to the police. A long line of uniformed police officers were walking with spooky slowness across the embankment, their eyes focused on the ground, looking for evidence. There were police dogs: German Shepherds. Ava didn't worry, though: the dogs were trained to look for more specific scents and, even if they sniffed their way to the Bonneys' door, Ava might have some explaining to do but she still hadn't killed Mickey.

White tape, uniformed police and flashing lights sealed off Cock Hill Lane's basin. Dad swerved right and then they were on their way, soundtracked by 'Fade to Grey' on the radio, a song that always transported Ava to another world. The Bristol Road South took them past their school to The Austin, the gargantuan car factory that dominated the area with its myriad roadways, huge plains of stationary new cars, stained brown buildings with mullioned windows, and thousands of men workers.

Dad asked about school and Ava answered with indifference. She suspected he knew how bad it was without being told. Ava swung the conversation to TV and music – but not the news. Ava was experienced at keeping secrets. The only person in the universe she trusted was her closest friend John but he was away on holiday visiting his dad in Ireland so wouldn't be back until next week, and she didn't even know if telling him would do any good. But John was sensible when it came to the serious things, and talking to him always made her feel better. There was no point telling Dad: he'd make his lips tight as a cat's arse then take them home so Mom would have to deal with it.

Why had she spoken up? Why had she told Delahaye about the Moors Murderers? Around strangers, in front of their mother, she usually remained shy and silent but there'd been something about the detective. Like her English teacher, Mrs Rose. Both made her feel it was safe to speak up, to be listened to, to be considered as a person. It helped that she'd really liked looking at him, the way she liked looking at David McCallum in *Sapphire and Steel*.

Ava daydreamed, and switched off for once until Dad patted her hand. Ava again wondered if her father felt guilt about having left them, not so many years ago. When he'd gone, life had been frightening: they'd no money, hiding from the Rent Man and the Telly Man and from any man who suddenly felt bold enough to make ugly passes at Colleen when they knew there was no husband to protect her.

Ava became a surrogate husband, therapist, cheerleader, guard dog and scapegoat. She was forced to write letters to the Solicitor and the DHSS because her writing and language surpassed her mother's: complex, adult correspondence she was expected to produce on command. Relentless worrying, and repeat visits to the DHSS building they had to pretend they never visited because of their mother's shame in having to. With its stuffy waiting room and dead-eyed clerks; Colleen's children lying around her feet like exhausted hounds.

Ava knew already that, if she was to survive childhood, she not only had to *understand* but she also had to make excuses, lie, keep secrets; keep her misery silent. Her mother was exhausting. Colleen saw all women as competition in a non-existent pageant, and any woman who slighted her in any way was 'just jealous'. Though jealous of what, Ava had no idea. Colleen was beautiful, but she was also a poor single mother with three children packed in a tiny flat, and a dodgy boyfriend no one was supposed to know about yet everyone did. People in glass houses shouldn't throw stones – especially if that glass house was mostly mirror and the only view was an embittered reflection.

The girls couldn't talk about *this* and couldn't mention *that*. They were Colleen's Mirror-Mirror-On-The-Wall, and Christ help them if their response was anything other than You Are, Mommy. Colleen was a terrifying short-cut troubleshooter who hit with anything to hand: hairbrushes, cutlery, keys; *Woman's Own*. She was irrational and her punishments were far too severe for the crimes committed. It was ridiculously scary how quickly their mother lost control. They were good girls due to fear, not love. They were scared of her and scared of losing her because she was all they had, and Ava could no more change things than she could change the weather.

The girls' relationship with their stepmother was complicated. Ava wanted to like Valerie but the woman had stolen Dad from Mom – that's what Mom always told them. They had to show loyalty to Mom, not only because it was the ethical thing to do but because Colleen so vehemently insisted on it, that the truth according to her was that Daddy had left *them*, not *her*, that his absence was *their* fault and not *hers*; that if they hadn't been born then he would've stayed.

* * *

They entered the museum through its majestic portico, Ava already happy as the familiar smells of old wood and stone settled on her like a welcoming touch. Voices echoed even though voices were hushed as in all mausoleums and the girls respected that hush, wanting to be good for their dad. In the art gallery, the sisters slid along the floors until their father whispered, 'Girls!' and they ran to his side, to listen and learn. He worked in the car factory but he should have been an artist, and he knew what he was talking about.

They loved the museum's zoology section: to Entomology – insects with their exoskeletons, their bones worn on the outside like armour. In Ornithology, Ava studied the flight birds' skeletons with their knees on back to front, their outsize rudder-like sternums, their hollow bones; their gossamer skulls.

In the Prehistory section, they laughed when Rita squealed with fright as she did every time the life-size model *Tyrannosaurus Rex* roared from concealed speakers. But Ava was at home with the

Mammals, especially the placentals rather than the marsupials whose skeletons always freaked her out. There were stuffed examples from every family, the old taxidermy worn through to suede in places. Ava studied the preserved beasts, wanting to know how the process worked, this craft of making animals last a little longer than mortality allowed. The polar bear (*Ursus maritimus* – 210 bones; 42 teeth) was close to the glass and Ava pressed her own cheek as if against its furry one, traced the lines of its massive head with her bitten fingernail.

'What part of the skeletons links mammal carnivores together?' her father asked her. Ava ransacked her brain for the main carnivore families: *ursidae, canidae, felidae, mustelidae* . . .

'The carnassial tooth,' said Ava, and her dad's smile of affirmation was worth a thousand tubes of sweets. Whole life stories were told through bones and their teeth – especially humans (*Homo sapiens* – 206 bones, 32 teeth). Bones exhibited behaviours under certain conditions: living bone had a lovely powder-blue tinge, and dead bone turned rubbery in acid, turned brittle when burned, and was especially beautiful when bleached.

She wondered about the fox, where he was now. She put her hand into her pocket and thumbed the tips of her blue pencil.

Chapter Five

L AID OUT ON A STEEL table, the corpse was a quiet atrocity, its reality almost impossible to comprehend: a once vital, noisy adolescent human stripped down to meat and mess. No amount of disinfectant could disguise its reek.

Yet the face was somehow recognisably Mickey Grant. Detective Sergeant Seth Delahaye presumed this was how the finder knew for sure it was Mickey Grant and not some other, random, corpse dumped in a place nobody knew about. Delahaye had worked homicide cases before, and he'd seen dead children, but he knew this was different. An implacable intuition bled dread.

The chief scene-of-crime officer, a forensic scientist who was only ever known as Mr Trent, had collected the clothing remnants carefully removed from the corpse. The rest of the SOCO team were still at the site. Delahaye left to cadge a cup of tea as the body was prepared for the autopsy. He needed respite, even if it was only to be found in a mug of weak Typhoo. His immediate superior, Detective Inspector Perrin, was with Mickey's parents. Delahaye preferred the morgue.

Time was a vital ally if evidence was gathered early but quickly became enemy when not.

Michael Anthony Grant was cut open and perused: samples then taken, bottled, labelled and stored to be sent on for analysis. Most of his organs had been pierced by the sharp points of his splintered ribs. His forearms were bent at oblique, unnatural angles, the skin punctured by fracture shards and circular marks. His face was pulled over his skull and his brain was removed, weighed, placed on a tray. A Y-shaped autopsy wound tracked raggedly down his torso. Much of the skin had sloughed away during the washing process. Delahaye swallowed down revulsion along with pity: neither helped.

The pathologist, Professor Simmons, was a tall woman, a little older than Delahaye, with eyes as blue as her face mask. She was accompanied by autopsy assistants: a slender young man called Hickman and a stocky powerhouse named Towler. Delahaye asked the relevant questions and received answers as close to the scientific truth as could be gleaned from disintegrating chaos. Time of death could not be accurately determined but the evidence suggested he was killed soon after going missing.

'Judging by hypostasis, he was in a seated position for a time,' Simmons said, her gloved hands and apron smeared with gorestains. She indicated the areas of darker discolouration. 'And he was kept in a relatively cool, dry place because decay would've been more advanced if he'd been left in the discovery site. The type of fly larva informs us he hadn't been there for long: those warmer days last week accelerated decomposition.'

'Rape?' Delahaye asked, because it always had to be asked.

'We can't tell,' said the pathologist. 'Bruising can be obscured by the discolouration. Semen degrades quickly, and a prolonged period outdoors with such robust decay ensures inability to detect it. Cause of death was a stab to the heart. The chest cavity appears smashed in by a large, heavy object, very likely before death but possibly after.' Simmons put her hands on her hips. 'There isn't very much blood left in him. And we can't tell how many wounds were pre- and post-mortem because of the state he's in.' Her eyes sparkled above the rim of her mask. 'Look at these . . .' She pointed out smaller wounds on the boy's arms, hands and shoulders – broken circles and crescents with uneven, almost serrated edges.

Delahaye looked then came closer. He frowned. 'Bite marks?'

'He's been mauled.'

'Mauled?'

'If you look here . . . and here, he has bites along his jaw, and the deeper ones on his neck are possibly an attempt to tear his throat. The injuries on his hands and forearms fit typical defence wound patterns – his hands in particular,' said Simmons. She indicated the more complete oval wounds. 'These holes are where flesh was pulled back as if the attacker was biting a moving victim, as if the victim was dragging himself away from the attacker. From the discernible marks, the perpetrator seems to have bitten in, tugged down, shook then pulled out.'

'Like an attack dog,' said Delahaye.

'Yes, *exactly* like an attack dog,' said Simmons. 'It could've been torture before he died or else part of the perpetrator's fight pattern.'

'Fight pattern?'

Simmons' eyes crinkled at the corners. 'Yes, DS Delahaye. Human teeth are still in our arsenal of physical weapons.'

'I suppose there isn't the possibility they *could* be animal?'

'No, the bites are very human,' said the pathologist. 'There's no deep upper and lower canine indentations and no carnassial impressions – humans don't have carnassials or long, curved canines like dogs. A forensic odontologist will take casts of the bites to see if we can get an imprint you could match to dental records but with the slippage so extensive, we'll be lucky to get a good cast.'

'Cannibalism?' Delahaye preferred the old-fashioned term: *anthropophagi*. Mention the word *cannibalism* and everyone panicked, then denied.

The pathologist and assistants glanced at each other. 'No flesh was removed. The typical areas of flesh usually found in historic cannibal cases are intact,' said Simmons. She pointed at the triceps, biceps, buttocks, calves and thighs as well as the back muscles – the usual areas taken for consumption in homicides where cannibalism was motive. She nodded to another table on which a sheet had been thrown. 'We also had this brought in with the boy.' She pulled off the cover.

It was a fox: its shrunken shell a russet outrage on the shining steel surface. Delahaye recalled seeing it when he'd shone a torch into the fetid den. It was the perfect place to hide a body in a built-up area: a person would have to be very familiar with the neighbourhood to know the sheltered enclave existed. It was, however, only the disposal site. Rubery was tucked beside a green belt, and the murder site could be anywhere.

'Roadkill,' said Simmons. 'Poor thing.'

Seth Delahaye stared at the animal. Two dead things found in the same spot. Mickey was also a *poor thing*, of course, even though he'd been a nasty little bastard by most accounts. But he'd been a nasty little bastard who'd had friends and potential. He'd been loved, he'd always be loved but he'd never learn how to be more of a good bloke, and it was a dreadful waste. *Poor thing* didn't even begin to cover it.

Chapter Six

THE FINE DRIZZLE UNDULATED IN the street lights as Paul Ballow left The Longbridge pub with Lucy in a haze of ciggie smoke and spent lager. Lucy pulled open an umbrella, and he joined her beneath it. The cars sloshed by, louder as they approached the breach of the Flyover, its concrete monstrousness rose then arched to divide the Village. Its stout pillars created pitchy voids beneath, and Paul saw Lucy's gaze switch to Rubery Hill Hospital. Lucy worked part-time at the hospital laundry but she was still unsure of the place, especially at night.

'Do you think they'll catch him?' she asked.

'I bloody hope so,' said Paul, thinking of his brother Matty.

'Do you think he's from ... *there*.' Lucy nodded to the asylum.

After a pause, Paul murmured, 'No, I don't.' There were more loonies out than in.

They walked up Cock Hill Lane until the Quarry's bulk over-looked them and, as a van whooshed by, its headlights cast a fan of light across a wedge of gorse. Lucy gasped, stopped in her tracks, and pointed.

'What the *fuck* was that?' Her eyes were fixed on the Quarry.

Paul, alarmed, followed her pointing finger. 'What?'

'There were eyes glowing in the dark. Like cat's eyes.'

Paul grinned. 'Then it was probably just a cat, Loops.'

Lucy wasn't convinced. Even in the street lights, he could see she was pale, her eyes focused on a point on the distant incline, and goose pimples rose in furrows along the skin of his arms. Cars were trundling up the Lane and the dual power of their headlights made her clasp the hem of his jacket as she pointed forward again.

'There! Quick! See?'

Paul saw. For a few fleeting moments, almost to the Quarry's uneven skyline, two large discs of gold reflected in the blackness, at least six feet from the ground.

'That's *not* a cat,' Paul murmured.

'An owl?' Lucy was transfixed as another car's headlights swept the same area again and this time the eyes were tipped, as if looking down at them.

'If that's an owl, Loops, that's a fuckin' tall owl.' He grabbed her hand and walked quickly, not quite running. When they slowed down, they laughed, out of breath.

'Probably a bear,' said Paul.

'We don't have bears in this country anymore!'

'We don't get tall owls either,' he joked, and then she kissed him.

Chapter Seven

THE GREEN FAMILY HAD ALWAYS been kind to the Bonneys, especially after Mike left. Their daughter, Becky, expert wrangler of temperamental pushchairs, had always been there to assist on day trips. She was older than Ava, and would leave school in the spring but she often accompanied Ava to school if Ava had to leave earlier than her sisters. Recently, however, Becky had a boyfriend, Kenneth, who was a member of the local punk band, War Dance, and they met every morning under the Flyover for a quick 'snog' before he left for college and she for school. Ava thought Kenneth was a patronising git but the others were civil to Ava; they gently teased her (if they weren't ignoring her completely) except for Paul Ballow who always said hello. Paul was the older brother of her friend Matty whom she'd known almost all her life.

The gang were smoking and chatting as the girls approached, Becky parting to give Kenneth a kiss, while Ava studied the others. Lucy, the singer, was cool, with a Debbie Harry vibe. The rest of the group were young men, and while Ava viewed young men akin to clumsy gorillas, these were human enough – especially Paul, despite his bristling Mohican.

Ava considered the graffiti on the walls. She read the band's name 'WAR DANCE' in its distinctive lettering and logo. Beside it was another graffiti message that seemed to be everywhere she looked over the past month:

BEWARE THE GRAB OF HARRY CA NAB!

Paul separated from the group, cigarette between his front teeth, to stand beside Ava. She liked him because she felt safe around him and he always treated her with respect.

'I wonder who our Harry is?' Paul asked referring to the graffiti she was looking at.

'I don't know. It's very neat and tidy. Not like . . .' She pointed to a very anatomically incorrect cock and balls scrawled above their heads. She couldn't resist a smirk. Paul shook his head in mock despair.

'I'd say Harry's trying to be a delinquent,' said Paul. 'Not really committing to a full-blown call for anarchy.' When Ava rolled her eyes, he grinned and asked, 'You like?' with a nod at his artistic handiwork. It was War Dance's insignia – a bloodstained arrowhead lodged between a W and a D.

Ava pretended to give the graffiti serious evaluation, like an art expert on *The Open University* programmes. 'It's a logo that will remain in the public consciousness for years to come.' She smiled. 'It'll look great on *Top of the Pops*.'

Paul huffed at her sarcasm, just as a silver Audi Quattro drove off the road and pulled up in the third arch. Its presence cancelled all the laughter and chat with immediate effect.

Car doors slammed and through the gap of the pillars walked a tall angular man alongside immaculate Detective Sergeant Delahaye. Delahaye recognised Ava but didn't say her name. Becky ran over, grabbed Ava by the wrist and pulled her away but Ava managed to steal a glance back: Paul winked at her and Detective Sergeant Delahaye gave her a small nod. Ava sensed the policeman and the punk were both good men in similar ways and it always helped knowing there were good men in the world because you never knew when you might need them.

Chapter Eight

DELAHAYE OVERHEARD ONE OF THE young men mutter to the blonde girl, 'Watch out, it's *The Sweeney*,' and she shoved him in the ribs. Their bandmates, Ben and Paul, straightened and snuffed out their cigarettes.

'Don't you ever go home, Detective Sergeant?' Paul asked.

'No,' said Delahaye. 'D'you mind if I ask you a few questions?'

'Not at all, Mr Detective,' said Kenneth. 'Go ahead. Make our day.' Detective Constable Steve Lines shoved his hands in his pockets and fielded their curious stares with great good humour.

They willingly gave their names and Delahaye asked, 'Did any of you know Mickey Grant well?'

'Not really,' said Kenneth. 'He was just around, hanging out with a couple of the older lads.'

'I did,' said Paul. 'His big brother, Joe, is one of my mates.' Corporal Joseph Grant would be home from Belfast to attend his brother's funeral.

'Were any of you around when he disappeared?' asked Lines.

They shook their heads, obviously too old for local discos in community halls.

'I bet it's Bob the Nonce that killed Mickey,' said Ben. 'I bet you a tenner.'

'We're looking at every possible suspect,' said DC Lines.

'You won't have to look far,' said Ben. 'He only lives near the Lickeys he does.'

'Mickey *did* spit at Aster once,' said Paul. 'Me, Joe and Mickey were walking past the outdoor when Aster came out with a bag of lager cans ...'

'Outdoor?' asked Delahaye.

'Off-licence', said Paul. 'Joe said, "Oh look, there's that pervy bloke" and Aster turned around so Mickey spat at him. It didn't touch him but the look he gave Mickey was furious.'

'*And* Mickey *did* have that run-in with the ice-cream man last year,' said Lucy.

'Did he?' asked Lines.

'Big time. Mickey pushed into the queue of kids and the bloke really told him off. Mickey gave him backchat and the ice-cream man actually came out of the van to give him a clip around the ear.'

'Do you know the name of the ice-cream man?' asked Delahaye.

Lucy shook her head, but Paul said, 'Pete Ancona. He drinks in The Longbridge pub most weeknights. His is the only ice-cream van that plays "Pop! Goes The Weasel".'

Delahaye liked this Paul Ballow. Like Ava Bonney, he spoke in full sentences containing a wealth of information.

'Mickey's bike and camera are missing,' said Lines.

'Mickey might've had a den somewhere,' said Paul. 'They could be there.'

'D'you know where that den was?' asked Lines.

Paul shook his head then said, 'Ask his friend, Dan Laws.'

'Ask any of the kids around the estate,' said Lucy. 'They've got a whole network of dens around here. I bet one of them could tell you.'

'Network of dens.' Delahaye wrote it all down. 'Anything else you could tell us?' He caught the glance Lucy and Paul threw at each other.

'There *was* something *weird* . . .' said Lucy.

Kenneth groaned. 'Not your spooky tale of alien eyes, Loops!'

'Yeah, but I saw it too,' said Paul. 'On Saturday night, we saw a creepy pair of eyes glowing on the top of the Quarry.'

'I wouldn't put it past a loony from the mental hospital having glowing eyes,' said Ben. 'We see some strange ones around.'

'Most patients in all the hospitals were accounted for on the night of Mickey's disappearance,' said Lines.

'Most isn't all, though,' said Ben.

'It was too tall to be an owl or a cat,' Lucy continued.

'There for a few seconds and then gone,' said Paul.

'It could've been anything,' said Lines.

'True,' said Paul. 'But what could that "anything" be in south Birmingham, with no natural predators, except a lunatic who killed a kid?'

'Could you show me where you saw these . . . eyes?' Delahaye asked, just as their lift arrived: a decrepit Ford van farting black exhaust.

'You go and we'll catch you up later,' said Paul.

Kenneth and Ben climbed into the back of the van and it pulled away. The small group walked to the Quarry, and Delahaye was glad he'd worn his jacket as they brushed through prickly bushes that tugged at their clothes.

'You wouldn't think this was all burned to a crisp five years ago, would you?' Paul said, halting. 'Here. Around here.'

They pointed at the ground. Delahaye and Lines looked to where the girl indicated. A series of footprints clearly marked in the damp earth. Their pattern was irregular; what looked like paw prints suddenly became human footprints further up the incline.

'Tall owl indeed,' Delahaye murmured.

Chapter Nine

BECKY AND AVA MADE IT to school just as the bell pealed for Registration. There was a rare whole-school *special* assembly, standing room only. Ava was aware of Brett Arbello's malevolent gaze drilling into the back of her head. Brett had been her nemesis, for reasons inexplicable, since nursery. She and her best friend at school, Maya Sandhu, sat in the midst of the Good Lads – Shawn Temperton (the hardest boy in their year), Tom Shelton and Matty Ballow. They were friends and allies. Around this island of nice were the seas of nasty: the spiteful Clackers who often stole from her or spat at her, the disdainful Cardboard Cut-outs with their backcombed manes sprayed into solid Elnett haloes; and then there were Brett's minions – the thuggish Trogs.

The headmaster snuffled his way through a speech about Mickey then waffled through another about why children should never talk to strangers. Some of the girls in Mickey's year were crying, and most of his friends were too shocked to join in.

Ava, not wanting to think of Mickey at all, had zoned out: she would be going to John's house at the end of the day to help celebrate his granddad's birthday as she did every year. She'd made a card for Mr Cadogan with a beautiful Welsh dragon on it. John would be waiting for her after school, and Maya would take Veronica and Rita home. Ava would trawl through this awful day just so she could have that happy occasion.

In the yard at lunchtime, Brett's runty mate Fred pushed Maya over. He sniggered as Maya got up and dug out the gravel embedded in her knee. To Ava, Fred, with his jagged Hartley Hare teeth, looked like he'd been blasted in the face with an incest grenade.

'How's your slag of a mom, Bon-bon?' Fred bleated.

'How's yours?' Ava drawled.

Fred marched up to her with an exaggerated gait, which was less 'hunky gangster' and more 'funky gibbon'. 'What *you* say, Bon-bon?'

Ava shrugged and slowly drew out her special, sharp blue pencil and, when he saw it, he backed off.

'You *wait*, Bon-Bon,' he said. '*I'll* get *Brett* on *you*.'

So, throughout the afternoon, Ava looked across the maths classroom to find Brett glaring at her. Her fear of him was perpetual, but she had adapted to avoid him – even though he made it his mission to seek her out. She had no idea why he hated her so much, and she'd given up guessing.

But maths had successfully pushed all thoughts of Mickey out of her mind. When a couple of the boys at the back of the room made farting noises, it set the whole class giggling, and because the teacher couldn't work out who was misbehaving, he decided to keep them all in for an after-school detention. When the home-time bell rang, the hordes of pupils streamed out until eventually the grounds became deserted. West Block's windows faced the main road, and she could see John waiting for her at the main entrance. John wasn't scared of other kids but as a Waseley pupil wearing his school tie, he'd be outnumbered by Colmers Farm pupils if they chose to react negatively to his presence so she could see he'd zipped his coat to the neck.

When their teacher eventually freed them, Ava walked outside, and recognised two prefects striding across East Block yard – Nathaniel Marlowe and Karl Jones. Both were impossibly handsome in different ways but Karl was a disdainful arsehole whereas Nathaniel was always friendly – Ava had never known a cruel word from him. He'd even given her a nickname – Lady A. Across the yard, he'd seen her too and he gave her a jaunty wave. She waved back as she rounded the corner, and saw John.

Ava had learned to ensure all aspects of her personal security were covered but she was so pleased to see John, so relieved the day was over, that she never heard Brett approach her from behind, his plimsolls ensuring his advance was silent. She saw John's eyes widen in horror.

'Ava!' His yell was a warning.

Brett punched Ava in the neck so hard she bounced off the wall and, as she rebounded into him, she quickly and instinctively stabbed her blue pencil into his hand then turned it so that the other sharp end pierced his thigh, making him yelp. There was no reason why he'd attacked her, no provocation on her part, and certainly no warning – he'd just wanted to hurt her. He could've punched her in the usual places – face, stomach, arms – but he'd deliberately aimed for her throat. John charged at him, and the boys fought, Brett's hand dripping blood onto the ground. Brett managed to escape John's grip and was about to kick Ava when the boy was suddenly thrown, literally, several feet away from her.

Nathaniel Marlowe towered over them. He regarded the squirming Brett with an almost academic curiosity, tilting his head as if considering the bully for a painful scientific experiment. As Brett struggled to his feet, his nose bleeding more than his hand, Nathaniel strode over and grabbed his shirt collar, lifting him off his feet then throwing him again, through the school gate. Brett saw him coming for him again, scrabbled to his feet and ran.

'Yeah, fuck off,' said Nathaniel, who then turned to face Ava, awestruck John, and a mortified Karl. Nathaniel took his bag from his friend. 'I'll see you tomorrow then, Karl.'

Karl nodded, obviously wanting to say something but too baffled to speak except for, 'Yeah.'

Ava subtly pocketed the pencil, sticky with Brett's blood. The boys hadn't mentioned the blood on the floor or noticed it on her hand, and she guessed it was because each thought they'd been the one to have made him bleed in the tussle.

Nathaniel turned his attention to Ava. 'Are you all right, Lady A?'

John gently drew her hand away from her neck and, judging by the boys' faces, the mark Brett had left on her throat wasn't pretty.

'Fucking *wanker*!' John spat in the direction Brett had fled. His anger on her behalf was too much for strung-out Ava so she burst into tears.

'Whoops! Now, now! Don't flood the school out, I'm shit at swimming!' said Nathaniel, who was quick to offer her his handkerchief. 'That's almost clean, that is. There's only one bogey on it from this morning.'

Ava laughed as well as cried, not caring her face was now a ruddy mess because what could she do about it? She looked up at Nathaniel with his high cheekbones and his auburn hair. The kirpan-shaped scar which curved its way into his hairline did little to obscure his appeal, and he had striking eyes – he was properly heterochromatic iridum with one eye darkest brown and the other brightest blue.

'What's your name?' Nathaniel asked John.

'John,' John said.

'That was a good tackle there, John.' Nathaniel dug into his jacket pocket, pulled out a paper bag and offered its contents to Ava and John.

'Have a cola cube,' he said. 'They're always good for what ails ya.'

Ava and John each took one of the small red cubes and popped them into their mouths. Ava was glad of the immediate tangy taste before the sweetness hit, the flavour always more cola than real cola. They were quiet as they ate their sweets.

'Thank you,' she said. 'Both of you . . . for . . .' She was starting to cry again.

'Shush!'!' Nathaniel demanded. 'Have another cola cube!'

Chapter Ten

DELAHAYE READ AGAIN THE INITIAL Missing Person report: Mickey was last seen behind Deelands Hall at 8.30 p.m., half an hour before the disco ended. His friends had told the police that Mickey had been his usual self, unworried by anything or anybody. Then he'd left, gone somewhere on his bike without telling anyone. He wasn't seen alive again.

WDC Olivia Gibson approached his desk with her notebook in her hand. She was a thorough and resourceful detective who always managed to find out information that eluded other officers, and he suspected it was because her previous job had been an investigator for a lost-heir-and-inheritance solicitor. The forensic analysis of the fibres found under Mickey's fingernails verified they'd been clawed from a purple carpet, and Gibson was assigned the exhaustive task of finding possible matches to it. 'Skip, about the purple fibres – I've been out and about in the local areas and in the city centre, visiting flooring stores and none of them has ever sold a carpet that colour ...'

Delahaye sighed but Gibson hadn't finished.

'I have a friend in West Mercia Constabulary who owed me a favour and she asked around carpet shops in Bromsgrove. One of them had fitted this colour carpet in a fashion boutique in 1972 but when she visited the shop, it had been refurbished and was now a café. The manager said they'd chucked the carpet in a skip ...'

'So, it's lost to landfill,' Delahaye said, disappointed.

Gibson shrugged. 'People pinch stuff from skips especially if it's in good nick. It could have been cut down into mats or the whole roll could have been recycled as a carpet.' She smiled sadly. 'Sorry it's useless info but you had to know, Skip.'

'Thank you, Olivia,' said Delahaye. He checked his watch and caught Lines' eye – it was time to talk to Mickey's closest friend, Dan Laws.

* * *

Mickey's older brother, Joe, had told Lines that he didn't know if Mickey had had a den, but Dan Laws informed Delahaye that, until the summer holidays of last year, they'd hung out in one of the lock-ups beside Quarry House block of flats.

'I think he had another hang-out but I don't know where,' said a tearful Dan. 'He'd started taking long walks by himself and when I asked him where he was going, he'd say, "somewhere else".' The boy shrugged. 'If I tried to follow him, Mickey would double-back home or I'd lose him in the gulleys.'

'Gulleys?' Delahaye repeated.

'The little passageways between back gardens,' said Dan. 'He said he wanted to be on his own more. I don't know why. But he was getting matey with a couple of the older kids like Karl Jones.'

* * *

Lines intercepted Karl Jones on his way to school, which plainly irritated the boy. Karl was tall, blond and good-looking, wearing an expensive pair of Wayfarer sunglasses and an air of superiority. He didn't know anything about Mickey's 'other' hang-out because he didn't hang out with Mickey. 'I talked to *him* when he talked to *me* but that's about it,' Karl said to Lines. 'We weren't, like, *mates*.' He sighed as if the interrogation was just too much. 'Can I go now?'

When Lines returned to the car, Delahaye smiled at his colleague's scowling face. 'How was your little chat with the Aryan Dream?'

'Moody little shit,' Lines muttered.

They drove up Cock Hill Lane and turned off at The Dowries, a short road of maisonettes and small semi-detached houses dominated by the apartment block. The wind whistled around the tall building as the two men exited the car and walked towards the cache of battered garages at its rear.

'Dan said third one along?' asked Lines.

Delahaye nodded. They faced the garage then entered its dingy interior. There were a couple of deck chairs, an old footstool, numerous cigarette butts as well as sweet wrappers and pop bottles.

'There's nothing here but rubbish,' said Lines, kicking a can into a dusty corner.

'Let's visit Mr Aster,' said Delahaye.

As with such cases, when it was acknowledged that the child victim hadn't run away but might have been abducted, the immediate suspects after the family were those people living within the county with criminal records pertaining to paedophilia – The Nonce Network as DC Lines charmingly referred to them. They had to be questioned about their whereabouts at the time of Mickey's disappearance. Detective Constable Kilborn had interviewed Bob Aster at the station after Mickey's disappearance during initial inquiries. According to DC Kilborn, Aster was very polite but aloof yet his alibi had appeared sound. His neighbours had no complaints about him because he kept 'himself to himself'. Six-foot tall, grey-haired and blue-eyed, Aster had once been a handsome man, but had been disfigured in an altercation while in prison. After a decade in prison, he'd lived the last four years in a secluded bungalow near the Lickeys. When local people initially discovered his address, his home had been vandalised and he'd been threatened. Because he went out in the daytime to go shopping once a week and went out on Friday nights to buy lager and cigarettes from the Village off-licence, he was mostly left alone except for the occasional altercation with local men when they were drunk. He also had a track record for occasionally living rough in squats or camping out in the more rural areas when he found the attention unbearable. He told Kilborn that he'd refused to move out of the area because he was 'too old to keep running'. He was on the dole but often worked as an odd-job man, and was an experienced gardener.

Uniform had searched around the house and property and found no evidence connecting him to Mickey Grant. Kilborn had written a concise report but Delahaye had noticed a slight inconsistency in the neighbours' statements. Both witnesses pointed out that Aster's routine of going to the Village off-licence at the same time every Friday night never changed. Aster's neighbour to the right, however, a Mrs Ellen Cutter, had noted a different time Aster had returned home from that of his left-side neighbour, a Mr Tim Hodder.

'Mr Hodder had stated that Aster had left his house at his usual time on a Friday night, about seven forty-five then had returned "around his usual time" which was habitually eight thirty. Yet Mrs Cutter reported that Aster arrived home "a bit later than usual, about nine thirty or so",' said Delahaye to Lines as they drove to Aster's address. 'His house is only a mile and a half away from Deelands Hall. A physically fit man like Aster could make the walk there if his intention that evening was to go that part of Rubery, and not the off-licence.'

'True,' said Lines. 'However, it stretches logic that Aster could make it to Rubery, kidnap and murder a teenage boy, dump him somewhere that wasn't where he was found, then race back home as if nothing had happened,'

'That's more than an hour's work, although if he'd had an accomplice with a vehicle . . .' said Delahaye.

'Not impossible,' agreed Lines. 'If he's given a lift most of the way home and walks the rest then he'd be a little late but not enough to concern the neighbours.'

'The trouble is still the complete lack of witnesses,' said Delahaye. 'He'd be recognised. Aster's pretty distinctive to look at anyway without his vile reputation.'

'His track record is befriending boys then luring them back to his home or an abandoned building to be assaulted,' said Lines. 'Snatching from the street *isn't* his MO.'

'It might be a recent development if he's recently acquired an accomplice with a car,' said Delahaye.

'Or *he's* the accomplice snatching a lad for someone else,' said Lines, a theory that Delahaye loathed to even contemplate. '*Or* he has his own vehicle which he is driving illegally. Aster hasn't had a driving licence since his arrest in 1967.'

They were driving along roads with detached bungalows with long front gardens, and surrounded by trees.

'Aster had motive to target Mickey,' said Lines. 'Mickey spat at him. I want to hurt people who spit at me.'

'But kill them?' Delahye asked.

Lines shrugged. 'Those discrepancies in the times weren't viewed as suspicious until those bites were found on Mickey.'

'Yes, but dental casts taken of the bites haven't matched any dental practice records yet. It doesn't help advanced decomposition distorted the imprints and made it difficult for accurate comparisons,' said Delahaye. 'Those bite marks are interesting because Bob Aster *had* bitten his victims during the sexual assaults. It *was* part of his MO and unfortunately there were no photographs taken of these wounds. Aster has never visited a dentist because he's never established the habit, having been born before the founding of the NHS and learned to live without dental care, free or not.'

'He could have gone to see a dentist in prison,' said Lines.

'According to WDC Gibson, who checked for that very detail, he never did because he apparently never had to. We're here.'

Aster's bungalow was secluded from the main road. The neighbours either side were close but far enough apart to almost mind each other's business. The property appeared well maintained to Delahaye as he and Lines approached the low-slung building.

'If he's in, be *nice*,' Delahaye said to Lines.

Lines tut-tutted. 'I'm *always* nice, Sarge.'

In Delahaye's experience cordiality always worked better than disdain and sarcasm – especially with paedophiles. DCI Brookes had wanted to bring Aster to the station again for questioning but DI Perrin suggested that DS Delahaye go to the man's home as a 'normal door-to-door' because he's more likely to answer questions with more than just 'no comment'.

Delahaye clattered the letter box and stood back. There was no boundary wall or fence separating the front and the rear of the property so Lines checked along the side passage in case Aster made a run for it through the back garden.

Bob Aster answered the front door. He was, even in his early sixties, powerfully built. His clothes were well worn but clean and his hair was clipped short. One side of his head was misshapen – his left brow bone was bulbous and slumped over his eye, reminding Delahaye of Charles Laughton's Quasimodo in the old *The Hunchback of Notre Dame* film. Aster had been attacked by another prison inmate wielding a hammer but the surgeons had managed to save his sight, and the sagging eye glittered as much as the other in the undamaged half of his face. He didn't look too perturbed by their presence on his doorstep.

'Good morning, Mr Aster,' said Delahaye as he and Lines showed him their warrant cards. 'I'm Detective Sergeant Delahaye and this is Detective Constable Lines.'

Aster crossed his arms. 'Good morning.'

'Just routine inquiries,' said Lines.

Aster looked him over speculatively. 'Aren't they always?'

'We just wanted—' Delahaye began but Aster cut him short.

'You just wanted to have a word with Bob the Nonce because he's the only suspect you have even though he's got an alibi?' Aster drawled. 'I answered police questions at the station when the boy went missing.'

'There are two reasons why we want to speak to you,' said Delahaye. Aster was obviously not going to invite them in for a cup of tea. 'The first is that there are time discrepancies in your neighbours' accounts of your whereabouts the night Mickey Grant went missing.'

Aster crossed his arms and leaned against the door frame. He regarded the detectives warily.

'Mr Hodder said you arrived home from your weekly visit to the Village off-licence around your usual time of eight thirty on a Friday night but Mrs Cutter stated that you arrived home about a full hour later than that. Can you account for what you were doing during that time, Mr Aster?'

'It's *only* an hour,' said Aster.

'A lot can happen in an hour, Mr Aster,' said Lines.

'It can,' said Aster. His crystalline gaze flickered from Lines's mouth to crotch then back again, a ploy to rile the young policeman, and Delahaye was relieved his colleague didn't rise to the bait. 'But it doesn't matter what *I* say, does it?'

'*Can* you account for that hour, Mr Aster?' asked Delahaye patiently. 'If so we can possibly dismiss you from our inquiries.'

Aster sighed, rolled his eyes. 'I was late back because I had to hide in the alley next to the outdoor while waiting for a bloke called Alan Shelton and a couple of his mates to leave the shop before I went in. They've roughed me up a few times before. They were in there a while, chatting to the manager, while I was next to the bins. It's Friday night and it can get busy, too busy if you're me.'

'Have you ever fought back?' asked Lines.

Aster tut-tutted. 'If I do then I go back to prison, DC Lines.' He pointed to his disfigurement. 'And I don't fancy it.'

'Can anyone verify you doing this?' asked Delahaye.

'Yes, the outdoor manager, Cal Mulligan. He commented on my tardiness, actually. You can ask him.'

'Mickey spat at you once, didn't he, Mr Aster?' said Lines.

'I'm used to it,' said Aster. 'I wouldn't murder anyone because they *spat* at me, Detective Sergeant. I'd be a *very* busy bee if I killed *every* spitter.'

Delahaye was aware of Aster's gaze on him as he wrote everything down in his notebook.

'You said there were *two* reasons why you were here, Detective Sergeant?' Aster's tone had become subtly smug and, when Delahaye looked up from his notepad, he saw it in his expression too.

'Mickey Grant was your "type", wasn't he? Blond and athletic. Early teens.' Delahaye kept his voice kind but the smugness had disappeared from Aster's face. 'During the post-mortem, human bite marks were found on Mickey Grant's body, Mr Aster. And biting was part of your *original* MO, was it not?'

Aster had blushed from neck to hairline. 'Bloody hell, I had nothing to do with that boy's murder . . .'

'No new accomplice then? With a vehicle of some kind?' asked Delahaye. His straightforward questions visibly rattled Aster.

'I've *never* . . . I would *never* . . .' Aster blustered and he couldn't make eye contact with either detective.

'Do you know anyone with a similar MO perhaps? Heard of someone with a penchant for such ... behaviour?' Delahaye snapped his notebook shut. 'Perhaps while in prison? Or members of your old peer group?'

'No. Er ... Look ... I *don't* have *any* contact with anyone like *that* anymore ...' Aster was withdrawing into the house.

'All right Mr Aster, such things have to be asked,' said Delahaye. Though statistically most paedophiles were loners, Aster had historical connections to a particularly vile paedophile ring in the South-East, supplying them with pornographic images of his young victims.

'Would it be possible for you to attend an appointment with a forensic dentist to take a cast of your teeth so we can eliminate you from our investigation once and for all?'

'Er ... yes,' said Aster reluctantly. 'When ... ?'

'We'll sort it out for you, Mr Aster,' said Lines. 'Do you have a telephone?'

'No, but Mrs Cutter next door does,' said Aster, retreating into the hall.

Delahaye pulled one of his contact cards from his jacket and handed it to Aster who took it gingerly at arm's length. 'Call me if there's anything you want to share, Mr Aster. We'll let you know about the dental appointment. Thank you very much for—'

The door slammed shut on them.

'What do we think?' Delahaye asked Lines on the way back to the car.

'He's up to something,' said Lines. 'But pervs always are.'

Chapter Eleven

O NCE A WEEK, AVA AND Veronica tidied and cleaned Trevor's flat for extra pocket money. It never seemed occupied, as if someone was about to move out or move in.

'Trevor was looking at your boobs again,' said Veronica unexpectedly as she dusted around the living room. 'I hate it when he looks at you like that. It makes me feel sick.'

It made Ava feel sick too. 'That's why I get dressed in the toilet or even in bed whether he's in our flat or not,' she said. It was a relief that she had a witness to Trevor's creepy behaviour, and that she wasn't imagining it. Ever since Ava had reached puberty, Trevor was often caught staring at her, his glittering gaze speculative. He forced Ava to surreptitiously observe him all the time, without making her mother angry. His interest wasn't constant but she dared not relax just in case his lapses were part of an insidious strategy by him.

'I know,' said Veronica. 'And those comments he makes when Mom isn't around . . .'

Comments that made Ava uneasy as they were intent disguised as flattery. 'You're getting big, aren't ya, gel?' he'd say. 'You could be on Page Three!' Considering a girl had to be sixteen to be a Page Three girl and she was miles off that age, it was double the dodgy factor when he said it. He complained to Colleen that he was 'hag-ridden' but to Ava, it was as if he was awaking to the reality of his being a caliph with his own ready-made harem.

'The trick is to keep out of his way or not be alone with him,' said Ava. 'And watch him when he is around.'

'Well thank God he isn't always around,' said Veronica as they finished dusting. Mom called Trevor a 'workaholic' because he had many jobs and his main hobby was fixing cars and repainting them for people. He also travelled all over the country going to car auctions or scrapyards. He often took the Bonneys with him on these trips, introducing them to new places and people beyond their flat and school. Ava had to admit it was this exposure to strangers that had stopped her and Veronica being so shy.

Sometimes, he would stay at work until late at night or if he was visiting a car auction or scrapyard far away, he'd stay overnight in a hotel. He still had his own flat and he still had his own life away from the Bonneys. Ava was grateful her mother had not yet given him a door key to their flat.

He was known as a 'womaniser'. It was how his marriage had broken up with his former wife. He had two children – a grown and married daughter and sixteen-year-old Luke whom the Bonney sisters adored because he was very kind and very camp, and treated them like they were his real sisters. He was also nothing like his dad.

'And Trevor is *always* up to something,' Veronica was saying. 'I've heard him creep out of our flat late at night many times.'

Ava nodded, though she'd also observed that he'd return just as dawn arrived. Colleen slept deeply and never seemed to notice.

'We can't tell Mom because she would accuse us of trying to cause trouble,' said Ava.

Veronica clutched her chest dramatically and accurately impersonated their mother. '*You just don't want me to be happy!*' She became serious again. 'But we have to be careful, Ava. Who do we tell if we can't tell Mòm?'

Ava didn't know. She knew she'd have to be vigilant. As for Trevor disappearing in the middle of the night, she had theories, but she dared not share them with her sister. Veronica was in competition with Rita for their mother's attention – a contest she would inevitably lose as Rita was the favourite. As much as she loved Veronica, any secrets were often weaponised and unleashed during arguments so she wouldn't risk even a theory.

For example, on the night Mickey went missing, Trevor had been out on one of his 'seeing a man about a dog' trips. He'd told Colleen that, when the police had gone door to door asking where everyone was the night Mickey Grant disappeared, he'd said he'd been with his brother. This confused Ava as she was sure Kevin and his family had still been on holiday at Barry Island and didn't come back until the Saturday morning after the Friday night Mickey disappeared. His lie might have been cover for his affair with one of his 'fancy women' or he could know more about Mickey's disappearance than he let on.

'The only thing that unites us with Trevor was that we hated Mickey,' said Ava to change the subject.

'Does it make me a bad person to be secretly pleased Mickey's gone?' asked Veronica.

'No, it just makes you honest and human,' said Ava.

'I wonder if Trevor is secretly pleased,' mused Veronica.

Mickey used to steal tools from Trevor's toolbox whenever he was under a car, working on it, black with oil. Trevor could never get from under the car fast enough to give chase so could only shout at the boy sprinting into the distance. Trevor had spoken to Mickey's father about it and Mr Grant had promised to 'have a stern word' with his son. And the tool theft had stopped, but Ava suspected it was more to do with it being winter then and Trevor was not out under cars as much and neither were teenage boys out causing havoc when the weather turned cold.

In Trevor's kitchen, car parts took up more space than utensils, and there was a table with a pile of paperwork sprawled across its top. Ava wiped around scrap, and Veronica shuffled bills into neat piles.

'Avie?' Veronica was holding a batch of letters in her hand.

Ava took the top letter and saw untidy handwriting. 'Have you read these?' Veronica nodded. Ava read quickly. They were love letters to Trevor from a lady called 'Amanda'.

'We should tell Mom,' whispered Veronica.

'All right – then *you* should tell her,' said Ava. She replaced the letters beneath the bills.

'Why me?' whispered Veronica.

'Because *you're* the one who wants to tell her, not me,' said Ava.

'Why?' Veronica was angry. Although Ava understood the misguided loyalty, she understood self-preservation more.

'Vere, Mom won't believe us about this any more than she'd believe us if we told her he's always looking at my boobs! She'll take his side because she always does. Remember?' Veronica looked down. 'She'll confront him; he'll deny it and she'll believe him and we'll pay for it more than he will.' Her hint was her warning: if Mom didn't believe them on this, then she wouldn't believe worse things he might do. It could allow him free rein for things Ava couldn't speak aloud, and she had to protect her sisters. 'We'll keep it a secret for now. Can you do that?' Veronica nodded. Ava kissed her sister's cheek. 'I think we're done here.'

Chapter Twelve

DELAHAYE AND LINES KNOCKED ON Mr Ancona's front door. On recent previous visits to Mr Ancona's house, his wife had answered the door by opening it only as far as the security chain allowed. She would tell Delahaye and Lines that her husband wasn't in. The property was the last semi-detached house on a secluded avenue just nudging the green belt. The ice-cream van was in a covered area beside the house, and a gleaming red Ford Cortina Mk V rested in the paved drive. The car had not been there on the detectives' preceding visits so they were in luck this time.

Pete Ancona answered the door and glowered at the detectives on his doorstep as they introduced themselves.

'So, what do you want?' he barked.

'We just want to ask you a few questions, Mr Ancona,' said Delahaye. When Ancona noticed a curtain twitch in the window next door, Delahaye raised his voice to add, 'About Mickey Grant.'

Harried and embarrassed, Ancona ushered them into the house.

'Where's you missus, Mr Ancona?' asked Lines.

'Out,' said Ancona. He led them through to a comfortable sitting room. 'Sit if you're gonna sit.'

The three men sat. Delahaye noticed how fidgety Ancona was despite his cock-of-the-walk demeanour.

'Nice motor you've got,' said Lines.

'Yeah, but it attracts a lot of unwanted attention,' said Ancona. 'Teenage lads mostly.'

'You can't blame lads for admiring a flash car,' said Lines.

Ancona frowned. 'My wife says you've been here on and off for a week. What's this about then?'

'We understand you had an argument with Mickey Grant last year,' said Delahaye. 'Several witnesses have come forward to say it got quite nasty.'

'Because he was a nasty bit of work,' said Ancona. 'Yeah, I gave him a clipped ear. Somebody needed to.'

'You aren't a fan of children,' said Delahaye.

'I hate the fuckers,' said Ancona. 'That's why I'll never have 'em.'

Delahaye wondered if Mrs Ancona had agreed to this decision wholeheartedly or to keep the peace.

'It's a bit odd you being an ice-cream man then, Mr Ancona,' said Lines.

'It's a living,' said Ancona. He smirked. 'Anyway, you can be a vet and still hate cats, y'know.'

'Was that the only run-in you had with Mickey Grant, Mr Ancona?' asked Delahaye.

'That was the last with me, yeah,' said Ancona. 'But I wasn't the only one who hated the little shit. I don't want to speak bad of the dead, but loads of us were sick of him.'

'Us?' Delahaye prompted.

'A few blokes who live around. Mack Hardy who owns the posh sweet shop in Rednal because Mickey was always shoplifting in there; Trevor Bax up the road had his tools regularly nicked by him. A couple of others.'

'I see,' said Delahaye, writing it all down.

Ancona's eyes narrowed. 'But that don't mean any of us killed him. He was just a kid. We've bigger fish to fry.'

'Your alibi for the time Mickey went missing was you being home with your missus watching *The Nine O'Clock News* and then *Knots Landing* on the telly with your wife,' said Lines.

Ancona rolled his eyes. 'Yeah, I hate that fucking programme. I usually go the pub of a Friday night ... '

'*The Longbridge* pub?' Delahaye asked.

Ancona looked put out that they knew his regular haunt. 'Yeah.'

'You say "usually". Why didn't you go to the pub on that Friday night?' Delahaye had hoped Mrs Ancona would be in so he could gauge her expressions for lies, of covering for her husband. On their last visit to the house, he and Lines had noticed the bruises on her forearms. When they'd asked her about them, she'd just said she'd 'bumped them against a cupboard door'.

Ancona smirked and shrugged. 'It was too fucking cold to bother.'

'But you have a car, Mr Ancona,' said Delahaye.

'Look, my wife wanted me to spend a bit of time with her so I did,' said Ancona. He winked.

Delahaye couldn't quite discern if he was lying. Ancona came over as the vindictive type, one who bore grudges, who could hit women and feel no guilt due to his inherent sense of self-righteousness ... or his permanent anger carried him above remorse.

'Thank you,' said Delahaye. 'Do you have a regular dentist, Mr Ancona?'

'Why? Because Mickey was bitten? It said in the news he'd been bitten? Bloody hell. Yeah, you can check my dental records.' Ancona sneered. 'Who *bites* kids? I didn't like the lad, but not enough to kill him.'

Chapter Thirteen

S ATURDAY WASN'T ALWAYS DADDY DAY: every fortnight it belonged to Nanny Ash and Granddad. The journey to West Heath was so long that there was time to appreciate the ordinary in a fresh light. In summer, ants surged from cracks in the pavement like megacity commuters and, after rain, giant tumescent earthworms surfaced in lilac Lovecraftian coils. There was the hum of the electricity substation that looked as if it had been plucked from *Metropolis*. And West Heath in sunshine looked forever stuck in the 1950s.

Nanny Ash was very tall and plain – until she smiled. Granddad rarely moved from his armchair, firmly rooted, as if potted. The TV was always on, always *Grandstand*, until Nanny would later switch over for the Saturday film.

Nanny Ash made the best cups of super-strong Blitz tea, and chatted to Mom, while Granddad talked to the children. It was the same routine – every other Saturday since their lives had begun.

Outside, it started to drizzle. Inside, the TV droned on. Ava's gaze fell on the front page of one of the newspapers on the coffee table. There was a photograph of the footprint casts taken from the Quarry alongside the headline:

THE MARK OF A MONSTER?

The police would have experts to tell them what kind of animal made such marks but there was nothing in the article that suggested which kind of animal. All it said was the human foot-prints were a size ten. The police saw the prints as 'possible important clues', and she suspected they were already desperate, because how useful were they, really? The prints were not those of a big cat or dog. She thought *all* the prints were human despite the animal-look of the 'paw' indentations. Humans move via bipedal locomotion, their elegant skeletons a bio-engineering marvel for this extraordinary method of getting about. Along with their big brains and opposable thumbs, it was how humans ruled the world, Ava thought, for better or worse. Quadrupeds, for the most part, carry their weight on their digits: equines on a single toe of each foot, pigs on two and dogs on four, making them digitigrades. Human feet distribute their weight from heel to toe. It is little more than a controlled fall, a skill which took time to master, as any toddler would tell you. Everything else about human anatomy fell in sync with this development: skull size, centred magnum foramen, hip width, premature birth, inner ear mechanism, stereoscopic vision.

From heel to toe: the newspaper photograph of the cast somehow didn't tell this story. The so-called 'animal' paw prints were of a human moving efficiently on all fours, not hands-and-knees all fours, but properly. She also noticed that both the heel prints for foot and palm were faint and marked with a soft outline – the person they belonged to was wearing thick gloves, likely mittens. And possibly thick socks on the feet, too. Ava needed to tell Detective Sergeant Delahaye what she'd deduced, even if what she'd deduced didn't make sense.

She needed to get to a telephone.

Last night on *Police Five*, Shaw Taylor had given out the investigation team's phone number and Ava had blinked, as if snapping a picture of it, and stored it in her memory.

Granddad, as if sensing her predicament, reached to the mantelpiece where he kept his loose change and said: 'Go and get you and your sisters some sweets, Ava.'

Ava kissed Granddad on the cheek and avoided her mother's glare. Ava walked fast: girls running outdoors attracted unwanted attention. She bought sweets for her sisters then entered the telephone box around the corner from the shops. Her heart beat against her ribcage like a trapped robin. But nobody gave her a second look. The street was deserted, as it would be on a cold rainy Saturday afternoon when the football results were about to be announced, and with the afternoon film starting. Fumbling in her pocket for money, she took a deep breath, pushed coins into the slot, dialled the numbers, and waited.

Chapter Fourteen

DELAHAYE HAD BEEN ABOUT TO leave his desk for home when the telephone rang, and Lines picked up the receiver.

'Good afternoon, CID: Detective Constable Lines speaking.'

'Good *afternoon*, Detective Constable Lines.' Lines froze on the other end then gesticulated wildly to Delahaye seated at his desk across from him. He clicked on the speakerphone.

'Can I help you, Miss ... Mrs ... ?'

'Your *footprint* casts in the newspapers ... They're *all* human footprints, dearie.'

'Pardon?'

'The footprints you found at the Quarry are *all* human – even the ones that resemble animal paw prints. The person was wearing thick gloves, likely mittens, and curled his fingers over to mimic the shape of paws. He was also wearing thick socks on his feet and moved on his toes – on all fours.'

Delahaye took over. 'We'd much appreciate it if you came in to talk more about this ... theory, as well as what happened last week, Mrs ... ?'

'Am *I* under suspicion?'

'No, of course not. We want to thank you, that's all.'

'No, *of course not*!' the voice said. 'Because women so *rarely* kill children!'

Lines called her out. 'Myra—' he began but she cut him off sharply.

'Please *don't* be a cliché and bring Myra *Hindley* or Mary Bell into it, Detective Constable. The *exception* to a rule is *not* the rule, now, is it?'

Lines blushed as if he'd been scolded by his mother.

'The Quarry *is* steep,' said Delahaye. 'Maybe they grabbed the ground in front of them to avoid falling back and that explains the paw-like prints.'

'One cannot *grab* with curled fingertips in the shape of a paw because one needs fingers and thumbs to grasp objects. When was the last time you saw a cat hold a stick, Detective?'

'Why would anyone move on all fours, with no shoes on, on a rainy night?' asked Delahaye.

'That, I can't answer,' said the voice.

Delahaye cleared his throat. 'Do humans have eye shine bright at night?'

She didn't even hesitate. 'Such delightful, tenuously linked questions! No, DS Delahaye. Humans don't possess *tapetum lucidum*, unfortunately.'

And with this statement, the line went dead.

Chapter Fifteen

'ALL FOURS.'

Lines folded his hands into paw shapes then placed them next to a copy of the prints taken from the Quarry. He then tried to grasp a pen and found it was really difficult.

'Well, that was a weird conversation with Miss *Play Misty For Me*,' said Lines.

Delahaye laughed. 'Is that what we'll call her? Miss Misty?'

'Might as well.'

'She's a resident in one of those blocks,' murmured Delahaye. 'I know it.'

'I don't recall meeting anyone in those flats who spoke like Princess bloody Margaret, Sarge,' said Lines.

'What did she call it? A *tapetum lucidum*?' Delahaye said.

Lines stretched out his long legs.

'Miss Misty sounds like she knows her stuff. I wonder what she looks like. She sounds like my type ... '

'Detective Constable Lines, the only type of woman you like is the type that never says no.'

'Harsh,' said Lines, grinning. He scratched his head then added: 'She mentioned Mary Bell though ... Everyone knows Myra Hindley. But then she added Mary Bell. Why?' He shrugged. 'Her point about women generally not being prone to murder kids could've been made with just that one name ... '

'Because most people only know of one female murderer, and that's Hindley,' said Delahaye.

'Yes, yet Miss Misty specifically mentions a female killer of kids who was a kid herself.'

'Mary Bell killed two toddlers about thirteen years ago,' Delahaye remembered.

'She was an eleven-year-old girl.' Lines offered Delahaye a cigarette, who accepted. Lines lit both, dragged hard, then exhaled. 'The police were looking for a male suspect because even with Hindley being so recent, we couldn't believe another woman could be such a monster.' He tapped ash into a chipped ashtray. 'And then it turned out to be a little girl who strangled little boys.'

'There was another girl with her when she did it.'

Lines nodded. 'Norma Bell. No relation to Mary, and Norma was older too – thirteen – but naive and just a tag-along. Mary's mom had even tried to kill Mary a few times, in little "accidents". Her dad was no better. Mary was a precocious little bleeder. She was her own star witness at her trial.'

'Why'd she do it? Did it come out in court?'

'The defence mentioned her background; said she'd been neglected, and I don't doubt it. I mean, when she was arrested, her hair was teeming with nits. But still, loads of us are raised in poverty and we don't murder people.'

'Why'd *you* think she did it, Steve?' asked Delahaye.

Lines's dark eyes narrowed. 'Rage and jealousy,' he said 'That's what I think. Because the little boys were loved and she wasn't, so she murdered them to get her own back on everybody.' He shrugged again. 'But that's just my opinion.'

'Children killing children *is* rare,' murmured Delahaye.

'But not unheard of,' said Lines. 'It's extremely unusual for a girl to kill. It *is* peculiar Miss Misty brought Bell's name into it, though, I think.'

They were quiet for a moment, contemplating, before Delahaye asked: 'Where's Mary Bell now?'

Lines mashed his cigarette out. 'She's out. Free as a bird. New identity, new life. Carrying on as if nothing happened. Meanwhile, the families of those two innocent babbies are ruined forever.'

Grey light from the window shifted tired shadows across the office.

'Do you know what Mary Bell said when they asked her why she did it?' Lines lit another cigarette. 'She said, "I like hurting little things that can't fight back."'

Delahaye sifted through his notebook and saw a scrawl from the previous week:

Dens. Kids. Ask.

Chapter Sixteen

'CATS HAVE TWO HUNDRED AND forty-four bones, thirty-eight more than humans, and their skeletons are constructed for agility and almost supernatural feats of acrobatics,' said Ava to her best friend, John Eades. 'They have free-floating clavicles and collapsible bodies so they can leap, bound, fall and fit into narrow spaces, as if they are poured oil.'

They were at the rear of the apartment block and at Ava's feet was a dead cat.

When Ava was in full flow, John could listen to her talk all day, but today he just wanted to talk about films and *not* deceased felines. 'He's a big tom in his prime, a rare silver mackerel tabby,' Ava continued and peered closer. 'See how his tongue is tinged grey at the edges? The papillae on its surface are dry white hooks when they're dead.' John pretended to see but he wasn't really looking. He supposed he was thankful it wasn't yet rotting. 'It probably died in the early hours,' Ava added.

In her crisp-packet gloves, because litter was everywhere and crisp packets made the best disposable gloves, she pushed a finger against its 'armpit'. 'There's no lingering warmth. It's in the latter throes of rigor mortis and there's an absence of flies, but then it *is* a rainy day and any self-respecting green bottle would have the good sense to stay inside!' She turned to John to see if he got her little joke. He'd got her little joke just fine, but he was struggling to find humour in this situation. The cat lay on its side, facing the wall, shattered like a Bull Ring toffee slab.

'I don't like the way it looks in this spot at the bottom of this building,' said Ava.

John didn't like standing in full view of someone's bedroom window as they were.

'Christ-on-a-bike, Ava, we'll be seen,' he said.

'Ssh then! Crouch down between the windows. It's a blind spot,' said Ava, without looking at him.

John did as she said, and glad he could now see Ava's face. He was just happy to look at her sometimes. It helped that she didn't know she was pretty. 'Ava, can't we just carry on talking about *Gregory's Girl*? Can we leave dead things alone just for today, please?' They'd been happily chatting about the film until her unerring death radar had helped her discover the cat.

'We will, just … not yet,' said Ava. She was totally focused on the cat now, and her hands travelled over its form as gently and nimbly as a vet's. Her eyes glittered with unshed tears as she stroked the animal as if it was still alive. John knew all about her roadkill body farm, as he knew a myriad other secrets, but that was all right because she knew all of his too. John was a year older than Ava, in the familiar throes of senior school, but at Waseley Secondary not Colmers Farm. He wished she'd come to his school. She would already have a gang of mates to protect her, not like at Colmers Farm where she was hunted by bullies every day.

John had met Ava when she was eight and he was nine. His mother, Carol, ran her own mail order business for bespoke baby clothes, and was roundish, blondish and, to John, an only child, she was sensational.

Carol encouraged John's friendship with Ava because, he thought, she liked Ava's influence on him. Ava was invited to the house any time she wanted. And it wasn't totally unselfish: his mom would talk to her for hours about so many things. Even his granddad thought she was 'glorious' and treated her like another grandchild. Ava had met John's school friends, and they neither knew she was being bullied nor cared that she was poor. They'd grown used to the fact she was a girl and liked her because she was funny and interested in seriously disgusting stuff. Little Adam Booth idolised her and, when she wasn't around, would always ask when she was going to be.

And John didn't like Ava's mother because she always seemed to be snapping or sulking. And he loathed Trevor.

John watched Ava's hands move over the cat again. 'It feels like a fluffy bag of knitting needles,' she said. 'Some of these breaks are brutal, not possibly just from a fall – even a great fall. Look how some of the bones protrude, splitting the skin and jutting forth as bloodied spines.' John didn't look – her description was enough. 'And see how a clear fluid has congealed in its ears, into the Henry's pockets,' she added. 'A fractured skull?'

Ava looked right, then left, then up.

'It fell,' she said. 'Or . . . it was chucked.'

'Holy-Christ-on-a-bike!' said John too loudly, and slapped his hand to his mouth.

Ava growled. 'It isn't right.'

'It was likely accidental, Aves. Come on, he must've jumped. He must've made a mistake and then *bang*, he's gone.'

'*Nobody* in this block has a cat like this,' said Ava. '*Nobody*.'

'You don't know that a hundred per cent,' said John. 'You aren't the . . . Cat KGB. It could be a . . . new cat.'

'I know all the pets in this block and nobody owns a superstar cat like this one,' said Ava.

'He could be a stray?' John suggested.

'He *isn't* a stray, John, he's in spectacular nick. I bet he's even had his injections.' She checked between the cat's hind legs. 'And he's been neutered, so he's definitely loved.'

John bit his lip. 'D'you think he fell off a balcony . . . ?'

'"Fell off"? Cats don't just *fall off*, John! No, he fell straight down.' They looked up at the apartment block. There were no open windows, no shocked faces peering down. 'I think from the roof. If he'd fallen from a balcony, he'd have bounced off a railing and landed on one of the other balconies. *Or* bounced off and landed on the grass *opposite* the balconies. If he'd fallen off a balcony and lived, you'd see drag marks in the gravel to this spot because he's a big, heavy cat. But there're no drag marks – he died on impact. It was a graveyard smash.'

'I know cats can get everywhere, but the *roof*?'

'Somebody must have taken him there.'

'But it's locked! They'd have to get a key!'

'Keys aren't unicorns, John. Grown-ups can get keys.' Ava pointed to the roof. 'They took the cat up there then they chucked him over on purpose – to see.' She was earnest as she looked at him. 'Imagine how scared the cat must've been, held aloft in the dark over the edge, in so much pain. Then, for one tiny moment, airborne and free like the birds he'd chased. Flight before final impact.' John thought she should write books when she was older. She had a turn of phrase that formed pictures in his head. It was a pity they could be pictures he *really* didn't want in his head.

Ava crouched beside the cat and bent its limbs. John heard a cracking sound, and he winced. She did it again.

'Stop doing that, Aves, it sounds rank, man.'

'Cats don't always land on their feet. They can still get injured or die if they fall from a building, especially if they can't engage their righting reflex. But this cat didn't stand a chance. Somebody *deliberately* snapped the bones in his legs like they were pencils then chucked him over.'

'"To see", you said,' said John. 'To see what?'

Ava's gaze was serene. 'To see what it felt like to kill something maybe. To see if they could get away with it.'

John felt sick. Bad people do bad things, the news said so, and a dead boy and a cat crippled on purpose proved it.

What if they're still around?

Once, Ava had showed John how eating grass turned your spit green, and then how to shoot the goo through the gaps in your front teeth like venom. She'd taught him how to draw a Tiger tank and a motorbike using basic shapes. She voiced hilarious impersonations of David Bowie singing nursery rhymes, or of John Lennon asking banal questions. And she could mimic all sorts of things – animal sounds, trains, machine guns, accents.. And all of her accents came with complete characters. She'd make words up and pretend they were real, and use them against him until he checked in a dictionary and found they weren't there. She had a labyrinthine mind, an imagination that astounded, and she possessed an animalistic quality which had John hooked. But she knew too much: she had instincts and intuitions that most grown-ups lacked and, in this moment, her *knowing* made him fluttery in the pit of his belly.

'Let's bury him.' Ava lifted the cat into her arms and, with John by her side, they made their way to the laburnum bushes. Ava retrieved the garden trowel she'd nicked from Trevor's brother and began digging a trench. She handed John a discarded length of wood and together they dug deeper.

John regarded Ava steadily.

'Aren't you going to body-farm the cat?' he asked.

Ava sighed. 'No. Let him rest now.'

'What if the cat's owner is looking for him?' asked John. 'Wouldn't they want to know where he is?'

Ava stroked the cat's head before placing him into his final resting place.

'I think it best they never know, and as long as we know he's safe, that's all that matters.' Ava looked at him – or through him, beyond him. It was sometimes like sharing space with a feral creature.

'Ava?' John said. 'Did you find Mickey Grant's body?'

'Yes,' said Ava instantly.

'I'm not going to ask why you were out at two o'clock in the morning, Aves.'

'You *know* why, you flump. I was there to check on the fox.'

The fox! She'd found him just before he'd gone on holiday. Having never observed a subject at night, she'd chosen the worst night to do so. Bloody typical Ava!

'I recognised Mrs Poshy-Snob when I heard her on the radio,' said John.

Her gaze was piercing but Ava was calm. 'Did you tell anyone?'

'No,' said John.

'Not even your mom?'

'No,' said John. 'Ava, you have to tell a grown-up because—'

'Why do I *have to*?' Ava was obviously pissed off now. 'If I tell a grown-up, I'd *have* to explain what I was doing out there at night, and they'd ask a billion questions about *me* and not about Mickey. *They've* got nothing else; so suddenly it's about what *I* did, even though what *I* did actually helped them out. Mom would be told and then I'd *have* to deal with the fallout from her, so I'd be exiled to Nazareth House.' Nazareth House was the huge Victorian children's home run by nuns, and it was bang opposite the Austin Works. Some parents threatened to send their kids there if they misbehaved. 'Instead, *nothing* has happened to me, has it?' Ava used her hands expressively when she was on a rant. 'Mickey's been found and now the police are investigating.'

'But weren't you *scared*?' John whispered. 'It must've done ... *something* to you.' He'd have been terrified. Dead humans were vastly higher on the terror scale than dead cats.

'No. I wasn't scared, and it hasn't done *something* to me.'

'No nightmares?'

'No, John.'

And John believed her. Ava could do that: separate parts of her life and feelings as if none bore any relation to the others. She dealt with her world in her own time in her own way. 'Weren't you afraid the killer was still around?'

'There was nobody there but me,' said Ava.

John had had mixed feelings on hearing Mickey's body had been found. Years ago, Mickey and a couple of his friends had shoved John and Little Adam against the walls of the underpass. John had kicked Mickey's legs, which made Mickey angry enough to smack John in the gob so hard it made his lip bleed. They then spat in Little Adam's hair and mushed it in. For weeks after, Little Adam was too scared to leave the house. John was bigger and stronger now, and would have loved for Mickey to try it on again, only this time in a proper fight. With Mickey dead, he'd never be able to beat seven shades of shit out of him. He supposed being dead meant Mickey had paid the ultimate price for being a wanker and that price was too high.

'Mickey *was* a tosser, Aves.'

'I'm glad he's gone,' said Ava. John breathed a sigh of relief, grateful he wasn't alone in feeling guilty for not feeling guilty. 'But the way he died wasn't right because somebody killed a kid and that puts all kids in danger, like you and my sisters ...' *And you*, thought John. *You're a kid yourself, Aves – don't forget.*

Their secret was gargantuan. It loomed above them both, greater than the building and the Quarry, the most serious thing to ever have happened to Ava, and now John too because he was part of it whether he liked it or not. It was scary and exciting, an adventure – but also a horror story. Ava was part of the investigation and nobody else knew it but him.

Ava patted the earth, folded her hand into a makeshift paw, placed it on the low mound of grave and murmured The Rabbit's Prayer. John tilted his head and said amen at the end, which made her smile.

'Did you say the prayer for Mickey?' John asked.

'Yes,' said Ava.

There was a loud whooshing sound from the road. Both children were obscured from view as Nathaniel Marlowe cruised past, hands-free, on War Horse. It was the name Ava gave Nathaniel's bike – a heavy black Raleigh Roadster modified with chunky wheels, a sturdy trailer full of bricks and tools at its rear. Marlowe whistled *The Dam Busters* theme under the hood of his *Quadrophenia* coat, cool as anything. Riding a bike hands-free was a skill Ava envied. But she'd only recently learned how to ride a bike, and that was only because John had taught her how on Winston, his orange Chopper. No-hands riding would have to wait.

Marlowe didn't see them as he sailed by, his arms outspread, the tails of his military coat flapping like wings behind him as he descended the hill and out of sight. As fearless as all teenage boys seemed to be.

'What if they find out Mrs Poshy-Snob *was* you?' said John as they got up and dusted dirt from their clothes and knees.

'How can they find out unless you or I tell them?'

John said nothing.

Ava told him about the footprint cast, and the telephone call she'd made to the investigation team yesterday.

'You've got steel bollocks, Aves,' John said with admiration. It struck him for the millionth time that the reason other kids were cruel to her was because they were afraid of her. Ava, perhaps bemused at his awe, shrugged.

'I'm chuffed you recognised Mrs Poshy-Snob,' she said with a smile. 'I knew you would.'

Chapter Seventeen

To Ava, the raindrops resembled glass beads thrown against the window, a multifaceted view through each globule, like a fly's compound eye.

The Bonneys' home smelled of Sunday lunch. Trevor and Luke were fixing wardrobe doors. Mom was washing up and listening to the radio, while Rita played with the cardboard puppet set Ava had made for her. The TV was off, but the record player was on, and Isao Tomita's *Snowflakes Are Dancing* filled the room with beauty.

'Arabesque' was Ava's anthem. She looked out the window as the music flowed through her, its pops and pipples, its soars and swoops – other-worldly and magical. At the table behind Ava, Veronica drew pictures and wrote stories.

Ava turned from the window just as the silver Audi Quattro pulled into the cramped cul-de-sac. She sat opposite her sister and resumed her own writing.

The letter box clattered and everyone froze. Veronica looked at Ava, their pencils poised. Rita's puppet play stopped mid-run. Rita turned the volume down on the stereo and ran to her sisters, just as she did when the Rent Man came.

'Who the bloody mc-fuckery is that on a Sunday, ay?' Trevor came into the hall in unison with Colleen, Luke trailing behind.

'It could be my brothers,' said Colleen. 'Or maybe it could be *your* brother, Trev.'

The letter box clattered again, accompanied by a thumping on the door. Trevor had turned a fascinating shade of green. Ava wondered about all those new things wrapped in plastic in his flat that had fallen off the backs of so many lorries. Maybe one of those lorry drivers had come to take it back. And all those times when Trev had gone to see all those men about all those dogs – maybe those dogs had come back to bite him? *One could only hope*, Ava thought.

'It could be your ex,' said Trevor.

'Who? Mike?'

'D'you have another ex, Coll?'

Ava found this funny. *Good one, Trev.*

'Why would Mike come here?' Colleen was genuinely baffled. 'There's nothing here he wants.'

Thanks, Mom, thought Ava. *Bitch.*

Another knock on the door. Whoever it was wasn't going away. Luke pulled a theatrically worried face behind his father's back and the girls smiled. If Luke was unworried then they'd be unworried too.

'It *could* be Mike,' said Colleen. Mike couldn't discover Trev was her boyfriend at all costs, Ava knew, as it might affect maintenance money. 'Trev! Hide in the bedroom and shut the door, just in case!' Trevor did as he was bid.

Colleen went to open the front door with her chin held so high Ava was surprised she could see ahead at all.

Ava recognised Detective Sergeant Delahaye's voice immediately.

'It's the police!' Colleen declared, as if announcing the arrival of Albert Pierrepoint.

Trev burst out of the bedroom with Luke behind him. Trev had two default forms of presentation indoors: oil-covered clothes or barely any clothes at all. Today, he'd actually managed to put on a clean shirt and trousers, for which Ava was thankful.

* * *

When the door opened, the angry-looking man standing at the threshold had his hands on his hips like a bullfrog impersonating Superman.

'Hello, sir. Sorry to disturb you and your family this afternoon,' said Delahaye, extracting his warrant card from his jacket pocket just as Lines did the same.

'What's this then? What you want then, ay, on a bloody mc-fuckin' Sunday?' In Delahaye's experience, Trev spoke in the manner of all criminals caught in criminal acts, Sunday or not.

'And you are, Mr ... ?' Detective Constable Lines pulled out his notebook and pen. The action had the desired effect on the man, who reeled his neck in sharpish.

'I'm Trevor Bax. I'm a friend of the family.'

Judging by Ava's expression, Delahaye could see he was no 'friend' of hers. He recognised Bax from the door-to-door inquiries after Mickey's body was found but he also recognised the name from Pete Ancona mention of it.

'I remember you,' Delahaye said. 'We interviewed you last week at your flat.'

Trevor said nothing.

The detectives were led into the living room to find the three girls huddled around a slim, dark-haired youth who stepped forward and said, 'Hello, I'm Luke Bax. Trev's my dad.' The policemen shook his hand, liking the lad immediately. Sometimes the apple falls miles from the tree.

'So, then, why're you here?' Colleen crossed her arms. 'We're a good family, we are.' She obviously dreaded having the neighbours watching police entering her home, Delahaye thought.

'I've no doubt of it, Mrs Bonney,' said Delahaye. 'We've come to talk to Ava, if you don't mind.'

'I *do* mind! What's she done, ay?' Colleen's eyes narrowed at Ava, and she took a step forward, hand raised. 'What've you done then, you little bleeder?'

Delahaye stepped forward and blocked Colleen's view of her daughter. 'I can assure you Ava is in no trouble whatsoever,' he said. 'We'd just like to ask a few questions.' Strangely enchanting music played on the stereo and he picked up the album sleeve nonchalantly. 'We hope Ava can help us.'

Trevor, however, had obviously thought they were here for him.

'Questions about what, ay?' Trevor laughed, though nothing was funny. 'Mate, no disrespect, but you'd better watch *that* one! She makes shit up, she does. Can be a right little bloody liar, can't she, Coll, ay? Away with the mc-fuckin' fairies. Can't trust a word she says, you can't.'

Delahaye listened to this little diatribe with interest because, in his experience, it was always the way of bad men to tell the truth about their own failings by accusing others – especially if those others were children. He suspected that the only person who needed watching, who 'made shit up', was Trevor Bax. Clearly Ava had him sussed and Trevor felt threatened. And Colleen not defending her own daughter against a man who was not the father – that appalled Delahaye.

'Perhaps we can talk in the car,' said Delahaye.

'What you need to say can be said here,' said Colleen. 'We've nothing to hide.' Trevor remained silent.

It was a dilemma. They needed to speak to Ava with an accompanying adult, but Delahaye suspected Ava would not speak openly with her mother and Trevor in the room.

'This has nothing to do with your family or Mr Bax,' said Delahaye. 'It's about Mickey Grant.'

'Oh.' Colleen clutched the dish towel to her chest.

Ava inhaled deeply and sighed. 'Luke can be with me. He's sixteen,' she said.

'We won't be long,' said Delahaye as he shepherded the teenagers towards the front door just as 'Footprints in the Snow' came on the stereo.

Chapter Eighteen

AVA WAS RELIEVED TO BE out of the flat – away from Trevor.

Inside the Quattro it smelled of cigarettes and clean men, and was the most modern car Ava had ever sat in. Luke sat in the back with DC Lines and Ava in the front beside DS Delahaye. This visit couldn't be about yesterday's telephone call from Miss Poshy-Snob, surely. Because how could they know Ava was she?

'Ava,' said Delahaye. 'Do you know anything about kids' dens and hiding places in this area?'

Ava nodded. 'Yes, *some* of them, but they do change around or disappear, especially after winter.' Also, children grew out of the need to make dens, and some teenagers preferred to call them hideouts or hang-outs.

Ava caught the detectives exchanging glances.

'Could you mark them out on a map for us?' Delahaye pulled an Ordnance Survey map from his jacket pocket. Ava balked.

'I could do but it would take me ages,' said Ava. She could only show them on her own hand-drawn maps. She'd never find the sites on an official chart.

'How come you know where they are, bab?' asked Lines.

'It helps to know where you can hide during Wolf . . . '

'Wolf?'

'It's a game. A really rough kind of hide 'n' seek,' said Luke.

'And it helps to know where to hide from the Trogs,' said Ava.

'Bullies,' Luke translated. 'Not the band.'

Delahaye shifted in his seat to properly face her. 'Trogs?'

Ava smiled. 'It's short for *troglodytes*, the classification name for chimpanzees.'

'Mickey Grant's old den is abandoned,' said Delahaye. 'We've been told he might've had another one, but nobody knows where.'

Ava scrunched up her nose. 'I don't know for sure. I *think* he *did* have another place he hung out. It was off the estates completely and I used to see him walk in that direction, towards Waseley Hills, lots of times last summer,' she said. 'I followed him once, just to see where he went when he wasn't going home.'

It was the day after Mickey had thrown gravel at Veronica and he'd enraged her, wearing his West Brom T-shirt with his cocky stride, as if he'd done nothing wrong. He'd stopped occasionally to stroke a cat or a dog – maybe the reason she hadn't hated him the way she hated Brett Arbello was that Mickey had genuinely loved animals. She'd shadowed him without knowing why and had kept a safe distance but Mickey, being a confident boy, never sensed a tracker because who would dare follow him? Boys had no need of peripheral vision or a sense for being observed. It must be nice being biologically programmed with such arrogance, to be kings of the world.

'I can take you to it if you like.' *Studying a map only wasted time anyway*, she thought.

Again, the men exchanged their shared relief with a glance. 'Yes please, Ava,' said Delahaye. 'But shouldn't we ask your mother if you can go with us?'

Ava rolled her eyes. 'She won't notice I'm gone.' *Or she'll stop me from going*, she thought. She looked at him. 'Can I ask *you* something now?'

Delahaye smiled. 'Yes.'

'What made you think I could help you?'

Luke shifted in his seat, just as curious to know.

'Something you said the first time we met – about the Moors Murders,' said Delahaye. 'You came across as a smart girl who might see things others miss.'

'Aw, she's a very clever girl, our Ava,' said Luke with pride, and Ava beamed at him. She didn't ask why the police needed to find Mickey's hideout. She guessed it was because it could be the kill-site. Delahaye's face, however, showed no urgency. She was surprised this possibility hadn't occurred to him, that he hoped only to find evidence of the boy's last movements, not anything as huge as a kill-site. Ava suspected it was because the words 'den' and 'hideout' just smacked of silly little kiddie business, playground nonsense.

Ava chose not to warn the detectives. She was aware she *should* warn them – it was a 'good girl' thing to do after all – but she didn't want to. Ava felt no need to share or divulge. And anyway, even if she did, they'd want to know why, because it wasn't something a child should suggest.

What's more, if they believed the den could be the kill-site they would insist she stayed at home. And Ava didn't want to go home. She was more involved than they knew, and *they* had come to *her* for help. They didn't know that they'd been helped by her before. Nope, she had to down-scope below the grown-ups' sight-line until they forgot about her; until it was too late to do anything about it.

'We ready?' Delahaye said, and Ava nodded. He started the car.

'Have you found out who the classy lady was – the one who made the phone call?' asked Luke. Ava fought off a grin. *Classy!*

'Nah, we haven't found our Miss Misty yet,' Lines said.

'Miss Misty?' Luke grinned. 'Like the crazy lady from *Play Misty For Me*?'

Delahaye smiled into the rear-view mirror. 'Well, we had to call her something.'

Miss Misty, thought Ava. *That's much better than Mrs Poshy-Snob.*

The windscreen wipers hit the same rhythm as 'Day Trip to Bangor', a song Ava despised as it was the main soundtrack to an uncomfortable journey to Wales last year in a battered, window-less Ford Transit van with few toilet stops.

At the junction, across the road, lay Frankley estate.

'Left here,' said Ava then added: 'Please.' When she'd seen Mickey walk along the old farm's drive, she'd gone straight back home. It wasn't safe for a girl to be caught in the middle of nowhere with a mean teenage boy.

On their way, Lines tapped the window on his side and said to Delahaye, 'That's Pete Ancona's house. Mickey had to have walked past it.'

Delahaye nodded. Ava was intrigued – it was true that the ice-cream man and Mickey had hated each other. Did the police think he had something to do with Mickey's murder? She daren't ask.

They remained on the road until the houses gave way to the countryside.

'This was a very long way for you to walk, bab,' said Lines.

Ava shrugged. 'I'm used to it.'

'And Mickey didn't notice you?' asked Lines, impressed.

'Ava's got serious ninja skills,' said Luke.

'Crikey, she should work for us,' Lines said.

'Boys don't notice anything,' Ava drawled before perking up in her seat, looking off to the right. 'There. Turn right there, please.'

Delahaye steered into the mouth of a narrow country lane. An orchard flanked the potholed surface; a faded sign hung lopsided on a rusting gate: BANLOCK FARM – PRIVATE PROPERTY.

'This is it,' said Ava.

Chapter Nineteen

THE CAR SLOWLY EDGED FORWARD, the ground beneath, pockmarked tarmac and cobblestones. The derelict farmhouse's timbers were bared like bones to the merciless sky, its hide chipped, and half of it slumped in falls of untidy bricks. Emerald moss blobs grew plump as cushions on every surface not already covered with white and yellow lichen. The front door remained, its small, mullioned window murky but intact. A tree had grown through the foundations, up through the chimney flume and spread with spindly victory above where the roof used to be. Strips of faded wallpaper flapped from exposed walls, and remaining windows beheld the brittle lenses of broken glass. The wind whined through drooping pylon lines which looped in lazy skipping-rope arcs.

'Christ Almighty, nobody's been here for years,' Lines murmured.

Suspended in the air, white and bright as spectral fireflies, were tiny blobs which moved whenever the wind picked up, as if gravity had no power over them, and shifted into drifts in corners and cornices. It was too soon for dandelion puff-balls; certainly too wet for ...

'What is that? Snow?' asked Lines. 'Blossom?'

A tiny fleck landed on the window beside Ava as if greeting her. She smiled. 'No, feathers,' she said. Feather down – light as breath – pulviplume.

Beside the broken house stood an equally broken barn and, on the opposite side, a set of mouldering stables and kennel block. A sagging wall bordered the property a little way beyond the outbuildings with a gap in its centre point. The rain eased but the windscreen wipers kept their incessant rhythm, marking time like a metronome while the detectives gazed at their decrepit surroundings. The policemen seemed unable to look away from the main house. Ava loved the state of it: this was the planet if people disappeared – the end of human rule.

The men believed the house to be Mickey's den. Ava sat very still, very quiet, and hoped they didn't ask her to confirm this. She'd fulfilled her purpose and, if she remained unobtrusive, they'd ignore her.

Without looking at either Ava or Luke, the men exited the car and shut the doors, stood looking at the house, suddenly boys again, busting to explore. Ava watched as they approached the building. The detectives hadn't *ordered* her to stay in the car; they'd temporarily forgotten her. She was free. Ava opened the car door a tiny bit.

'Aves? What're you up to?' Like John, Luke was attuned to Ava's strangeness, and would be more of a hindrance than help if she wasn't canny.

'I'm just ... going to ... stretch my legs,' said Ava. 'I'll have a look at the stables.' *Of course* Ava would want to look at stables. She loved horses, so Luke wouldn't suspect her of mischief. She kept her voice neutral: 'You can come with me if you want.'

Luke pulled his coat tighter around him. 'Nah, it's too damp for me. You just be careful though, yeah?'

'Yes,' said Ava, and eased out of the car. She stood beside the car as the men disappeared around the ruins. Still barely as tall as the Quattro, even if they turned back they wouldn't have spotted her.

It was too quiet. There were birds in the trees but not on the farmhouse grounds, only their feathers. This was a wild place, free of human interruption: there *should* be birds *everywhere*. Their absence usually indicated heavy predation, with rangy carnivores killing everything remotely edible until extinct, or scared off permanently. Cats and foxes were the likely culprits. Abandoned properties usually teemed with them. But Ava could see no sign of either.

Ava breathed in through her nose deeply. The damp day made scents harder to discern and the wind shoved in fits and starts. Time was of the essence: the detectives might be finished at any minute so she couldn't falter. To the right, she passed the barn, with holes in its roof, its floor stained with oil. Inside, ancient hay bales had turned gunpowder grey; disintegrated matter seeped from mouldy boxes. Smashed flowerpots and shattered glass – more feathers. No signs of rodents and no sign of feline pest control: no cat-scat, or acrid stink, or fluffy faces peering out at her. No bird nests in the eaves. Weeds thrived in gnarled batches. A corroding hulk of a Land Rover slumped in the corner like a shot rhino, tethered by ivy, its bonnet a crumpled grimace.

She turned to see the car then stepped out of sight of its windscreen with one small, casual step.

The wind was a whine in the wires. The place was haunted – though not necessarily with ghosts. Ava believed in ghosts, but only as maudlin residue of extreme actions in unhappy places. Like Harry Price had said about Borley Rectory. Ava used her senses to explore the world, and while she was cynical about the presence of God or the Devil, she knew about hostile things and miserable places, that death was very much at home in this wretched zone. Something had occurred here; extreme actions that had not ended well.

A block of loose boxes stood opposite, paint peeling, their latches rusted orange. Ava stepped into view of the car again, waved to Luke and then peered into the stables. This wasn't the den – only storerooms for broken objects. Her quick eye sought a souvenir in the first loose box, but there was nothing except corroding columns of water bowls and a stack of large dog beds. In the other stable, Ava saw a rope with a small leather collar and muzzle at the end of it, attached to a metal ring in the wall. There was a bowl, old straw and a duvet folded into a bed in the corner. On it, she spied a stuffed toy – a black teddy bear with distinctive yellow feet and one eye missing. Newspapers, yellowed and curled, were scattered on the floor, and Ava saw that the youngest was from 30 December 1967 – three days after Ava was born.

The kennel block gates creaked whenever the wind whipped through them. Ava didn't want to show the policemen the real den until she'd seen it first; she wanted this time to be completely her own before all the noisy grown-up stuff started.

Her eyes were drawn to a single boy's shoe – a black trainer caked with mud.

This was Mickey's shoe.

The wall was a crumbly mass of weathered brick with a collapsed centre; and through the gap spread a scrubby piece of land occupied with nettles and weak-linked clovers. Down feathers landed on Ava's nose, hair and coat. She pinched one between her fingers and studied it closely: the little bits were tipped brown at the ends. But, she knew, that the brown had once been red, bright red. *Blood.* These feathers hadn't been moulted or plucked – they'd been torn out.

Ava stepped across the threshold, into the kennels and rounded the corner, pulviplume billowing in her wake.

The smell hit her with the force of a hammer-strike.

The wall concealed its secret but it had also concealed odours. Ava considered her sense of smell excellent for a human, but a dog would never have ventured further. Old smoke, spent fire, burned fabric; she could taste it all on the arch of her palate. Beneath it all was the vile ground note: death.

Ava paused.

In the field beyond lay more ruins and a row of standing stones as grim as decayed teeth in a phossy jaw. To her immediate left, tucked among withered elm trees, were two lock-up garages. A short apron of cracked concrete lay before the building, exuberant weeds sprouting from beneath. Ava's feet crunched on the ground. Instinctively, she looked down and crouched. Below her feet were bones – thousands of them. Stained, bleached, weathered, marking a path to the garages. Smashed ribs and pelvises crunched underfoot. Tiny bones, hollowed bones: nothing bigger than those of a badger. There were more feathers too. Ava picked up a handful and sifted them in her palm: mostly avian but there were many *Theria* pieces; paw phalanges with cat claws attached, mice teeth, fur fronds. Ava's sharp gaze shifted around her: no skulls. *Where were the skulls?*

This was why there was no life in this place: something was killing everything. Ava had followed Mickey only as far as this spot and then turned back. Back then, the carpet of crushed skeletons hadn't been laid but last year was a while ago and since then a predator had been busy.

The first garage was securely locked down. The second was open a little at the bottom. A thick brown stain spread out from beneath the door not just in front but around the corner. Dried blood. The mess had dribbled out then set in gobs on the door's architraves. At the base of the jamb was a single bloodied handprint: a desperate grasp, the thumbprint clear as if stencilled. Up close, the bloodstain was colossal and roughly the shape of South America. It didn't sweep *away* and around the corner, as she had originally thought, but *towards* the garage door, then inside.

Ava faced the door. She studied the frame and the lip of the bottom. Trevor had taught her that such garage doors needed to be thrust upwards with decisive force otherwise they were prone to sticking part-way and then you had to heave – a waste of energy for such a simple task.

Ava reached down and curled her gloved hands around the bottom of the door then threw it wide open. Trevor was right: shove like you mean it.

Chapter Twenty

THE GARAGE DOOR SAILED UP and tucked into its niche above with ease. Ava immediately coughed – old smoke and petrol acrid to taste. Her eyes adjusted to the gloom. Ash was caked into corners by stale draughts and damp. Ava looked around slowly: this was it. This was the den.

Mickey's bike lay on the floor to her left, his Grifter: chain rusted and wheels partially melted. Shelves had burned to a crocodile-underbelly texture.

A charred rug made from a large piece of tatty purple carpet was on the floor. There was a melted plastic chair, and a battered armchair. The armchair was stained with a filthy outline where Mickey had 'sat' steeped in his own effluvium. A wastepaper bin filled with burned litter was next to a weight-training barbell. On a small side table sat scorched copies of magazines, editions dating from last summer. A tipped-over ashtray, used butts smattering the floor alongside empty cigarette packets.

On the floor was a heap of burned fabric and the other trainer. These had to be the rest of Mickey's clothes. Ava touched nothing because she knew better. She studied the bulkier stains, the blood spray and the blood spots. This was both kill-site and temporary storage, but it did not tell the whole story.

On the floor, in its own blotch, was an ordinary carving knife sheathed in gore: the murder weapon? The killer had left crucial evidence to be found – or perhaps he'd assumed this place would never be discovered.

Or he'd panicked, thought Ava. He'd panicked because he was surprised he'd done it, he'd done murder; he'd actually killed a *person*. The battle ended here but didn't begin in this space.

Ava played through the most likely scenario in her mind. The killer had dragged the body in and propped it in the armchair – Mickey hadn't simply been discarded on the floor. The killer had fled after the fire then returned a while later to discover Mickey's body was about to morph into an out-of-control mess. *What to do?* The killer couldn't just leave the body here, even though the den was far enough away from civilisation. If the killer had wanted Mickey to be found, wouldn't he have dumped the body in a more obvious location than the bramble den Ava found it in? And this place was *not* Mickey's den, but a monster's lair. Only the monster was gone.

And there was more: older, chunkier stains; partial remains of the other slaughtered animals. Ava's gaze narrowed on a metal container tucked behind the plastic chair. She stepped forward and crouched in front of it, spotting a thin pile of Polaroid photographs. She saw something in the top image.

She snatched it as she heard her name being called from a distance. *Delahaye.* She shoved the photograph into her pocket and backed out of the garage. Her exploration was not over yet, but the garage, with its burned, bloodstained den inside, would soon keep the detectives preoccupied.

'*Ava!*' Luke called out in harmony with Lines. Delahaye was closer now, visibly worried.

Ava stood in the gap in the wall so she was visible. The men approached; she could hear the crackle of their feet on the bones and stones, their forms fondled by the down-feathers in the air. She saw the horror in their eyes as they realised what was causing the snapping under their shoes. Delahaye was at the apex, with Luke and Lines flanking him, as they ran towards her. She lifted a hand and pointed at the garage. They'd have to work out for themselves that it wasn't Mickey's den. She needed them distracted so she could go and find the missing skulls.

Ava watched them see, heard their grunts of disgust as the stench hit; saw them cover their mouths with ineffectual sleeves, heard their coughing, observed their policeman instincts kick in. She jumped when Delahaye appeared, crouched before her, grabbing her hands.

'Ava? Are you all right, sweetheart?' His concern was genuine: he was sorry, guilty that he'd left her. But Ava forgave him – both because he was a good man, and because it suited her. She nodded. His eyes were massive, and in them she saw that he believed her. Then Delahaye turned to Luke.

'Keep an eye on Ava for us,' he said, but Luke was transfixed by the big bloodstain. Ava watched the detectives move into the den. She saw Luke move closer to the brown mark.

This was her cue.

Ava rounded the corner of the garage and found a slight incline of mud lined with smashed vertebrae and tiny ribcages. Her burning calf muscles told her the path was becoming steeper, and she tried to clear her mind of all thoughts and feelings. Tomita's rendition of 'Arabesque' played in her head, as if to protect her from what was to come, from what she would see.

She was at the top of the slope now. In front of her, two rows of standing broomsticks marked a path, and atop each perched a large dog skull, all of them glaring down at her from eyeless sockets, their mandibles hinged by fragile dried tendons. Around their weathered pates were desiccated crowns of daisy chains. These were the main focus of the display, crude totems that heralded her passage.

Ava moved further into the macabre garden. And then stopped abruptly. Spread out before her was the ossuary arrangement of a truly deranged mind. Cat, rabbit, rodent and hedgehog skulls discarded on twigs lined the shabby path, margined with barbed wire, twisted brambles and dog roses. More skulls of bigger birds – hawks and ravens – and a chunky badger skull. The tall bushes either side gave Ava the impression she was in a labyrinth, their fronds clasping above her head, creating a mystical chamber. The musk of spilled blood and old meat pervaded the cold air. Above her hung a gruesome mobile: a starling's wing and a raven's tail twirled in a helix on thorns. Bells from cat collars chimed in the wind.

She turned briefly to look down the bristling funnel and pondered that awful handprint, brown now, and dry. Mickey had grasped to purchase anything solid, desperate, terrified beyond imagining, but holding on so that he wouldn't be pulled under. He'd still fought to the end. And the only witnesses were the severed heads of slain animals.

The earth had taken the stains away: the blood percolated into the soil though its scent of rusty iron and boiled sugar remained. Before Ava, the ground dipped then rose in a dry ravine. The bushes huddled closer: their dead fruit shrivelled baubles. The spiked skulls leaned in too, a scene despicably beautiful, wrought from a Grimm fairy tale plucked from Baba Yaga's bliss. Discarded on the ground was another barbell and, still clinging, was gore and bone shards, tiny as a bird's. But not a bird's – these were human. Ava stared at it and blinked. In her head, she tried to match the barbell with the wounds she'd seen on Mickey's corpse. Was this the tool used to smash his chest? As Ava approached an altar-like structure directly ahead, she saw it wasn't an altar but a slab of solid granite; a worktop balanced on oil drums, with a giant crack in its centre, like Aslan's resurrection stand in *The Lion, the Witch and the Wardrobe*. There were cups and playing cards, used batteries, a smashed torch bulb with blood flaked on the surface: more evidence of a fight and not a sacrifice. Not ritual then – but resistance.

Ava tried to imagine what occurred that night. Mickey had come here on a whim after the disco and on arrival, he'd found his sanctuary had transformed into a charnel pit over the winter. All these bones and feathers had been a shock to the boy because Ava knew Mickey had loved animals, especially cats.

Mickey was known as a 'hard rock' by the local boys. He was a scrapper; fearless. So he'd confronted his killer. There'd been shouting into the night, screams. When Mickey had threatened to tell, that was when he'd been attacked. Mickey was lifted high then thrown down onto the makeshift table, hard and agonising – cracking it with the force. Fighting broke out, but not the typical way men fight, because the experienced predator had weapons and was not afraid to hurt in ways most people considered taboo. A terrified boy against somebody much stronger: somebody with no morality, or fear of law and consequences. Was that all this was? Mickey's desire to confront a criminal, and his attacker's desperation to prevent his crime's disclosure?

In nature, every species recognises its own, and in human culture every tribe knows its kith. Ava descended from ferocious women who'd escaped a starved Ireland for the bellowing factories of industrial England, and from stubborn men blackened and bent from generations in Welsh coal mines. Yet she possessed no root into her history, no pull in her genes. In this place, however, she sensed a rogue in her species, a predator that preyed on his own.

'DS Delahaye!' Luke yelled.

Dear Luke, darling Luke, running towards her, his face a Greek mask of tragedy. She pondered how Red Riding Hood won in the better versions: the beast had met its match in hers. It was why Ava was here. It was why she was Ava. With this beast, she was not the hunted but the hunter. Ava pulled her hood over her head and the wind lifted her onto her toes. Her tears made clean tracks in the ash on her cheeks.

Ava was custodian of the dead; this she understood. The idea of hurting an animal, by accident or on purpose, was anathema to her. Even at the height of her curiosity, she would never cut them open to explore their interior anatomies – she was content with books to learn such details. All her subjects were buried intact, they were mourned, and they were given back to nature as nature intended. In the moments before giving them back, they were loved. It was Ava's calling.

In this atrocious place she had discovered another custodian. But, unlike her, their calling was taking – a thief who stole not only respect from the dead but also life from the living. With this monster there was desecration instead of reverence. His hate poisoned the spikes of wire and thorns. Ava's mind rattled faster and faster as her body slowed into an inexplicable exhaustion. Perhaps it was because of the weight of secrets: Mickey's savaged body, the fox, and the tortured cat.

'Ava!'

The shout came from behind her but Ava could barely hear it. She knew that the monster was not like her; that it had no desire to respect the dead. But her brain was too tired to fight off another awful epiphany: that this killer was just herself turned inside out: her fatal inversion.

'Ava!'

Luke. It took all of Ava's effort to focus on Luke as he ran to her, and she tried to capture him in her mind like a snapshot: the highlight along his cheekbones, the glint of gold in his ear, and the tuppence-bronze of his eyes. Her knees buckled. She hadn't asked them to, they just buckled even when she tried to stop them they still dropped, as if crumbling like the wall.

Luke reached and caught her before she hit the ground, Delahaye in his wake, and Ava collapsed into him. He held her close. But the darkness held her closer still.

Chapter Twenty-One

RETURNING AVA TO HER HOME after the discovery at Banlock Farm, Delahaye had suggested to Mrs Bonney that her daughter 'have a day off school because she'd been sick on the way back'. This was a lie: Ava had quickly recovered from her faint and, when he and Lines had suggested taking her to hospital, she'd resisted and insisted that 'hospital was for births, deaths, cancer and serious accidents, not my fannying about'.

As Delahaye drove back to the Bonneys' flat the morning after, he hoped Colleen Bonney had followed his advice and not sent her daughter to school. He wouldn't put it past Mrs Bonney to disregard another person's concern for her daughter – she came across as a very hard, self-centred woman. He wasn't looking forward to meeting her again today but it couldn't be helped. He wanted to thank Ava again for her assistance, give her a small gift for doing so then he'd be gone.

As he drove down the cul-de-sac towards the apartment building, he briefly saw a pale face at the window of the Bonneys' flat, and knew it was Ava's.

Delahaye took the stairs instead of the lift – it had questionable fluids on the floor and a massive gob of phlegm on the ground-floor button. He was about to clatter the Bonneys' letter box when an old lady appeared from next door and squinted at him. 'Hello,' she said.

He showed her his warrant card just as the Bonneys' door opened and Ava stood there, her huge green eyes serious as she regarded him without surprise.

'Your mom asked me to keep an eye on you, so I am,' Edna said to Ava. 'This is a nice policeman but keep your door open just to make sure, you know.'

'I will,' said Ava. She smiled at Delahaye. 'Hello, DS Delahaye.'

'Good morning, Ava,' he said.

Ava stood aside to let Delahaye in. She closed the door behind him and he followed her down the hall to the small kitchen. The view from the window was part of Cock Hill Lane and the Quarry.

'You're not surprised to see me?' said Delahaye.

'I saw Suzi through the window,' said Ava.

'Suzi?'

'Your Quattro.'

Suzi Quattro. He grinned, delighted by the pun. 'I get it! Yes, I like that. That's her name from now on.'

'Would you like a cup of tea, Detective Sergeant?'

'Yes please, Ava.' He smiled. 'Your mother is out?'

'I'm perfectly fine to be by myself.' Ava frowned.

'I've no doubt.'

She turned and smiled as if regretting her sharp tone. 'My mom's taken my sisters to school and then going to Northfield so she won't be back until lunchtime.'

'How're you feeling, Ava?'

Ava shrugged. 'I'm fine. How're you?'

'I'm a little tired but still standing,' said Delahaye. 'Did you tell your mother about what happened?'

Ava looked nonplussed. 'No. Why would I?' She shrugged then added, 'She hasn't said anything to me but it's good because it proved to my sisters that there's nothing to worry about.'

'Do you think Luke will say anything about yesterday to his father?' asked Delahaye.

'No,' said Ava. 'We can trust Luke. He's not like his dad.'

Delahaye didn't doubt that either. He looked around. 'How long has your mother been … friends … with Mr Bax, Ava?' Ava said nothing. 'I'm sorry. It's none of my business. I'm just a very nosey policeman.'

'He's nowhere to be seen since yesterday,' said Ava. 'He thinks the only reason why you came here yesterday was for him.'

As she made the tea, she kept her body at an angle so her back was never to him. She evidently didn't trust men and Delahaye wondered if Trevor Bax was compounding her wariness. He didn't want to make her uncomfortable. His mother once told him that the male gaze carried weight and could be felt everywhere it bounced and lingered so he made sure he only looked at her face.

'Are you *sure* you're all right after yesterday, Ava?' Delahaye asked gently. 'Some young people would have viewed what happened at Banlock Farm as a life-changing event.'

Ava leaned against the sink with her arms folded and smiled. 'Like an epiphany? Did you know that, historically, epiphanies don't serve children well? Look at Joan of Arc, who ended up burned to death for hers. And Stephen of Cloyes, who ended up a slave during the Children's Crusade.'

Delahaye was impressed and it showed because Ava rolled her eyes and said, 'I read a *lot*. Too much, Trevor says.' She handed Delahaye a mug of tea.

'Ava, I can't stress how important your information has been for us . . . and for Mickey's family, of course.'

Ava handed him a mug. 'Shall we sit in The Front?'

'The Front?'

'The living room.'

He could sense Ava watching him as he studied the place. But when he turned to look at her she quickly switched her gaze to the carpet. The room's window looked out to Lea Walk and the curve of Deelands Road. Delahaye wondered if Ava had been awake on the night of the Gail Kinchin shooting.

'Can I look through your work, Ava?' Delahaye asked. He saw the hardcover Oxford journals on the large table by the window.

'Yes.' Shyly, she opened her book on illustrated stories as he sat at the table to look at it. Her drawings were beautiful but dark in subject, of dragons, and big cats, and wild horses galloping through twisted trees. But it was her handwriting that really caught his attention.

'You've lovely handwriting, Ava,' he said. 'And you can seriously draw.'

'I get that from my dad,' said Ava. 'He taught me how to write when I was small. That's why I don't hold my pencil "properly".'

She sounded disdainful of what was 'properly' as she showed him how she gripped writing implements by using the blue pencil from her pocket. It fascinated Delahaye – a claw-like grasp that could switch from precision to manual grip in a moment – beauty to brutality. He turned the page and found her drawings of skulls – human and animal, wonderfully detailed and shaded. There was a sketch of a cat skeleton, labelled and annotated.

'You've an interest in skeletal anatomy.'

'We are our bones,' said Ava.

Delahaye paused, struck by the profundity of her simple statement.

'I was told to ask the local kids about the dens by one of the War Dance band members,' Delahaye said. 'And I thought, if there is someone who would know the den system on a housing estate full of kids it would be you.' He smiled. 'So, if you can think of anything else that could help the police ... '

Ava's face remained impassive.

'You'd get on with Miss Misty,' he said. 'Between us all, we might crack the case.'

Ava became very still then she said, 'Would you like another cup of tea?'

Delahaye looked up from the picture. 'No thank you. I have to go.' He smiled again. 'In gratitude, I've bought something for you. For helping us.' Delahaye handed Ava an HMV carrier bag.

She peeked inside and drew out a Tomita album – *Pictures at an Exhibition* – then looked at him with shining eyes.

'I hope you like it,' said Delahaye. 'I noticed you were listening to Tomita yesterday.'

'Thank you,' said Ava. Her smile was lovely when it happened.

Delahaye reached into his inner jacket pocket, pulled out a small card and handed it to her.

'That's the CID office number, along with my extension. Let me know if you remember anything else, all right?'

Ava nodded. She studied the card, both sides, and sniffed it.

Chapter Twenty-Two

I T WASN'T LIKE COLLEEN TO sleep in. Usually, by now, their mother would be dressed, with her face done and radio on. But today her mother was dishevelled, having slept in her makeup so her mascara had dried in Alice Cooper streaks, her hair a mess.

So, Trevor had hurt her again.

As Ava came in, with her offering of tea held out like the Holy Grail, she said nothing. Ava knew that any word uttered in the next few minutes could tripwire Colleen's full detonation.

Colleen, however, wasn't in the mood for confrontation: she appeared defeated.

'Oh, you are lovely,' said Colleen, hand outstretched. She gave Ava a cursory glance. 'How are you?'

'I'm all right,' said Ava. Should she brave the big question? Her mother's answer might be a smack or a sigh. The trick was to stand out of Mom's retaliation zone because Colleen had the reach of an orangutan.

'Are you all right, Mom?'

A long pause then a tight-lipped, 'Yeah, I'm all right, bab. Have to be, don't I, ay?'

Ava didn't respond. Colleen didn't want responses, she didn't want advice and she certainly didn't want to hear anything negative about Trevor. Telling her the problem was Trevor wouldn't end well. But, Ava knew, the real problem with Colleen was Colleen. She was proof that being beautiful bestowed a woman no advantages whatsoever. Her mother's sadness was her own fault and Ava observed it from afar, with indifference, as if watching Dresden burn through binoculars from a Lancaster Bomber cockpit. Colleen had made her bed and was now lying in it.

* * *

An hour later, Colleen was dressed. The curtains were open, the bed was made, and Rita lay across it, flicking through *Woman's Own* magazine. Colleen took money from her purse and handed it to Ava.

'Go the shops for me,' Colleen said.

Veronica asked to go with her, so they both surged out into the blustery morning. As they reached the curve of the road, they peeked into Deelands Hall, with its squat drabness and train of over-spilled rubbish bags.

'Avie!' said Veronica. 'Look!'

Tied to the post outside the Small Shop was Starsky, Mickey's dog. Both girls stopped in their tracks. Not so long ago, they would've waited until Mickey had left the shop before going in as it wasn't worth the hassle. They'd halted out of habit, as if Mickey was still alive. Ava marched towards the dog and the Labrador greeted her like an old friend, his tail wagging. Veronica joined in the petting and the dog twisted around them, pleased to be with young humans again.

'Oh, he loves that he does,' said Mr Grant as he stepped out from the shop, smelling of wet pennies and nicotine, newspaper under his arm. The girls stopped pampering the dog, but Mr Grant smiled at them. Ava thought the smile didn't show in his eyes. 'No! Carry on! Don't mind me!'

Mr Grant had always been polite and jovial. A round-faced man with a paunch, lately the skin hung off his bones in folds, as if he'd melted and set like the sagging clocks in a Salvador Dali painting Ava had seen in one of her father's art books. He looked haggard: a man not yet forty-five who looked twenty years older.

'We're taking him up Cofton Park,' Mr Grant went on. Ava felt his yearning like a cartoon creeping vine.

'Oh, lovely,' said Ava. The man's lip trembled, and Veronica took a step back.

'Well, you know ...' Mr Grant swallowed. 'My son Mickey used to take him ...' He sighed hard, emitting a small sob.

A car horn beeped and Mr Grant turned. An Allegro pulled up to the kerb. He was obviously relieved to escape. He took

Starsky's lead and the girls watched them both climb into the waiting car.

'Poor man,' said Veronica.

'Yes,' said Ava.

'He's nice. You wouldn't think he was Mickey's dad,' said Veronica.

'No,' said Ava.

In the Small Shop, as the girls perused the back aisles, they heard other people enter, big boisterous people – young men. Ava's hackles rose. She loathed encountering local kids – they were unpredictable and prone to arbitrary savagery. She heard the boys talking to the manager.

'What're we getting again?' Veronica murmured.

Ava relayed the items in the order of importance. 'Cigarettes, bread, matches, margarine; a sweetie mix-up if we've enough change.'

Veronica snapped her fingers and did a little dance around her sister, chanting: 'Ciggies! Bread! Matches! MARGE! A 10p mix-up if the change is LARGE!' They giggled. 'Could we get liquorice pipes?' she asked, as she looked at the sweets in the glass cabinet below the cash till.

'If we've enough, maybe,' said Ava, who knew they wouldn't.

The shop was suddenly busier. The stacked shelves were taller than Ava and she couldn't see over them, but she knew there was somebody there, listening. It wasn't the manager – she could hear him talking to one of the young men outside – Karl Jones. The pressure in the air was bent like a fist pushing down on a pillow. Ava touched the blue pencil in her pocket.

Veronica held up a loaf of bread. 'Green Sunblest?'

Ava frowned. 'No! It smells of feet and goes stale in ten seconds. Get the blue Mother's Pride.'

They approached the counter. The cigarettes were on display behind the till, a wall of colour in cardboard pixels. As they waited for the manager to return, Ava caught movement in her peripheral vision. She relaxed when she saw who it was – Nathaniel Marlowe.

Browsing the cold drinks fridge, he pulled out a bottle of pop. Had he been listening to them? He smirked at Ava as they formed an awkward little queue. The girls stared at him.

'How's your neck, Lady A?' he asked, obviously referring to the injury she'd sustained from Brett punching her.

'Much better now, thank you,' she said, politely. Trevor had gleefully insinuated the bruise on her neck was a love bite. Her mother had gone to slap her until Ava had lied about bumping her neck on a shelf at John's granddad's house and she could ask him to verify this. Mr Cadogan knew what had really happened and would stick up for her even in this lie.

The positive outcome from Nathaniel's intervention was now Brett Arbello left her alone. His avoidance of her was temporary, but she would enjoy it for as long as it did. She'd always be grateful to Nathaniel, and John, for coming to her aid.

Nathaniel did a comical bopping dance and whistled Veronica's shopping tune. 'So, Sunblest smells of feet and goes off in ten seconds,' he said, nodding as if seriously contemplating her opinion. 'Good to know.'

'You shouldn't be listening,' said Ava. Her tone was just a little bit strict and he Groucho'd his eyebrows at Veronica, whose face suddenly glowed red, stricken with the double-barrel blast of a shotgun crush.

'Yeah, well, *you* were loud as a crowd,' Nathaniel said. In the wan overhead light that made everyone look jaundiced, his eyes were large black pits, his distinctive eye colouring obliterated by the pupils.

The manager bustled in. The change Ava received was barely enough for a mix-up to share, certainly not enough for the liquorice pipe Veronica really wanted. They took the full bag and left the shop, Ava seizing Veronica by the shoulders so she couldn't sneak a backward peek at Nathaniel. Outside, they chewed their meagre sweets.

'Oy! Lady A! Hold on!'

The sisters turned to see Nathaniel striding towards them, his shirt tails billowing. The sunlight had made his pupils contract so his incredible eyes were obvious. He held out two liquorice pipes, pointing one at Veronica, who, in Ava's opinion, was close to swooning like a ditzy skirt from a Victorian melodrama.

'Bodie or Doyle?'

'Doyle,' said Veronica because he was her favourite agent from *The Professionals*.

Nathaniel pointed a liquorice pipe at Ava. 'Bodie or Doyle?'

'Bodie,' said Ava because Lewis Collins was Lewis Collins.

'Right answer, Lady A!' he said, and gave Ava the liquorice. His gaze switched to Veronica's fallen face, and he bopped her on the nose with the other pipe then handed it to her. Both girls were wary as they thanked him.

'Why?' asked Ava, and Veronica gasped. Ava wasn't usually so brave around Really Big Kids.

'Why what, Lady A?'

'Why're you being nice to us? People aren't nice to us ... usually,' she added.

Nathaniel shrugged. 'People aren't nice usually.' He hadn't answered her question, but he smiled when they did. 'How'd you get your scar, Lady A?' he asked, indicating the old white mark on her lower lip.

'I fell on a desk,' said Ava.

'Yeah, I fall on desks too,' he murmured.

She'd spoken the truth and he'd used her truth as his own euphemism.

'You have heterochromia iridum,' said Ava. Nathaniel was the ultimate science textbook example.

He stared at her.

'I do.' His odd eyes narrowed. 'You know what it is.'

'Yes,' she said. It was like there were two different people looking at her from the same face. 'Which is your favourite side?' Ava asked.

'Which is *your* favourite side?' he threw back.

'Both,' said Ava.

'Right answer, Lady A,' said Nathaniel, and grinned.

Veronica, feeling left out, tugged on her sister's sleeve.

'We've got to go,' Ava said.

'Yeah, so have I.' He jerked his head in the direction of his bike, War Horse, with its large, covered trailer full of groceries ready for delivery, and began to back away from the girls. 'See you around, Lady A.'

As the sisters resumed their journey home, Veronica said, 'He calls you Lady A!' Ava said nothing. She could feel her sister's envy spike, and she didn't want Nathaniel Marlowe to be used against her in a future bickering contest.

Veronica tried again. 'I think he's nice.'

'*Obviously*,' drawled Ava, and her sister blushed then shoved her. *Nice* was not a word she'd use to describe Nathaniel Marlowe. She suspected *nice* was too fey for the likes of him.

Chapter Twenty-Three

O, HAVE YOU EVER SEEN A COPPER
WITH HIS POCKET BOOK AND PENCIL
A-LOOKIN AT A-BODY WITH ITS EYES
FUCKED UP??
HARRY CA NAB!

'WELL, IT'S GOT A GOOD rhythm,' said Delahaye, studying the graffiti on the Flyover wall. It was scribed in spray paint like so much of the surrounding cacography, but instead of the usual sprawling letters, these were neat and tidy, in capitals the size of tabloid headlines. 'It'll stick in your head all day if you sing it loud with a bit of percussion.'

'Nice,' said Lines without humour. 'It's familiar.'

'It's based on the "Dear Boss" letter Jack the Ripper allegedly sent to the police,' Delahaye said. 'I suppose it's more original than "*Shaz woz ere*".'

'Jack's Greatest Hits then,' said Lines. 'It's a poke at you, Sarge.'

'Yes. Thanks'

'I'm hoping it's kids,' said Lines.

'Well, if it's the killer, it's about time we had *something*,' said Delahaye, though he didn't think it was. He thought it was simply a little note to the police, telling them to get a shift on. It didn't mention Mickey, but it was obviously about him.

'Harry Ca Nab . . .' Delahaye said.

'The mythical Devil's huntsman who rides his horse with hounds over the local hills,' said Lines. 'But I doubt he'd be down here writing crap on the concrete!'

As they headed towards Suzi, young Police Constable Morgan loped over to them from a patrol car.

'Sarge! A call's come through to tell you that Mr Coleman is lucid and will be able to see you today at Joseph Sheldon Hospital.'

To find Banlock Farm's owner, Delahaye had assigned the task to WDC Gibson. Meanwhile, Banlock Farm was processed for evidence, and they'd confirmed it as the location of Mickey Grant's murder. There were no matches for the degraded fingerprints lifted from the crime scene, but the purple fibres from under Mickey's nails matched those of the rug in the garage den. Professor Simmons believed the knife was the murder weapon that had delivered the final coup de grace.

The photographs of the farm possessed a Gothic beauty, Delahaye thought. There was no explanation for the hundreds of dead animals and the sinister outdoor ossuary of their remains. The Polaroid photographs, possibly taken by the missing camera, obtained in the garage were faded and probably taken sometime last summer: images of happy Mickey playing Solitaire in sunshine, snaps of the ruined house, and little else. But no pictures of the person who took the photographs – most likely just another kid.

WDC Gibson found the estate agency's owners, the McIntyres. The farm hadn't been occupied for ten years. It used to be a dog-breeding establishment, a small enterprise that produced bespoke police, military and guard dogs. The owner refused to sell the land even though the housing authorities had offered him thousands for it.

The owner was an elderly man with Alzheimer's Syndrome, currently a resident of Joseph Sheldon Hospital: eighty-one-year-old Mr Neville Coleman. Previous attempts to interview him had been thwarted because Mr Coleman had major lapses when he didn't know who – or where – he was, and was prone to violent outbursts. The hospital manager promised the police that as soon as Mr Coleman was having a 'good day' he would let them know.

Today was apparently a 'good day'.

The detectives drove Suzi down the Bristol Road South, narrowly missing a British Telecom van exiting its headquarters without indicating. Delahaye pushed down on the horn and was rewarded with the driver's hand-wave apology. Delahaye swore under his breath.

'Somebody got out of the wrong side of somebody's bed this morning,' said Lines.

Delahaye scowled. 'It was *my* bed.'

'Exactly, Sarge. That's your trouble. It's always *your* bed. Have you ever tried someone else's bed for a change? Like WDC Gibson's, for example.'

'Pardon?'

'Olivia Gibson. She fancies you, Sarge.' Lines grinned.

'Really, we're talking about this *now*?'

'I bet she'd OK a drink if you asked her.'

Delahaye said nothing. He wasn't happy talking about the personal during the professional, and he loathed talking about women to other men.

'And it's not like she's ugly, Sarge,' said Lines. 'She's a bit of a smasher, is Olivia.'

Delahaye shook his head as if he'd misheard.

'Come on, Sarge! It's her thirtieth birthday shebang at The Prince of Wales tonight. She's hoping you'll go, like, and wish her many happy returns.'

'She told you this, did she, DC Cupid?'

'In a manner of speaking, yes,' said Lines. 'Well, in the manner of: I overheard her chatting to some of the plonks – sorry, *WPCs* – in the canteen.'

Plonks. Delahaye had made a vow long ago not to date women in the Job. Previous experience proved that it just became a nightmare when it all went wrong. But Gibson *was* part of the team.

'I'll pop in and wish her a happy birthday,' Delahaye said finally.

Friesian bullocks grazed in fields beside the school as they cruised towards the John Connolly Hospital and Joseph Sheldon Hospital. Hollymoor Hospital's red water tower – what the local kids called the 'Tower of a Thousand Maniacs' – reached into the sky beyond it.

'Why're there so many loony bins around here?' asked Lines as they parked.

'These hospitals treat patients from across the country,' said Delahaye. 'During the wars they were military hospitals. This would have been a rural area back then. It was believed green space and fresh air healed damaged minds.'

* * *

In the hospital, Mrs Brown, the manager, supplied information with little prompting.

'Mr Coleman came to us from another care home in Bromsgrove five years ago,' Mrs Brown said. 'He was diagnosed with dementia, and he's been getting steadily worse. It's a shame because when he's lucid, you'd never know he has Alzheimer's. He was a man of means, and he's still not short of a penny, but there's not much he can do with it where he is.'

'Family?' Delahaye looked through the man's strangely sparse file. A few black-and-white photographs, a few documents, little else. As a young man, Coleman had been striking, with a glint in his eye that suggested either a good laugh or a good fight.

Delahaye spotted the Next Of Kin section on a document:

Wife – Deceased
Daughter – Deceased

'His daughter died in an accident about thirteen years ago,' the manager said unprompted. 'He doesn't get any visitors nowadays, but he's made good friends here, when he's able to recall he's made them. They're a good bunch – they make allowances.' She paused. 'He's not in any trouble, is he?'

'Not at all. We're here to tell him Banlock Farm was the scene of a serious crime. We'd also like to ask him a few questions about the place. For extra colour, if you will.'

Mrs Brown smiled with relief. 'He's developed the habit of talking to himself late at night. Entire conversations with an invisible friend. Sometimes, in the early hours, we find him with his face pressed to the window, chatting away. It's such a shame he's been reduced to this state, it really is.' She stood. 'I'll ask

Maureen to attend your interview, as she always gets on the right side of him if he ... has a moment. She'll be your yellow canary today!'

The detectives followed her down the long corridor.

'He sometimes wears sunglasses because his right eye is sensitive to light.'

Maureen was Mr Coleman's keyworker, a thin woman, worn out but kind. She escorted them to Mr Coleman's room.

'He's lovely really when he's having a good day,' Maureen whispered. The detectives nodded. 'And please, Detectives, don't mention Tess.'

'Tess?'

'His daughter.'

Sunlight streamed in bright stripes across the carpet. There was a sideboard with a small record player, a few framed photographs and an old black teddy bear slumped against them. One of the pictures was of a pretty girl with her arms wrapped around a magnificent German Shepherd. Another was of the dog on its own. An armchair faced the window.

'Nev? You've got visitors!' Maureen stood aside, and the armchair scraped back.

A man unfolded his long length from its corduroy embrace and stood. Delahaye had no doubts this was the man in the file pictures, despite the wrinkles and white hair. He was smartly dressed and wore sunglasses with very dark lenses perched high on the bridge of his nose. Old age had only made him a little stooped nothing more.

'Detective Constable Lines and Detective Sergeant Delahaye,' said Delahaye, and both reached forth to shake Mr Coleman's hand. When the right cuff of the old man's shirt pulled up on his wrist, Delahaye noticed a white oval scar in the pale flesh.

'I'm very pleased to meet you, gentlemen,' said Neville Coleman in a gravelly drawl. 'Detectives! Well! Hark at this!' Maureen sat down when Coleman did; the detectives remained standing. 'Excuse these,' said Coleman, pointing at his sunglasses. 'My right eye streams like piss.'

'You've quite a collection of sunglasses now, ay?' said Maureen. 'It's a pity about them favourite ones. They were proper vintage, them were.'

'Some sod's pinched them,' explained Coleman. 'Now, how can I help CID?'

'Banlock Farm ...' said Lines.

'Yes.' Coleman shrugged. 'I suppose you had to go through the old McIntyres to find me.'

Delahaye nodded.

'He used to breed Alsatians there back in the day,' said Maureen, before turning to Mr Coleman. 'Didn't you, Nev?'

'Not *Alsatians*, Maur! Shepherds!' He pointed at the picture of the dog on the sideboard. 'Banlocks, like Zasha there. Best dog I ever had, she was.' He waved a dismissive hand. 'Go on.'

'A few weeks ago,' Delahaye continued, 'a serious crime was committed on your property and it was temporarily sealed by the police during the investigation. We tried to contact you sooner, Mr Coleman, but—'

'When I have one of my turns, I'm no good for beast or man,' said Coleman. 'What kind of serious crime?'

'Murder,' said Delahaye. When Coleman leaned forward on his knees, Lines instinctively stepped back. Coleman remained silent, his face impassive. 'You don't seem surprised that a murder was committed at Banlock Farm, Mr Coleman.'

'I'm not,' said Mr Coleman. 'Cruel shit happens everywhere. Who was murdered then?'

'A local lad, a teenage boy,' said Lines. 'Fourteen-years-old.'

Coleman's mouth tensed. 'Oh *no*, not a babby.' The old man was quiet for a moment then, with a snapping change, Coleman added, 'Tell me: were the fields touched?'

'No,' said Delahaye. What did Coleman mean by *touched*? And why were the fields shown concern but the farm itself was not? Delahaye wrote it down in his notebook.

Coleman relaxed. 'Have you caught the murderer?'

'We're still investigating,' said Delahaye.

'Bad luck, that place, eh?' said Lines.

'It used to be a happy place,' said Coleman. 'We were happy. Like paradise it was, just us . . . Sometimes I dream that he comes back.'

Lines glanced at Delahaye.

'Who comes back, Mr Coleman?' asked Lines.

Maureen caught Delahaye's eye. Coleman turned his face to the window and removed his glasses. He fidgeted with them, his hands shaking, agitated and unlike the calm man he'd been when they'd first entered the room.

'That night, the first time, black as pitch it was, but the moon was massive. He came here and I could tell he was hollow inside, with nothing left.'

The old man's left hand rubbed the scar on his wrist and, in profile, Delahaye saw the lines etched deep into Coleman's face.

'Who comes here, Mr Coleman?' Delahaye prompted.

Coleman turned his head slightly. The curve of the old man's watery iris resembled the Earth as seen from space before he put the sunglasses on again. He was still anxious but he had collected himself, as if he'd suddenly remembered who he was talking to. His voice was almost a whisper. 'Good pups become bad dogs if you're cruel to them, Detective. I should know. Punish 'em too much, and they turn rogue, they do. Shame. He was a good 'un, once.'

'Who was good once?' asked Delahaye, but the old man wouldn't answer.

Chapter Twenty-Four

JOHN HAD BEEN BOASTING ABOUT his new hang-out for ages. When Ava showed up, he was lobbing a tennis ball against the wall with an old racket. He smiled, until he clocked her outfit.

'Oh my Lordy-Lord,' said John. '*What*'re you wearing?'

Puffed-sleeve polyester, Ava's new dress looked as if it could generate electricity if she walked fast enough. Ava struck a pose.

'It's my new frock! Don't you like it?'

'No,' said John. 'It's vile.'

'I'm sorry,' Ava said. 'I'd no idea *you* were the new editor of *Vogue*.' She hated the dress too, but she couldn't tell her mother because Colleen seemed to be going out of her way to buy Ava terrible clothes. Ava had grown out of everything except her school uniform, and she needed a proper bra more than this crappy dress. She would never admit it, but John's reaction disappointed her.

They set off for John's granddad's house which was just around the corner. ('I'm fixing Winston's tyres,' said Granddad Cadogan. 'So, make yourselves at home.') The house had a large garden and John's granddad owned a short street of three sheds at the bottom of the property. The newest shed was John's to do what he wanted with, to store his bike and his collections, as his own bedroom was becoming too cramped. He even had a key and he opened it to show Ava with a big arm flourish.

'Ta-dah!'

Ava stepped in, John watching as she looked around ... She wondered if he saw her as a girl. He was going to be fifteen in the autumn and she knew he must fancy girls – he must have a crush on someone. She didn't care – he was her best mate and his attitude towards her hadn't changed. But one day it might.

'Anything kept in here will be safe,' John said.

It's our War Room, Ava thought. She hauled her bag onto the table and pulled out her notebooks, and a couple of huge black ring-binder files. They were her father's collection of bound *Crime & Punishment* magazines and they were an excellent source for learning about criminal history, especially that of the last hundred years. They'd be more useful here.

'I'm shutting down the body farm,' said Ava. 'Just for a while. The days are longer and there'll be too many kids about trampling everything. I'd like to keep my old Red Books here if that's all right.' She intended to keep the latest with her. She always used the same brand of red-covered notebooks and they filled quickly – she'd brought several years' worth of observations.

John flicked through the notebooks, and she suppressed a grin as she watched his face twist at the drawings. People's disgust at natural things always amused her.

Ava had retrieved her Red Book and had drawn what she'd seen at Banlock Farm. Every detail of her rough map of the property was annotated and labelled. She'd written John a long letter describing everything that had happened then sent it and she could see it pinned on the wall of the den already.

The Polaroid photograph she had taken from Banlock Farm was of three graves – she had studied the image close up and she couldn't decipher the names inscribed on each marker. She also couldn't work out where they were situated in the world – certainly not any churchyard or cemetery as there were no other graves around them. They might be somewhere on Banlock Farm. She didn't know why she took the picture with her – she suspected it was because it was of gravestones and it appealed to her macabre nature, but it mostly piqued her instinct for mystery.

The Red Book was one of a series over the years, packed with information concerning her body-farm subjects – tables, bar graphs, diagrams. Ava's heroes were the most famous forensic pathologists: Sirs Francis Camps, Sydney Smith and, her all-time favourite, Sir Bernard Spilsbury. But she believed that Professor John Glaister's – a nineteenth-century Scottish forensic pathologist Ava was also very fond of – maxim was truth: bodies decompose in air twice as quickly as in water, and eight times as rapidly as in earth (especially for small mammals and amphibians).

And then she'd redrawn the original drawing of Mickey at the den, and in even greater detail, this time portraying the development of fly species and beetles, the source of light, depth of shadow. And the state of the corpse's decomposition, the rate of it: her theories and suspicions. She'd drawn a rough body outline of Mickey and marked the wounds, particularly the stabs and the dreadful bites.

John pulled up a box with a lock, the kind of box her dad kept his vinyl albums in. Its label proclaimed '*BEANO*'. He dropped the notebooks inside then covered them up with copies of the *Beano* so a nosey person would see nothing was amiss.

'For the noticeboard, I've got a huge poster of Madness to cover it every time we leave,' said John.

'Brilliant,' said Ava.

Ava slid the Polaroid photograph she'd stolen from Banlock Farm from the cover of her notebook and handed it to John. He studied it closely. 'To actually hold it in my hands feels really ... weird.' He squinted at the picture again, trying to make out the names carved on the marble as she had done many times. The image was stamped on her memory: two big headstones and one smaller marker. The area around the graves was festooned with hawthorn flowers.

'But Ava, this is vital evidence, and you took it from a crime scene,' said John, his face worried.

'It's not *vital*. I'm going to find those graves. I know they're on that land. The police have the murder weapon and they have the place Mickey was killed, thanks to me. The picture isn't important in light of those things.'

Not yet anyway, she thought. 'And it's just three graves. Nothing to do with the murder,' she said.

John put the photograph down.

'Ava.' His voice was quiet. 'Ava, this is too big for us.'

Ava stepped into the shade away from the window.

'Oh, yes,' she said. 'But let's make it *our* project for a while. We'll be Sherlock Holmes and Dr Watson!'

'But which of us is Sherlock?' he asked, and grinned when she rolled her eyes because wasn't it obvious?

Chapter Twenty-Five

'**G**IRLS!'

At the sound of their mother's voice, Ava and her sisters froze. It didn't sound as if they were in trouble, but with Colleen you never knew – their laughter could annoy her.

They hurried from their bedroom to find their mother seated at the big table in The Front room. There was an officious-looking letter in her hand.

'I just want to tell you now that we'll be moving to a house in Frankley by the end of the year,' said Colleen, her eyes bright with excitement. Ava's sisters gasped with surprise. 'We're on a list, but because you girls are getting older and you're all sharing one bedroom, we'll be put on an even shorter list!' She grabbed Rita's hand and squeezed. 'Isn't that great?'

'Will I get my own room?' asked Ava. She knew that Trevor would be going with them and she dreaded to ask even to confirm it.

'Yes, because you're the eldest and your sisters get on better,' said their mother. 'We need to start preparing. You need to sort stuff out, what you've grown out of. It's going to be a new start!'

Her sisters skipped about, chatting about their new house and what it might look like, and Colleen kissed the top of Ava's head and returned to the kitchen.

Ava, however, went to The Front room window. Rain fell in long drops like diagonal wire, but she wanted to go out in it, to be alone and think about what she'd just learned. She asked her mother and Colleen nodded.

'Ten minutes,' her mom said.

Ava marched down the lane, shoving her hands deep into her coat pockets as the wind shoved her about. She walked backwards to look at the dump site. It seemed an age since she'd discovered Mickey's body. She turned away and thought of happier things: *I'm getting my own room!*

She walked alongside the wall that bordered Rubery Hill Hospital then passed the empty sixty-three bus stop. To her left, she spotted a pale figure flit amongst the trees that lined the avenue to the hospital. The apparition floated too close to the edge of a steep dip to the stream, and Ava paused to look. The spectre paused too, to stare back. Ava was familiar with this woman. Some locals called her 'Lady Mary' or 'The Ghost Lady' but Ava called her 'The Wraith': a thin lady who might've been old or young, with pale skin, wild white hair, wearing nothing but a white nightgown and grey cardigan. Some people had seen her come into the Village, some said she'd even sometimes wandered into the schools. But Ava had only ever seen her on this road, wringing her hands and gliding about, her lips mouthing silent words, her eyes glistered with tears.

Ava walked and The Wraith walked too. Ava walked faster and The Wraith followed suit: copying her, mirroring her, a peculiar yet comforting contact. The lady wasn't right in the mind if her forever home was a mental hospital – but Ava had yet to witness her being threatening or dangerous.

Ava reached the edge of the avenue and saw The Wraith approach, at almost supernatural speed, her stride short, on tiptoe. The woman's hospital slippers were soaked through, her bare legs mud-spattered. A fair distance behind The Wraith, concerned hospital staff followed, reluctant to spook their charge so close to a hectic main road. Traffic on the Bristol Road South whizzed and hissed in a constant torrent.

Ava stopped and waited.

The Wraith stopped and waited.

Ava hoped the attendants would hurry up.

'Lady A.'

Ava whirled around to find Nathaniel Marlowe astride War Horse, in a greatcoat and hood that obscured most of his face. She hadn't heard him approach because of the road noise.

Nathaniel's gaze narrowed at the pale figure of The Wraith. Then he cycled around the corner towards The Wraith as his whistled rendition of *Dr Zhivago* cut through the wind and traffic. Ava watched in awe and trepidation as the music seemed to lure The Wraith towards him, her arms outstretched like a toddler's for sweets, a beatific smile on her face. Nathaniel made a slow circle in the empty road to make sure he had her full attention and then languidly pedalled towards the grateful attendants with The Wraith in his wake: a teenaged Pied Piper leading a crazy lady to safety with a trinket box tune.

Ava ran across the road to shelter beneath the colossal bulk of the Flyover, her legs grateful for the exercise as they'd become numb with the wet. She could barely feel her hands they'd become so cold. As she crossed beneath the concrete mass, Nathaniel skidded to a halt in front of her with the flourish of a speedway rider. He kicked down War Horse's stand and threw back his hood. The huge pupils in his eyes were blank voids. He raised the tarpaulin cover off the trailer hooked to the back of his bike and ushered her over.

'Get in.'

'Pardon?' Ava said.

'Get in.'

Ava got in.

Nathaniel handed her his big old sheepskin mittens with huge rips in the backs. His own hands in fingerless gloves, he checked her knees were drawn up and that she was seated securely.

'Stick your hands in your armpits,' said Nathaniel 'It keeps them warm,'

Ava obeyed. It was so strange to be so low to the ground, but even stranger to be scrunched into a trailer at the back of Nathaniel Marlowe's bike on a rainy day. He closed the trailer's cover as far as it would go and secured the tarpaulin. It was, she supposed, a kind act – but there was no kindness in his manner. No warmth or presence whatsoever. He was as different from the boy she'd spoken to last Saturday as a barracuda was from a bear. Ava, veteran of moody people, knew better than to initiate conversation.

'Lea Walk, right?' he said.

'Yes.'

'House, maisonette or flat?'

'Flat.'

'All right, hold tight.'

Ava's heart thudded fast as Nathaniel began to pedal. They swooped into the plummeting rain, along the path towards home. The trailer's thick tyres absorbed most of the bumps in the pavement, but they flew off the kerb into the road with a thud which made her coccyx tingle. The road was dangerously close and a blur. But it was exhilarating: her breath caught in her throat and she giggled, unable to voice the delicious terror any other way.

Peeking from under the tarpaulin, Ava could see the tail of Nathaniel's coat flap and snap; saw how hard the boy's long legs worked to keep them speeding up the hill, the wind behind them, aiding their flight. They crested the hill then dipped so fast Ava's tummy lurched, as it did on the Pirate Ship at Drayton Manor, down the potholed road to Rushmore House. Nathaniel braked to a halt in the foyer and helped her out of the trailer like the Prince assisting Cinderella from the pumpkin carriage. She beamed so wide her face hurt.

'Thank you so much!' Ava said. 'That was ace!'

Nathaniel looked at her. There was no trace of his heterochromatic distinction today, not in the darkening light.

'I'll sew these up for you,' Ava said. 'I'm good at sewing. You know, as a thank you.'

Nathaniel swallowed hard and she heard a click of cartilage.

'Cheers.' His voice was a Phil Oakey monotone.

'Bye, Nathaniel.'

He nodded. 'Take care, Lady A.'

PART TWO

Chapter Twenty-Six

Mid-June

I T WAS BRY'S WAY: TO wait until his brothers fell asleep and then creep downstairs to be with Mommy whilst she watched telly. Mommy told him off, but her scolding was such a soft thing and Bryan knew she couldn't send him back to bed without a cuddle.

He was the baby who still needed Kelly, as her eldest sons grew more into men every day. Rob was fifteen: in lust with Kim Wilde and moaning about spots; Tom was simply Tom, immature for his age but growing up too. Kelly and little Bryan snuggled on the settee and watched the television. Kelly enjoyed her last cigarette of the day. She nuzzled her son's temple, with its fine fuzz which smelled of teddy bears. He giggled because she tickled, so much younger when he was in her arms, so much like her with his large eyes and round forehead. In his hand – as always, as if grafted into the palm – was his toy Comanche brave riding a pinto mustang. He'd had it since he was a toddler and it went everywhere with him.

When the adverts came on, Kelly saw his eyes close.

'Come on you, Sunshine Blue. Off to bed.'

Bryan was immediately alert. 'I'm awake!'

'You little fibber!' Kelly said. 'You're dropping off! It's a school night.' She stood and held out her hand which Bryan reluctantly took as she heaved him to his feet.

'Where's my wolf suit, Mommy?' Bry was obsessed with Max from *Where the Wild Things Are* and his grandmother had made him a replica wolf suit from a pair of old baby blankets and a tail from a real fox-fur scarf bought from the Rag Market.

'It's in the wash, Bry.'

'When're *you* going to bed?' he asked with a big yawn.

'Soon, after I've put the rubbish out and I've got your clothes ready for tomorrow,' said Kelly.

His eyes brightened. 'Can I help? Can I put the rubbish out? Please, Mommy!'

Kelly laughed. 'All right!' she said. 'I'll get the bag ready and you can take it out. But be quick: it's late. Yes?'

Bryan nodded. Kelly handed the bag over.

'Quick,' she said. 'Leave the door open so you don't have to worry about the latch.' She kissed the top of his head. 'Go!'

Bryan slung the sack over his shoulder like one of the Seven Dwarves, and plodded out of the front door. Kelly turned to the living room and smiled as she arranged the laundry piles on the armchairs and settee. She heard the front door click shut, a neat sound, decisive – unlike his usual slam.

'Thank you, Bry!'

Kelly paused. Her smile slowly disappeared. Her head was cocked to one side as she listened and waited. She switched the television off and the silence deafened. She stepped forward into the quiet.

'Bry?' she said softly. And then, a little louder: 'Bryan? Sweetheart?'

No answer.

No concern – not yet – just puzzled curiosity. She searched the house and gardens, inside cupboards and under beds. But Bry wasn't there. She called his name softly so as to not wake her older boys. Bryan's bed was next to Tom's, empty, still warm from his small body. He wasn't in the bathroom either, only the tap drip-dripping with ominous rhythm. She looked out of the window into night. The moon was dark, the stars dim.

Bry wasn't a boy to play such games: he was good and would never worry her in this awful way. Kelly felt panic hatch and squirm in her stomach. She wrapped her cardigan tightly around herself as if to keep the anxiety contained; as if fearful it might burst her open. Her heart thundered in her chest as she yelled her son's name.

'BRYAN!'

His small voice never answered.

124

Chapter Twenty-Seven

THEIR MOTHER'S BAD MOOD OSMOSED through walls and under doors like toxic gas. She'd already smacked Ava around the face for making her sisters laugh too loud, so they all slunk away to get their school bags.

Colleen's bad mood was because of Trevor. Sometime in the night, he'd left her in bed and gone out without saying a word. Ava had been up and staring out The Front room window as she often did when she couldn't sleep and needed to think. She'd heard Trevor get up so she'd ducked behind the big table. He'd been naked and he'd silently padded in to The Front room to quickly get dressed in the dark, loose change and keys jangling in his pockets. She'd listened to him quietly leave the flat then she'd scurried to the kitchen window.

The wall clock's luminous hands stated it was quarter past two in the morning. If he'd returned to his own flat on the level below them, she'd not see him, but she'd watched him run up the steps to the main road and switch right. He was no doubt going to visit one of his other women or attend a rendezvous for a dodgy deal. Ava had returned to bed and, a few minutes later, as she settled, she heard her mother open her own room door and whisper into the night, 'Trev?'

Of course Ava couldn't tell her mother what was regularly going on with Trevor's nocturnal excursions. She just had to endure her mother taking her frustration out on her daughters instead.

Ava returned to The Front room while Mom put on lipstick in the mirror, getting ready to go nowhere. Rita opened her mouth and flipped over a penny on her tongue, an impressive skill but one not appreciated by the eagle-eyed Colleen.

'And get that out your gob or you'll get canker!' Colleen said.

Rita removed the penny sheepishly and put it in her pocket. Ava resisted the urge to challenge her mother's assertion: the possibility of contracting canker through sucking pennies was highly unlikely. Germs yes, but not canker. But Ava didn't want to get hit again so said none of this as she ushered her sisters out of the front door.

In the foyer, they met Susan Shaw, who was taking her children to school too.

'Ava?' she said. 'Have you heard?'

Ava shook her head, and Susan's mouth pinched. 'Another kid's gone missing!'

The Bonneys stopped in their tracks.

'Around here?'

'Yeah! But they haven't said who it is, only that it's a six-year-old boy. He went missing last night.' Susan pointed towards the Quarry. 'Police are all over again. Look.'

In the tepid sunshine, on the very crest of the Quarry, Ava could see the search teams waving sticks in the gorse. Ava's stomach fluttered. She thought of Trevor out last night.

At school, during form-time, Ava looked for absentees. Two faces were missing: Tracey Wilkes and Tom Shelton. Her stomach fluttered again. Tracey had older brothers. Tom had a six-year-old brother.

Oh, please, please God, no. Don't let it be Bry.

Ava tried to be rational, tried not to worry. There were hundreds of six-year-old boys; the missing pupil could be from any of the many primary schools in the area.

It could be someone else. But Tom's empty chair exuded disquiet. As the class filed into the hall for assembly, everything was typically unbothered. None of the teachers mentioned a missing child, their faces as impassive as church statues.

It was on the way out of assembly that one of fourth year kids murmured, 'It's Tom Shelton's little brother. My mom said.'

Chapter Twenty-Eight

DRIVING TOWARDS RUBERY, PERRIN GLANCED at Delahaye.

'I want you to meet the Sheltons because you're great with kids, Seth,' Perrin said. 'I want you talking to the boys. I'll talk to their mother. And you have a good look around, too. I'm not suggesting that there's anyone to worry about in the family, but we all know the statistics.'

'This shouldn't have happened. We should have caught this monster by now.'

'Rubbish,' said Perrin. 'How? We work with what we've got, Seth. It's always been the way. Think about those great coppers who worked on the Jack the Ripper case – Abberline and Reid. And the brighter lads working on the Yorkshire Ripper case for years. The former was never caught and the latter was only caught by accident. We're not mind readers, we can't solve crimes with clues we don't have. And we can't pull happy endings out of our arses. Seth, Ava Bonney was a gift and she found the murder site, but *you* found her. You've made headway with the local teenagers too – eyes and ears in the community are just what we need right now. Doubt helps nobody.'

Delahaye said nothing.

'And don't let the squad hear it, either,' said Perrin. 'They see you as much a guv'nor as me and DCI Brookes.'

Delahaye suspected he was a mystery to his superiors. They wanted him on fast-track promotion schemes, despite his dropping out of university to join the police force. He knew it wasn't the 'done thing' but Delahaye didn't want to fast-track – he hadn't joined the police to climb the ranks. It had been a calling, not to 'do good' but to 'do right', which are two very different things, though neither were often achieved.

As they approached the car factories, Delahaye realised he didn't want to go any further.

'I think we're looking at the worst-case scenario,' Delahaye said. 'I don't think Mickey's killer is finished.'

Perrin said nothing for a long while, until they turned into the underbelly of the Flyover and onto Cock Hill Lane.

'I don't want to see that look on your face near the mother and her boys,' Perrin said. 'I want her to see hope glowing from your face like fucking neon.'

* * *

Delahaye followed Perrin into the Sheltons' living room, which instantly shrank with their presence. They introduced themselves to Kelly Shelton, who sat on the settee with two boys, and beside them an older woman in her fifties whom Kelly introduced as her mother. PC Daryl Morgan stood immediately when the detectives came in. Morgan had dark rings around his eyes and Delahaye could see he was still high on the last streaks of adrenaline in his system. The collar of his blue shirt was grubby. He'd been in this house since first-responding the night before, and it was obvious he'd established a rapport.

'Go and have a break, son,' said Perrin, taking the young officer to one side. 'Get some kip.'

Morgan nodded but Delahaye could see he was reluctant to leave. Delahaye patted his shoulder, and the young officer smiled through his tiredness, leaving to a chorus of goodbyes from the Sheltons. Perrin made the introductions and Delahaye shook hands with the boys then showed them his warrant card. They stared at it, impressed. Kelly laughed at their expressions; a bright sound which punctured the worry in the room. Kelly had a birthmark the size of a penny on her throat, which her sons had inherited, though in differing locations: Tom's was high on his cheek, and Robert's was a streak of brown under his chin. Bryan's mark was on his forehead.

Whilst DI Perrin began his courteous but forthright questioning of the mother, Delahaye asked her sons to give him a tour of the house and tell him all about their little brother. There was nothing amiss – it was a normal family home. Alan Shelton had been fifty miles away on a driving job when his youngest son went missing, and was currently on his way back to be with his family.

The boys showed him to Bryan's bed and Tom offered his own for the detective to sit on.

The boys sat on Bryan's bed opposite him. He asked them friendly questions about routines. He asked them about their dad and if he liked talking to their mother. About school, and people the family knew. Was there anybody who was nasty to them, who might bear a grudge against them, who might steal Bryan away as a bad joke? The boys answered in that blasé, honest way well-loved boys with nothing to hide answered.

Delahaye looked at them. 'Is Bry being bullied?'

Robert shook his head. 'Nah, everybody loves Bry. Even Mickey Grant left him be.'

Delahaye experienced a weird bump in his equilibrium hearing the name in this house, with one of its own children missing.

'And you heard nothing at all?' Delahaye said.

'We were fast asleep,' said Robert.

Tom brightened. 'D'you want to look in Bryan's treasure chest?'

Delahaye smiled. The brothers each had a large box kept under their beds for the things they loved most. Tom pulled Bryan's box out. It was made of pine, and a good size, with a hinged lid carved with Bryan's name in a Gaelic font.

'Dad made us one each,' said Robert.

The few objects within were typical little boy 'tranklements' and toys. Delahaye saw a picture with Ava Bonney's name on it.

'Do you know Ava Bonney?' said Delahaye.

'Yes, we're in the same form at school,' said Tom, blushing. He seemed very young for thirteen. 'Ava drew these for Bryan.' He leaned against the detective as he unfolded the pictures. 'She teaches as she talks.'

'I know,' murmured Delahaye.

Rob came to sit on the other side of the detective, so close now that he could smell their apple-shampoo scalps and their toothpaste-minty breath.

'These are Bry's favourite books,' said Tom. He pointed at a tatty copy of *Where the Wild Things Are*. 'When Ava and Vere come round, Bry gets into his wolf suit and makes them read it in their different voices.'

'They can do accents and impressions,' said Robert. 'Mary Poppins, and wolf howls ...'

'Speaking of wolves,' Delahaye interjected. 'How is the game Wolf different from hide-and-seek?' Delahaye had wanted to know ever since Ava first mentioned it.

Robert shrugged. 'Well, you start off with a bunch of kids and they go and hide, and the lead seeker is the Wolf. With every person they find, they join his – or her – pack, then they become wolves and the more people you have the more people you find.'

'It can get scary sometimes,' said Tom. 'Last year, two of the big kids found us, but let us go in the end.'

'Nathaniel and Karl,' Robert supplied. 'Karl's a snobby git but Nathaniel's all right.'

'Yeah,' said Tom. 'But because of them we won the game.'

Delahaye made notes in shorthand. The boys watched as he jotted the strange symbols as fast as they talked. He shifted, and they sat a little apart from him, suddenly aware that they were too close.

'D'you think Bry will be back soon?' asked Tom.

Delahaye had to be careful not to make his answer a promise. 'We're working hard to find him,' he said.

Rob frowned but said nothing.

Tom lifted the copy of *Where the Wild Things Are* from the box, revealing an object beneath. Then his eyes widened and his jaw dropped.

'Rob!' he said. 'Look!'

At the bottom of the box, cradled on white tissue paper, was a sugar mouse.

The sugar mouse was roughly twice the size of a real mouse; ivory with rose-gold blushed ears and snout. It glistened in the daylight, a gorgeous confection, with its soft scent of vanilla. It sat there on its crepe cushion, too beautiful to eat.

Delahaye was suddenly invisible as the brothers spoke in harsh whispers over his lap. Where did Bryan get it? How could he have afforded it? Or was it a gift – and, if so, from who? Could he have stolen it? Surely not: Bry knew stealing was wrong, and anyway the expensive sweets were kept behind glass.

Most importantly, why hadn't Bry told them he had it?

The boys stared at each other, suddenly remembering Delahaye was still sitting between them.

'But I don't think Bry nicked it,' said Robert quickly, and then, under his breath: '*Shit.*'

It was a load of fuss and palaver over a sweet but, however small, it was still a clue in a case with very few clues – a secret Bryan had kept from his family. A little secret that disconcerted the children and piqued Delahaye's curiosity.

Using the tissue paper as gloves, he picked up the sugar mouse, as the boys watched in wonder.

'Shall we ask your mother about it?' asked Delahaye, and the boys nodded. They trooped downstairs and Delahaye showed Kelly the sugar mouse.

'Have you seen this before, Mrs Shelton? It was in your son's treasure chest.'

She stared at it, confused. 'Only in the posher sweet shops. They're too expensive. Was it really among Bry's things?'

Her sons nodded, sombrely. 'We never knew he had it,' said Robert.

'It's just a sweetie,' said Kelly with a smile. 'Perhaps he found it in the street and that's why he never ate it then kept it because it's pretty.'

This was the most plausible explanation, but there was something about it that tugged at Delahaye's copper intuition.

'Do you mind if I take this with me, Mrs Shelton?'

Mrs Kelly nodded. 'But don't eat it all at once, Detective Sergeant. It'll rot your teeth.'

When the boys' grandmother called Robert and Tom into the living room, Delahaye asked Kelly to re-enact her and Bryan's movements in the moments before he went missing. SOCO had tried to lift fingerprints from the door but without success. The killer knew enough to wear gloves.

'And you heard the front door click shut,' said Delahaye.

'Yes,' said Kelly. 'He never clicks, he slams. I'm always telling him off for it. It bothered me last night, the way the door closed. I can't describe it, but I'll try and make the same sound ...' She closed the door to, as Bryan had the night before, then she pulled it tight in the frame. No footsteps. No voices. Just a prissy click and a separation of worlds: light from dark, warm from cold, safe from unsafe.

The sheer balls it took to take a child from outside his own home were astounding.

'Daddy!'

A burly man was walking down the path and the Shelton boys ran out of the house and threw themselves at him. The man ruffled their hair and carried them towards the policemen and Mrs Shelton.

Kelly ran to her husband who enfolded her in his donkey-jacketed arms and kissed her fiercely on the top of her head. She sobbed, and then their sons burst into tears as if allowed now their father was home. Over the crying lump of his family, Mr Shelton extended a hand to Delahaye and Perrin.

'I'm Alan Shelton.'

Chapter Twenty-Nine

GRAFFITI ON THE SIDE OF a white van parked outside The Plough pub:

> **There was a vicious king**
> **who had a vicious sting**
> **right in the middle of his smile.**
> **When he was nice**
> **he was very, very nice**
> **but when he was cruel**
> **He was vile.**
> *Harry Ca Nab!*

'Ava!' Ava's mother called. 'It's John!'

Ava could hear her mother asking him to come in, but John refused, claiming he had to be home soon and just wanted to ask Ava a quick question about homework. John attended a different school and was in a different year, but the lie worked like magic on Colleen.

Ava stepped out and John's relief at seeing her was palpable.

'Bryan,' John said. 'What do you think?'

She put the door on the latch and closed it behind her.

'I think he's gone,' she said simply.

'D'you think it might be ... the *thing* ... at Banlock Farm?' he whispered.

Ava nodded. It couldn't be Trevor. The news said Bryan had gone missing about 9.30 p.m. and Trevor had left the flat hours later so it couldn't have been Trevor who snatched him. Her deep disappointment: if he was the murderer then the murders would stop ... and when he was in prison, he'd be gone from her life forever.

Spotting Suzi cruising the hill, she wiped her eyes on her sleeve and murmured: 'DS Delahaye's here.'

John leaned over the balcony railing to see the silver Quattro parked on the kerb.

'I'll see you later,' John said.

Ava watched as Lines and Delahaye approached the foyer of the flats.

'Go,' she said.

John descended the stairs two at a time.

* * *

The detectives looked pleased to see her, despite the circumstances.

'My mom's in if you want to speak to her,' said Ava.

'Actually, it's you we've come to see, Ava,' said Delahaye. From his inside jacket pocket, he extracted a plastic bag and removed a white-tissue parcel. In the centre of the crackling paper was a perfect sugar mouse, which he held up to Ava. 'This was found at the bottom of Bryan Shelton's treasure box. We think it was deliberately hidden. We've asked around and nobody can recall him buying it, and it's apparently impossible to steal. Nor was it a gift from his family or friends.'

Ava huffed. 'I don't think they're worth a pound. It's ostensibly just a lump of sugar.'

Lines raised an eyebrow. 'Ostensibly?'

She paused. 'So, Bry kept it a secret?'

'We think so,' said Delahaye.

'He might've found it,' said Ava.

'That's possible,' said Delahaye.

'But it *is* weird if Bry kept it a secret because he's *very* close to his mom.' Bryan would have definitely showed it off to Kelly, Ava knew.

'That's what his brothers told us,' said Delahaye.

Ava took a deep breath. 'How're the Shelton family?'

'They're worried, as you can imagine,' said Delahaye, returning the sugar mouse to his pocket. Ava decided she never wanted to see another one again after today.

Over the detectives' shoulders she could see dogs in harnesses and police officers on the Quarry. Delahaye watched her watching the dogs.

'Ava, can you tell me the difference between Alsatians and German Shepherds?' he asked.

'There isn't a difference between Alsatians and German Shepherds because they're the same breed,' said Ava. 'German Shepherd is the proper name. It's to do with history. After World War I, there was so much anti-German feeling that the first breeders of German Shepherds in this country couldn't show the breed and, as the first puppy brought back to England was allegedly found on the Alsace–Lorraine border by a British soldier, it was decided they'd be called Alsatians instead.' She paused then added, 'The same reason why the Royal Family changed their name from Saxe-Coburg Gotha to Windsor in 1917.'

'Good Lord, Ava.' said Lines. 'We could do with your brain back at the nick instead of those soddin' computers!'

Ava shrugged. 'Why d'you want to know about German Shepherds?'

'Because Banlock Farm used to be a breeding centre for police and army dogs,' said Delahaye.

'Is the owner . . . still around?' Ava thought it might seem rude to say *dead*. 'Does he know about . . . everything?'

'Yes,' said Lines. 'His name's Neville Coleman. He's in Joseph Sheldon Hospital because he's very old and senile. But he knows about the murder. He's the only one left – all his family have died.'

Ava logged this information and blinked. 'Are you visiting the Sheltons today?' she asked and Delahaye nodded. 'Could you tell them that we're thinking of them?'

'Of course, Ava,' said Delahaye, and Ava knew he would. 'There's a television appeal on the news tomorrow. We're holding a press conference earlier in the investigation than Mickey Grant's, because Bryan was so much younger.'

Bryan *was* so much younger. *Was*. Past tense – a slip. Ava sensed more truth in that tiny mistake than everything else Delahaye had said, and he had a habit of telling the truth. Ava had no intention of watching the television appeal. She didn't want to see Kelly Shelton's shattered face and she didn't want to hear the desperation in her voice. Ava knew an appeal wouldn't bring Bryan home and it wouldn't make the kidnapper return him either.

Bryan is where the wild things are forever, she thought with a shudder.

Chapter Thirty

ONCE A WEEK, JOHN WENT out before dawn. On Thursdays, his mother shared a stall at the Rag Market in town with other single-mom entrepreneurs, and she was excited about market day, often regaling him with tales of banter and errant customers, and the characters she encountered.

She always asked him to go to the newsagent's and buy her assorted magazines to read during rare quiet moments between customers. This small errand was the reason John loved Thursdays so much – because he got to walk along empty streets like he was the last human on earth.

He wasn't the *first* human – the milkman beat him to that accolade, whistling cheerfully as he passed alongside John in his humming float, which chimed with glass bottles. A few night-shift workers were returning home, too, but John was the only *kid*.

His joy was tainted, however, because of Bryan Shelton's disappearance. He didn't personally know the Shelton family but Ava did, and anyway, you didn't have to know someone to feel empathy for their distress. Before he started to worry and think too much about it, he took a deep breath and walked faster.

In the distance, traffic grew louder along the Flyover. Leach Heath Lane forked left and right to Leach Green Lane and was divided by a grass holm Ava called Three Tree Island.

But as John walked opposite the junior school, he was no longer the only kid around. He kept walking uphill, shooting surreptitious glances at a tall, rangy youth on Three Tree Island. The boy faced away from him, and was crouched on his haunches, looking at something out of sight. When John recognised the big bike on the ground not far away, he knew who the boy was.

Nathaniel Marlowe.

John, not wanting to disturb, remained quiet and, he hoped, invisible. He was just thinking he'd successfully retained the last of his dawn solitude when Marlowe turned and looked straight at him. He stood upright. John kept his eyes averted but to avail.

'Oy! John!' Marlowe called out. 'Oy, mate! Can you help me out a sec?'

John stopped, as if his own free will was momentarily short-circuited. He saw what had held Marlowe's attention – a small, dead dog was lying at his feet. John wanted to say no, but instead he crossed the road as if compelled, his inherent politeness driving him like a heavy goods vehicle. He stopped a few metres from Marlowe.

John hadn't spoken or been this physically close to Marlowe since Marlowe had chucked Brett Arbello across the ground for attacking Ava outside the school. He saw Nathaniel and his fellow delivery boy, Karl, zoom around on their bikes, but that was the limit of his acquaintance. Marlowe's odd eyes were distinctive in the morning light, and, at full height, he carried his weight across both feet like a boxer. On his scarred forehead rested the coolest pair of sunglasses John had ever seen – like goggles explorers wore from the 1920s.

John looked down at the dead dog: a little fluffy thing of indeterminate breed, with no collar, and yellowish fluid and blood sticky about its ears. *Fractured skull*, thought John, a long-time pupil of Ava's. There was no fly activity – probably because the dog was freshly dead. He looked up to find Nathaniel watching him with his head cocked to one side.

'Poor dog,' said John. 'Is he yours then?'

'No,' said Marlowe. 'I found him.'

'Maybe he escaped.' John looked to the road. 'Hit by a car most likely.'

'Yeah,' said Marlowe. 'I just want to move him into the bushes. Will you help me carry him over?'

Marlowe looked strong enough to carry a Shetland pony all on his own, and certainly this dog. But maybe he didn't want to be seen carrying a dead animal alone.

'We don't have gloves so ...'

'Hold on,' said John and, recalling Ava's trick, he scoured the area and found several empty crisp packets which had been blown into a corner by the wind. He handed a couple to Marlowe, who watched as John slipped his hands into them then did likewise with his own.

'Good plan, Batman,' said Marlowe.

Between them, they carried the dog to the gorse bushes across the road then laid it on the ground behind them. Marlowe stroked its ears as if it was still alive, with a gentleness reminiscent of Ava and the dead cat all those weeks ago. With the same sadness and reverence. Quickly, and out of habit, John mouthed The Rabbit's Prayer.

John stepped back as Marlowe straightened.

'Ta for this,' said Marlowe, removing his makeshift gloves.

'That's all right,' said John, and turned to go.

'I'm Nathaniel.'

'Yes,' John said. 'I know. We met when Ava ...'

' ... was attacked by that wanker outside school,' said Nathaniel. 'How is Lady A?'

'Lady A?' John frowned. He'd forgotten Marlowe's nickname for Ava. He didn't like it much.

'Ava Bonney,' said Marlowe.

'Oh, yes.' John took another step away. 'She's fine.'

'Good,' said Nathaniel. 'Take care of her, yeah?' He picked up War Horse without effort then cycled away on it. John thought it would be so easy to like Marlowe, but he didn't want to. He supposed it was because Marlowe was too good-looking, and because he called Ava 'Lady A'.

Chapter Thirty-One

DELAHAYE SAT AT HIS DESK, staring at the photograph of Bryan his family had given the police and the press. Delahaye had noticed that many of the police officers had become fond of the Shelton family, especially young Constable Daryl Morgan. The Sheltons now kept strange, sleepless hours so, at midnight, Delahaye took them up Beacon Hill to spend time unhindered by press and well-wishers; to sit and stare out across a glittering Birmingham sprawled out beneath. One night, they'd been on the hill playing night footie when they heard a chorus of mournful howls carried on the wind. The boys and policemen had stopped playing, but not Alan Shelton.

'It's just them massive scrapyard dogs,' Alan had said.

Alan insisted the police arrest the Old Nonce, Bob Aster, or at least bring him in for questioning. Aster, having the worst track record of sexual offences against boys, was always highest on the list of suspects. His fingerprints hadn't been found at either Banlock Farm or the Sheltons' house. They couldn't prove he was the culprit – although he would know enough about forensics to wear gloves this time.

The police had visited Aster's family, but they had disowned him a long time ago. His elderly mother had died during his incarceration. When Bryan went missing, police called around but there had been no answer then or since. His recent inexplicable absence from the area was proof enough of guilt for Alan, who was feeling helpless and demanded action. This was the general feeling across Rubery.

Rubery: from the old English word *rowbery*, meaning 'rough hill'. Where combustion engines roared in rivalry with birdsong. Delahaye loved Rubery and its confusion of ancient and modern landmarks, perched on the outskirts of the once soot-blackened city. Lines, on the other hand, didn't think much of it. 'There were nice streets, sure,' he would say to Delahaye, but he described the estates in the green belt 'like gunshot wounds on a pretty face'.

Brummies bore grudges more eternal than Mafia Dons, but their community spirit was genuine. Locals reached out to the Sheltons, leaving letters and cards on the doormat, in the garden, on the windscreen of Alan's van. Mickey Grant's mother supplied casseroles and stews, handing them to PC Morgan to give to the family, unable to confront her own agony in another mother's eyes.

'Sarge?'

Delahaye snapped out of his reverie and Lines added, 'A member of the public has just rung in to say they think they've found something on their property, Sarge. Something of Bryan's.'

Chapter Thirty-Two

MR AND MRS JACKSON HAD returned from their holiday in Weston-Super-Mare four hours after Bryan Shelton went missing. They'd backed their caravan onto the drive and parked the car on Callow Brook Lane.

A week later, Mr Jackson had decided to move the caravan so that he could access the garage. By this time, the whole area was buzzing with police. Mr Jackson had spotted something odd at the bottom of the garage door. At first, he'd thought it might be a dead animal, but as he'd stepped closer he'd seen it was a mass of fabric. It looked dry and squashed, as it would be, having been flattened by a caravan. Mr Jackson had bent to pick it up then paused. He'd felt the colour drain from his face and his hands had grown cold. The media's descriptions of little Bry Shelton and his clothing had been constant, so he'd known straight away what he was looking at.

Bryan Shelton's dressing gown.

* * *

Outside the Jackson's semi-detached house, Delahaye and Lines watched as another police officer approached with a dog by his side. On first viewing it looked like a German Shepherd but on closer inspection Delahaye could see this dog was taller, bigger boned, less tucked up at the back. It was a different colour from the Shepherd standard; white and blue-black fur covered its heavy, muscled body. The dog looked at the detectives with almost primate intelligence then dismissed them.

The handler introduced himself as PC Tanner.

'And this,' PC Tanner said, pointing to the dog, 'is Zeus.'

Tanner buried the dog's nose in Bry's dressing gown, unclipped its harness and then ordered him to go find. Even if the dog discovered nothing, Delahaye found a raw joy in watching the beautiful animal at work, knowing its job, its connection with its handler as powerful as telepathy.

Zeus sniffed the base of the garage, back and forth. He seemed to lose the scent a metre from the site, lifted his muzzle in an attempt to recapture it, and then continued around the driveway.

'I've never seen a German Shepherd that colour before,' said Delahaye.

'Petrol and platinum?' Tanner grinned. 'I was lucky to get him: there's a waiting list for Banlock Shepherds. Zeus is a descendant of dogs bred at Banlock Kennels up the road.' He paused. 'Y'know, where ...'

'Really?' said Delahaye with keen interest.

'Yeah, my old guv'nor, Chief Inspector Harry Marshall, personally bred a direct line of dogs from his first Banlock Shepherd. Every dog he's used throughout his career was bred from that original. Says there're no better dogs than Banlocks.' Zeus continued his meticulous rootle around the Jackson's drive. Tanner then nodded in Zeus's direction. 'Ay-up.'

The dog circled, barked once, sat down and looked up at Tanner, then stared at a spot deep in the short hedge. Tanner went to his dog and praised him with a rub. Zeus watched, head tilted, as his handler crouched and pulled gloves and an evidence bag from his pocket. He carefully scooped the small object into the bag and handed it to Delahaye, who held it up to the light. A half-eaten chocolate mouse. And, as it still retained vestiges of Bryan's scent, it was also evidence. It must have fallen out of the dressing gown pocket when the garment was discarded on the drive. In her statement, Kelly Shelton hadn't mentioned giving Bryan any sweets in the run-up to his disappearance. Did Bry's abductor give it to him?

First a sugar mouse, and now its chocolate twin. Bry liked mice and Delahaye had a hunch that his kidnapper knew it.

PC Tanner reclipped Zeus, who now sat at his side. 'Anything useful?'

'Possibly,' said Delahaye, and held up the half-eaten chocolate. There was only one place the other half could be.

Chapter Thirty-Three

A FROG HAS 159 BONES, THOUGH its skeleton gives the impression of fewer because it lacks a ribcage and its lower limb bones are fused together. It has no cervical vertebrae, so no neck, and its pelvis can slide along its spine. Last summer, Ava had studied a frog decomposing at her body-farm and it had rapidly liquefied in the heat, quicker than a mammal of equivalent size, its remaining skeleton made cartoonish by its large skull.

She and John were going to the Rezza to collect frog spawn for John's garden pond, as they did every year. Few frogs ever returned to John's pond to breed – it was an area heavy with cats, birds and motorcycle wheels – but it was always worth trying again. The Rezza was an oval stretch of water surrounded by banks of wire gabions in which spiders skittered. It was a flood-pool for the Austin, a fake lake beloved by ducks and mythical monster pikes.

Nanny Ash and Granddad were on holiday, and Trevor was working, so Colleen had gratefully accepted the Greens' offer of a drive to Cannon Hill Park leaving Ava to her own devices.

It had become cold and wet again despite it being summer. Cars hissed on wet roads gleaming with oil rainbows. Few people were out because of the rain.

Ava and John chatted as they crossed through the gate leading to the hospital grounds; the road noise disappeared as if they'd passed through an aquatic portal. Cattle grazed in the field across the road and Ava skipped alongside, holding on to the barbed wire fencing. The bullocks swung their chunky heads to look and lumbered towards her, lowing and nudging. There was something odd in their behaviour, Ava noticed. They weren't grazing across the field as they usually did, and seemed reluctant to separate.

The cows were at the fence line now, and Ava showed John how to scratch under their lower jaw, told him how a cow could climb upstairs but not down them, as their stifle joint didn't allow for such movement. She lifted the thick top lip of one of the beasts to show him that they had no upper front teeth. When they patted them goodbye, the bullocks remained, whipping their ropy tails around their shit-caked arses.

The road swooped down to a bridge before its gradual ascent to the hospital area and surrounding fields. On either side of the bridge was a treeline, sparse on the left but a wooded area on the right which led to the Lanes. As they approached the bridge, a smell hit Ava and she stopped in her tracks.

John smiled, unaware.

'What?' he said, his smile fading when he saw her expression. Ava took a few steps back and lost the scent, then stepped forward and found it again, almost imperceptible, not yet in full bloom.

The wind lifted and pushed the scent towards them.

'Can't you smell it?' Ava whispered.

John nodded. 'Sort of like a cross between Camembert cheese and over-boiled cabbage,' he said.

Ava walked around to the patch of trees in front of the John Connolly Hospital. There was no barbed wire required here: the trees were dense and perched on a disconcerting slope down to the stream. Ava negotiated the root-twisted incline with careful grace, down to the streambed and the mouth of the bridge tunnel. The yawn of the tunnel on this side of the road was narrower than the other side, and deep in shade. A smell of damp advanced and Ava sensed John's nervousness rising. Blackbirds sounded alarm chirps in concert with the chuckling stream. Ava jumped to the far bank and scanned the length of it, searching for the source of the smell.

'There's nothing,' John whispered. 'I can't smell it anymore.'

Ava agreed, but not entirely. From where they stood, they were below the road and out of sight of people walking or driving. This part of the bridge never encountered sunshine and teemed with cyanic slime and obese mosses. She blew air out through her nostrils, her mouth closed, then she straddled the stream with her feet in the water and faced the tunnel.

Suddenly, Ava caught the scent again, and she was certain now of the source.

Dead flesh.

Not totally rotten yet, she guessed, perhaps preserved due to the cooler weather. She peered into the tunnel mouth. The remains – of what she wasn't yet sure – were either in the middle of the tunnel or at the other side. But she couldn't see anything in the darkness, only a crescent of light.

Ava looked up at John.

'Ava?' John replied, his voice shaking.

Ava scrabbled back up the slope. Something was about to happen – something she had to be strong for. Something that John couldn't be a part of, except as a bystander. Her suspicions might be wrong; it could be a dead duck or vole, or anything other than what she felt it was. Nanny Ash always said, 'God judges, Fate listens, Cancer waits.'

Fate listens.

Ava could not believe Fate would call on her twice for the same horrible job. To find a human body is one thing – but to find two? It should be impossible, and it wasn't fair.

Yet here she was.

Ava looked John up and down. He was dressed in dull tones, so he wouldn't be spotted from the road against the treeline. Ava grasped his arms, looked into his eyes, and kept her voice ever-so-slightly Miss Misty.

'John, stay here,' she said. 'I'm just going to look over the bridge, all right?'

'I'll come with you,' said John. Ava shook him – not hard, not frantically, but enough to warn him not to disobey her – and he gasped.

'No, John. You're waiting for me right here.'

'Why can't I come with you?'

'Because you can't un-see what you see,' said Ava. 'It could be the worst thing of all.'

147

'Why can't we just leave it and call the police?'

'*I* need to see if it is ... if it's *him*, and *then* we'll call the police. I need to be sure. *Please.*'

It was the *please* that did it. Ava desperately wanted John to remain Normal, because if he couldn't un-see what he saw he might never be Normal again. Ava was inured to the horror because she'd seen it before.

Finally, John nodded, and Ava firmly pushed him further amongst the trees.

'Stay here and be lookout,' she said.

Ava was aware cars or people could arrive at any time, and the smell would only get worse if she dallied. She looked over the edge of the bridge. Barbed wire was wrapped around the rusting handrail so she had to tiptoe for a good look over. Initially, she saw little of interest except the widening stream, the mudbank on one side and an old chequered blanket on the other.

Ava's gaze narrowed on the blanket, and she swallowed a sob. Icy dread trickled through her as steadily as the stream on its way to the city. This explained why the bullocks had stayed at the top of the field; why there were so many green bottle flies lazing around as if drugged. She focused on the object peeping from the blanket edge. Ava squeezed through the gap between bridge and fence post, careful not to get snagged on the barbed wire.

Ava drew level with the tunnel mouth, wider on this side and high enough that she could almost stand up straight – a suntrap with no moss or shade, bright with paintball splashes of lichen. The draught from its arched maw reeked of minerals and mould, and kept the air around the body relatively cool but not cool enough. The motor-like hum of flies turned to a roar when Ava approached the old blanket. Ava looked straight ahead, took deep, slow breaths, preparing for the initial horror. The smell was not all pervasive but it did intrude, and would only get worse if the temperature warmed by even a few degrees which it would do because it was summer.

Ava looked down.

Floating on the pebbles in crystal-clear water, among the lazy trails of green hair-like weed, was a small hand in a weird rubbery glove. It was a child's left hand, half closed but not clenched, with middle and ring finger digits missing. Her gaze travelled to the small head poking out of the blanket, chin tucked into its folds. Ava stepped closer and saw grit in the scalp and hair, the birthmark on the forehead which proved this was little Bry Shelton, wrapped in a blanket as if sleeping. Closer, his skin was ashen with delicate black veins tracing beneath the surface. The glove on the hand wasn't a glove at all, Ava noticed – it was the skin of his hand. *Degloving*, she thought – when the skin has been in water so long that it swells, loosens then pulls away. Ava could just see the grey tendons and the white bones beneath the hand – the same hand she'd sometimes held, warm in life, now disintegrating in death. The water relentlessly tugged at the flesh, tearing it little by little right before her eyes. His half-open eyes were no longer brown but dark blue, and the whites now brown-red (the result of petechiae, Ava knew); the inner canthi rife with fly eggs ready to erupt into jubilant larvae. From her viewpoint, Ava could see the jagged rip in his bruised throat.

And then she saw them: bite marks stamping his thin forearm.

The whole scene was bloodless, sedentary. Like the bramble hollow, this was a dump site. But Bryan hadn't been thrown down recklessly – he'd been carried and wrapped, then tucked in as if sleeping.

Ava could see material packed under the remaining fingernails, and she knew this crucial evidence would soon be washed away by the stream if she didn't do something about it. She wouldn't touch anything else, for this was a crime scene, but if the finger-nail evidence was precious then she needed to save that hand.

Ava pulled out the clear plastic bag and two rubber bands from her pocket then wiped the bag clean of any fingerprints. Her feet were sodden, but she didn't notice as she carefully pulled the bag over the hand and gently secured it at the wrist with the rubber band, disliking the feel of the lifeless form. She then quickly secured the area around the hand with a pebble corral, stone on stone, until the water flowed either side of it and no longer troubled the flesh. The rest of Bryan's body rested on land, sheltered under the bridge. Bryan was at least still recognisably Bryan, not the shredded mess of Mickey Grant, but that was set to change if she didn't get a move on. She rinsed her hands in the stream and, even though she knew The Rabbit's Prayer wasn't good enough, she murmured it anyway – it was the only prayer she truly trusted.

A lowing close behind made her whirl around. The cows had silently approached, were on the verge of crowding, unsure of her presence. They wouldn't stampede and trample her if she remained calm, but it was another incentive to leave immediately. She waded through the water to the opposite bank and noticed the peculiar footprints in the drying mud, so she sidestepped to avoid them, crouched then sprang up the bank, grabbing at dry grass to haul herself into the opposite field. She squelched to the gap in the barbed wire and slunk beneath on all fours, careful not to let the spikes gouge skin and hair.

She ran over to John and drew him further into the trees, her shoes squeaking with the wet. A car zoomed by without slowing, and they watched it speed around the corner and disappear. 'It's Bry,' said Ava.

John turned from her and vomited his alphabet spaghetti lunch in one brutal heave.

'Are you sure it's Bryan?' he asked shakily.

'I'm sure,' said Ava. 'We need to call the police right now.'

Ava told him about the plastic bag, and stones, how she'd created a *corral* in a bid to preserve evidence on Bry's disintegrating hand. She threaded her arm through his, and together they marched towards the main road.

Next to The Longbridge pub was a telephone box, one of the new metal ones. Cars rushed to and fro but there were still few people about. Before they stepped on to the main path, Ava pulled John to one side.

'You're making the phone call,' she said in a tone that allowed no debate.

'What?' John looked horrified.

'If Miss Misty speaks then that's going to look suspicious. They won't believe I've found two bodies ...'

'*I* can't believe you've found two bodies!' said John.

'If I use my real voice, Delahaye might recognise it. So, you'll speak, but you repeat *exactly* what I say, OK? Just concentrate on that and you'll be fine.' Ava's patience was waning. 'John?'

John nodded reluctantly.

They crossed the road at the pedestrian crossing, giving both of them time to process and accept.

Huddled tightly together in the telephone box, Ava said, 'Ready?'

Chapter Thirty-Four

T HE SPACKLE OF POLICE RADIOS was interrupted by gargled voices and the irregular clicks of a camera. White tape flapped and snapped in the wind, and crows spiralled in loose murders above. Bullocks shoved and slid far from the static of traffic. White-suited scene of crime officers trailed a ghostly glow against the mouth of the tunnel. Chief SOCO, Mr Trent, organised his team with almost military efficiency, then, with DI Perrin, set about telling the uniformed police officers where and how to conduct a search of the surrounding area. Mr Trent concentrated his own examination of the body and its immediate situation.

There was a hush and reverence around the boy, as if he only slept. Bright evidence markers collected mostly on the corpse, although it was possible precious clues had washed downstream.

The corpse *was* Bryan Shelton, Delahaye knew. No mistake: the child's face wasn't disfigured, but even if it had been, the forehead birthmark was a sure indicator of his identity. He'd hoped there had been an error; that the children who'd called it in had been playing a sick joke, or had made a mistake.

He'd hoped that the boy would be found alive ...

Delahaye knew better. Knew to ignore any comforting delusions in cases such as these. The fur of his parka hood sparkled with moisture and he squeezed it out. His shoes and trouser cuffs were soaked from standing in the stream. A few yards away, a despondent Lines sat on a tree stump smoking another cigarette.

According to the grid-search records, this area had last been searched four days before, in the morning, with a helicopter overhead. No body had been found because it hadn't been there then. Delahaye noted there were very few cow footprints around the boy, even though it was their favoured drinking spot.

Delahaye noticed something interesting in the earth of the steep bank across the stream, opposite the body.

'Mr Trent,' said Delahaye, and the chief SOCO waded across the stream to him. 'Do you see these footprints in the bank?'

Mr Trent peered at the marks in the earth. 'They appear similar to those found on the Quarry.' He asked the photographer on his team to take pictures of the marks. 'These smaller footprints – shoe prints – discovered on the bank and the relatively fresh alphabet spaghetti vomit in the trees on the opposite side of the road suggests the recent presence of children in this vicinity. But the vomit and the shoe prints could've been made *before* the body was disposed of here.' He looked at the detective sergeant. 'This area is a link between Rubery, Rednal and the Frankley council estate. Children attend the school beside this field and if they live in Frankley, they'll walk home this way.'

'There *are* the Lanes,' said Delahaye. 'But they become mudbaths in wet weather. If children had found this body, they'd have run home and told their parents. We'd be here yesterday.'

'What do you make of this, DS Delahaye?' Mr Trent pointed at something on the corpse. One of the boy's hands, the one closest to the water, was wrapped in a clear plastic bag secured at the wrist with an elastic band. Surrounding the hand, in the water, was a crescent made of large stones and pebbles. Delahaye was puzzled at the sight.

Mr Trent asked the SOCO photographer for the camera then he took pictures of the curious scene. He cocked to his head, studying it without saying anything then he beckoned Delahaye closer.

Delahaye crouched alongside the corpse and looked to where Mr Trent's finger pointed.

'Can you see material packed under the remaining fingernails?' asked Mr Trent. Delahaye saw it through the hand's transparent cover and nodded. 'I would say that material is possibly evidence, wouldn't you?'

'Yes,' said Delahaye.

'My SOCOs generally use paper bags to conserve evidence, especially on hands,' said Mr Trent. 'It's cheaper but paper also prevents moisture and mould growth from contaminating original evidence stores unlike plastic bags. But if we were to arrive at a crime scene and we had run out of paper bags and we had only plastic ones ...'

The penny dropped. Delahaye nodded. 'You'd have to use plastic in an emergency.' He studied the elastic band tying the bag to the body's wrist. 'So, you're supposing *this* is a deliberate attempt to preserve evidence?'

'I am *supposing* that, yes. The hand was beginning to shed its skin after being submerged for so long.'

'You think that somebody, possibly the person who called nine-nine-nine, put the bag on the hand to preserve evidence?' asked Delahaye, not quite believing Mr Trent's theory. 'Would a passer-by have that much common sense? And why would they be already carrying a plastic bag and elastic band? It might've been the person who put the body here. It's possible the killer has done this,' Delahaye mused.

'True but the damage is done so why bother?' said Trent. 'Why would the perpetrator help us out like this?'

'The body is wrapped in a blanket and placed on its side with care,' said Delahaye. 'That measure of care could possibly extend to preserving the hand from harm.'

Mr Trent thought about that for a moment then shook his head. 'My guess is that the body has been here for a couple of days but that plastic bag is very recent. There's no evidence of condensation.' He indicated the pebble and stone crescent. 'I think this odd little extra to the scene is even cleverer.' He briefly removed his latex glove and briefly touched the cuff of the child's clothing. 'Judging by the damp cuff, the hand was in water for a while but isn't as soaked as it should be.'

Delahaye could see that Mr Trent wanted him to work out for himself the meaning of the rock crescent. The water swerved around it and Delahaye guessed that, without the rock barrier, the stream would flow against the hand, engulf it, speeding the degloving process and washing away the material under the remaining fingernails.

'It's a little dam,' said Delahaye, impressed though confused.

'That's what I think it is,' said Mr Trent. 'It's successfully protecting the shedding hand from further damage by the water. There's no indication that the bagged hand and the little dam were done by the same person, but I think they were – it's the same kind of resourceful common sense.' Delahaye agreed.

Mr Trent straightened. 'Perhaps it was a well-meaning member of the public who knew enough to save evidence then made the nine-nine-nine call. They did their duty but didn't want to be involved, didn't want to be questioned.'

'But there are no adult footprints anywhere near the site, there're only the child-sized ones. There're also the peculiar prints like those found on the Quarry. Perhaps whoever made those sorted out both hand and dam,' said Delahaye.

'The smaller prints *are* child-sized but you *do* get adults with small feet and they're usually female,' said Mr Trent. 'Though, again, there's no way of telling if they were formed before or after the body was placed here. They could still have been made by children before the body was placed here. The mud is saturated by constantly flowing water and too soft to retain prints close to the corpse so would be washed away. Because of this, notice there are no footprints around the body. The person who put him here stood in the stream to do so, and a different person stood in the stream to bag the hand and create the dam.' Mr Trent straightened. 'Let's take a closer look, shall we?'

Delahaye called Lines over. Lines stood, brushed himself down and trudged over to his sergeant's side. On and around the bridge, more police officers stopped to watch the unveiling.

The SOC photographer took snaps as Mr Trent gently lifted the blanket, eased it off then upwards, careful not to obscure the camera's lens. A peculiar collective moan sounded from the gathering. In his makeshift cocoon, the boy lay in a foetal position on his left side, barefoot, dressed in the blue pyjamas he was wearing on the night of his disappearance. His throat below his chin was a ragged mess. The spectators strained closer, eyes wide. Their mouths fell open when they saw what the boy held in the crook of his right arm. Delahaye felt a chill that had nothing to do with the cold water lapping at his feet.

A little dead dog.

It was a touching but disquieting vision, not gore-stained but still appalling: the deep bite marks, the severed fingers and ragged throat put paid to the notion of boy and dog in eternal rest together.

DI Perrin watched from his vantage point on the bridge. His eyes met Delahaye's who glanced at Joseph Sheldon Hospital – not deliberately, more a subconscious nudge. Delahaye and Lines clambered up the far bank, struggled through the gap in the barbed wire fence and met their governor on the road next to Suzi the car.

'DCI Brookes is on his way. I want to tell the family before the media get there first,' said Perrin. 'I don't say this often but thank God for rain.' They looked up the road towards the police barricade and the diversion stop signs.

'The only bloody witnesses are these cows,' said Lines. 'The farmer's coming to collect them. He told me he checks on them every Sunday and Wednesday at the top of the field by the iron gate. Said he always makes sure the stream is clear of rubbish for their drinking. He didn't see anything amiss.'

Perrin had sent police officers into the nearby hospitals to question staff and patients. Delahaye supposed it was a good thing it was summer so they had enough daylight left to examine the area further. It appeared to Delahaye to be less of a dumping and more of an exequy: a ritual tainted with regret. At the top of the road, the barriers were moved aside, and the few onlookers were pushed back as an ambulance drove through escorted by a police car. Both rolled slowly down the incline, lights flashing but no sirens.

Mr Trent told the team it was time to lift the body. He unfolded a sheet of plastic, and he and the photographer lifted the whole parcel of boy, dog and blanket onto it. They folded the sides of the sheet over carefully and placed a big pebble atop to secure it.

Delahaye and Lines assisted with carrying the stretcher from the ambulance, over the wire and down to the crime scene. All the while, Lines averted his eyes from the little corpse. The child was lifted as a piece, still on his side so as not to disrupt the original pattern of hypostasis. Lividity had a habit of changing to the demands of gravity, making it difficult to estimate time of death. The bundle was zipped into a body bag then strapped onto the pallet passed hand by hand to the bridge above.

As the paramedics slid the cot into the ambulance, a commotion at the top of the road stole everyone's attention.

'Oh, Christ no,' said Lines.

There was a squabble of police holding back a man who was trying to wrestle himself free. Delahaye heard the man's begging and bellowing.

Suddenly free, the man ran with his arms pinwheeling and legs pumping. He stumbled momentarily and managed to steady himself, while the police stood watching in mounting horror.

Chasing the flailing man was PC Daryl Morgan, who'd dropped his police helmet while running. But it was too late, Delahaye knew. The paramedics looked to the detectives. Perrin, Delahaye and Lines stepped forward to form a barrier.

Alan Shelton slid to a halt like a cow pony, his breathing ragged, haggard with exhaustion and dread. PC Morgan rested his hands on his knees as he fought for breath. The detectives moved forward as one, hands raised and faces impassive.

'Is it him?' yelled Mr Shelton. 'Is it Bry? Is it our boy? It's not. Tell me it's not. Is it?'

Delahaye had been delivering terrible news to families his entire career, and it never got any easier. This was why *transference* was the real devil – not the criminals, not the paperwork, not the Top Brass – but empathy. But this was the worst by far. Shelton spotted the body bag in the ambulance and let out a long, thin keening sound too animal for PC Morgan to bear, and the young policeman sank to his knees like a shot horse. Shelton stumbled forward and shambled back, lost and unsure, frightened and frightening. Nobody told him he shouldn't be there – in that moment the rules no longer applied.

'Can I see him? Please?' He looked desperately to Delahaye. Perrin nodded his approval.

Delahaye stepped towards the open doors of the ambulance. Up close, Shelton looked so much older, and his whole body was shaking, as if he was in the throes of a standing fugue. The paramedics stood back, their heads down. All was quiet except for the trees, the snapping tape and the crackle of radios. This would be the formal identification; not in a hospital morgue or an undertaker's, but metres from where the boy had been found.

Shelton stood as close to the body bag as he dared, his trembling becoming an intermittent jitter. Delahaye met the father's stricken eyes.

'Mr Shelton?' Delahaye murmured. He wanted to say, 'Are you ready?' But how could any father be ready for this?

Shelton rubbed his nose on his sleeve and nodded. Carefully, Delahaye unzipped the body bag, just enough to show the child's face, not the savaged neck or the broken hands. For a second, Shelton dared not look and instead stared out of the tinted windows to the woods beyond.

In a manner so tender, the father tipped his head to view his son's face. In the vehicle's bright white interior the boy looked asleep. Old-fashioned Mr Trent had seen fit to close the boy's eyes – Delahaye owed him a pint for that simple kindness.

Alan Shelton gazed at his youngest son, his features now softened by love and grief. His hands had balled into fists. He knew where Bry was now, Delahaye thought, and the next crushing stage could begin.

'It's him,' Shelton mumbled. 'It's our Bry.' He looked up at the detective with all of Dante's hells in his eyes. 'What do I tell my Kelly, Sergeant? What do I tell our boys?' Delahaye said nothing. Shelton returned his gaze to Bryan. 'Can I touch him?'

It was such a small question. Bryan was evidence now, the essential element of a crime scene, but Delahaye nodded. Shelton's hand gently cupped the boy's cheek and he leaned in and kissed the birthmark on his forehead.

'We love you, Bry.'

Lines disappeared behind the ambulance to vomit his lunch onto the road. Delahaye carefully zipped up the bag, tried to remain stoic against the racking sobs.

'Oh, Kelly! We've lost our baby! Oh, man, oh man, he's gone.'

The paramedics assisted Mr Shelton down from the ambulance where he sat by its tyres and wept. Delahaye spotted PC Morgan, still on his knees in the road, sobbing his heart out. Delahaye picked up Morgan's dropped helmet and returned it to him.

'Get up,' Delahaye said, offering the man a hand.

Morgan stared at the hand without comprehension.

'Police Constable Morgan, get up,' Delahaye said. 'Now. It's an order.'

Morgan took the sergeant's hand and was pulled to his feet, unsteady as a newly born colt. Delahaye held the constable long enough for the sobs to abate then he took out his handkerchief, dipped it into a nearby puddle, and rubbed most of the grime from the man's unlined face. Morgan was unable to meet Delahaye's eyes as he straightened the constable's shoulders and placed the helmet on his damp head.

'Alan overheard the radio call about a body found at the bridge in Park Way,' PC Morgan explained between sobs. 'And nobody could stop him taking his van to get here. He abandoned his vehicle at the diversion signs when they wouldn't let him through. I almost crashed the car trying to stop him.' His gaze switched to the ambulance. 'I've got to tell Kelly,' said Morgan, barely audible. 'I don't know how. I don't know . . .' Fat tears rolled from his eyes in ceaseless streams.

'I'll come with you,' said Delahaye.

'Will you?' Morgan looked surprised. Steve Lines approached, jaw tight with anger, but his bleak gaze softened at the sight of the younger man.

'*We'll* come with you,' said Lines.

Chapter Thirty-Five

AVA, AN AVID NEWS-WATCHER, KNEW of many terrible places in the world, all of them terrible because of humans: the stinking rubble of Beirut; the ash-caked soil of Chelmno. But the worst place in this moment, the emotional ground-zero, had to be the Sheltons' home. Ava couldn't begin to imagine their utter despair and its crippling annihilation. She was glad to be here and not there, glad to be her and not them.

Ava turned on her side and saw Rita shaking with sobs in the top bunk and, in concert beneath her, she heard Veronica doing the same. Ava, however, was tearless – she'd done all her crying after seeing John to his granddad's house. She had run home, sobbed, then washed her face, ready to blame her sore red eyes on hay fever.

By the time her family had returned home, she had been sitting composed in front of the telly, pretending to be shocked by Bry's death on the news. They'd all loved little Bry. It was so terrible that Colleen even refused comfort from Trevor, who slunk back to his own flat without complaint.

Rita slid out of her bed, climbed in beside Ava and hugged her, face blotched from crying. Then Veronica joined her sisters, cramped but united. The younger girls swapped memories, all of which began with 'Remember when Bry ... ?'

Ava shared nothing. Instead, she stroked their smooth cheeks in slow, hypnotic circles, their bodies becoming heavier as they drowsed.

'Is Bry really gone, Ava?' Rita murmured.

'Yes,' said Ava, before falling asleep between her sisters.

Chapter Thirty-Six

THE DETECTIVES DROVE TO RUBERY in silence. Lines looked shattered and Delahaye didn't look much better. Dawn had arrived too early, as it always did at this time of year. Informing Kelly Shelton and her sons about Bryan had been worse than finding the body itself. But it also proved that this case wasn't just a job – every on-duty police officer had flanked Delahaye, Lines and Morgan on the doorstep as they relayed their catastrophic message. If words were bombs, the effect on the family could not have been more devastating. Delahaye thanked God the aftermath was a blur. He didn't envy those fellow officers who were so used to delivering bad news they had become inured to the subsequent suffering, but he understood its protective mechanism. Although the day he felt the same would be the day he resigned.

DCI Brooks's briefing was, for once, brief – mostly because there was nothing to add to what they already knew. The post-mortem was not until Tuesday, and they'd have to wait for the test results from SOCOs' findings. The door-to-doors were ongoing, mostly local hospitals with transient staff shifts so everyone who had been working the week before had to be questioned and logged.

Delahaye glanced at Lines, who was staring out of the window. He thought of Ava and her sisters. They would have heard the news by now.

Lines shifted in his seat. 'It's enough to make you never want to have kids,' he murmured.

'Don't think like that, Steve,' said Delahaye.

'I do, Sarge,' said Lines. 'Christ, I don't ever want to feel the way the Sheltons or the Grants feel. I don't think I'd survive it.'

Delahaye didn't have many friends and the few he had weren't colleagues, but he counted Steve Lines as one. 'You should take some time off.'

Lines gave Delahaye a sideways glance. 'Yeah, I will when you do, ay, Sarge?'

'You're just knackered,' Delahaye scoffed.

Lines sighed. 'We're all knackered.'

None more so than Daryl Morgan, who was on official leave. Yesterday had blasted a hole in the young officer's expectations of police work, and the chat going around was that he might resign. Delahaye doubted it. He knew Morgan would return before his leave was up.

Delahaye turned into Park Way, down to the bridge where Bryan had been found. One of the uniformed officers questioning staff and residents at Joseph Sheldon Hospital had some news – apparently a couple of the care assistants had shared a 'weird story'. One of those staff was Maureen.

'You can't possibly think that old git did it, Sarge,' said Lines, as he sat up.

'I don't think he did it,' said Delahaye.

They passed the bridge. The farmer had moved his cattle so the forensic teams could peruse the area without hindrance. The SOCO team was out on the field, walking in slow steps with heads down, fanning out from the main site.

At the hospital, the care workers were assisting residents to the main dining hall for Sunday lunch as the detectives walked in, and an agitated Mrs Brown led them to a small staffroom where Maureen was taking her break.

'How is Mr Coleman?' Delahaye asked.

'Not too good I'm afraid,' she said. 'He took a nasty fall last Monday and has been at Selly Oak Hospital all week. Silly accident – he fell out of his bed. The usual kind of thing that happens with the elderly.' She checked her watch and went to stand, but Delahaye sat her back down.

'We've heard there was an interesting incident last Thursday evening?' Delahaye said.

Maureen frowned. 'Yes, almost midnight, it was. I don't know if it has anything to do with that poor babby . . .'

'You tell us and we'll see,' said Delahaye.

Maureen set her cup on her knee. 'Well, firstly, me and Greg heard this massive dog barking its head off outside.'

Delahaye paused. 'A *massive* dog?'

'Yeah, it sounded, you know, like a *big* dog. You can always tell, can't you? A Rockwyler don't sound like a Shewawah, does it, ay?'

Rottweiler. Chihuahua.

'I suppose not,' Lines said, fighting back a smile.

'We were all a bit scared, you know. Nobody wanted to go out there. It just kept barking. We didn't see its owner. It might have been a stray.'

'Can you show us where?' asked Delahaye.

Maureen took the detectives to an exit door at the far end of the building.

'This door leads out to the Lanes,' Maureen noted.

Delahaye spotted a gap in the hedge, presumably used by schoolchildren as another short cut to and from Frankley Estate.

Next, Maureen led them to Neville Coleman's room, which overlooked the field.

'It sounded really close then it stopped,' Maureen said. 'That's when the second strange thing happened – me and Greg had come out with torches, and then we saw something odd in the bushes.' She pointed to the hedgerow which concealed the Lanes and the reservoir.

'That was brave of you,' Lines said.

Maureen smiled. 'We flashed our lights at it. It was the weirdest thing we'd ever seen.'

'Weird, how?'

'Well, *I* thought it was a *dog* at first. It looked ... raggedy ... like its skin didn't fit anymore. And then, when we shouted at it ...' Maureen shuddered, her eyes round. Goose pimples popped along Delahaye's flesh. 'Well, it grew.' She pointed to the sky. 'Upwards.'

He stopped writing and met Lines's gaze. 'It grew ... upwards?'

'I'm not joking,' Maureen said. 'Greg'll tell you. It grew tall, as if it was standing on its hind legs, not just for a moment but for a long while.' She shook her head. 'I know dogs can't do that, not even circus-trained ones. It was man-sized.'

On a whim, Delahaye asked, 'How tall would you say?'

Maureen bit her lip. She looked up at Delahaye, then Lines. 'I'd say as tall as Mr Lines.'

Lines was about six foot two – and that was very tall. Maureen was a pragmatic, down-to-earth person who wasn't likely to indulge in flights of fancy and monster-making. This was clearly no joke to Maureen.

'It sounds mad but Greg thinks it was a man in a bear costume,' said Maureen, blushing, as if embarrassed by her colleague's theory. 'Like a bloke on his way to a fancy dress party or something, taking a short cut and stopping for a poo because it was dark and thought nobody would see him. What else could it be, ay?'

'That is possible,' said Lines. 'Perhaps the barking dog belonged to the costumed man.'

'Or just two different people and one had a noisy dog. We get all sorts in those lanes,' said Maureen. 'Whoever it was might have seen something to do with the murdered boy. It's the same area.'

'This is true, Maureen,' said Delahaye.

'It . . . he . . . whatever disappeared in the gap at the bottom of the hedge there. See it?' Lines and Delahaye squinted, nodding. Maureen stood. 'Anyways, I've got to get back to work. I feel stupid for bringing you out here to tell you about a bloke dressed as a bear . . . I suppose it could be just a coincidence but the news did ask for anybody who saw or heard anything *unusual* that night to come forward. And you can't get any more unusual than what Greg and me saw and heard so . . . '

'Thank you, Maureen,' said Delahaye. The whole case was not so much unusual but downright macabre.

Chapter Thirty-Seven

THE COOL, TILED ROOM HARBOURED broad worktops, deep steel sinks and roomy drawers. In one of these drawers lay Bryan Shelton – six years, two months and four days old.

Delahaye and Lines were relieved they'd missed the autopsy. The pathologist was once again Professor Simmons, with Hickman and Towler in attendance. For some unknown reason, Delahaye was pleased Simmons was working the case. Because she explained her findings so clearly, she never made him feel like a layman more a student of her practice. *She teaches as she talks.*

'I'll send you the full transcript of my autopsy notes when we get the biopsy and blood test results in,' Simmons said. 'But I'll give you something to work with now.' She removed her mask to reveal her lovely face and Delahaye blinked rapidly. Lines stared in rude awe until Delahaye nudged him.

'As you know, death's stopwatch is unpredictable at the best of times – with or without insect activity. There were fly eggs found on him, but they hadn't hatched. The unseasonably cool temperatures and the rain slowed further development, but their presence puts the body on site only a day or so before he was found.' She took a breath. 'Your senior officer informed me that the boy's last meal was consumed at about five p.m., and, from initial perusal of Bryan's stomach contents, I estimate he died at least an hour or two after he was abducted.' She switched on the light box, illuminating an X-ray of a small human skull. 'Bryan was dealt a traumatic blow to his head, which fractured his eye socket. There's a blood clot on the brain where the injury occurred, and a fracture. A blow this hard would have rendered him immediately unconscious.' Simmons shuffled through the photographs and presented them on the table.

Lines moved closer. 'He has a red rash around his wrists – restraint marks?' suggested Lines and Delahaye nodded.

Simmons handed them another photograph. 'Rigor mortis had dissipated by the time of his discovery, but the hypostasis patterns suggest he was stored on his back after death, until he was laid outdoors on his right side. The secondary lividity pattern is fainter but present. See?'

They saw.

'The child must have regained consciousness, and was attacked again. The bites on his palms and forearms are defence wounds. I'll wager they share the same signature as those bites found on Mickey Grant. His fingers are bitten off at the carpals and meta-carpals on both hands. He may have been small, but he fought back ferociously.'

'As Mickey Grant had,' said Lines.

'Their attacker had to have offence wounds where the victims scratched and bit him. This child died very differently to Mickey.' She handed them more photographs taken during the autopsy. 'His throat was torn out by human teeth. The typical upper and lower crescent indentations are human bite marks. And the bites were deep, to gum level. If you see ... here ... the carotid was successfully bitten through. The attacker kept going in until he was successful.' The pathologist referred to the X-ray light box again. 'Exsanguination was the cause of death but he was also manually strangled – see the finger marks around the throat?'

The detectives nodded.

'I found bruising to anterior neck structures. There is cyanosis around the lips and extensive petechial haemorrhaging on the sclera, the lining of the eyes, tongue and on the mucosal lining of the mouth. His hyoid bone was ruptured.'

Simmons paused.

'We found human tissue packed under the nails of the remaining fingers,' she continued. 'Very little was found under the nails of the right hand. The left hand, despite its lacerations, proffered far more evidence. It's been removed and taken for analysis. Thank goodness someone had the presence of mind to bag it when they found it.'

'We think it might be the same person who called nine-nine-nine,' said Delahaye. 'But we don't know for sure.'

Professor Simmons looked suitably impressed. 'So they haven't come forward?'

'No,' said Delahaye.

'Bryan has no other bites anywhere else on his body other than the defence wounds on his arms, hands, jawline and throat. The attack possibly stopped as soon as the perpetrator succeeded in killing him.'

A telephone rang in the office at the other end of the mortuary.

'Forgive me,' she said, walking to the phone while shedding cap, gown and apron. The two detectives stared up at the X-ray in silence.

'Gentlemen!'

The detectives switched their attention to Simmons, who was beckoning them.

'Apparently we're *gentlemen*,' murmured Lines. They shuffled towards the compact office as Simmons took a seat at a desk littered with paperwork and notes stuck down with Scotch tape.

'Sorry about the interruption,' Simmons said. She turned to Hickman. 'Could you get these fellas a cup of tea?' Hickman nodded and left the room. 'The body was in good condition when it was disposed of, and probably kept in a very cool, dry place from time of death. However, if the temperature had been even a few degrees warmer, we would have been looking at a less recognisable Bryan.'

Delahaye recalled Alan Shelton running towards the ambulance and thanked the unseasonably cool weather for a small grace.

'The hand must have been submerged from the moment he was laid by the stream,' she added 'The water level might have been higher when he was placed, and the dismembered fingers would have taken water into the tissues quicker than if they'd been intact.'

'Was there evidence of sexual assault?' asked Lines, because it had to be asked.

'No.'

Lines breathed a hefty sigh of relief.

'But that's no indication that there *wasn't* sexual motive,' said Delahaye. 'If this *is* a lust murder, it's possibly sexually motivated by the complete destruction of life.'

'But if it *isn't* a lust murder and it's not need or greed, then what can be the motive for *this*?' asked Lines.

'Just because there were no semen traces doesn't mean there was no semen,' said Simmons. 'Bryan's body had been washed.'

Both detectives regarded her with steady interest.

'Usually, with strangulation, people involuntarily defecate and urinate. Now, there *was* evidence that this had happened: his pyjama trousers were stained but they'd been given a perfunctory rinse, as had the body. There's no smell or chemical evidence of detergent.' Simmons sat firmly back in her chair. 'Then he was roughly re-dressed.'

They sat in silence until Hickman brought in cups of strong, sweet tea.

'Mickey was half-naked when found,' said Lines. 'Could be the attacker attempted to clean up, but the body was too far gone to do so.'

Delahaye nodded. 'Bryan might've been washed to get rid of any evidence.'

'Yeah, and the murderer is smart enough to wear gloves because he hasn't left fingerprints,' said Lines. 'And it seems he has no dental records either.'

'If this perpetrator killed Mickey Grant too – and that looks very likely – then he might've learned from his mistakes,' said Simmons quietly.

'Murderers such as this progress from petty offences to murder,' said Delahaye. 'Voyeurism, burglary, animal cruelty . . . '

'There was plenty of evidence of animal cruelty at Banlock Farm,' said Lines.

Delahaye nodded. 'But the care with the dogs . . . '

'Even Adolf Hitler liked dogs,' Simmons added, and smiled.

Delahaye cleared his throat.

'We've concluded the motives for killing the boys are different,' he said. 'Mickey must've surprised the killer on his turf, so he was attacked to keep him from calling the police. God knows why he killed Bryan Shelton. There're no signs of prolonged torture or restraint.'

'None of this is making sense to us,' said Lines. 'Robbery and sex we understand, but if neither of the usual is the motive then where do we stand?'

'The biting,' said Delahaye.

'Oh, Bryan had bitten back,' said Simmons. 'He lost the rest of his baby teeth in the process but we found flesh tissue mashed against his molars.'

Good for Bry. It wouldn't make the suffering any easier for the Shelton family, but if they knew that he'd been brave and fought back . . . Sometimes, these small details helped.

'The Casualty departments might aid you with details of patients with recent hand infections. The infections caused by human bites are more dangerous than that of a dog's, you know,' said Simmons.

Lines shut his notebook with an exasperated snap. 'I don't get it: how can *that* be true when *we* brush our teeth and dogs eat their own shit and lick their own goolies?'

Simmons frowned down a smile at this colourful question. 'Our mouths simply contain the more toxic bacteria,' she replied. Lines rolled his eyes and shook his head.

'Biting in self-defence is common but biting to attack is rare,' Delahaye said. 'You mentioned before that it might be part of the killer's fight pattern.'

Simmons nodded. 'Hmm, yes, it's uncommon for men to bite while fighting because it's generally considered unmasculine. Men will usually bite as a last resort or during aggressive sex. For women and children, however, their teeth are their most effective primal weapons given their more limited upper-body strength. In general, people recoil from biting because it's so intimate and they see it as dirty somehow. Personally, I find biting more terri-fying than fists and weapons. It means the attacker has no inhibitions, likes to get as physically close as a lover.' Simmons sipped at her tea then added, 'There's no typical evidence of cannibalism in either. I think Bryan's fingers were collateral damage not the prize.'

Delahaye agreed. 'And nothing stopped the killer from biting a terrified little boy. Nothing stops dogs, or any animal, from biting us. They rarely pause before they bite and never consider the consequences of their action – it's both attack and defence. Maybe this is how it is with our murderer.'

'Animals are all over this,' murmured Lines.

Simmons leaned forward, interested. 'Pardon?'

Delahaye briefly outlined each piece of evidence connected with animals. Principally canines: dogs, wolves and foxes. He mentioned the barking dog and the ridiculous yet disturbing sighting of a man in a 'bear' costume on the night and in the same area Bryan Shelton was dumped. Professor Simmons listened in rapt silence, clearly fascinated.

It couldn't be a coincidence. Not anymore.

'And you think Neville Coleman is the eye of the storm?' Simmons asked.

Delahaye's gaze switched to the ring finger of her left hand. 'I believe so. It's not much to go on, but Mickey Grant was killed on Coleman's property, and Bryan Shelton was found close to the care home Coleman lives in as well as strange activity seen and heard around the building – opposite Coleman's room, in fact.'

Simmons walked out of the office and returned to the morgue. The detectives followed her to the table, on which rested a small, shrouded form. She removed the sheet to reveal the dog found by Bryan's body.

'An old friend of mine is a vet,' said Simmons. 'He checked this little fellow over. It appears to be a straightforward hit-and-run – died of internal crush injuries. He hasn't a collar but he was well nourished, looked after. Has anyone come forward to claim a missing dog?'

Delahaye shook his head. 'We're keeping the information from the public so we can filter false confessions. We've had quite a few of those.' The police were also keeping back the extent of Bryan Shelton's injuries, especially the torn throat. It was another piece of evidence a person had to give to police if they telephoned into the incident room and claimed they were the killer.

'The way Bry was laid out with this dog,' said Lines. 'It was almost ritualistic.'

Delahaye agreed.

* * *

Delahaye and Lines left the mortuary with full notebooks, including some information the Sheltons could endure – that the boy had not been sexually assaulted and that he had fought back very bravely.

'I don't understand how but I feel better for talking to the pathologist about all this,' said Lines as they climbed into the car. 'We're no closer to finding a suspect, let alone making an arrest. But at least we've got a fresh perspective.'

Delahaye said nothing as he processed the post-mortem and what it meant for the investigation. Lines was right.

'She doesn't know, does she?' said Lines as they drove away from the mortuary.

'Hmm?'

'Professor Simmons. She doesn't know she's stunning.' Lines grinned when Delahaye shrugged, as if he hadn't noticed this.

Chapter Thirty-Eight

THE ATMOSPHERE AT SCHOOL WAS despondent on Monday morning. During break time, in the staffrooms, teachers drank tea in silence. Girls huddled like penguin chicks in corners. Some boys slid a ball around in half-hearted play while others, led by Shawn, gathered in a little gang, faces serious and angry.

Ava was puzzling over what had been mentioned on *Midlands Today* about the mysterious barking dog and the man in a bear costume who were in the same area on the same night Bryan's body was dumped. People had come forward to say there *had* been a fancy dress party on the Egghill Estate not far from the place the costumed man was seen, and one man had turned up as Yogi Bear, but he had insisted he hadn't been anywhere near the Lanes on that night and his fellow partygoers were his alibi.

Ava had been toying with a theory since she'd seen those bites on Mickey's and Bryan's bodies, and since she'd discovered that Banlock Farm had been a dog-breeding facility. She had played out other hypotheses in her mind because she didn't want to believe what she truly believed in her heart what the killer might be. She needed to say it out loud and the only person she trusted to share her findings with was John. She needed to see John. When the bell rang out, the pupils lined up. Ava felt a nudge in her back and turned to find Shawn.

'Some of the lads from around are going to trash the Old Nonce's house tonight,' he whispered. 'This lad from Turves Green figures we should be like those Glaswegian kids who hunted down the Gorbals Vampire back in the day. We should be out there, getting the bastard.'

Ava frowned. In the early 1950s, a rumour had bounced around every playground in Glasgow that a seven-foot-tall monster with metal teeth had killed two boys. The children had gone out into the night to hunt for it, searching the largest cemetery, armed with clubs and sticks. They never found it because it had been just gossip, yet Ava had always found the children's courage remarkable anyway. 'But the Gorbals Vampire was a myth.'

Shawn winked at her. 'Not the part where the kids went hunting with weapons and dogs. Tom's dad thinks it was the Old Nonce who killed Bry and he wants in on the fight. He and a bunch of his mates are going to get stuck in too.'

A witch-hunt, thought Ava: *a lynch mob*. Shawn was usually immune to rumours and hearsay. She supposed it was because he was devastated over Bryan's death too and he wanted action, to *do something*. But she wouldn't be able to convince Shawn or Alan Shelton to not terrorise a suspect – they were too far gone.

'Please be careful,' said Ava, and it sounded lame even to her own ears.

As the line shuffled forward, Shawn said, 'Tom's not coming back to Colmers, Ava. The family is leaving Birmingham after Bry's funeral.' Ava had suspected the Sheltons would leave, but it was still an awful blow. Shawn knew because he and the Shelton boys were close, and their mothers were friends. She could think of nothing to say in response to this extra bad news.

'But he gave you the best goodbye present,' he added, nudging her again.

'What?' she said.

He gently touched her lip with a fingertip. 'This scar. I wish I had it.'

Chapter Thirty-Nine

ARMED WITH STICKS AND STONES, the ragtag band of boys walked quietly through the Village streets; any yelling would attract adult attention that might thwart their quest. It was late but still light. Shawn did a head count – they were at least twenty strong, their ages ranging from ten to seventeen, and they were from all over: Rubery, Rednal, Frankley and West Heath. The Scottish lad, Trigger Magaw, who had inspired this vigilante procession, led the way.

The Shelton boys were absent. They weren't allowed out for obvious reasons, and it had been Tom who had told Shawn that his dad and a few of his mates were going to get drunk then 'sort out' the Old Nonce. Alan, frustrated and grief addled, was fired up with the idea that Aster murdered both his son and Mickey Grant. Tom said that, apparently, the police couldn't find the Old Nonce so he must be in hiding, but his dad would find him and beat the shit out of him. Shawn thought that was fair enough, but if the boys could get to the Old Nonce first, all's the better – the police couldn't charge them the same way they would a grown-up. Alan in prison was the very last thing Kelly and their sons needed.

The Old Nonce's bungalow was at the end of a long drive, its garden unkempt and its windows dirty. The boys started shouting for Aster to come out, to try it on if he thought he was hard enough.

Nobody came out.

Shawn sensed the house had been empty for some time, but their blood was up now, there was no retreat, so they banged their sticks against the doors, threw their stones and smashed the windows. Some of the older boys pissed through the letter box and spat on the path. There was a pure, pleasurable joy in meting out such deserved destruction, and Shawn's heart was racing so hard it felt more like a hum than a beating in his chest. Trigger wordlessly handed him a bottle filled with clear fluid and a piece of fabric stuffed in its neck – a Molotov cocktail. Shawn had only ever seen them on the news, during the riots. He lit its rag fuse with a lighter and the flame bloomed hot and bright against his tear-stained face.

This is for you, Bry, he thought, and launched the missile through a broken window, the bottle exploding like a burst of temper.

Chapter Forty

'WHAT A BLOODY MESS,' SAID Lines as he and Delahaye carefully traipsed through the drenched interior of Bob Aster's home the next morning. Only the bedroom had been incinerated during last night's vandalism but most of the property was still soaking wet from the fire hoses. The places untouched relayed evidence of a home unlived in for a while. The garden, so tidy on their first visit, looked like it hadn't been tended for weeks.

The house was comfortably furnished but sparsely so. There were no knick-knacks, and few pictures hanging on the walls. A fine layer of dust settled on surfaces. The kitchen cupboards were stocked with tinned foods, while the fridge contained gone-off milk, and half a block of crusty butter. By the small table in the kitchen sat two chairs, one of them pulled out a fraction, and on it was a mouldy cup of tea There was a clump of envelopes beneath the letter box, red warnings for unpaid bills and rent, all drenched in what smelled like urine.

'When was the last proper sighting of Mr Aster?' asked Delahaye.

'A month ago, shopping at Lo-Cost supermarket,' said Lines from the other room. 'The neighbours on both sides haven't seen him since.'

'Did the neighbours recognise any members of the gang?' asked Delahaye.

Lines came through to where Delahaye stood. 'They claim they didn't,' he said. 'They were probably chuffed to see this place get torched.'

On cue, as if conjured, one of those neighbours tapped the living-room window. Mrs Cutter in a ragged fur coat and slippers waved at them. Delahaye met her outside and she said, 'I think Mr Aster went off to be a tramp again.'

'Again?' Aster did go AWOL into the countryside occasionally but these circumstances were different. He was missing, wanted by the police.

'Yes, he sometimes just takes a backpack and a quilt and off he goes. To the streets in town or the hills for thinking space so he says,' said Mrs Cutter. 'This is the longest he's been away though. He's usually back after a week.'

'Do you know when he left, Mrs Cutter?' Delahaye asked.

'Not sure. Before the last babby went missing? He must've left in the night because I never heard him go like I usually do.' She smiled a toothless smile. 'Just thought I'd let you know in case you want to check them Lickeys.'

'Thank you, Mrs Cutter, said Delahaye, and went back inside and returned to the kitchen area again. He pointed to the cup of tea. 'Left in a hurry or planned to leave?' Lines shrugged and returned to the living room.

A newspaper rested on a footstool by the armchair. Delahaye picked it up and read the date aloud: 'Friday, twelfth June – that's a week before Bryan Shelton was snatched.'

'Aster never went to that dentist, did he?' said Lines.

Delahaye entered the hall to view the hooks by the front door. A thick cardigan hung beside a heavy grey winter coat. In the pockets were a set of keys, and receipts for supermarket goods. On the floor beneath: wellington boots and a pair of good leather shoes.

'He left the house without his keys,' said Delahaye.

'Spare set?' Lines called.

It was possible they were spares, but who would keep the spare set in an outdoor coat?

'Would a man leave the house without a proper coat on? And footwear?' Delahaye said. 'Especially if he's planning to live rough for a while?'

'He could have another coat,' said Lines from the other room. 'And other shoes.' It was a fair point. But the whole scene reminded Delahaye of the cover Andrew Gold's album, *What's Wrong with This Picture?*

He found Lines in the living room, studying the spines of scrapbooks in the corner bookshelf, no titles just dates, the earliest 1977 and the latest 1980. Lines picked out the 1979 edition and flipped through it, frowning.

'Oh dear,' he said, and opened it to show Delahaye.

There were pictures of pre-teen and teenage boys in swimwear or underwear, cut from retail catalogues and glued in. Delahaye looked through the most recent scrapbook to find similar images of semi-naked boys. No girls. The last page had a Polaroid photograph of a naked boy, perhaps mid-teens, from the neck down and with no distinguishing features. There was no telling when the picture was taken or of whom. He recalled the Polaroid picture of Mickey Grant at Banlock Farm, a more innocent image but still . . . Mickey had been Aster's type. Was this naked boy Mickey? Was his photographer Aster? It wasn't certain: paedophiles had a habit of swapping trophies. Had Aster occasionally lived rough at the old farm and somehow befriended the boy, just to groom him for abuse? Had Mickey gone to see him that night, and had Aster then attacked him?

And Aster had a score to settle with Alan Shelton. Bryan's father had beaten up Aster and what better way of getting his own back than by abducting and murdering Alan's youngest son then going on the run? This scenario would explain why Aster felt the need to leave home in a hurry.

Delahaye's heart sank and his hope rose. Perhaps tired of creating amateur pornography, had Aster reverted to his old perverted, predatory ways but with a new twist. He'd graduated to murder?

The police would have to search the hills.

Chapter Forty-One

July

J OHN HAD WATCHED THE NEWS story on *Midlands Today* concerning the 'man in a bear costume' who had been seen in the same area the Bryan's body was located. The police believed he might be a 'witness'. John was incredulous – surely it must be some sort of prank? Then, the next day, the news reported that a man had come forward and claimed *he* had worn a bear costume that night but at a party where he was seen by hundreds of witnesses therefore couldn't have been anywhere near that area. John couldn't wait to hear what Ava thought of this. He didn't have to wait long.

The doorbell rang. It was Ava. She didn't say hello, only: 'War Room. Now.'

In the War Room at the back of his granddad's garden hung a huge blackboard, and pinned to it were pictures cut out of newspapers – of Mickey Grant and Bry Shelton – alongside Ava's drawings. John's chalked Venn diagram showed the similarities and differences between the two cases. There were recent bulleted notes, too:

- *Banlock Farm's original purpose:– German Shepherd stud*
- *NEVILLE COLEMAN owned Banlock Farm*
- *Dog skull with a crown of daisies at Banlock Farm*
- *Bite marks on both victims' bodies*
- *According to the news, a large barking dog was seen not far from where Mr Coleman stays at Joseph Sheldon Hospital and where Bryan was dumped and*
- *A man wearing a bear costume was seen in the same area too at the same time.*

As additional information, under the title 'Lunatic Asylums', they'd written the names of all the mental hospitals in the area. It left a great deal of space for theories and ideas. They contemplated the rough mind-map before them. 'The only pattern I can see,' said John, 'is that a loony probably got both of them.'

Ava stepped forward and, in the middle, in capital letters, wrote:

- LUNATIC – LUNA, GODDESS OF THE MOON.
Lunatics believed they were controlled by the moon.

She stood back and reviewed the board. 'There's a pattern,' she said.

John peered at the scant evidence they'd accumulated, Ava waiting patiently for him to find the pattern too. *Bite marks. Lunatics controlled by – Moon – Dogs – German Shepherds which look like wolves – man in a bear costume – bite marks – human wearing a fur costume – human bite marks. What do you get if you cross a man with a dog or a wolf? Man–wolf?*

'Werewolf,' said John. Ava nodded. 'Ava! No!'

'Not a *real* werewolf because there's no such thing,' she said. 'But there *are* people who truly believe that they *do* change into werewolves. History has many cases.' She wrote on the blackboard, the chalk squeaking locations, a name beside each:

Bedburg – *Peter Stumpp*
Allariz – *Manuel Blanco Romasanta*
Dole – *Gilles Garnier*
St Severs – *Jean Grenier*
Livonia – *Thiess of Kaltenbrun*

'All these places were home to men who genuinely believed they were werewolves. Their victims were mostly children. It even has a scientific term: 'Clinical Lycanthropy'. She circled *Dole* and *St Severs* then put the chalk down. 'And two of them – Grenier and Garnier – wore dogskins when they attacked their child victims.'

'Oh no,' John murmured, his head swimming with this far-fetched but awful possibility. Miss Misty was back in the room, he noted. 'Did the boys go missing during a full moon?'

Ava paused. 'No,' she said. 'They went missing during a *dark* moon. And "werewolves" wouldn't need a full moon's permission to transform: they could change at will because mad people are mad all the time.' She wrote 'WEREWOLF' under 'LUNATIC' then added '*Lycanthropy*'. 'It could be that he *believes* the time of the full moon ... *revitalises* him, but by the end of the month he runs out of energy. He becomes moody, angry maybe.'

'So, he thinks he needs to kill to feel better,' John murmured. Outside, he could hear his granddad working on the vegetable patch and listening to old music on his battered transistor radio. 'The dog skulls at Banlock Farm,' he added.

'Yes. And they were big, too – almost as large as wolfhounds'. And they were the only skulls balanced on poles – like totems – as if they were too special to be with the other dead animals. The largest skull even had a daisy chain crown.'

'Like he ... *worshipped* it?' John didn't like the idea of that at all.

'Perhaps,' said Ava.

'It would explain the cats then,' said John. 'The cat thrown from the roof. The dead cats at Banlock Farm. Dogs hate cats, don't they?'

'Well, yes, unless they're raised with them,' said Ava. She stepped forward and stared at the chalk writing. 'According to my dad's *Crime & Punishment* files, psychopaths start their killing careers with animals first. Usually cats, because cats are practically feral and people aren't supposed to care about them as much as dogs. If cats go missing it's a *c'est la vie* moment. If the killer likes killing cats he'll carry on the habit. We just haven't found them yet.'

John didn't want to find them.

'So,' John said. 'Do we know anyone whose eyebrows meet in the middle?' He ransacked his brain for facially hirsute grown-ups and recalled several teachers at his school.

'John, that's ridiculous. There're probably more people who believe they are werewolves without monobrows than with.' She tapped her temple. 'Their *mind* is the werewolf.'

'If he *thinks* he's a werewolf, wouldn't he be acting vicious?'

Ava's eyes narrowed. 'Only during the killing.'

'But how does he do it?' *Monsters should look like monsters*, John thought, *otherwise it was unfair.* 'A disguise maybe?'

'Possibly, but I think the boys knew their killer.'

'So, if Bry and Mickey knew the killer then that means we might know him too,' said John.

'Yes,' she said. She pointed at the last two bullet points. 'Now we come to this interesting little development: the mystery "man in a bear costume".' Her eyes were bright. 'Because it had occurred the same night and in the same area Bry's body was deposited, the police have loosely connected both incidents. The fact it's mentioned in the media at all means that the police view it as somehow important, not as a joke. I don't think this "man in a bear costume" was wearing a bear costume at all. I think he was wearing a dog costume instead.'

This whole scenario was mad. 'Do you think the police *know* it wasn't a man going to a fancy dress party as a bear?' he asked.

'They *must* somehow guess it wasn't,' said Ava. 'But I think they hope it's really *just* a man going as a bear to a party. I mean, think about it: the terrible truth or the beautiful lie? The lie is that it's just a bloke dressed as a cartoon bear going to a silly party because that's more likely and less horrible. And the truth is it's a man in a dog suit who kills children because he absolutely believes he's a werewolf. Which one would most rational grown-ups choose?'

They'd choose the lie, John thought. 'Where'd he get the dog suit from, though?'

'Oh, he could've made it himself or bought it from a specialist fancy dress shop. In the news, the man who came forward and who's been eliminated from inquiries, the one who was dressed as Yogi Bear, he'd have hired or bought that from a shop,' said Ava. She studied the blackboard. 'You know, he doesn't wear it when he's catching them.'

'He has to show his human face to make them go to him?' John asked.

Ava nodded. 'Because we're taught to trust adults we know, or are in authority – parents, relatives, teachers and police, it must be someone from one of these groups.' She recalled the drive she'd made with DC Lines and DS Delahaye on the way to Banlock Farm that fateful Sunday and remembered what DC Lines had said as they passed a road of semi-detached houses just before it became countryside: *'That's Pete Ancona's house. Mickey had to have walked past it.'* 'Or an ice-cream man,' Ava concluded. She briefly told John about what she'd overheard DC Lines say and he nodded.

'He *does* hate kids,' agreed John, not surprised. 'He especially hated Mickey. And he knows the area really well and where all the kids live.'

'And he knows Trevor,' said Ava. She had never liked Mr Ancona because of the way he looked at her mother.

'Has Trevor stopped going out at night?' John asked.

Ava sighed. 'Yes, ever since he and mom had that massive row about it. But he'll start doing it again because he always does.'

John said, 'If Mr Ancona is on the police suspect list with Bob Aster then there must be something to it.' He paused. 'But I can't see Mr Ancona as a werewolf.'

'That's how these murderers got away with it for so long,' said Ava, pointing at the names on the blackboard. 'People saw them as harmless.'

She underlined Neville Coleman's name with her finger. 'And some of the strange activity seems to centre on *him*.' Ava wanted to meet Mr Coleman. She had to think of a way of doing so.

They were quiet for a moment then John said, 'I don't think the police know about lycanthropy. I think *you* really need to tell them. Or rather, Miss Misty needs to tell them.'

Ava shook her head. 'I don't know when I can do that.'

John nudged her. 'The six-week holidays start next week, you can do it then. You need to do it soon. I'm going on holiday from next Monday until Thursday night. Go to my house on Monday and borrow our phone. I'm allowed to make short calls so Mom won't notice the number on the bill. If Miss Misty gives the police lycanthropy as a clue then they'll talk to doctors in the mental hospitals who might know more about it. Come on! We're surrounded by mental hospitals! One of the doctors must know about it.'

'Maybe even treated someone with it,' Ava mused.

'Yes!' said John. 'They might even give the police a name.'

'But it's unlikely for the police to follow this lead because a random person says so. It sounds too . . . mad. Anyway, they might know about clinical lycanthropy already and are at the hospitals as we speak, talking to the doctors . . .'

John pulled his keys from his pocket and held them out to her. 'Ava, no excuses. The neighbours might see you but, if they ask, just say you're feeding my hamster whilst I'm away.'

'John, you don't have a hamster,' said Ava.

'True. But they don't know that,' said John, grinning. 'And I trust you *not* to look in my pants drawer.'

Ava pulled a doubtful face. 'I've got better things to do than sniff your Y-front collection.' She rolled her eyes. 'And I certainly don't want to see any cheesy gussets.'

'You're disgusting, Ava. You know that?' John felt his cheeks grow hot.

'I was *born* knowing it,' said Ava. Finally, she took the keys from John and tucked them into her jeans pocket. 'I'll do it.' John sagged with relief.

'Ava?' said John. 'What do you think he's making the dog suit from?'

'Real dogs, obviously,' said Ava, and walked out into the sunshine.

Chapter Forty-Two

THE EADES HOUSE WAS OPPOSITE the park. Ava *could* turn back and choose *not* to telephone the police in the mad hope of helping them catch a child killer. It was funny when she thought about it; so silly in its seriousness, like she was in a film or on TV given the stage fright she felt. To make this work she had to perform, pretend to be somebody she wasn't – someone brave and confident.

Ava crossed the road, her stride long and sure, like she was meant to be there. She pulled the key out of her jeans pocket.

The property was flanked by thick hedges and a tall fence so Ava was able to casually walk up to the front door without hindrance. She turned the key in the lock and walked in.

The house was silent.

In the living room, she stood over the rotary telephone, pulled out her notebook and, very quietly, panicked. Being called upon to act alone was terrifying. And so Ava decided to warm up. She stretched and made wide lunges and explosively huffed as if she was doing kung fu. She studied her script as she didn't want to spring off the subject in random tangents. Dictionaries and her trusty thesaurus had been checked for all the correct terms in correct contexts, as well as the rare books on the subject, to ensure everything was just right. There were many foreign names that she could spell, just hoped she could pronounce. She would be perfunctory, precise, professional then gone.

She also had to make sure it was Miss Misty that came out of her mouth – there could be no trace of Ava, even to her own ears.

Her throat was too dry. She went into the kitchen and drank directly from the tap.

Ava picked up the telephone receiver and rang the number of the incident room on the card Delahaye had given her, nervous but breathing normally. Yet she needn't have worried: when the receiver was picked up the other end, Miss Misty snapped on instantly, as if she'd been waiting in the wings for just the right moment.

She closed her eyes.

'Good afternoon, Bournville Lane CID, Detective Sergeant Delahaye speaking. How may I help you?'

Ava would have faltered on hearing Detective Sergeant Delahaye speak with such immediacy at the other end of the line. But Miss Misty didn't miss a beat.

'Good morning, Detective Sergeant.'

* * *

It was Miss Misty. Delahaye's pause was too long.

'Misty, hello,' he said eventually. 'Long time, no hear.' He gestured frantically to Perrin and Lines then set the telephone onto speaker. The team froze and fell silent. His colleagues looked as gobsmacked as he felt.

'Indeed,' said Miss Misty.

'How are you?' asked Delahaye.

'Fine, thank you.' A pause, then, 'I have some information *you* might find useful regarding your investigation.'

Delahaye grabbed a pen. 'Please continue.'

'You'll be tempted to disbelieve what I tell you, but I advise you to take it very seriously, for the sake of Rubery's children. Are you ready, Detective Sergeant?'

'Yes,' said Delahaye.

'Have you recognised a pattern thus far?'

Delahaye paused. Perrin nodded. 'Yes,' Delahaye said. 'The pattern involves dogs.'

'Correct. Canines of all kinds: wolves, dogs and foxes. Bites found on the children suggest the killer is attacking the boys the same way dogs attack people.' Miss Misty paused once more. 'Bryan Shelton was found with his throat possibly torn out.'

'That detail wasn't disclosed to the press. How would you know that, Misty?'

190

'Have you forgotten that I was the one who found Mickey Grant's body, and saw for myself the damage done?'

She hadn't answered the question. Delahaye was sure now he knew the identity of Miss Misty – it was the girl who'd helped make the 999 call on the day Bryan Shelton's body was discovered, a girl canny enough to preserve evidence on that body and would have seen the wounds inflicted on the child's neck.

Delahaye looked to Perrin, who nodded his consent. 'Mickey was discovered with a fox ... And Bryan Shelton was found wrapped in a blanket with a little dog.'

There was a long pause.

'Thank you,' she said. 'We see a developing pattern. It was once believed that unstable people became uncontrollably violent during the time of the full moon. This is fallacy.' Another pause then: 'So, what do you get if you cross a man with a wolf, DS Delahaye?'

It wasn't a question you got asked on an ordinary day – and Delahaye thought he'd heard everything.

Then the penny dropped.

'A werewolf,' he said. The other squad members turned to look at each other, bemused.

'Yes, but the proper term is *lycanthrope*. Lycanthropes don't exist, DS Delahaye. He *doesn't* physically *change* into the beast, he just *thinks* he does. Clinical lycanthropy, however, *does* exist and has existed in spots and spats throughout human history. That's *clinical lycanthropy*.' Helpfully, she spelled it out while Delahaye scribbled. 'History has many cases of clinical lycanthropy. These are real-life accounts of men who truly believed they were werewolves, believed *absolutely* that they transformed into animals at will. It is known in modern psychology. The famous cases in *criminal* history will interest *you* more. Am I speaking too quickly?'

Delahaye paused. 'No.'

'Good,' she said sharply. 'These cases match the criteria of the murderer you pursue. In each case, a small community was terrorised by a lone man who suffered with clinical lycanthropy, and children were the victims.' Miss Misty slowed down as she listed. 'The names of the places are, amongst others ...' She made every name clear and singular. 'Bedburg. Allariz. Livonia. St Severs; Dole.' She paused then added, 'Of this list, take a closer look at Dole's Gilles Garnier, and especially St Severs' Jean Grenier – these two are the closest you will find in comparison to Rubery's predator.'

'Mickey's murder was different from Bry—'

'But not *so* different, DS Delahaye.'

Delahaye closed his eyes. She had put into order what had been disordered for months. Her theory fitted and it threw light on the whole case. It might *not* be clinical lycanthropy, of course, but it was something to move forward with. How did she know so much about such things?

'There aren't many books on the subject, and most of those available aren't very good. But might I recommend a shortcut?'

Delahaye smiled in response. 'Yes, please.'

'Rubery has a mental hospital, and then there *is* Hollymoor Hospital. There must be a rich store of knowledge amongst their *faculties*. There might even be a case history of clinical lycanthropy amongst their patient records. At least one doctor there *must* have *some* interest in unique psychologies – or will *know* of a colleague who does. I suggest you start there for your research.'

Delahaye glanced at Perrin, who nodded. DCI Brookes leaned against the door jamb of his office.

'A werewolf . . .'

'No,' said Miss Misty. 'A *man* who truly *believes* he *is* a werewolf. Those who suffer this condition are usually male. You're literally looking for a lone wolf in sheep's clothing – someone local to the area, well known to local people especially children. He ensures his everyday mask stays in place but somebody close to him must know when it slips.'

The police had always suspected the killer was a local man, and if their main suspect believed he was a werewolf, it was a dramatic, surreal yet comfortable fit for the evidence, and his method of operation.

'You *mustn't* tell the public this,' said Miss Misty. 'You'll have gangs on the streets hunting anyone they perceive as odd and mayhem will ensue. You'll have to pursue this quietly for now.'

She was right.

'I would like to ask you a question, DS Delahaye.'

'Yes.'

'Why release to the press the story about the man in a bear suit seen around the site of Bryan's body?'

Delahaye clicked his pen. 'Because we don't believe it was a man in a bear suit ...'

'*I* don't think it was a *bear* suit either,' agreed Miss Misty. '*I* think it was a *man* in a *wolf* suit making mischief of one kind ... or another.'

Where had Delahaye heard that line before?

'I think the suit is ... *bespoke*,' Miss Misty continued. 'I suspect he's made the wolf suit himself – from fake or possibly even real dog fur. This thing he is: it's private, all his own. He wouldn't risk sharing any part of it with an outside ... *agency*.' She pronounced some words with the delicacy of a person eating expensive food for the first time.

'Where would he get real dog fur?' asked Delahaye, horrified.

'Detective Sergeant: many dogs are killed by cars on the roads every year so it would not be difficult to find the right materials.'

On the other end of the line, in the background, Delahaye made out the loud, trilling tones of an ice-cream van, and Ancona's van no less – 'Pop! Goes The Weasel'. He heard Miss Misty's gasp: a startled intake of breath, as if she'd been goosed from behind. In that gasp, Delahaye heard Ava, all Ava as her disguise collapsed for a brief moment. Robert Shelton's voice was suddenly in his head: '*They can do accents and impressions ... Mary Poppins, and wolf howls ...*'

Where the Wild Things Are, Delahaye thought, remembering that Bryan had been buried in his home-made wolf suit ... Hadn't Ava's Miss Misty just quoted the *mischief* line from that story? '*The night Max wore his wolf suit and made mischief of one kind and another ...*'

'You mentioned before about him walking on all fours,' he said. 'Is that physically possible for a human to move like that for long periods of time?'

'Yes, with practice.' A short pause, then, 'I hope this information will be useful.'

A click, and then the dial tone buzzed in Delahaye's ear. The squad exchanged glances.

Delahaye sat alone in the growing disquiet. They'd been fooled into thinking they were speaking to an educated, upper-class woman. The emergency telephone call alerting of the police of Shelton's location had been made by children. The tape of the call had been played several times and it was two children they heard – a boy and, in the background, seemingly telling him what to say, a girl. Both refused to give their names when asked by the controller. Delahaye had exchanged a glance with Lines because they knew a girl bright enough to avoid making the call herself as she knew Delahaye would recognise her voice – Ava Bonney. This beggared the possibility that was both impressive and chilling – Ava bagging the hand and making the little dam. Now he had a decision to make: to tell the rest of the squad that Ava was Miss Misty, or not to tell?

Don't tell.

She gave us a wad of clues.

She's too useful.

She doesn't interrupt.

She doesn't get in the way.

Leave her be.

'Was that a hoax call?' DC Hicks asked. 'Are we getting our legs pulled?'

Gibson watched Delahaye with intense interest.

'No,' said Delahaye, Lines and Perrin in unison.

'I'll call Rubery Hill Hospital,' said Gibson, and turned away to the telephone on her desk.

Delahaye checked his watch then snatched his car keys from the desk. Miss Misty's call had been timely for he had a meeting with former Chief Inspector Harry Marshall, and the drive to Rubery would be time to consider all she'd said. The police wouldn't be able to utilise the information until they'd spoken to an expert about it, but it was a new lead.

Chapter Forty-Three

THE VILLAGE SWELTERED BENEATH A mauve sky. Union flag bunting hung above shop windows as the royal wedding fast approached, and homes displayed posters of Lady Di and Prince Charles in front windows in anticipation.

Delahaye had arranged to meet former Chief Inspector Harry Marshall at the New Rose & Crown. Delahaye was a familiar face in the pub, as were many of the police officers over the past weeks. At a corner table by the window sat a man with skin bronzed from a lifetime outdoors. The man rose from his seat and extended a hand. Delahaye stepped forward and shook it.

'Harry Marshall,' said the burly man.

'Detective Sergeant Seth Delahaye. Please, call me Seth.'

Harry grinned. 'Seth it is.'

As Delahaye settled into the chair opposite, Harry watched him in that way police always watch people, even when retired – looking for secrets and hidden behaviours, even in the innocent.

'You're older than you look on TV,' said the former policeman. Delahaye smiled.

'I did some homework on you,' said Harry 'You received a commendation for finding the murderer of little Kim Johnson. West Midlands Police were lucky to nab you. So, why'd you leave the Met?'

'The atmosphere became poisonous after the anti-corruption reshuffle and nobody trusted each other anymore. I just wanted to do the job, but if you didn't choose a side you were scabbed. It broke up good teams, so I wanted out.'

'With what happened in Brixton, I think you had a lucky escape in more ways than one,' said Harry. 'Why Birmingham?'

Delahaye grinned. 'Because I get all the excitement without the politics.'

'Aw, West Midlands Police has got plenty of politics, Seth,' said Harry.

'Not like the Met. The Met is part Hoxton Mob and part hen party from hell.'

Harry laughed. His mirth was infectious and Delahaye chuckled too.

Harry studied Delahaye's face. 'So, you want to know about Nev Coleman.'

'As much as you can tell me,' said Delahaye.

'Is he a suspect?' asked Harry.

'No, he isn't,' said Delahaye. 'But I think he's linked to the investigation somehow, and not just because Mickey Grant's body was discovered on his property.'

'How'd you know where to look?' asked Harry. 'I've been following the investigation on the news and through former colleagues, but that little piece of information wasn't disclosed.'

'A teenager showed us where it was.'

Harry almost choked on his drink. 'I'll do you a deal,' he said. 'You tell me as much as you're allowed about the investigation, and I'll tell you all I know about Neville Coleman.'

Coppers always want to know what other coppers are doing, retired or not. Delahaye gave a stark recap of the investigation: the autopsy findings of both murders; the canine link; the fox and dog companions found with the boys' corpses. He told of the dog spotted on the night the murderer disposed of the body. Even about the mysterious Miss Misty, Ava Bonney leading the police to Banlock Farm, and the children's telephone call on the day Bry Shelton was found.

But Delahaye didn't mention clinical lycanthropy. He needed to talk to a qualified doctor about the condition first.

'And then there was the interview with Neville Coleman,' Delahaye said. 'But his illness has stolen his capacity to make sense most of the time.'

Harry shook his head, sad that an old friend had fallen so far. 'You're right – dogs do seem to thread through the case.'

'That's why Nev Coleman is important.'

'Well, it's a long story so we're going to need extra liquid sustenance.' Marshall raised a hand to catch the attention of the barman.

'Poverty drove Neville Coleman into the army – he'd lied about his age when he signed up a year after the Great War began. He found his calling in the mud of Flanders: the British Army had seen how the Germans were using dogs in warfare and hadn't caught on let alone caught up. Neville had noticed how some German soldiers had brought German Shepherds with them. A POW had a puppy and Nev traded for it with a bar of chocolate. That was his first dog – Troy. He smuggled him back to England, intended to set up a stud, but he needed capital to buy land. He didn't want to work in the factories, so he joined the police instead, Seth.'

Delahaye's pen stopped mid-flick. Harry smiled. 'Yes, Coleman had been in The Job back in the day.'

'Nev gave us no inkling he'd been police when we interviewed him,' said Delahaye. It is generally understood, he'd thought, that coppers gel with coppers even after resignation or retirement – the old tribal pull.

Harry shrugged. 'The job wasn't Nev's be-all and end-all. But he did make it to sergeant. In the summer of 1940, his beat was the city centre.'

Harry extracted a plastic wallet from his jacket pocket and handed it to Delahaye. Inside was a laminated newspaper clipping from the *Birmingham Mail* from 1 August 1942, with a faded photograph featuring a uniformed policeman crouching in rubble with his arm around a German Shepherd dog. The officer's face was unmistakeably Neville Coleman's. Delahaye read how Coleman and his 'remarkable canine comrade Apollo' successfully rescued survivors of the bombed shelter on Coleshill Street, and how the duo attracted a crowd of awestruck onlookers as the dog discovered more people under the wreckage. Neville received the George Medal for his contribution that day.

Harry tapped the clipping with a forefinger. 'This started it all for me,' he said. 'I wanted to be a policeman with a police dog by my side. I got in touch with him and we clicked. Coleman had saved his money in a proper bank account at a time when most people stashed their cash under mattresses. He bought Banlock Farm in 1945.

'A year before West Midlands Police set up its Harborne dog unit,' Harry continued, 'I'd volunteered to take on a dog as part of an early experiment, thus was sent to Banlock Farm. Neville was married to Sophia with a daughter by then.'

'Tess,' said Delahaye, but Harry shook his head.

'Nah, Seth, not Tess: *Tiss. Tisiphone.* Can you believe it? Who calls their baby girl *that*? But Neville loved the name. It was in keeping with the dogs', I suppose. They'd grand names too, and all from mythology.'

Harry watched the detective write the girl's name correctly and he smiled.

'Tiss had authority over the animals even as a tot. She'd be playing out in the fields surrounded by a pack of twenty or so Shepherds. She'd communicate with them using their own sounds and body language.' Harry turned his near-empty glass on a beer mat, lost in reverie. He shook his head when Delahaye offered to buy him another. 'I bought my first dog from Nev – Kronos. He'd already created his Banlock Shepherd-type, and began producing bigger-boned stock with diverse colour differences – and white dogs. Her father built Tiss a set of kennels and she bred a line of Snow Shepherds and sold them as pets. They had odd eyes, just like Tiss and her father had. By aged twelve, she was earning her own living.

'When Tiss was eleven, Sophia died of ovarian cancer. Nev was devastated, but work, and his daughter, kept him going. His business boomed. He bought real estate and became a landlord. Became a rich man. But by then he had help.' Harry's eyes darkened, his smile now sad. 'That's when a bloke called Jip started working for Nev.'

Delahaye waited, pen paused, ready to roll. 'Jip?'

Marshall shrugged. 'I never knew his full name. Jip might be short for gypsy, for his looks. But he was quite well-to-do, obviously from money, and with a solid work ethic. He was about nineteen or twenty at the time. He and Nev got on. Jip and Tiss fell in love, and she was sixteen when she became pregnant. I expected Nev to be angry but he wasn't – she was his daughter. After Tiss died, though, they blamed each other, and Jip must've moved on.'

'Where did Jip end up?'

'No idea. The last time I saw Tiss she was obviously expecting. I didn't visit Nev again until about three months after she died in that car accident. When I saw him, he was so grief-stricken and full of rage. I didn't know how to help him, and I never went back. I should have. He never mentioned a baby though, and I didn't see a child so I assumed the poor girl must've miscarried or put it up for adoption.'

Harry shrugged. 'I was told Nev suffered a nervous breakdown, that he sold most of his property portfolio and became a recluse. He lost interest in his stud, shut the kennels down, gave the dogs the run of the place. I understand the conditions became so bad and he had lost his mind to such an extent, police had to go in. But most of the dogs had become wild and so vicious they had to be destroyed. Nev was sectioned and sent to Rubery Hill Hospital then diagnosed with early-onset Alzheimer's Syndrome soon after.'

Harry returned the laminated newspaper clipping and pulled out a photograph tucked behind it: a small black-and-white picture, with '*Banlock Farm, 1963*' written on the back. It depicted Coleman with sunglasses on, his arm around the slim shoulders of his teenaged daughter, and between them sat a Banlock Shepherd.

'I took that picture,' Harry said. 'The dog is Zasha, Nev's favourite of all time. She was always mothering Tiss, mothering any younger animal, no matter the species.'

Coleman had mentioned Zasha. Delahaye sat back in his seat. .

'And there's no other family?'

Harry shrugged. 'All I know is what he told me: his own parents had died before he married, his older brother had been killed in the Great War, Sophia was an only child raised by a widow who died a year after Tiss was born.'

'He's on his own,' said Delahaye.

Harry studied Delahaye. 'You're not on your own, Seth – remember that. You've a good squad, you turn up in a suit without fail every morning; you've solid hunches and a wealth of experience. Bear with yourself and you will catch this bastard.'

Chapter Forty-Four

PAUL BALLOW HAD ASSUMED THAT being a pest control officer was, at the very least, a conversation starter. He was, after all, killing things for a living.

He'd shaved off the Mohican and didn't miss it. The band had accused him of selling out, but Lucy said he looked like Midge Ure, so it was worth the sacrifice.

Paul liked his job, and the other lads. Even liked his boss, Charlie Flint.

'Have you been to Marlowe's before?' Charlie asked, as he drove the van through green and gold countryside.

'No,' said Paul. It was the largest scrapyard in the region, and he wondered where such an ugly blot could hide.

'Then you're in for a treat.'

They turned into a country lane that Paul would have completely missed if he'd been driving. The trees gave way to reveal tall wrought-iron gates.

'Bloody hell and bugger me,' Paul murmured in awe.

Charlie grinned. 'I told you!'

Marlowe & Son Breakers Yard was a vast, unhallowed kingdom – both a mass grave and a hollow town for scorched and smashed metal. Its streets were lined with bent, rent columns of battered vehicles. Chrome grilles were rictus grins in steel skulls; windscreens were either absent or cracked into webbed cataracts. Dissected for parts, only the rejected corpses of countless vans, lorries, family cars and trophy machines remained.

Paul couldn't help but think of the irony: only a few miles away, in Longbridge, cars were built glistening with new paint and polish. Here, a sauropodic crane clutched wrecks in its giant claw and swung them into the roaring crusher or shredder.

Men's laughter boomed from the open door of the farmhouse. As Charlie and Paul approached, the tallest man Paul had ever seen stepped out. He greeted Charlie warmly then regarded Paul with intense curiosity. Charlie made brief introductions and Nick Marlowe extended his hand. Paul shook it: the man's hand was the size of a grizzly's paw. Marlowe towered over Paul, with biceps like melons strapped to his arms. His thick forearms were covered in fresh and healing scratches and bruises. Marlowe's weathered face was flanked by Dickensian sideburns. Lucy would think he was 'dishy'. Paul thought he was a man you wouldn't want to get on the wrong side of.

'Have a quick cup of char and a bacon cob,' Marlowe said. His voice wasn't posh, but Paul heard money in it.

They followed him into the farmhouse. Inside, the place was grubby, with Page 3 girlie pictures curling against their pin restraints on the wall above the cluttered desk; the stench of body odour, dog and lard beneath the veneer of fried bacon. Tim and Minty were in the kitchen, frying breakfast and buttering bread rolls. At their feet sat two dogs, at first sight both German Shepherds, but of a type Paul had never seen before. One was white and very elderly, and the other was grey and very pregnant. Both were big-boned, big-headed and dense with presence.

'Sit down,' said Marlowe as he retrieved extra chairs from the office then snapped the kettle on. 'Don't mind Luna and Asta – they won't bite unless you do.'

Paul sat, and Luna shuffled to him, placing her head in his hands and looking up into his face with her odd eyes: one hazel, one blue. 'That's Luna,' said Nick. 'She likes you.'

'How's your Nathaniel, then, Nick?' asked Charlie. Tim and Minty glanced at each other.

'He's working,' said Marlowe after a short pause.

Charlie shrugged. 'I haven't seen your lad since he had his accident last year. He needed surgery for his head injury didn't he?' He turned to Paul. 'Nick's son was hit by the crane claw. He almost bloody died.'

'He *almost* did. He's all right now,' said Marlowe. 'He's doing well in school and he earns all his own cash, so ... I don't see him much these days.'

'So, what d'you need doing?' Charlie asked.

'The house and the meat store,' said Marlowe. 'Asta's pups are due and I want her in, but the rats are getting brave and setting up in the attic. We'd have your terriers in but they'd disturb our lot. Better the traps, yes?'

'I'd say so,' said Charlie as mugs of tea were placed before them at the kitchen table. 'We'll be done by mid-morning, and you should be clear by tomorrow morning at least.' Tim handed him a plate of bacon, egg and sausage buns.

When offered a breakfast cob, Paul shook his head. 'It's why he's so skinny,' Charlie lamented, and winked at Paul. 'Why don't you have a quick look round whilst you're waiting for me?'

'He should know about the dogs first, boss,' said Minty.

Nick nodded, disappeared into the hall, and returned with a sheepskin jacket, and a yellow hard hat. He handed them to Paul. 'This jacket's covered in my scent. And you need the hard hat anyway.' Paul put them on. Nick treated the young man to a rough saccade. 'The dogs are trained but you don't fuck about. If they confront you, walk backwards, eyes down and *do not* run. Yes?' Paul nodded, suddenly under siege. Nick saw his apprehension and grinned. 'My son's out there and they'll always be where he is.'

'And mind the dog shit,' said Tim. 'It's like landmines – you won't know you're in it till you're in it. Seriously, they shit like fucking elephants.'

Outside, Paul shucked further into the man's jacket and began exploring the twisted avenues of Marlowe's scrapyard. Around him, dogs barked and howled together, making the hairs stand up on his nape. The wind whizzed through the metal shells in pulsing intervals, as if following him.

He stopped at a barn and peered in: tyre piles, headlamps and tail lights, broken combustion engines, exhaust pipes. A couple of charabanc buses slumped against each other in companionable obsolescence. Beyond the barn, an old Ferris wheel arched in falling, its spokes cankered, and the few gondolas remaining were flecked green with mould.

Paul strolled around enjoying the sculptures rendered unintentionally in the twisted ugliness, the roar of the crane claw and shredder a constant background noise, as unpretty as punk music but just as invigorating. He kept his distance from the crane, which swung the old wrecks into the crushing maw.

It was only when he looked at his watch, then around him, that he realised he was lost.

He'd ambled into a shaded cul-de-sac of tangled machines. The damp air was cold, closer to autumn dusk than summer dawn. Then, when he took a step back to retrace his path, he heard a low growl.

There were dogs – on the roofs and under carriages. They glared at him with pitiless eyes, electric green in the dingy light. They assembled as if they were the jury of a makeshift court and he was the offender in the dock. Like the house dogs, these were not German Shepherds: they were too tall, too heavy; and wild. Like Luna, some were pure white, their coats an ethereal contrast against the dull scrap.

Paul stared.

The dogs stared back.

His primeval brain screamed at him to run but he knew that, if he ran, it would be the last thing he'd ever do. His breathing was rapid; his heart thundered until his pulse points hurt. Suddenly, he felt entirely unsubstantial, certainly not a member of an apex species at the top of its game. A caveman without weapons facing a pack of wolves.

He stepped back.

The beasts growled: a rhythmic rumble, like a chorus of engines revving then falling away. Their muzzles corrugated and their lips ruched to reveal merciless teeth. They snapped as they snarled: ears flat against their heads; hackles spiked. The noise was tremendous, their barks echoing in the metal arena. They dipped their heads below their shoulder blades and he could have sworn he felt the tremors from their displeasure ripple through the ground beneath his feet.

Paul took another step back. In unison, they stepped forward. Panic was setting in. He wanted to run and sod the consequences. But instead he kept ... stepping ... backwards. They were still in sight and there was no corner to hide behind and it was then, just as he was sure the dogs were about to charge, that he saw the boy.

Or, rather, a young man. The figure materialised from the fur and metal of his surrounds. Taller than Paul but younger, with auburn hair and mismatched eyes.

Then, the youth growled, and the animals fell silent.

He wore a welding apron over a grey boiler suit. No yellow hard hat. It wasn't hard to see the family resemblance: this was Nick Marlowe's son.

Paul recognised him as the delivery boy who rode a massive, customised bike and trailer. The teenager tipped his head to one side as if to study Paul, revealing a scar along his temple. The youth made another sound – not quite a whistle, more like a whine – and the dogs poured from their perches and huddled close to his legs. The boy walked forward with peculiar, fluid grace, and they moved with him.

With an elegant sweep of their master's hand, the dogs immediately swarmed Paul – swirling round him, sniffing him thoroughly – and he kept still, not daring to move, staring at the ground.

'We'll take you back,' said the boy, with no trace of emotion.

'All right,' said Paul. 'Thanks.' No introductions, no handshake.

The dogs were relaxed now, totally different from the vicious, snapping beasts just moments before, reacting merrily to the Marlowe boy's occasional growls and whines. There was no conversation with his human companion, and the chilly silence ensured the hairs on Paul's nape remained standing, warning him to remain absolutely vigilant.

Paul cleared his throat and said, 'Mate, what's with the Ferris wheel, then?'

The boy smiled. 'A fairground went bust and sold it as scrap,' he said.

Paul counted seventeen dogs in total. 'Your dogs scared the crap out of me, I can't lie.'

He watched the boy pull further ahead and then spotted Charlie waving at him. Paul waved back and jogged ahead. He turned to thank the boy but both he and the dogs were gone; disappeared into the scrapyard, as if they had never been.

Chapter Forty-Five

AVA AND JOHN PERCHED ON the climbing frame on the flats' lawn while her sisters played with their friends at the park. They talked about the Bonneys' prospective move to Frankley.

'It's official. We should be moving just before Christmas,' said Ava. 'The paperwork is signed, sealed and delivered.'

'Do you think you'll miss the flat?' John asked.

Ava looked up at the Bonney's kitchen window. 'I think I'll always miss it, in my way.' She smiled. 'But I can't wait to finally escape Rita's bloody snoring!' She proceeded to mimic her sister's nocturnal snorting and twitching, making John laugh.

Ava brushed down her grass-stained jeans. Lately, she'd taken to wearing Trevor's old shirts with a studded black belt around the waist – sort of like Annie Hall. She marched up the incline towards Cock Hill Lane. It was then she saw the detectives cruise by in Suzi. Had they spotted her?

Ava grabbed John, and he laughed in surprise.

'Quick,' she said. 'Hide in the den.' But it was too late: Suzi purred down Lea Walk just as Ava shoved John into the bushes opposite the climbing frame.

John crouched to hide. Ava knew they'd seen her, knew that they would come to speak to her. Every pessimist knew it was always shit that hit the fan, and never chocolate. She posed nonchalantly on the climbing frame as Delahaye and Lines exited the car and approached. Ava waited to be beckoned, climbed down, and walked over. She had wanted to see Delahaye again, but now a piquant sadness tainted her joy. The last time was on the day of Bryan's funeral, when he'd been standing on the crest of the Quarry with binoculars.

But today she had to be on her guard.

'Hello, Ava,' said DS Delahaye. 'How've you been?'

'I've been fine, thank you,' said Ava. He was wearing a short-sleeved shirt and, for the first time, she saw he had tattoos on his arms; more tattoos than she'd ever seen on anybody. Some words and sentences. She wanted to read what they said.

'Are you all by yourself there?' DS Delahaye asked. A smile brought out his dimples, but Ava wasn't fooled. Anyway, dimples were genetic imperfections.

'I'm waiting for my sisters,' said Ava, which wasn't exactly a lie because she was almost always waiting for her sisters.

'We haven't seen you for a while, so we thought we'd just stop and say hello.'

Ava knew this was a lie folded in a truth.

'Have you seen the graffiti about the Village?' DS Delahaye then said.

Funny how he called Rubery 'the Village' like a native. Ava nodded slowly.

'The corrupt nursery rhymes,' she said. DC Lines grinned.

'Exactly,' said Delahaye. 'They *are* corrupt nursery rhymes. Well put, Ava.' He stepped closer. 'You don't think it's the handiwork of the punk band, War Dance, do you?'

'No,' Ava said quickly. 'And anyway, it's only writing.'

'Vandalism *is* a crime, you know, bab,' said DC Lines, his eyes full of wry humour.

'But not the crime you're investigating,' said Ava.

'Touché,' said DC Lines.

'I suppose you were busy the Saturday Bryan's body was found,' said DS Delahaye, changing the subject. Ava didn't falter; she'd been expecting this.

'Yes, my family went to Cannon Hill Park.' This was true – though Ava had not gone with them. 'It was raining though.'

'Yes, it was,' said DS Delahaye.

'You could ask my mom about it if you want.' Ava nodded to the kitchen window. 'She's in right now.'

'No, that's all right, thank you, Ava,' said DS Delahaye. He turned as if to walk away. 'One last thing,' he said, stopping. 'The emergency call we received about Bryan Shelton's body was made by a couple of kids. You haven't heard anything about them, have you?'

Here it was. The real reason for their visit. But Ava was prepared. She took a deep breath and said, 'Are they in trouble?'

'No,' he said. 'No trouble at all. We're just worried about them, that's all. Both the boy *and* the girl. It's a horrible thing to do so young. They might want to talk about it, get help. They did a very brave thing.'

'No, I haven't *heard* anything about them.' Ava managed her facial expression into just the right mix of unsure-and-I-could-be-wrong. It was difficult because DS Delahaye's gaze felt like it was pecking at her face, and she could see he wanted to say a great deal more. In a flash of panic, she realised that he *knew* she was Miss Misty. She didn't know how he knew but it was there, tucked behind his eyes and in his seemingly harmless questions. Disquiet fluttered in her belly. 'Perhaps they were kids from Frankley or Rednal.'

'Yes, of course,' DS Delahaye said. 'We hadn't thought about that, had we, DC Lines?' DC Lines shook his head. 'Well, we'll let you get on,' he added. 'And Ava.'

'Yes?'

'Please don't spend so much time on your own, all right? We'd prefer it if you kids stayed in groups at the moment. You need to keep safe.'

'I will,' she said, backing away then skipping to the climbing frame, tugging at a twig she'd plucked inches from John's head as she went.

* * *

'Ava reminds me of Rynn Jacobs,' Delahaye said, clicking in his seat belt.

'Who?' asked Lines, rolling down the window, a cigarette between his lips.

'Rynn Jacobs. You know, the character Jodie Foster played in *The Little Girl Who Lives Down the Lane*? Ava's got the same cool, uncanny self-possession.'

'I've never seen it,' Lines admitted. 'So, d'you still think it was Ava and her friend who made the call?'

Delahaye straightened. 'Yes, but I can't prove it.' He turned the ignition and the car thrummed into life.

'We *could* ask her directly, Sarge,' said Lines with a wry grin. 'We *are* the police in this scenario.'

'I think she'd lie outright if we did. She deflected our questions the entire time, but a direct call for the truth would make her defensive, because it's not herself she's protecting. It's the boy.' Delahaye turned Suzi onto Cock Hill Lane. 'And I don't want to be her enemy. She did the right thing that day.'

'I think she's a smashing kid,' said Lines.

Delahaye agreed but he was not stupid. He knew someone had been hiding in the bushes during their little tête-à-tête. He would've bet a month's wages on it being the boy who'd spoken during the 999 call. Ava had found the body of Bryan Shelton, of that he was certain. She had bagged the boy's hand. It was such an awful thing to do – for anybody. But for a girl to have the presence of mind to actually do it . . . Girls were supposed to be appeasing and Ava exhibited none of this characteristic. Perhaps, Delahaye thought, it was about time he reconfigured his idea of what a girl should be and model her on Ava.

PART THREE

Chapter Forty-Six

Late August

T HE TREES WERE GREEN CROCHET blotting out the sky, and the woods looked like a theatre backdrop, the peculiar light lending an artificial dullness to everything. There was no wind so nothing moved. Thunder grumbled in the distance.

Gary paused.

It was hot, too – *damn* hot. Like a jungle– steamy, sweaty. Unbearable. It was just as hot under the trees – there was no escaping it.

The further into the woods Gary ventured, the more overgrown it became. Perfect cover for predators. But his brother Cal said there were no big predators in Britain anymore, so it was all right. Not many super-poisonous creepy-crawlies either – unless you were allergic to adder venom, and Gary didn't know anyone with that allergy. Although there was one kid in his class who'd ballooned when stung by a bee.

Gary's friends, Billy and Jez, were behind him . . . somewhere. They were playing Hunter, which was just their own name for hide-and-seek. Billy was the Hunter and Gary and Jez were the Hunted but whoever was found first became a Hunter too. You had to up your game and find the best hiding place to dodge two Hunters. With a bet on Gary being caught first, the stakes were high: if he was caught before Jez, then Gary had to share his pound note and buy sweets for them all. His pound note had been a bribe from big brother Cal so Gary would not bother Cal and his new girlfriend when Mom and Dad were out, even though they had told Cal he had to 'keep an eye' on Gary while they did the big shop. Gary didn't mind – he thought it was a *bostin* deal.

It was almost the end of the summer holidays and he was out with his best mates.

Somebody he knew had thought it was a bostin deal too. He called him Somebody because Gary didn't know his real name but that was OK because Somebody knew Gary's name so they weren't strangers.

But this Somebody was to be kept a secret, even from his mom and dad because Somebody said they wouldn't understand but also because he gave Gary cool sweets. Gary was only allowed sweets at the weekends because having sweets all the time was bad for you. Gary didn't really know why he had to keep Somebody a secret, but the sweets were great and it *wasn't* like he was taking them from a stranger – he knew Somebody.

Gary had chatted to Somebody outside the paper shop whilst his friends had been in the queue buying crisps for their long journey to Beacon Hill. Today, Somebody had given Gary the rest of his sweetie mix-up, which had flying saucers in, and Gary had told him about their plans for the afternoon.

Somebody had said that sounded great, but if Gary really wanted a fantastic hiding place no one knew about then he'd have to find the Dead Hollow Tree. Gary could hide there and win the game and keep his quid. Gary had been gobsmacked by the idea so Somebody had given him directions then had walked away just as Jez and Billy left the shop, but Gary said nothing because now he had a secret plan.

They'd bought ice creams from Mr Ancona's van – and Mr Ancona had actually been in a good mood for once – then they'd walked to Beacon Hill, chatting along the way, oblivious to everything else around them. On the castle-thingy, Billy was left to count to one hundred whilst Jez and Gary ran into the woods, giggling – separating, as one person is easier to hide than two will ever be. Gary had followed Somebody's directions and now he was in deepest woodland he'd never been in before, and the path was lost. But he kept going.

Every time Gary paused to look around, he heard a big branch – or something – smash against a tree, as if the trees were in on the game too, urging him to not falter, to keep going. The crashing always came from behind, and instinctively he moved in the opposite direction to its source.

Gary finished his last sweet and threw the paper bag away. Cal said the Lickeys were safe because you were never far from Civilisation. It wasn't the Amazonian jungle. Lots of branches must be falling today, another right behind him, closer this time.

Thunder rumbled again, louder, nearer. There was going to be a storm! He kept walking, glad he was now away from the Slanting Trees. In the Lickeys, many trees grew on a steep incline, their roots braced against gravity's pull, trunks defiantly straight above them. Gary thought they looked too much like the slanting trees in the landslide scene in *The Railway Children* film. It'd been creepy, and he'd been scared. But Cal had reassured him that the trees hadn't *wanted* to move, that they'd *had* to move; that gravity had pulled them down. Gary understood but he still didn't trust slanting trees.

Gary stopped. He'd come to a clearing that had materialised like a mirage before him. There was a giant old oak, fallen, hollowed out – not only a perfect hiding place but also a perfect den for future games. He couldn't wait to tell Billy and Jez about it. As he stepped closer, he saw something else, something unbelievable. Familiar yet at odds with its surroundings. He wondered how it'd got there, so fast, so deep in the Middle of Nowhere.

Twigs snapped behind him. Gary whirled around, scared then not scared as he looked up. He smiled a lovely smile.

'Oh,' Gary said. 'It's you.'

Chapter Forty-Seven

AVA AND HER SISTERS WERE jolted awake by a commotion. Something was ricocheting off the walls of the flat. Ava sat up.

'What is it?' Veronica whispered. Rita whimpered.

Ava waited until the source of the noise was at the far end of the landing then opened the door.

'Mom?'

'It's just a dog!' Trev bellowed. 'Go back to fuckin' bed!'

'A *dog*?' Ava must have misheard.

Colleen stepped out. 'Yes, bab,' she said. 'Trevor got us a dog.'

Ava couldn't see the animal in the darkness. 'What's his name?'

'Fizzog.'

Her mother shut the door.

Ava could sense her sisters' excitement but also their trepidation: how big was this dog? Would it bite?

'Fizzog!' Ava whispered. 'Fizz!'

She smelled it: warm fur, meat breath. It approached, close enough that she could see its eye-shine. It was a squat block of a terrier, and he was as scared as she was. Ava reached down, felt its warm tongue lick her hand. Trevor had been to see a man about a dog, and had brought the dog home at last.

Chapter Forty-Eight

GRAFFITI ON THE OLD BAKERY, Rubery:

Little Boy Blue has far to roam
Out in the woods – come home, come home!
Where's that boy? Where can he be?
Hope and pray and wait and see.
Harry Ca Nab!

Gary Clarke – nine-years-old for just a week – was last seen wearing a grey T-shirt, blue jeans, and red and white Nike Blazer trainers. Such distinctive footwear was a clear point of recall – but nobody had seen either Gary or his shoes since he'd stepped into the woods.

Nobody had seen anything at all.

Lines was searching the drawers in Gary's bedroom when he spotted something and beckoned Delahaye over. Delahaye peered into the open drawer. Tucked beneath an envelope labelled 'Birthday Money' was a big, red jelly crocodile, as grotesque as a Cartier overstatement.

'Cal?' said Delahaye. Callum Clarke entered the room immediately – he'd obviously been hiding just out of sight, eavesdropping. Delahaye waved him over and pointed a latex-gloved finger at the garish confectionary.

'Ooh, a jelly croc!' said Cal.

'Did you know Gary had this?' Lines asked.

Cal shrugged. 'Nah, must've bought it with his pocket money.'

Bryan's sugar mouse flashed in Delahaye's mind. Surely it was no coincidence.

'Cal, where can you buy jelly crocs?' asked Delahaye.

Cal didn't hesitate in answering. 'Hardy's Gifts in Rednal.'

'That's very specific,' said Delahaye.

'I don't know of anywhere else,' said Cal. 'All the flashy sweets you don't see anywhere else are sold at Hardy's.' He frowned. 'But Gary never said he'd gone to Hardy's unless he'd bought it as a present for someone. And kids aren't allowed in the shop without a grown-up. Plus, it's the longest walk.'

Pete Ancona had mentioned Mack Hardy as one of the people with a grudge to bear against Mickey Grant – for shoplifting. Hardy was also a regular at The Longbridge pub and he'd been drinking there the night Mickey went missing. Because the unusual sweets connected two cases and appeared to source from the same retailer, Delahaye would pay a visit to Mr Hardy's gift shop. DC Lines would look in on Mr Ancona as he had been the last adult to speak to Gary and his friends on the afternoon the boy had vanished. 'But you've been to Hardy's Gifts, Cal?' Delahaye asked.

Cal nodded. 'I went with Dad to buy a present for mom's birthday last year.'

Lines took a picture of the drawer's contents, then picked the crocodile up and turned it over carefully. Fingerprints scored its white marshmallow underbelly. Delahaye took it gently and placed it in a clear evidence bag.

Cal was all eyes. 'Is jelly croc being arrested?' he said. He sat on his brother's bed and watched the detectives move around him, quiet as burglars. 'It's my fault Gaz's missing,' he murmured.

Lines and Delahaye exchanged glances. Lines sat next to the boy.

'Callum, listen to me.' Cal looked at the detective, his eyes welling up. 'This is *not* your fault.' The boy nodded unconvincingly. 'You are *not* to blame. Am I clear?'

Cal wiped his cheek with the heel of his hand. 'Do you think it's . . . ? Could it be the . . . ?' Delahaye could see fear in the boy's eyes; his reluctance to say what they were all fearing.

'Does Gary have any adult friends?' Delahaye asked, ignoring Cal's unfinished questions. 'Any grown-ups he talks to who aren't your parents, or teachers?'

Cal shook his head.

'All he knows are kids. We talk to mom and dad's friends sometimes, but they aren't, you know, our *mates*.'

Other detectives on the team were talking to Desmond and Pat Clarke's friends at that very moment. The Clarkes were famous and wealthy because Desmond wrote jingles for adverts and lyrics for pop songs so it was initially suggested that their son had been kidnapped for ransom. However, no ransom demands had been posted or telephoned.

Lines drew out a picture from his jacket and showed it to Callum. 'Have you seen this bloke about recently?' It was a photograph of Bob Aster.

Callum clearly knew who it was because everyone did. 'No.' He looked even more worried. A silence passed between the three of them. Then Cal sniffed, looked up at Lines and said: 'Do you like being a copper?'

Lines paused then smiled. 'Most of the time.'

Chapter Forty-Nine

DELAHAYE PUSHED OPEN THE SHOP door of Hardy's Gifts and a bell chimed above his head. It was late in the day so he was the only prospective customer. The shelves were laden with expensive giftware and the cashier station was in the centre of the space, affording a wise 360-degree view of the store. A man in a linen suit was behind the counter.

The counter was polished glass and, as Delahaye approached it, he saw it was a cabinet of extraordinary confections.

Sugar mice. And giant jelly crocodiles.

There were other, almost fairy-tale-quality candies, but Delahaye was fixated on the sugar mice. The giant crocodiles were displayed in a crystal bowl, twisted around each other like a rainbow Escher lithograph. The man behind the counter walked around to greet him.

'Can I help you, sir?'

Delahaye showed him his warrant card. 'Hello, I'm Detective Sergeant Delahaye.'

The man extended his hand. 'Yes! I'm Mack Hardy, the owner-manager of this shop. How can I assist?'

Delahaye shook the man's hand which had a peculiar powdery softness. 'I'd like to ask you a few questions about some of your stock, Mr Hardy.' The man's mouth was lopsided, scar tissue pulling the lower lip out of shape.

'Ah! I saw you admiring the rose-point sugar mice! Exquisite, are they not?'

Delahaye reached into his jacket pocket and drew out Bryan Shelton's sugar mouse in its clear evidence bag. He placed it on the counter. 'This was found among Bryan Shelton's possessions, Mr Hardy. His family have no idea how he came to have it.'

Hardy moue'd his lips. 'And you think it was bought from this shop?'

MARIE TIERNEY

'You sell the rose-points. The only other shop who sells sugar mice like this in Birmingham is on Corporation Street and they sell only the blue-points.' WDC Gibson had also found out that the things were made in Switzerland. 'You are the only shop who sells these rose-point mice.'

'I see,' said Hardy. He had grey almost metallic eyes. 'It isn't inconceivable that someone well meaning bought it for the poor boy.'

'I hear you have a problem with shoplifting,' said Delahaye.

'Not since I rearranged the cashier station and maintain the strict rule of *no* children allowed unless accompanied by an adult,' Hardy said with a smile.

'I understand Mickey Grant had shoplifted from you a few times,' said Delahaye.

'Yes, he was the main reason why I enforced the rule. He was problematic but ... not anymore,' Hardy said.

Delahaye couldn't work out if Hardy was sad about that. His face was expressionless, the steely eyes revealed nothing. He didn't blink much.

'As for Bryan Shelton, that poor child! This mouse might've been a gift from a friend,' said Hardy.

'An *adult* friend? The boy kept it a secret at the bottom of a box under his bed,' said Delahaye. 'So, if an adult bought it for him, and he never told his family about it, I'd say that was dubious.'

'He might've found it,' said Hardy. 'Some people are *so* careless with their possessions.'

'Entirely possible, Mr Hardy,' said Delahaye. He didn't like Hardy. There was a mechanical falseness that underpinned the man's every move like he was a stringless puppet. Like Pinocchio.

Delahaye reached into his other jacket pocket and extracted Gary Clarke's red jelly crocodile and placed it beside Bryan's mouse. Hardy cocked his head to one side and studied the sweets but Delahaye could see that the man was unsettled.

'This was found in Gary Clarke's drawer,' said Delahaye. 'His family have no idea how or when he got it. His brother claims the only place he knows where Gary could've got it is *your* shop,

224

Mr Hardy.' There were no matches yet for the fingerprints other than Gary's on its marshmallow underbelly.

'Again, it's an unfortunate coincidence but it still could've been a gift bought or a thing found,' said Hardy. He clasped his hands in front of him. 'I do hope you aren't suggesting that I have anything to do with these frightful murders, Detective Sergeant.'

'Your shop with these unusual sweets *is* a connection between Shelton and Clarke other than their manner of disappearance,' said Delahaye. 'The police must follow every clue and investigate each piece of evidence, Mr Hardy, no matter how small and seemingly irrelevant. I am sure you understand that.'

'Of course. Yes. You could take *my* fingerprints so that you could eliminate me from your inquiries but you won't find them on these confections, DS Delahaye – I use hygienic plastic gloves, tongs and scoops and I *never* pick up with my bare hands.'

Although Hardy remained unctuous, he was clearly rattled by the presence of the evidence presented before him. Hardy was so otherwise expressionless Delahaye couldn't tell if the man's unease was due to guilt, of knowing something he should tell the police about or knowing someone who bought these things for the boys with ill intent. His knowing his fingerprints might be asked for and saying so without prompting was interesting. The police would take his prints anyway.

'Gary's father and brother came in here last year to buy a present. Do you remember that?' Delahaye asked.

Hardy pretended to think hard. 'I *do* recall the Clarkes purchasing a silver frame, yes. But that was all they bought. No sugar mice or crocodiles!'

Delahaye returned the packaged sweets to his pockets. 'How did you get those scars, Mr Hardy, if you don't mind me asking?'

Mr Hardy relaxed, and smiled, which looked awful because the damaged lips couldn't quite make a full curve. 'Oh, a farmer's dogs attacked me while I was apple-scrumping on his land as a child. Thank God I was unconscious for the worst of it. Alsatians they were – nasty things! I had thirty stitches in my poor head and face!'

There it was again – the canine connection.

The bell chimed above the shop door and Karl Jones sauntered in wearing his reflective Wayfarer sunglasses. He stopped when he saw Delahaye.

'I've delivered everything you put on the list, Mr Hardy,' the boy said, walking no further. Delahaye didn't need to see Karl's eyes to know there was animosity there, and Delahaye wondered if hostility was just the boy's nature. 'I'll go home now.'

'Yes, Karl, thank you,' said Hardy, his eyes shining. When the boy left, Hardy smiled at Delahaye. '*Gorgeous*, isn't he? Cheaper and faster than Royal Mail!'

* * *

Lines found Pete Ancona on his drive, chatting to Trevor Bax, who was tinkering underneath the Cortina. Their laughter stopped when the detective constable strode into view.

'Good afternoon, gentlemen,' said Lines. 'Mr Ancona, can I have a private word?'

Ancona folded his arms. 'Nah, I've nothing to be ashamed of. What do you want?'.

Lines shrugged. 'You were the last adult to speak to Gary Clarke before he disappeared on Saturday ... '

'Oh, here we go,' said Ancona.

'Was there anything about the boys or anybody around them that made you at all suspicious that afternoon?' asked Lines, amiably. He'd pulled out his notebook.

Ancona sighed, his cockiness given short shrift by the detective's civility. 'The boys bought ice creams from me. They were chit-chatting about fuck all as kids do, and happy enough. I *did* hear Gary say he couldn't wait to get to Beacon Hill because somebody had told him about the best hiding place but that's it. Off they went.'

'Thank you, Mr Ancona,' said Lines. 'That's genuinely very helpful.'

As Lines turned to go, Bax, from beneath the car, said, 'Catch the fucker doing this, Detective. I've got my Luke to worry about.'

Chapter Fifty

AVA HAD OBSERVED THAT, AT Joseph Sheldon Hospital throughout summer, some of the residents would sit out in the sun, facing the fields. They would chat with each other and the staff and it seemed a lovely way to spend time.

'If you think DS Delahaye somehow knows you're Miss Misty, why aren't you in trouble?' John asked her as they walked and sucked on Tip-Tops in the late afternoon, Fizz bouncing ahead.

'Maybe he hasn't told other grown-ups and is keeping it to himself,' said Ava. 'I panicked at first but I trust him. He'll ask me about it eventually, but he's got bigger things than me to worry about.'

'Let's hope he finds a psychologist that knows all about clinical lycanthropy,' said John.

Ava was steering them towards the Joseph Sheldon Hospital. John must have picked up on her train of thought because he said, 'You think Mr Coleman is the murderer, don't you?'

'I know it's a high task but I just want to see if I can somehow "meet" Neville Coleman,' said Ava. Her interest had been piqued since she'd been told Banlock Farm had been a dog stud. It was curiosity and a hunch she couldn't quite shake. 'I think he has *something* to do with it all. I know it's silly. He bred dogs at Banlock Farm and dogs are so much a part of the Rubery Wolf's standard. And because Mickey was murdered there I feel he *might* know something.' John was too quiet. 'You think I'm mad, don't you?'

'Yes, but I'm used to you by now,' he said. 'Like a carer.' She nudged him. 'I'm not disagreeing with you. Anyway, we might *not* meet him.' He grinned. 'We don't know what he looks like.'

'Fizz will be our Coleman-detector,' said Ava. 'A man used to dogs, who probably really misses dogs, well, he might be happy to see Fizz.'

'What if *all* the old men sitting outside are happy to see Fizz?' asked John.

She sighed impatiently. 'Then Mr Coleman will be the happiest.'

'Do you think we'll ever be able to hang out without you going all Nancy Drew every time?' John drawled. Ava noticed his voice was mostly absent of its adolescent squeak. He was becoming taller and bigger but then, he was a fortnight from being fifteen.

'The way to get a dog-obsessed person's attention is to talk about dogs. I just want to ask him some questions,' said Ava.

'If he'll let you,' said John.

Fizz pulled on his lead. She'd constructed an extended lead and harness from chains and Rita's old reins but it didn't stop Fizz pulling like a tubby testosterone engine. They walked through the Lanes, and Fizz pulled Ava up the steep incline to the track surrounding the Rezza. The recent storms had fattened the lake, the water clear as glass with feral goldfish darting like bronze spearheads in its paperweight stillness. Magpies bickered, and giant dragonflies swooped above the surface as if the Mesozoic was still in vogue.

As they approached the hospital, there were elderly people sitting out on chairs, chatting to each other or staring out into space or reading newspapers. Ava ignored the sudden flurry of shyness that assailed her and she marched over the grass towards them, Fizz pulling ahead, John in her wake.

'Oy!' said one of the old men. 'Let's have a look at him, then.'

He was wearing dark sunglasses but his attention was on them. Fizz paused in perfect show-ring stance with his tail slightly wagging as if he recognised the gentleman. The man leaned forward in the chair, his arms outstretched to greet the excited terrier, and when man and dog finally met, it was as warm a reunion as the end of *Lassie Come Home*. There was a skinny woman standing behind him, and she turned to see what all the fuss was about. Although some of the other residents peered to have a look, nobody else bothered to make a fuss.

The old man studied Ava as if he recognised her. 'Orla?' he asked. He didn't even look in John's direction.

'No, Ava,' said Ava.

He shrugged. 'Well, I'm Mr Coleman,' said the man and Ava's heart felt like it gambolled in her chest. 'What's this little fella's name, then?'

'Fizz,' said Ava.

'Fizz,' he repeated, and the dog wagged his tail. The old man handled the dog's barrel body with an expert touch. Though his face was wrinkled and his hair was white, Ava guessed he'd been handsome when young because he was handsome when old. The sunglasses obscured his eyes but some vague recognition tugged, a viable perception prodded. The shape of his face and the height of his cheekbones were familiar – maybe he resembled a famous actor or pop star whose name escaped her at the moment.

'I think he's got bull terrier in him,' she said.

'Yes!' he said with a grin that knocked decades off his face. 'You've a good eye, sweetheart. Hasn't she, Maureen?' He turned to the care assistant who smiled.

'There's not much our Neville doesn't know about dogs, bab,' said the woman.

Neville. Neville Coleman. Ava was overjoyed that her plan had worked – that a man who loved dogs would react first to a dog in his midst. She glanced at John who almost smiled.

'I like big dogs,' said Ava. 'Y'know: huskies ... German Shepherds.'

Coleman took the bait, his gaze switching to the care assistant. 'See, Maur?' he said. 'Didn't I say this babby had a good eye?'

'You did, Nev.'

Detective Constable Lines had told her that Neville Coleman was *senile* but the man in front of Ava didn't seem senile at all. Maybe the dog's appearance had sparked a cognitive response, she considered – reminding him of who he still was.

'This lead's all wrong for him,' said Mr Coleman

'I know,' said Ava. 'But it's ... ' Even as she spoke he was removing the leads, his hands strong and quick as they rearranged the chain and leather. All the while he mumbled to the terrier, which sat and listened, his small head cocking this way and that, as still as Ava had ever seen the creature. Within a few minutes, Coleman had made a proper harness that meant Fizz would no longer be able to choke himself to death.

'Thank you!' said Ava. Because Maureen the care worker didn't seem displeased of their positive effect on the old man, Ava dared to ask, 'Are you the Mr Coleman who used to breed police dogs back in the day?'

'I did,' Mr Coleman said. 'Banlock Shepherds.' His focus remained on Fizz.

'Banlock Farm,' said Ava.

'That's right, bab,' Mr Coleman replied.

Ava took the plunge. 'It's terrible what happened there, isn't it?'

Mr Coleman was quiet for a moment then he said, 'Terrible things happen everywhere, sweetheart.'

Ava's heart was pounding with excitement. 'Like murder.' She made it a statement not question.

Despite the sunglasses, she felt his hard gaze on her. He knew to whom she was referring when he said, 'The daft lad was trespassing though,' said Mr Coleman. 'He *shouldn't* have been *trespassing* on *my* land.'

'His *murderer* was trespassing *too* though,' said Ava, her voice gentle, but she found his response odd even wrong because it was as if he was blaming Mickey for being murdered on his land. Maureen's gaze was sharp but she didn't interrupt and John's eyes flashed a warning not to go too far. When Mr Coleman didn't react to her comment, when he became very still, she wondered if he was on the murderer's side, which was a horrible thing to think about a senile old man who loved dogs.

'Anyways, Nev, shall I get you a cup of tea?' asked Maureen, smoothly covering the awkward silence and Mr Coleman suddenly smiled at her and nodded. Fizz licked Coleman's hand then stood facing the direction of home.

'He's had enough of me, and who can blame him?' said Mr Coleman. He stroked the dog's head one last time then looked at Ava, his gaze soft again. 'Now, off you go' he ordered. Ava pulled the newly strapped Fizz away and Coleman watched them leave.

Chapter Fifty-One

DELAHAYE SURVEYED THE DAPPLED INTERIOR of the watching woods. He lifted the clear evidence packet, its contents a small, dried-out paper bag. He tipped it upside down and a fine white powder puffed out – kali, the stuff Lines called kiddie cocaine. It was found a few metres away from the dead tree, discovered by a police dog following Gary's scent; protected from the thunderstorms by the close-knit tall trees.

This was the place Gary was taken. It was a densely forested section of the Lickeys, the sky mostly hidden by canopy, and cloaked in the woods' Grimm penumbra. The ground was uneven, raised roots ready to trip unsuspecting feet, crammed with lush bushes and ferns.

There had been evidence of someone having lived rough or briefly camped in this spot – a rock fireplace in which dead ashes coagulated, and, beside it, a filthy quilt stuffed into the old tree's hollow trunk. After Mrs Cutter had suggested Aster occasionally lived rough in the hills, the police had organised a manhunt across the area but had found nothing. Delahaye wondered if the search had discovered this little nook, and doubted it. SOCO had taken the quilt for analysis, to see if any trace evidence was matched with the blanket found around Bryan Shelton. There wasn't, but there were grains of that strange cement found under Bryan's fingernails so the police knew it was likely the same person who had snatched both boys.

According to Lines, Ancona told him that somebody had 'told' Gary about a special hiding place. Gary's two friends, Jez and Billy, couldn't recall anybody telling Gary about it. The only adult they'd spoken to that afternoon had been the ice-cream man. Delahaye wondered who that 'somebody' could have been. No signs of footprints, the ground too hard to maintain any lasting impressions, even after the weekend rain.

Delahaye smoothed a pebble between his thumb and forefinger, and surveyed the dogs' scent detection line. The land was briefly level, then dipped to match the incline of the surrounding woodland. A dead tree lay partially hidden from view – a potential hiding place?

Delahaye walked until the trees thinned out and the road appeared. He checked his watch: from the dead tree to this spot cost fifteen minutes at a fast walk. It was doable for a strong man carrying a child. But this point, in the exposed treeline, a man carrying a child would've been noticed, particularly on a hot summer afternoon – especially a man as loathed and recognisable as Bob Aster. What if the boys were being abducted *for* Aster by an accomplice?

If Gary had struggled, people would've noticed. But if he hadn't struggled, if he'd been rendered unconscious, then it would've looked like the man was carrying a *sleeping* child. If the child had been bleeding, alarm bells would've sounded in every passing bystander – but not all head injuries bled. A vehicle to transport the child must have been used but the path from the hollow tree was too narrow and rough for a car. A few of their suspects had cars but their main suspect, Aster, didn't have a licence – not that you needed one to drive someone else's vehicle illegally.

Delahaye frowned. Then how?

Chapter Fifty-Two

WITH FIZZ, AVA WAS ALMOST invincible, and because he was aggressive towards men, Colleen allowed Ava to walk him whenever she liked.

Ava liked 5 a.m. The excitement of going out in all weathers, alone with her dog, at a time when few other people were about, was addictive. Ava could take stock of the day before, and prepare for the day ahead.

It was a Sunday and most people enjoyed a lie-in. Ava, emboldened by her short conversation with Mr Coleman, was going to Banlock Farm to see if she could find the three graves pictured in the Polaroid she'd pilfered. She just wanted to see if she could find them, infused as she was this bright morning with an implacable curiosity. She really wanted to discover the names inscribed on them.

Fizz pulled Ava across the road to the Quarry side and immediately found something reeking to roll in. Dogs loved rolling in crap, and Fizz was the king of crap discovery. Ava prevented him from sliding into what had once been a cat. She discerned that the cat had been dead for a week or so, but the hot weather and storms must have caused its decomposition cycle to accelerate as it was mostly skeletonised. She couldn't possibly tell how it had died but she made a note in her Red Book anyway, which she always carried with her on her walks. Fizz pulled to move on. Ava may have retired her official roadkill body farm, but Fizz gave her cover for a more casual form of study.

Ava checked her watch – she still had ages before she'd have to return home. She couldn't dawdle; she needed her wits about her. It was far too early for a girl to be out walking in the boonies but she was on alert, with her blue pencil in her pocket and the furious Fizz beside her.

It was a year ago – almost to the day – that she'd followed Mickey to Banlock Farm. Ava saw the mouth of the driveway that led up to the farm, and her breath quickened. Fizz caught her anticipation and pulled harder. The earth was even more rutted due to the heavy diggers passing this way to plough up and knock down what was left of it. It smelled of brick dust, of turned earth, of green gone wild – but not death.

They scrambled up the short incline engulfed in brambles where scrub grass and wildflowers fought for the sun. Ava gazed across the field beyond. The concrete pillars of long-gone outbuildings remained untouched. She climbed over the fence (Fizz shuffled under it) and together they ran, sliding to a halt just before the markers behind the kennel ruins – a small pet cemetery.

The forensic team and police must've been here to find further evidence, Ava assumed, but lost interest when they discovered nothing of value. There hadn't been heavy feet wearing a path into the earth for years.

A little further back was a small but dense copse with a daisy path leading to a hollow, which she was certain led to another, secret place.

She bent to enter the arched portal, Fizz by her side, and they stepped into an antechamber created from tree branches and hawthorn bushes; its vaulted ceiling bristling with leaves so thick only spatters of sunlight reached the earth. It was quiet and the wind had no voice here, lending a peace usually found in chapels.

Further in and along, past a bush that grew in the centre of the aisle, she spotted them: the same three graves pictured in the Polaroid. There were two headstones for humans, and one with a smaller marker at its side. Ava saw the larger stones were of marble, white as Polo mints, the roughly chiselled letters were shallow, uneven. The smaller plaque was made of wood painted white.

The grave on the left had inscribed: *Beloved Sophia Coleman – 6th September 1910–15 May 1960.*

The stone in the middle: *Tisiphone Coleman – 17th April 1949– 12th November 1967.*

The smallest marker had simply *Zasha* scribed in black paint.

When she saw what was placed on Tisiphone's and Zasha's graves, she froze. The hairs on her nape rose, and goose pimples popped their way along her arms. On Tisiphone's grave was a bouquet of large daisies tied with string. They looked freshly plucked, no doubt from the verge outside this hallowed chamber.

On Zasha's grave was a cat skull.

It was placed in the middle of the grave, and its contours speckled with dappling sunlight. It had been cleaned out of all of its tissue, its pate stained with blood and the mandible still attached by dried tendons.

Fresh daisies. A cat skull. If it had been just the daisies, Ava would have been curious about them but would've dismissed them. Flowers on a grave were not unusual. The cat skull, however, set off alarm bells. Ava deduced, with a fear that settled in her belly like solid rock, that the killer of cats and wildlife at Banlock Farm, the killer of Mickey and Bryan, and possibly Gary, had returned to visit these graves. And this meant that the people lying within them were important to the killer. They were still loved enough to be honoured with small gifts that were symbolic in some way. And the killer had been around here recently. In fact, a small voice whispered with glee in her mind, *He might be still here! And you're trespassing!*

Mickey had trespassed on Mr Coleman's land. He'd been killed on it. 'Get a grip, you silly cow, it might not be the killer *at all*,' she murmured to herself as Fizz sniffed each grave. 'You're jumping to conclusions, the worst-case scenario.' *But, just in case, I will let the police know.* She'd contact DS Delahaye – not as Miss Misty, but a simple letter sent direct to his desk.

Her hand felt for her blue pencil. She couldn't stop looking at the cat skull. Delahaye had told her that Neville Coleman's family were dead and he was the only one left but if that was so, who was visiting these secret graves? It could be a friend who had loved them too who came to pay their respects, but the cat skull seriously unnerved her. Did Neville Coleman steal out of the care home at night without being noticed and come here? It was unlikely but not impossible. The dead women in the graves shared Neville's surname – wife and daughter? *Family*. It was the cat skull that made Ava suspect that the killer came back here. And the daisy bouquet? *Daisy crowns on a dog's skull.*

'Let's go,' she murmured. Ava ran across the field with Fizz jump-running to catch up, the undulating grass whipping at his legs.

At a distance, Ava turned to face the gravestone nook, invisible to anyone not looking for it. Having met Neville Coleman, she didn't *really* think he could be the killer, but perhaps her bias towards old people being harmless was working against this possibility. Look at Albert Fish, the so-called Werewolf of Wysteria, who had been a child-eating killer in his sixties. Perhaps Mr Coleman *was* entangled within the horror but unaware of it, his dementia shielding him from its sordid reality – unless he was using dementia as a cover. After all, a physically fit old man could easily make the walk from the hospital to this farm, especially under cloak of night.

If she'd made it in without seeing another person, she bet the killer could too.

Chapter Fifty-Three

WITHIN A DAY OF GARY Clarke's disappearance, the CID squad investigating the Rubery child murders had become a bigger team and moved to a larger incident room at West Midlands Police HQ. Detectives were interviewing every single adult the Clarkes knew in a bid to find the person who had given Gary directions to his abduction site. There was a television reconstruction of Gary's last known movements, the last resort when there were no new leads. They were inundated with calls from well-meaning people claiming to have seen Gary that afternoon but nobody had seen him after he'd gone into the woods.

Rubery Hill Hospital's Dr Tremblay, a specialist in rare psychological disorders like clinical lycanthropy was at a conference in the USA and wouldn't be back for another fortnight. Delahaye was desperate to speak to him and the waiting was as frustrating as that for forensic test results.

A larger team meant more officers taking calls and more officers on door-to-door duties but the original core of the team remained. Delahaye had a new, slightly bigger desk. Unfortunately, as a result of this move, his post arrived a day later. He sliced the top of the envelope and slid out a letter folded around a Polaroid photograph. His heart double-bumped in his chest: three gravestones. He turned it over to reveal beautiful, cursive handwriting he recognised:

These graves are on Banlock Farm in a hawthorn hollow to the right of the old kennels. I went there on Sunday and there are fresh daisies on one grave and a cat skull on the other. If Mr Coleman's family are all dead, who is visiting the graves? I'm just curious.
A.

Lines sat at the desk opposite, took a sip of his first morning cup of tea then caught his sergeant's eye. Delahaye passed the photograph and letter over to him.

Harry Marshall had called him revealing that he and his wife failed to find the graves of Tisiphone and Sophia Coleman in Bromsgrove or Lodgehill cemeteries. Ava's picture solved that mystery. It gave a solid reason as to why Coleman had been eager to know if his fields had been 'touched'.

Because Coleman had treasure buried in them.

Lines handed the photograph back to Delahaye. 'Is it worth a look then, Sarge?'

* * *

Delahaye parked at Banlock Farm and grabbed the Nikon camera from the back seat. 'I've asked Gibson to work her magic,' he said. 'And I've asked Professor Simmons if she can shed some light on the family's birth and death certificates.'

Lines raised an eyebrow at the mention of Simmons and suppressed a grin. 'A side project, is it, Sarge?'

Delahaye considered. 'Yes, it is. It might be nothing, it might lead to something. It'll do until I can meet Dr Tremblay and shed some light on clinical lycanthropy.'

Delahaye and Lines clambered over the fence and into the paddock with its kennel ruins and pet cemetery. It perturbed Delahaye that Ava had returned to this place by herself. He hoped at the very least she'd been accompanied by the boy who had spoken on the 999 call.

The men saw only trees that rustled in the breeze. Delahaye walked forward a hundred yards, squeezed himself behind a tree and immediately understood how they'd missed the graves during their initial search of the property. Delahaye had to bow down to enter what was an organic sepulchre – not dingy and mouldy like a stone crypt, but rife with birds and flowers.

They stepped in to the wild sanctum. There were the three graves.

'Tisiphone Coleman,' Lines said. 'And Sophia Coleman. Neville buried his family here.'

'And Zasha was his favourite dog,' said Delahaye.

'But why was *this* dog buried *here*, favourite or not?' Lines asked. His eyes glittered with dark humour. 'You don't think there's a *jackal* buried here, Sarge? Like in *The Omen*?'

Delahaye made a sarcastic face then crouched to study the objects placed on two of the graves. There was the daisy bouquet now starting to wilt, and there was the cat skull. He recalled the dog skull with its crown of dried daisies and the crushed bones of animals underfoot when he'd first encountered this macabre property. He took photographs of the graves. When he looked at Lines, he saw that the detective constable remembered too.

'It *could* be our killer visiting these graves,' said Lines. 'But then, what connection does he have to this place and this family? A friend?'

The Colemans had been a very insular nuclear family. Their blood relatives were dead. Harry didn't know where Tisiphone and her mother were buried so it wasn't him paying his respects – and he couldn't see Harry placing a cat skull on a dog's grave. He remembered Harry saying he'd seen Tisiphone heavily pregnant but knew nothing of what happened to the baby, had never seen a child with Coleman when he'd visited his friend months after. If the child had died – stillborn or cot death – wouldn't it have had a grave of its own, here? Not with its mother – she died years after so where was it buried? Or, born alive, was it then given up for adoption? If the kid was still alive, it would be a teenager by now. Delahaye wondered if childbirth showed up on the skeleton post-mortem.

'We are our bones,' Delahaye said, to no one in particular.

Chapter Fifty-Four

'OY! LADY A!' A VOICE yelled from above as Ava and Fizz rounded the corner of Dowry House.

She squinted to see Nathaniel Marlowe waving from the top floor gallery of the apartment block. 'Come on! I want to meet your new friend.'

Ava frowned upwards. 'Come down then!' she yelled back.

Nathaniel tut-tutted. 'I've got to be up here for a bit. Could you bring the packet of fags from the trailer, please?'

Good manners were Ava's weakness. War Horse was leaning against the foyer wall, and she noticed it had been further modified with a motor. Ava retrieved the packet of Benson & Hedges from the trailer.

She'd never been in any other block of flats except her own and, although the layout was the same, it was unfamiliar. With Fizz's panting loud in the quiet of the building, she pressed the button for the elevator.

The lift doors opened to reveal Nathaniel crouched on his haunches. Fizz bounded over and sniffed every detail of him. Nathaniel's face was impossible to read, and it had a fresh bruise marring his cheek but Ava sensed he was in a good mood. She handed him the cigarettes.

'War Horse has an engine,' she said.

Nathaniel grinned, puzzled. 'War Horse?'

Ava shrugged. 'It's what I call your bike.'

He nodded in approval. 'War Horse it is.' He stood and smiled down at Fizz who sat and looked up at the boy. 'He's a chunky young fella.'

'His name's Fizz and he usually hates all men,' said Ava out of habit.

'Who doesn't?' said Nathaniel.

'He was treated badly by men,' said Ava, also out of habit.

'Who isn't?' Nathaniel's hands caressed the bustling canine, then reached into his pocket and gave the terrier a biscuit. As Fizz munched, Nathaniel looked to Ava, his odd eyes startling in the amaranth light. 'I've got the coolest den to show you,' Nathaniel said. 'The Sky Den.'

Ava nodded. There was an interlacing of familiarity, no shyness, no awkwardness.

'But before we go, we must do this,' said Nathaniel. He rolled the sleeves of his shirt to his elbows and Ava noticed the bandages wrapped tight around his forearms. He snapped the lead from the dog's harness, circled the lead around Ava's waist, threaded the clip end through the handle then re-attached it to the harness. Suddenly she was hands-free. Nathaniel moved with efficient speed, and he hadn't touched her once. Often boys – especially older boys – snatched any opportunity to touch a girl in places they shouldn't, as a 'game', even if the girl was younger.

He pulled out a key from behind a section of loose concrete in the wall then unlocked the door to reveal stairs that led up to the roof.

'We'll get into trouble,' whispered Ava.

'We won't,' he said.

Ava and Fizz walked past maintenance cupboards then up the short flight of steps. The turret door opened to the roar of the wind which snatched their breath away.

They were on the roof! Gusts pushed Ava this way and that, but with the lead wrapped around her waist both she and Fizz were secure with each other's weight. She'd never imagined being on the roof of these apartment blocks in her life.

Nathaniel laughed as he leaned against the wind, which was so strong it held him upright.

She walked slowly, distrusting of the wind, not wanting to be scooped aloft and thrown to the ground below. They pushed on to the furthest corner of the right wing of the building until she saw it – a perfect den. Ava grinned. Perhaps seeing her response as his cue, Nathaniel smiled too. The den was tucked into the corner, out of the wind, about as big as an Austin Mini, raised on wooden pallets for the floor, and constructed of breeze blocks, wood fencing and, on one side, a window made entirely of Corona pop bottles, their thick bottoms facing out. Its roof was corrugated iron draped in a black tarpaulin. A length of thick tarp material covering the entrance flapped in the wind.

Nathaniel pulled back the tarp and Ava bent to look inside. Fizz, jumping in, began sniffing everything: a sleeping bag, camping kettle and stove, and a tin mug. Milky light filtered in through the bottle window.

Nathaniel was watching her reaction.

'It's like *Stig of the Dump*,' she said, delighted. 'How'd you get away with it?'

Nathaniel pointed behind her. 'Look at the view.'

Ava gingerly approached the edge then looked out, not down. It was like being on the prow of a galleon sailing through the skies, the rose clouds rolling past as if they were not the ones moving, but the building. Up here, they seemed to sweep forth on the crest of a wave of green hills and fields, and the houses of Frankley Estate. The wind snatched at her breath, her smile puncturing dimples in her cheeks.

'I come here to think,' said Nathaniel. 'I've got dens all over, but this is my best one.'

'Why show me?' said Ava, because it had to be asked.

Nathaniel considered for a moment then said, 'Because you're all right, Lady A. You're all right with me.'

Ava wasn't sure what he meant by this. She supposed it was similar to how she felt around certain people who managed to slip through the chinks in her armour as if she never had any, people she felt safe with. It was strange but symbiotic alliances came in all shapes and sizes – like plover birds cleaning the mouths of crocodiles.

The scar on Nathaniel's head was pale against his recent tan. Ava kept her face impassive as she wondered at the scar and the bruise on his cheek. Did he get into fights? Were his parents hurting him? It was difficult to imagine anyone hurting Nathaniel because he was tall and strong and he'd thrown Brett Arbello like he was thistledown.

Nathaniel sat on the edge of the building with his back to the drop, lit a cigarette, and crossed one leg over the other, his gaze inscrutable.

'How'd you get that scar?' Ava asked before she could stop herself.

'Last September I had an accident at my dad's junkyard.' It was obviously a popular question, as he answered it with ease. Trevor had once taken them to the Marlowe junkyard, but children weren't allowed inside so they had waited in the car. The yard had *huge* guard dogs. 'The crane claw clipped my head as I ran around a corner. I don't wear a hard hat, see, like I should. I ripped my head open and pushed bone into my brain. I was in a coma for a week, but I got better.'

'Does it still hurt?' she asked.

'Nah. I get migraines now. They get so bad I can't go to school or work but I get through them.'

This would explain his irregular but long absences from school. He was a prefect so she'd always noticed when he wasn't at his usual post at the bottom of East Block stairway.

But Ava sympathised – her father had also suffered terrible migraines for most of his life.

'You could've died though,' she said.

Nathaniel stood, stomped on the cigarette stub, his face relaxed. He said nothing.

'How'd you get that bruise?' she asked, emboldened by his easy-going attitude though it was cheeky and none of her business.

For a fleeting moment, she saw anger ripple across his features, but she felt the anger was not aimed at her. Then he said with sardonic humour, 'I fell on a desk *again*.' He shrugged. 'It's nothing much. My dad and I have the same bad temper when we disagree and we're blokes so sometimes . . .' He shrugged again. 'We scuffle.'

Ava was angry for him because she suspected Nathaniel was being loyal to his abusive father, taking on some of the blame for his father's violence. She no longer blamed herself for her own

244

mother's habitual cruelties, and she wondered if, like her, Nathaniel had a mother who wouldn't protect him. She pointed at his bandages in a silent question.

'You're a bit nosey, aren't you, Lady A?' There was no bite in his tone just amusement.

Ava blushed. 'Sorry.'

'I play rough with my dogs, that's all,' said Nathaniel. 'They forget sometimes who's boss.'

'Oh,' said Ava. His explanation could be true – she'd seen the Marlowe dogs from behind a fence and they looked ferocious. Fizz whined, and looked up at her.

'Come on, Lady A,' Nathaniel said. 'I'll take you down.'

As Ava turned away, she caught Nathaniel hiding the key in a hole in the concrete above the door before replacing it. To anyone else but them, it would just look like a crack in the wall.

Chapter Fifty-Five

'I THINK THE BIGGEST OBSTACLE TO solving crime stems from a single demographic: the Ones Who Know Yet Do Fuck All,' said Lines as the squad waited in the incident room for Mr Gann, a lab technician who was referred to as 'an expert in dirt'. It had taken the team a while to find a specialist in cement, and Gann had insisted on relaying the test results concerning the grit found under Bryan Shelton's fingernails in person. 'The wives, girlfriends, parents, work colleagues; all the "peripherals" who know there's a bad 'un in their midst but won't report it to the police.'

'It's often due to misguided loyalty, or laziness,' said WDC Gibson quietly.

'Sometimes it's out of fear,' said DC Kilborn, and Delahaye remembered Mrs Ancona's bruised arms. She had told the police that her husband was in bed beside her the night Bryan Shelton went missing. Even when she'd said it, she hadn't looked convinced or comfortable but then, this was probably her habitual manner being married to Pete Ancona.

'Somebody out there has to know *something*,' Lines went on. 'We've reinterviewed and rechecked; we've sifted and studied every detail. Bob Aster's in the wind, Ancona's got an alibi we can't dig under unless we torture his wife and I think she's tortured enough.'

'You mean she's one of those "who know yet do fuck all"?' WDC Gibson gently teased, and Lines rolled his eyes at her.

'Ancona hates children but he *is* known to them,' said DI Perrin. 'He lives close to the Sheltons. And Ancona had taken Mickey Grant to task about pushing the little ones around. He may have been seen as a hero to Bryan.'

'Ancona's the same blood group as the material found under Bryan Shelton's fingernails,' said DC Kilborn.

'But so is Aster. Blood type O is the most common blood type,' said Delahaye. 'Thirty-eight per cent of the population is blood type O.'

'Would Bryan have gone willingly to Aster though?' asked WDC Gibson.

'Aster is very charming when he wants to be,' said DC Kilborn.

'But he got his face hammered in prison,' said DCI Brookes, overhearing and coming out of his office. 'That face would scare children now, surely.'

'Aster had motive for getting his own back on the Sheltons,' said Delahaye. 'He told us that Alan Shelton and a few cronies had "roughed" him up a few times in the past, and, although the off-licence manager, Mr Mulligan, backed this up, Alan Shelton wasn't in the shop for that long. A few months before Mickey went missing, Alan and his friends waited for Aster to leave the shop and then dragged him into the alley next door for a "kick-about". Mulligan came out and stopped it. Aster had a black eye.'

'I'd say that was motive,' said DC Kilborn.

'And that's probably why he's on the run,' said Delahaye.

Bryan had willingly gone to his killer. It had been someone he trusted. The boys, like all children, had been raised not to trust strangers. If not trusted, then somebody known – and Bob Aster was *too* well known with an ugly face. But Aster had been charming, generous when he'd been hunting, and this charismatic mask might have tricked a sleepy, gullible little boy into talking to him, and might have worked on Mickey, in secret, over time. Secrets were bad for children because they knew how to keep them.

'Aster is a rapist,' said Delahaye. 'Why weren't the boys raped before they were murdered? Rape would be motive for the attacks. Or is he just turned on by bloodshed and violence now?' The squad were fixed on Aster being the culprit because he fitted the criteria so well. He understood why, but Delahaye had doubts.

'If that's how he gets turned on now then possibly yes,' said DCI Brookes.

'Maybe he can't get it up anymore,' said DC Kilborn.

'Maybe that knock on the head made him even crazier,' said DC Lines.

Delahaye couldn't get a 'feel' for the crime scene at Banlock Farm; there were too many crossed wires. The sooner he interviewed the psychologist about clinical lycanthropy the better.

There'd been a covert police presence at the boys' funerals, for it was a habit of many habitual murderers to attend their victims' services. But the only person who had blipped the radar was Pete Ancona turning to look directly at the police cameras high on the Quarry ridge as Bryan Shelton's hearse had rolled down the street, his expression inscrutable.

If, however, the killer was as instantly recognisable as Bob Aster, he wouldn't risk turning up in such a public place. He'd have been torn to pieces.

The forensic odontologist report stated the bite patterns were not recognised by any local or national dentist, and Ancona's dental records hadn't matched the original bite analysis results. This didn't mean that Ancona was absolved completely – he might be an accomplice with the car who might possibly have assisted Aster in transporting the victims to their demise – and disposal sites. However, Ancona's Cortina and ice-cream van were clean of all trace evidence – both had smelled literally of roses. And he had his wife as his alibi.

The bite pattern found on Mickey matched those found on Bryan. The footprints on the opposite bank were again corrupted by their radical positioning. The stains on the boy's clothes were indeed faeces and urine – but neither provided any further clues. The blanket was old and of a popular type with grime weaved into the fabric over time.

Time: It had been a week since Gary had gone missing.

The office door opened and a short, round-shouldered man was escorted in by a uniformed policeman. 'Hello, sorry I'm late,' Mr Gann said as he approached the large desk in the middle of the room. He placed photographs on its surface and spread them out. The team gathered around him and he seemed excited to be a part of the investigation.

'The grit found beneath Bryan Shelton's fingernails is cement: a heterogeneous mixture of a type used *before* the 1960s yet *after* World War II. It's not the highest quality and it has gradually degraded.' He moved photographic images taken of the material under the microscope. 'Hence the reason why this species of mould was found among the grit samples. These spores flourish in dark, cool, airless underground spaces.'

'We retrieved local maps from housing organisations in a bid to find which houses had basements and cellars then we knocked on those doors again. But most of the cellars and basements had been filled in or developed, using more modern concrete,' said WDC Gibson. Delahaye knew there would be another press call for properties to be searched again for nuclear-fallout bunkers.

'I've matched it to similar samples from different sites and it's a concrete very commonly found in post-war apocalypse bunkers,' said Gann.

Lines folded his arms, his tone incredulous. 'What?'

'The end of the world is nigh, Detective Constable,' said Gann. 'Some well-off people, right after the war, built themselves shelters to save them from the oncoming nuclear firestorm. I believe this concrete is from such a bunker, and such bunkers aren't necessarily built in basements. Many are built in back gardens or in fields, in hillsides, even woodland.' He gathered his resources together. 'Some will be abandoned over time and possibly under our very noses, rotting away in the dark.'

Chapter Fifty-Six

D ELAHAYE AND LINES HAD BECOME regulars at the café, their cups of tea often presented before they'd even ordered food.

Now Delahaye sat alone, staring out the window and half listening to the animated gossip of the off-shift nurses from nearby Selly Oak Hospital.

Outside, the rush hour traffic was relentless in the pulsing heat, drivers desperate to get home for tea and telly.

The bell above the door pinged. A glorious redhead entered, looked around, spotted him, then smiled with relief and approached the table. Delahaye straightened.

Professor Angela Simmons took a seat opposite. She blinked at the tattoos revealed by his short-sleeved shirt, then parried his gaze as it travelled over her. Delahaye cleared his throat.

Angela called the waitress and ordered a glass of orange juice.

'You have tattoos,' she said. 'Well, well.'

Delahaye smiled. 'And?'

'Seth Delahaye – not so much an experience but a story to be read.' It was the first time she hadn't used his police rank to prefix his name. As if he was a proper person.

'You're not a fan of tattoos then?'

Angela shrugged. 'My dad says the only people who have tattoos are rough sailors and tough whores.'

'Well, I'm not a tough sailor,' said Delahaye, and she laughed. There followed a shy silence.

'Gary Clarke,' she prompted.

'We've sod all,' said Delahaye.

'So, we're just waiting for the inevitable,' she said, as the waitress delivered her juice. Angela took a sip, glancing out at the street beyond. Delahaye studied her face surreptitiously, looking away quickly when she returned her attention to him. She pulled a cardboard file from her bag and placed it in front of him.

'I brought what you asked.'

Delahaye read the document quickly and frowned.

'Tiss Coleman only had an external post-mortem?'

Angela nodded. 'There was no need for an internal autopsy because it was clear from the head injuries how she'd died. Also, the lorry driver was the one to blame as he was drunk at the wheel. He claimed full responsibility. The doctor who'd completed the examination stated that she would have died instantly so there was no need.'

Delahaye read on. 'And she had stretch marks ...'

'Yes, of the type usually caused during advanced pregnancy.'

'Were there no other external signs of childbirth?'

'No,' Angela said. 'All possibilities are on the table. She could have carried the baby to full term and given it up for adoption. Or maybe it was stillborn. She could've miscarried or even have had a late abortion. But for that information you'd need a full internal autopsy.'

'There would have been ... imprints ...markings on the pelvic structures ...' said Delahaye.

'I'm impressed,' said Angela.

'We are our bones,' Delahaye murmured. Angela gave him a confused look. 'The girl I told you about? The one who helped us find Banlock Farm? She said that once. It's always stuck with me.'

'Well, she's right,' said Angela. 'The only way you'll know a child was born to Miss Coleman is if you exhume her body and have an experienced pathologist perform another autopsy looking for that specific evidence.'

'Nev Coleman owns the land outright; he could bury his family on his land and, anyway, I don't think it matters to the case. I just wanted to know.'

Angela rustled through the file and pulled out another piece of typed paper. 'There are two more very important details related to this. Firstly, there is no death certificate for Sophia Coleman. Towler and I discussed the possibility that she died at home, and Neville

Coleman and his daughter held a private – or secret – funeral on the land.'

'It's illegal not to register a death,' said Delahaye. 'He'd know that, being an ex-copper. And you'd need a death certificate to arrange a normal funeral.'

'But he didn't arrange a normal funeral. He buried her himself.'

Delahaye sat back in his seat. 'Does Tiss have a death certificate?'

Angela pulled out copies of both Tisiphone's birth and death certificates, passed them to Delahaye.

'If Tiss's child *was* born,' she said, 'he or she would be about fifteen or sixteen now.'

'Difficult to miss or hide,' said Delahaye.

'Yes, and a birth must be registered too. But there isn't a child's birth certificate related to Tisiphone Coleman at that time in any of the records. So there's no grandchild – at least not officially.'

'Well, this is where the plot thickens,' said Delahaye. From his satchel, he pulled out WDC Gibson's research: a thin wad of papers; copies of records, all stamped, dated and signed. He handed Angela a social services report summary:

On the morning of 14th August, 1969, a male child, whose approximate age was estimated to be three years-old, was taken into emergency social care from the property of Mr Neville Coleman, of Banlock Farm, Worcestershire. The Social Service team was in attendance with West Mercia Constabulary's armed officers. The complainant had been a man who had claimed to have been the boy's biological father with no evidence to support this claim. He had tried to 'rescue' the boy from the obvious neglect, but discovered he could not enter the property because of the pack of large aggressive dogs, and Mr Coleman's firearm. The child is Mr Coleman's grandson and both had been living in squalid conditions among his animals for some time. The boy was thin and malnourished, and suspicious of strangers. He also preferred to use animal sounds instead of speech and opted to move on all fours instead of walking. Mr Neville Coleman was suffering severe mental health issues and could no longer cope with the child or the animals. Mr Coleman was admitted to Rubery Hill Hospital for treatment and the child was fostered then adopted out of county . . . to Staffordshire.

'It's helpful to have a birth certificate for a child you're trying to adopt,' said Angela. 'But so much of this child's information would be missing, not least the actual birth date and the name of the father, so . . .'

Delahaye pondered this. 'So, there *is* a grandson.' He looked to Angela. 'It does put the rumour to rest.'

'But it doesn't explain why there's no birth certificate,' said Angela. 'Unless the deadline to register the birth was missed. For example, if mother or baby had been too ill, they may have just forgotten to do it.' She shook her head.

'Somehow forgetting to register a death can be forgiven. But not registering a child's birth – that's more than just sloppy, it's deliberate, has to be.'

Angela turned her glass. 'But think of that poor man, going mad and having to give away his only surviving family, and then him being taken away from him forever. It's shameful.'

Delahaye rummaged in the file and pulled out the official list of evidence and observations by the authorities for why the child was removed so forcefully from his grandfather's care. He handed it to Angela. 'Check out point 10A to D.'

Angela read, her hand creeping up to her mouth, her eyes wide with dismay. 'My God, how does a child ever come back from *that*?'

They sat in silence for a moment, the chime of the other diners' cutlery washing over them.

'Thank you,' Delahaye said eventually. 'I know it's not a pathologist's job to do my research for me.'

Angela smiled. 'It made for an interesting change from my own paperwork.'

'Coleman is somehow right in the middle of it all, but he is totally innocent.'

'You believe that?'

'Yes, I do,' said Delahaye. 'It's the other stuff I find difficult to believe, frankly.'

'But it makes sense, doesn't it? Clinical lycanthropy ... Using sweets to lure these boys. It's so old-fashioned, almost cliché.'

'I don't think the sweets are the lure,' said Delahaye. 'I think he himself is the main attraction.'

Angela studied his face. She drank the dregs of her juice and stood. Delahaye shook her strong, capable hand with its short, practical nails and subtle callouses. Sensing he'd held on for too long, he released his grip, reached into his jacket pocket and passed her a small white card.

'That has my number on it in case you ... need it.'

Angela smiled.

'Thank you.' She slid the card into her blazer pocket. 'Until I need to use it.'

When Delahaye returned to the station, his calm mood was blighted by WDC Gibson's horrified face as she handed him the telephone: 'Sarge, a body's been found.'

Chapter Fifty-Seven

THE ABANDONED ANDERSON SHELTER WAS in an allotment field. Delahaye's torch beam hit the rusty walls, and sent beetles scurrying for the shadows. On the curved, ridged ceiling was a single, bold handprint – too big to be a child's – etched in the filth but even he could see without getting too close it was smooth, without prints. He brought the beam down onto the old cot that had long ago collapsed; earth, detritus and litter ushered in by winds and weather to form a crusty mattress. Lying upon it was a swaddled form and, sprouting from the top of it, a spray of dirty curls. He concentrated the beam on what once had been the living face of Gary Clarke.

* * *

In the mortuary, Mr Trent pulled back the stiff canvas to reveal a dead boy, curled in the foetal position, his hands tucked under his chin. He was clothed in a T-shirt and jeans. His feet were bare, wrinkled as if he'd been in the bath for too long. Held in the child's arms, its small head tight under the boy's chin, was a dead puppy.

Mr Trent took a photograph of the tiny animal and Delahaye bent forwards.

'It looks newborn,' Delahaye said. 'Or stillborn.' Professor Simmons pointed to the side of the boy's head, and he saw the indentation just above the temple. Towler raised the boy's arm and Hickman extracted the tiny dog and took it over to the sink to process.

Mr Trent and his team retreated, and the corpse was placed on a clean table. Professor Simmons and Towler felt around with light, experienced touches, talking through their findings all the time. Hickman wrote everything down as Delahaye observed.

Hickman and Towler began the task of straightening the contorted limbs. Free from rigor mortis, the limbs relented but the execrable sounds made during the process made Delahaye cringe. When the boy was supine, his head resting on a block, Professor Simmons again gently tilted the boy's head. And there it was: a torn throat with a deep, wide bite mark beneath.

With sadness came fleeting panic. How could nobody have noticed? In the old days, Delahaye would've indulged the clichés – escaped in booze, boobs and brawling just to untether from the stress and the chattering doubt – but he was too old for the old days. He was as exhausted by the past as he was the present, and the future only offered endless more of it all. He wanted sleep.

Professor Simmons placed her hand on his arm. 'Detective Sergeant Delahaye, we'll be here for a while, and the post-mortem is scheduled for tomorrow. Why don't you go home?'

Delahaye frowned. 'But—'

'I wasn't really asking, Delahaye,' she said. 'Please. Go home.'

Towler and Hickman exchanged a glance as they worked and heard the policeman's retreating footsteps along the corridor.

Chapter Fifty-Eight

September

Graffiti on the wall of the fish and chip shop:

> Copper, Copper
> Have you stopped the cull?
> 'No sir, no ma'am,
> Three graves full –
> One in a garden,
> One in the rain
> And one in a tatty den
> Up Cock Hill Lane.
> *Harry Ca Nab!*

Rubery Hill Hospital bled majestic charisma, and its sombre function only contributed to its mystery. Its rooftops rose above the trees like the turrets of Aurora's castle, a fortress as well as sanctuary to the unsound of mind. Its labyrinthine corridors stretched in all directions through vermilion walls, the windows of the generous wards bestowed light, and the kempt gardens were worthy of any stately home. Some later extensions were unlovely, admittedly, yet its elder beauty outmatched the dour modern brick.

But it was still a lunatic asylum. It beheld dangerous psychosis and incurable sadness, and decades of suffering had seeped into its walls, its ceilings, and the very earth beneath its foundations. The faces at the windows aged without experience, trapped in their hectic nightmares or muted melancholies, ensconced in their deranged minds yet free to express their pain in shrieks, in rage, in destruction, or catatonic desolation. Only those strong of humour, compassion and dedication could work there and not be infected by such misery and madness.

Dr Walter Tremblay was tall and lanky, his manner bursting with inquisitive ebullience. His suit was outdated, and his tie knot just too wide.

Delahaye liked him immediately.

They passed light-filled wards along the myriad corridors until they reached a door, which Tremblay unlocked to reveal an untidy office. Here were desks covered in the scree of paperwork, and walls lined with framed certificates. Tremblay locked the door behind them. He offered Delahaye the comfortable chair as he sat in a plastic one, unclipped his tie and laid it on the desk.

'Anti-garrotte,' Tremblay explained cheerfully.

'It takes a very special kind of person to work here,' said Delahaye.

'Yes, we get that a lot,' said Tremblay. 'I expect you do too, as a police officer.'

'No, just riots and spitting lately,' said Delahaye, and Tremblay chuckled even though Delahaye hadn't meant to be funny.

'I was very intrigued by your telephone call, Detective Sergeant,' said Tremblay. 'I apologise for not getting back to you sooner.' He sat back. 'There are so few details in the media about how the boys were killed.'

'We aren't sharing that information with the media,' said Delahaye. 'And we won't be sharing anything discussed today. It might spark civil unrest, and I think this community could do without that.'

Tremblay nodded. 'I understand and that's a wise course of action.' He tapped his fingers on his desk, pondering while gazing briefly out of the office window then looked at Delahaye. 'According to the media reports, the victims are all boys, and the youngest siblings,' said Tremblay. 'They were well loved from secure nuclear families.'

'It had crossed my mind that perhaps the murderer is not from such a loving background, and he's destroying those families in a way to feel ... justified,' said Delahaye.

'Yes, that's a plausible hypothesis because there *are* offenders who blame their behaviour on such formative reasons. Is your leading suspect still Bob Aster?' asked Tremblay. When Delahaye nodded, he continued, 'Aster originated from a troubled, chaotic family with a weak widowed mother allowing a string of men into her life; one of those men possibly abused Aster, which might have led him to commit these crimes against boys as a grown man.'

'Yes, but he seems to have disappeared off the face of the Earth,' said Delahaye. 'We're getting desperate if we can't at least eliminate Aster from the investigation.'

'Aster *could* be dead,' said Tremblay. 'His type of offender has a high suicide rate, especially when cornered. Or he could have been murdered. His body just hasn't been found. Aster might not be your man.'

'True,' said Delahaye. 'But we don't know for sure so he's still our top suspect.' He shook his head. 'This theory that the murderer is suffering from clinical lycanthropy is a very recent one.' How does one begin a conversation about such things in real life, Delahaye wondered.

'Understood,' Dr Tremblay said. 'Let's begin at the beginning then, shall we? You tell me all you know about clinical lycanthropy, and I'll see if I can fill in the gaps. Perhaps even help you understand what it is – separate fact from fiction, so to speak.'

Delahaye read from the notes he'd taken during Miss Misty's call – the examples she'd given him from history – and spoke of the dead canines found with all three victims.

'You've mentioned most of the historic examples of clinical lycanthropy,' said Tremblay. 'It's not information people are wont to know offhand, even if they're interested in the monster element. Everything you've told me I would've told you today,' said Tremblay. 'The person you seek must be under a tremendous amount of stress to compartmentalise their lives in this way.'

'If the specific historic cases have anything in common with the present investigation ...'

Tremblay sat back in his chair. 'In 1572,' he said, 'a recluse named Gilles Garnier lived on the outskirts of a French town named Dole. He was married, but his family was poor and starving and, soon after, several children were discovered partially eaten, with their throats torn out. Local workmen discovered what they thought to be a wolf standing over the corpse of a child but it turned out to be Garnier, and he was arrested. At his trial, witnesses claimed to have seen him both as a human and as a wolf. He confessed to the murders. He said a spirit gave him some magic salve that he rubbed onto his body so he could turn into a wolf and become successful at hunting. He was burned at the stake for his crimes.'

The doctor continued. 'In 1603, around St Severs, Gascony, several small children went missing and were never found. Young women in the area claimed they'd been attacked by a werewolf or large dog. Jean Grenier was a young man who claimed that he'd been given a wolf skin – and an ointment that would indeed turn him into a wolf – by the Lord of the Forest. He boasted to a local girl about his murders and he was subsequently arrested. He was put on trial at Bordeaux, confessed to cannibalism and murder, and was interred in a monastery for the rest of his life.'

Delahaye's pen paused above his notebook. There were similarities between the Rubery murders and the historical cases.

'These cases both happened in France ...'

'All the historic cases happened in Northern and Eastern Europe,' said Tremblay. 'It must be something in the water.'

'And all male,' said Delahaye.

'With one exception. The historic cases where homicide was involved were male. And most modern-day clinical lycanthropes are male with rare exceptions. It is this statistic that possibly lent the werewolf legend its all-male bias.'

'Are all the cases linked to cannibalism?' asked Delahaye.

'Yes. And possibly witchcraft.'

'There's no evidence that cannibalism or witchcraft is the motive for these murders,' said Delahaye. 'The victims were killed as if by a specially trained guard dog.'

'And then ritualistically deposited with a dead canine as a companion,' Tremblay mused.

Delahaye handed over the photographs showing the boys' wounds and the dead dogs. The psychotherapist studied each picture.

'Does this evidence support the theory that the murderer is a clinical lycanthrope?'

'Yes,' said Tremblay.

'Have you ever come across it here?'

Tremblay shook his head. 'No. I've checked, and there's never been a case of clinical lycanthropy here at the South Birmingham hospitals or at All Saints. I'm a psychotherapist who specialises in rare disorders such as multiple personality disorders and the even rarer species dysphoria – when a person believes totally that they're a different species to their own. Both conditions can have foundations in schizophrenia or dysthymia – as will clinical lycanthropy.'

'But you *have* come across it before?'

'Yes, at a Welsh asylum. The patient believed he was a werewolf all the time, not just at the full moon. He believed he could change at will. It was only then that he would become very dangerous to staff and the other patients. He would attack by biting rather than punching. He could move on all fours – not hands and knees but properly quadruped. And very fast.'

'Is that really physically possible?'

'Yes,' said Tremblay. 'With practice.' He'd given the exact same answer as Miss Misty.

Delahaye reached down for his satchel and pulled from it another photograph, this time of the clearer footprints found around Bryan Shelton's body; of hands curled into forepaws and the feet high on the toes, like a dog. Delahaye spoke about Neville Coleman, Banlock Farm and its original purpose, and the thousands of animal bones found by Mickey's body.

'Let's say Bob Aster is alive and well. He knows the area well enough to know Banlock Farm was abandoned. He's still a strong man with a history of biting his victims. He might have progressed to such savagery and murder,' said Tremblay. 'His target demographic was exclusively boys.'

'But the bites on his victims were more like deep love bites with extensive bruising,' said Delahaye. 'I mean, he could've been planning these attacks for years, changing his MO with his growing needs. He could've groomed Mickey, Bry and Gary over time or ...'

'It is unusual for such an offender as Aster to give up sexual pleasure from rape to gratification from bloodlust,' said Tremblay.

'Unless he has erectile dysfunction and it's the only way he can find such gratification?' Delahaye wondered.

'Hmm. Have you considered Aster having a young accomplice? A youngster he might possibly have groomed or is paying to lure boys for him? Somebody who is "his type" whom he enjoys having around for other purposes?'

Delahaye's memory flashed to Mickey Grant and the naked boy in the photograph found at Aster's home. But he also remembered Karl Jones walking into Mack Hardy's shop. 'I haven't considered that possibility at all,' said Delahaye, miserable now he had to consider this on top of all the other complex theories.

Tremblay nodded. 'It's worth considering even though the historic profile of this type of murderer is exclusively a lone male. Anything else?'

'We've also interviewed witnesses who claim to have seen a strange dog-like creature standing on two legs outside Joseph Sheldon Hospital,' he said evenly. 'A man dressed, we believe, in a wolf suit.'

'A wolf suit?' Dr Tremblay said with interest. 'Samuel never thought to do that.'

'Samuel?'

'My patient in Wales.'

'What happened to him?'

Tremblay cleared his throat. 'Samuel escaped the hospital and disappeared into the countryside. That night, he attacked a flock of sheep and killed as many of the newborn lambs as he could get his hands on. He tore out the throats with his teeth, just as your murderer has done with these children. The farmer had to shoot him to stop him, like a rogue dog. Said he didn't even have to aim – Samuel came straight at him. Samuel died of his wounds on the way to hospital.'

Delahaye was silent for a moment then said, 'Had he been born that way, do you think, or made?'

Tremblay smiled sadly. 'Nature or nurture? That's *The $64,000 Question*, isn't it?' He tapped his fingertips on the desk again. 'In Samuel's case, his mother traced it back to when he was sixteen and had meningitis. He'd almost died, and they thought he'd have permanent brain damage but he seemed to return to a normal life. When he was eighteen, Samuel began to experience debilitating migraines and violent mood swings and, as these worsened, so his condition manifested and exhibited as clinical lycanthropy. You'd be surprised how many homicidal murderers have been found to have had head trauma of one kind or another.'

Delahaye looked up from his notebook. 'Like Charles Whitman, the Texas Tower Sniper.'

'Yes, a perfect example. They discovered a brain tumour, didn't they, at Whitman's post-mortem? It was pressing against his amygdalae, the clusters of nuclei that control emotional responses – our fight or flight reactions.'

'And Bob Aster had had a head injury from a hammer strike while in prison,' said Delahaye. *But then, Mack Hardy had also obtained a debilitating head injury – from German Shepherds no less.*

Tremblay nodded. 'Even in history, we can hypothesise it was head trauma that created monsters out of men who'd previously been relatively human before it. Most sufferers of clinical lycanthropy aren't dangerous, they can be treated, and they can live their lives without hurting anyone. However, if there is a base mental disorder *before* a head injury, that's where you'll find the overlap with homicidal tendencies. When not in thrall to his condition, Samuel was charming and erudite. But it was a deflection from his true psychology – and it wasn't clinical lycanthropy.'

'What goes through their heads when they think they change?' asked Delahaye.

'When they "change",' Tremblay said, 'the beast is pure in intent, it has no ego – it is the id. It is primal nihilism and possibly rooted in self-destruction. It's free from guilt and inhibitions. They don't have to ask permission – they're free. Some claim they can't remember what they did after "changing". Suicide or suicidal thoughts aren't uncommon in sufferers of clinical lycanthropy. If remorse is experienced, it is only after the rage is spent, even if murder is the result of that rage. Most sufferers of clinical lycanthropy don't harm anyone else, let alone kill. They can exhibit animalistic behaviour that can be elegant and fascinating to observe. But those that do harm . . .'

'Samuel was a psychopath,' guessed Delahaye.

'Detective Sergeant Delahaye, Samuel was the typical psychopath cliché. As a small child, he often tortured small animals. His parents took him to a doctor who suggested he was hyperactive and prescribed Ritalin. When he was twelve-years-old, they took him off Ritalin because his parents believed their son was magically cured. But he wasn't. His energies had diverted to other pastimes: shoplifting, voyeurism, vandalising property.'

'But those *are* all the typical warning signs of a homicidal psychopath, cliché or not,' said Delahaye.

'And you've come across as many psychopaths in your line of work as I have, probably more,' agreed Tremblay. 'A child that exhibits these behaviours will continue these traits into adulthood. And they've no idea that they have a disorder. You won't find a psychopath wanting to get better. He thinks he doesn't need to get better, he *is* better. And psychopaths can be found from loving, supportive backgrounds – just like Samuel.'

'Ian Brady has said, "We do whatever we enjoy doing. Whether it happens to be judged as good or evil is a matter for others to decide",' said Delahaye.

'And that's the typical cop out of a nihilistic, narcissistic psychopath. The human mind is an incredible and mysterious organ, capable of great innovation, creativity and genius. But it is also just as capable of unspeakable evil.'

'It is strange to hear a man of science use the word "evil",' said Delahaye, surprised.

'I'm not a bleeding-heart liberal and I've no faith,' said Tremblay. 'I'm a pragmatic realist. The modern terminology faffs about in our bid to *understand* but when we understand too much we start making excuses. And for human evil, too many excuses means we turn a blind eye to the warnings that alert us of its presence, and its oncoming. Mad, bad or deluded, nature or nurture, human evil has nothing to do with Satan and sinning. It's to do with choosing to do the wrong thing because we want to.'

'The murderer must feel some remorse if he places the boys with canine companions, as if he doesn't want the children to be alone in death ...'

'But have you considered it could be the other way around?' said Tremblay. 'That this supposed remorse has nothing to do with the children but all to do with the dogs? That it's the *dogs* he worries about being alone in death? Because he sees the dogs as more like him than the boys are?'

Delahaye hadn't considered this theory at all. He remembered Zasha's grave hidden at Banlock Farm.

On the wall beside the doctor's desk was a black-and-white photograph of a little girl walking on all fours. Tremblay turned to see what Delahaye was looking at and smiled.

'Ah, the nature versus nurture argument again – feral children. That girl was named Kamala and she had a younger sister Amala and they were allegedly raised by wolves in the Bengal, and subsequently rescued. They both died in childhood. It's a pity there are suggestions the whole story was a hoax.'

'Like the legend of Romulus and Remus, like Mowgli,' said Delahaye. 'Do you believe that such children exist? Do you think that there're children raised by animals – like wolves?'

'I do,' said Tremblay. 'There're some interesting cases of children being raised by packs of urban dogs in the Soviet Union.' A silence settled between the two men. 'Have I been useful to you, Detective Sergeant?'

'Everything you've said makes sense to this case,' said Delahaye. 'Thank you.'

'It should assist you in creating a profile of the type of perpetrator you seek,' said Tremblay.

'Profile?'

'The conference I attended in the USA was about the kinds of habitual offender we're seeing more and more of, murderers like John Christie, Peter Sutcliffe, and their ilk. The FBI are organising these offenders into categories and creating descriptions for each type. A *taxonomy* of such species, if you will. They've a new term for such murderers that might catch on – they're calling them "serial killers".'

Tremblay scribbled on his notepad and tore the page out, handing it to Delahaye.

'If you've any more questions, please contact me on that number. I'll be glad to assist in any way I can.' The men shook hands. 'I've enjoyed our conversation, Detective Sergeant. I haven't had such an interesting chat in a long time.'

PART FOUR

Chapter Fifty-Nine

THE LANES IN AUTUMN REGALIA blazed with incandescent hues cast from leaves flickering from the trees in cascades. On the horizon, the sunset rivalled then bettered the leaves with its own bright palette, making the clouds a rolling inferno. Ava had stopped to stare at the display and John fought the temptation to stuff his pockets with conkers until they bulged. Ava picked up a few to study their auburn colour and rub their smooth texture.

For a fleeting crazy moment, he wanted to hold her hand but he resisted. He had no idea how Ava would take such a presumptive gesture because he was sure she didn't feel for him the same way. It was ironic because there were girls at his school who said they 'fancied him' yet the one girl he really liked didn't fancy him. He knew Ava loved him in her way, only not *that* way. He was supposed to be used to her by now, but he wasn't. He knew why, and he wanted to stop it. His feelings towards her had changed with the same stealth as the final acts of puberty – he'd grown taller and broader over the summer holidays and he wondered if Ava had even noticed.

John had been chosen to play rugby for his school, and he'd a paper round so he was earning his own money. His O-level studies meant he was overloaded with extra homework so he and Ava hadn't been in the War Room for a while. His gaze slid to Ava's elfin face. Her hair had been cut like Sheena Easton's and, he'd noted, she'd filled out here and narrowed there. She seemed older somehow, even though he was now fifteen and she wouldn't be fourteen until Christmas.

Ava caught John gawping and he glanced away, his cheeks bright pink.

'What are you staring at, weirdo?' she said.

'I dunno,' John said. 'But it's not recognised by science.' Ava's smirk told him she appreciated his lame wit.

In the earth at their feet, they both noticed a set of tiny footprints.

'Hedgehog,' said Ava. 'Probably on its way to find a hibernation site for winter.'

'I bet *you* could tell if it was limping due to an injury it had on its right femur an hour after birth,' said John and she pinched him for his sarcasm. He winced.

As they walked on, John said, 'Wouldn't the Wolf's body show signs of long-term four-legged movement?'

Ava drew out her Red Book from her jacket pocket. 'I've already surmised how a human body would adapt to a regular quadrupedal stance over a prolonged period of time. It helped that my dad bought me a copy of *Grey's Anatomy* so I can study the bones and the muscles attached in detail with all the correct names. I'm guessing but I'd say that the Wolf has developed larger bones in his wrists as his muscles and tendons in his arms become stronger – the bones grow to compensate.' They were walking past Joseph Sheldon Hospital. 'It's how anthropologists know what a person did in life when they find their skeletons thousands of years later – if they were a carpenter or a gladiator. Everything we physically do, especially if we do it a lot, shows in our bones.'

'The human head is too heavy to carry at that angle on all fours for too long, I bet,' said John.

'Yes,' said Ava. 'But if he's been doing it for a long time, since childhood say, his body must've adapted.'

The sun was setting and the air was cooling, already perfumed with that smell of burning autumn always seemed to manifest.

As they left the Lanes, they saw a flash of movement by the Shapes near the Infants' playground. The Shapes were concrete climbing frames of a steam train, a huge pair of cat's ears, and a series of humps. Ava, always wary of her schoolmates, stopped walking and listened. They both heard the rattle and hiss of a spray can of paint being used. Somebody was there in the already creepy deserted playground and they were up to no good behind the hollow steam engine structure. John, bigger and unafraid of other kids, yelled, 'Oy!'

The spraying stopped then they heard the scurrying of running trainer-clad feet.

'Harry Ca Nab?' Ava joked, firing John into pursuit. He ran, thanking his recent improved fitness as he took long strides after the offender. From what he could tell from behind, the graffiti artist was a boy, but he couldn't tell anything else as he was wearing a beanie hat and a black bomber jacket. The little sod obviously knew the huge, empty school's layout very well because when John swerved around a building, sure that he would catch him in a corner, he found another passageway and the boy gone.

John bounded back, sweaty, grinning, flushed with the chase.

'Get him?' she asked though it was obvious he hadn't.

'Nope!' he said. 'I lost the little bugger.' He caught his breath then added, 'Shall we go back and check out what he wrote? Make sure it was our Harry?'

Ava's tone was sharp. 'No. Let's just go home before any more strange shit happens.'

Chapter Sixty

G RAFFITI ON THE STEAM TRAIN climbing frame in the Infants' school playground:

Darling monster ever so sly
tortures lads to make 'em cry!
When they beg him just to play
Monster kills 'em anyway . . .

The boy had written this message only yesterday evening but hadn't tagged it because he'd been disturbed and chased away. He'd returned this morning to sign his pseudonym but somebody else had got there first with their own cryptic response to his work. Beneath his sprayed rhyme, somebody had added in black crayon:

I DON'T TORTURE

He was so distracted staring at the competing message that he didn't hear the caretaker sneaking up behind him.

'Got you, you little sod!' the caretaker hissed.

* * *

When Delahaye came through Rubery police station's door, he found a very forlorn teenage boy sitting on a chair. Delahaye's presence, however, made the boy sit up, his face sheepish, unable to make eye contact. According to the desk sergeant who had called him about the 'capture of Harry Ca Nab', Adam Booth was nearly fifteen but didn't look it, slight and small for his age.

Delahaye sat beside Adam. He'd seen the boy around the Village hanging out with Ava's friend, John. This meant it was possible that Adam knew Ava. Did the girl know of her friend's alter ego?

Did Adam know about hers, about Miss Misty? It bothered him that these children were pretending to be adults and involving themselves in the case. Could they not see that they were putting themselves in serious danger?

The desk sergeant knew Adam's father and had told Delahaye that the boy had never been in trouble before, that he was doing well in school, and was from a good family. The detective saw all this, and utter remorse, on Adam's stricken face.

'Hello, Adam,' said Delahaye. 'I'm Detective Sergeant Delahaye. I understand that you're Harry Ca Nab, the delinquent who's been spreading disturbing graffiti all over the area.' Adam had twitched at the word 'delinquent', but he nodded anyway. 'You've caused alarm, mocked the police, and defaced public buildings.' He paused then added, 'These are serious offences.'

Adam was silent, his eyes tearful. 'I'm really sorry.'

'The community is terrified with a child killer on the loose,' Delahaye said. 'I've heard some people say that the killer is this Harry Ca Nab ...'

Adam's blushing shame retreated to deathly pale. 'No! I'm not!'

Delahaye sighed. 'That may be, but people are so frightened and angry they'll blame anyone for the murders, Adam. They might think your rhymes are making fun of their misery.'

'I didn't do it for that reason,' said Adam. 'I'm just sick of being scared all the time. I just wanted the fear to go somewhere else and the graffiti's my way of getting it out.' He shrugged. 'My parents won't talk about what's going on.'

'But you might have caught the murderer's attention,' said Delahaye just as a warning, but the boy's sudden expression of horror made him pause.

'Sir, do you have a pen and paper?' Adam asked.

Delahaye handed him his unofficial notebook, and pen. Adam scribbled on it then handed it back to the detective. Delahaye read the rhyme that had got the boy caught.

'I promise I *never* wrote that last line,' said Adam. 'That's *not* my work. I wrote mine last night and *that* message was there this morning.'

I DON'T TORTURE

'So, the murderer might have seen you and knows who you are now,' said Delahaye. It wasn't a typical tit-for-tat graffiti-to-graffiti response: it was a simple correction. 'Can you see the potential danger you've put yourself in?'

'Oh . . . sugar,' Adam said. 'I'll never do it again. I promise.' He held out his hand and Delahaye shook it, not doubting the boy's integrity in any way.

'Will you tell my parents?' Adam asked.

'I'll take you home and tell them you got caught in a bout of mischief and you're let off with a warning,' said Delahaye. Adam's relief was palpable as Delahaye tucked the notebook into his jacket pocket.

* * *

After taking Adam home and explaining to his shocked and disappointed parents that their son had been caught 'in a minor act of vandalism, nothing serious, he's apologised and he'll never do it again', Delahaye drove to Colmers Farm Infant School. He collected his camera from Suzi's boot and arrived in time to find the caretaker about to sandblast the graffiti off the concrete structure. He asked the man if he could take a picture of it before removal, and the caretaker nodded.

'I hope the lad's all right – I didn't mean to scare him,' said the caretaker.

Delahaye took a picture of the graffiti, concentrating on the bottom message and how very different it was from Harry Ca Nab's style.

I DON'T TORTURE.

Was this a message from their child killer? If it was, and his instincts insisted it was, the murderer might not think he tortured his victims but Delahaye believed otherwise because the bite marks suggested a relish that had little to do with killing them outright.

277

This key detail had not been released to the media, and only the police and forensic team knew the post-mortem particulars. Delahaye looked out across the deserted playground, the silence unnatural in a place usually loud with children's voices.

Chapter Sixty-One

Mid-October

KEITH 'TRIGGER' MAGAW CLAMBERED OUT of the window as the rest of the house slept. Beacon House was a six-bed children's home at the base of the Lickey Hills, surrounded by gardens, but no fences. It was a good place and very few of its residents ran away, but those that did could do so easily. There was nothing wrong with the food, the rooms or the treatment. Trigger didn't know why he was running away, again, for the third time since he'd been placed there. And that was a year ago. He was beset with a restlessness that nagged like an itch under his skin. He couldn't settle or relax because foster homes were never *home* – the only place he called home was Aunt Maxie's on Scotland's Isle of Skye. She'd wanted to adopt him but his mother had always obstructed her, so he certainly wasn't going back to Glasgow. The last time he'd returned, his smack-addled mother had demanded cash from him before he'd even said hello – one of the many reasons he'd been in care since the age of five. Trigger's nickname originated from his temper – a hair-trigger ferocity that could be frightening even to most adults. He saved his anger for the bastards who deserved it but there were still a great many bastards willing for a square-go.

The streets were quiet and deserted. He'd lived on the streets before, too many times. He carried a backpack carrying only essentials: two bars of soap, a water bottle, matches and his two favourite books. He also took a notebook and pencil, as well as his trusty flick knife. He wore thick clothing under his parka coat and sturdy brown shoes. He had decided to hole up in the hills for a month or so, just for the adventure of it, before heading to his Aunt Maxie on her tiny farm on the Isle of Skye. He'd saved for the fare – he could do it. He'd left a note on his bed to say that was where he was going – he didn't want home manager, Sarah, panicking, assuming the murderer had got him. Besides, the subsequent police search would ensure he was found and sent back to another horrible foster home.

Trigger wasn't scared of anything or anyone and the recent murders didn't even dent his objective, didn't even cross his mind. He believed the Old Nonce was long gone, scared off by the gang's vandalism on his home. Trigger's immediate worry was to evade capture, but he had all the time in the world to make his mind up. He'd have an adventure like Huckleberry Finn. He was only twelve years old, after all.

Chapter Sixty-Two

NANNY BEA WAS VERY DIFFERENT to Nanny Ash – more rounded, jolly. Her house was untidy and dust-covered. The radio or record player was always on: old jazz records soundtracking her every waking moment. Her dog, Meena, was kept in the back garden during visits because it couldn't be trusted not to bite Rita. Ava empathised – she herself couldn't be trusted not to bite Rita either.

It was an unusual day. Dad had picked them up after school so he could take the kids to wish Nanny Bea a happy birthday. They'd made her cards and drawings and the joy on their grandmother's face upon receiving them made even Dad smile.

While her sisters played with Nanny Bea's assorted knick-knacks, Ava visited the loo upstairs. On the landing, she noticed her nan's bedroom door was open, and it was never open. Ava had never been in any of the upstairs rooms, except the toilet, and she was curious to see what her grandmother's bedroom looked like. She crept to the door.

All the standard furnishings of a bedroom were here, along with the smell of cigarettes and Shalimar. Photographs lined the walls, some that Ava had never seen before; mostly black and white, some sepia-toned – all very old indeed. One captured a huge crowd of suited-and-booted, flat-capped men with horses. A couple of impossibly beautiful little girls – they had to be sisters, Ava thought – stood in the foreground, and she recognised Nanny Bea as the younger of the two. Nanny Bea had been gorgeous as a young woman (a 'man magnet' according to Nanny Ash) and, although Ava saw herself in that far-ago face, she refused to see the beauty she might one day possess herself. At the bottom of the inner frame was a handwritten caption:

The Scullion Clan, Scullion Farm 1936

Ava knew exactly where Scullion Farm was, except now it was called Marlowe & Son Breakers Yard and it belonged to Nathaniel Marlowe's dad. Ava had decided she didn't like Mr Marlowe for hitting Nathaniel. It didn't matter that parents and teachers smacked children for misbehaving because there was a difference between smacking and beating. It wasn't right.

The Bonneys had been there in summer whilst on a night visit with Trevor, and it had huge dogs that were not German Shepherds. The Bonneys had waited in the car but they'd been excited to see puppies watching them through the fence.

That land had once belonged to her family.

'What're you up to, my darlin'?' Nanny Bea's voice at the door startled Ava. But her grandmother wasn't angry at Ava being there because it was Ava.

'I'm looking at your pictures, Nanny,' said Ava. 'I like these two.'

Nanny Bea smiled. 'We were a huge family back then. Irish we are – the wildest kind.' She kissed the top of Ava's head.

'Who is the girl next to you?' Ava asked.

Nanny Bea sighed. 'That's my lovely sister, your Great-Aunt Orla. She died very young, God bless her soul.'

Orla? Ava ransacked her memory for where she'd heard that name before and quite recently: Neville Coleman. Coleman had called her Orla.

'You're starting to look more and more like her as you're getting older,' said Nanny Bea. 'You'll break hearts, my lovely.'

Ava seriously doubted it but said, 'So, we had a farm ... '

'It was a grand place back in the day. We bred horses.'

'It's a scrapyard now,' said Ava.

'Aye. An old friend of ours bought it from us to pay our debts, then sold it to his son-in-law years later.'

Nanny Bea held out her heavily ringed hand, which Ava held. As she was led out of the room, Ava asked, 'What was your friend's name, Nanny? The one who bought the farm.'

Nanny Bea smiled. 'Oh, he was a smashing bloke. His name was Nev Coleman.'

Chapter Sixty-Three

DELAHAYE, LINES AND OTHER POLICE officers had spent most of the week at Banlock Farm with a group of archaeology students from Birmingham University, and metal detector enthusiasts. The students volunteered to search for a bunker at other properties and related areas using Ground Penetrating Radar equipment. They'd gone over the ground at the farm after searching the allotment field where Gary Clarke was discovered. The students and detectorists were lively volunteers, their positive excitement at being part of the investigation the fuel that had kept the police team motivated.

Detectives had visited fancy dress shops across the county, asking the staff if anyone had been in asking for a bespoke dog or wolf suit but, other than the factory-made costumes hanging in the stores that were more cartoonish than realistic, they hadn't had anyone asking for a specific costume to be made.

Delahaye visited a taxidermist, Mrs Giltrow, who specialised in large animal subjects. The shop was full of dead animals with glass eyes that seemed to follow the detective as he was shown around. It was slightly unnerving.

'I've never had a customer ask for a bespoke wolf suit,' she said. 'You'd need to learn how to prepare skins for making into clothing. A lot of pelt and a strong needle as well as possibly animal sinew as thread like the Native Americans do. It's hard work. If I was doing it, I'd work while the flesh was still wet. But I've never tried to do it!'

* * *

Driving back to HQ, Delahaye pondered how close Adam Booth had possibly been to sharing space with the Rubery boy-killer. Delahaye knew it was time to confess.

'Guv, can I have a word?'

DI Perrin jerked his head towards his office, and Delahaye and Lines followed him in. Perrin shut the door behind them.

'Ava Bonney is Miss Misty, guv,' said Delahaye.

Lines was delighted. 'Christ, of *course* she's Miss Misty! Who else could it be, when you think about it?' Then he frowned at Delahaye, 'Why didn't you tell me sooner?'

'Seth, how long have you known this?' asked Perrin.

'Since the nine-nine-nine call. I recognised her voice – it was a girl not a woman,' said Delahaye.

'That's not all,' said Lines. 'Ava's isn't just the Miss Misty who found Mickey Grant, guv. She's also the girl who found Bryan Shelton, bagged his hand then got her friend to call it in.'

Perrin sat down in his chair and buried his face in his hands. 'Bloody hell! And neither of you saw fit to share this with myself and DCI Brooks?'

'She's a kid, guv',' said Delahaye. 'We didn't want to make her life any harder than it already is.'

'How can a girl find two dead boys' bodies? Unless she's *colluding*...' said Perrin.

'No, sir.' Delahaye cleared his throat. 'Only Ava knows how she found those bodies, and it's best to ask her directly.'

'When the media get hold of this ...' Perrin said.

'Why would they?' Delahaye said. 'Only we've had contact with Miss Misty, and the public don't know the nickname we gave the "woman" who made that first emergency telephone call. I doubt the public even remember it now.'

'But the accent ...'

'The Sheltons told me that Ava and her sister Veronica are accomplished at accents, mimicry.'

'Well, my God, the mind boggles, lads. Why tell me now?'

'Because I fear she might put herself in serious danger. She's meant no harm. In fact, she's helped.' Delahaye told Perrin and Lines about his encounter with Adam Booth, aka Harry Ca Nab. He showed the detective inspector the photograph of the graffiti with its cryptic correction at its foot:

I DON'T TORTURE.

'What the bloody hell are these kids playing at?' asked Perrin without a trace of irony. 'Does she know you know?' When Delahaye shook his head, he added: 'Go and speak to her about it ASAP, before she gets herself into some serious shit.'

Chapter Sixty-Four

SINCE FINDING OUT FROM NANNY Bea her own family connection to Mr Coleman, Ava's curiosity demanded she find out more about him. Her instincts were on high alert, but she had to be careful because she was prone to jump to conclusions.

The cat skull was what kept her hooked because of the dog-skull totems she'd seen on Banlock Farm. She couldn't help believing that whoever put the cat skull on Zasha's grave was responsible for the massacre of animals at Banlock Farm and, possibly, the homicide of the boys. She couldn't dislodge from the notion that the old man knew more than he let on about Mickey's death at least.

She'd read that dementia sufferers experienced lucid moments, but it was how sharp his voice became when he'd said Mickey had been trespassing on his land. Ava was cautious not to read too much into an old man's opinion, but it had sounded as if he blamed Mickey for being murdered *because* he'd trespassed on Coleman land.

What *if* Coleman *was* hiding behind his illness? And if so, why? Ava was aware that she was just a teenager and she should be doing normal teenage stuff, but she was heavily invested in the case, she was nosey, and she honestly saw no harm in finding out more. Unless the Wolf had died or retired from hunting, he would kill again soon. If there was anything she could do to help the police in preventing it then she would try.

Ava bundled up and put a cap on her head so that she didn't look like a girl, checked her watch and left her sleeping family for the dark outside. Fizz marched ahead as they took the route through the grounds of Rubery Hill Hospital, the buildings looming gauntly as they passed. When they approached Joseph

Sheldon Hospital, it was already bright with lights. Ava saw a man her father's age smoking a cigarette at the rear by the fire exit doors. She advanced with Fizz pulling ahead, ready to attack. The man had a name badge on his tunic which declared him to be 'GREG HICKS'.

'Hello, bab,' the man said in a concerned, fatherly tone. 'It's too early for you to be out by yourself.'

Fizz immediately snarled at the man, who grinned, impressed by the pint-sized dog's protective instinct. 'You're the lass and dog who passed by a while ago. You made our Nev happy.'

This was Ava's cue. 'Is Maureen here today?'

Greg nodded. 'Yeah, she is.' He flicked the stub of his cigarette onto the ground. 'I'll go and get her. She's due her last break before handover.'

'Thank you,' said Ava.

When Maureen opened the heavy doors and saw her, she smiled. 'Ava, isn't it?'

Ava nodded. 'I was just walking my dog and I thought I'd say hello to Mr Coleman.'

Ava was playing up the grown-ups' belief that children had no concept of adult realities, responsibilities and time so her turning up on a whim wouldn't be a great surprise. If Maureen wouldn't allow her to see Nev now then she'd try another time. Ava crossed her fingers and hoped Maureen wouldn't turn her away.

'Animals aren't allowed in here, especially dogs,' Maureen said. 'But I'll give you five minutes.'

'Thank you,' said Ava. Fizz sat and looked up at Maureen. When she smiled at the animal, Ava asked, 'Is Mr Coleman all right?'

'Yes, he's fine, sweetheart,' said Maureen.

'Does he get many visitors?' Ava asked.

'No, bab. All his family died years ago, and any friends he's made are all here,' said Maureen.

Ava still suspected Mr Coleman could leave the hospital and walk to his old home to place flowers on his daughter's grave. 'My nan recently told me that our family know Mr Coleman because they sold land to him many years ago.'

'Really?' said Maureen.

'He called me Orla because that was my great-aunt's name,' said Ava. 'I think I remind him of her.'

Maureen considered. 'Nev's in a great mood this morning so he'll appreciate a visit from this little fellow.'

Fizz knew where he was going and marched into Nev's room like it was his right. The old man's face lit up with surprise and pleasure at the sight of the animal. Nev was dressed, his sunglasses on, and he bent to pet the bustling terrier.

'Orla,' said Nev. Maureen kept watch at the door, looking out for other member of hospital staff who might object to Nev's unscheduled visitor.

'I'm not *Orla*, I'm *Ava*,' said Ava. 'Orla was my great-aunt. I'm Beatrice Scullion's granddaughter.'

He was astounded. 'Well, my God! Bloody hell! Maur! Did you hear that? I know this girl's family!'

Maureen nodded and smiled.

'How are they all, sweetheart?' asked Mr Coleman, sitting down in his armchair whereupon Fizz jumped into his lap.

'Orla died a long time ago,' said Ava because that was all she knew. Mr Coleman's smile faded at this news but he brightened when she added, 'But my nan, Beatrice, she has two sons. One is living in Australia and the other is my dad.' She smiled. 'Beatrice says hello.' This wasn't true because Ava had said nothing to her grandmother about meeting Mr Coleman but it conjured the right response. He smiled again.

'Smashing,' he said and, in that moment, Ava liked him.

As the old man fussed about the dog, Ava studied the framed black-and-white photographs on the sideboard. The picture of a family, of Nev, his wife and daughter, was a happy one. There was also a picture of Nev with his daughter as a teenager with her arms around a white Banlock Shepherd.

'She's very pretty,' said Ava.

'She was my clever girl,' said Coleman, the dog in his lap.

Ava took a deep breath and exhaled softly.

'Tiss ...'

Maureen shot Ava a warning glance but the old man didn't seem upset at the mention of the name. Instead, he nodded.

The picture beside it was of a magnificent Banlock Shepherd.

'I love this picture,' said Ava.

'That's Zasha, isn't it, Nev?' Maureen asked like she didn't already know.

'Yes,' said Nev. 'Best dog I ever had.' *Zasha*. The dog buried in the hawthorn hollow gifted a cat skull in remembrance. Ava paused. She blinked as she saw what could not be here, in this room, tucked behind the photos as if hiding from her.

The black teddy bear. The black teddy bear she had seen lying in the stable on Banlock Farm that awful day. She could argue with herself that there could be more than one like it in the world except it had the same missing eye as the toy she'd seen all those months ago. How did it get here from there? And when?

She wanted to ask about that bear. It might make Mr Coleman angry, but if it did then his anger would reveal more about him than her question intended. Ava stood by the black bear, leaned forward to study it closer.

'You like Winky, eh?' asked Nev with a smile in his tone.

'Winky?' Nev's daughter and dogs had had such extravagant names and Winky was not one of them. John had told her that Tisiphone was one of the three Furies from Greek legend who punished the crimes of men.

'He's always had one eye, like he's winking at you,' Nev explained.

'I swear I've seen a bear just like him before . . .' said Ava.

'I doubt it, sweetheart,' said Nev. 'My wife made him for our girl. He's a one-off.'

'I'm sure I've seen one exactly like him,' said Ava. 'In the countryside somewhere . . .'

The silence behind her was telling until he said, 'Well, maybe you have then.' She turned and found Nev watching her, his expression calm. Fizz licked his face, and he smiled at the dog.

'Can I bring Fizz to see you again, Mr Coleman?' asked Ava. She was going to find out about that bear even if she had to visit him a hundred times because that thing was in this room with the owner of that awful place where a boy was murdered.

'Yes', said Maureen when the old man turned to her. 'A proper visit next time, ay Nev? Outside though, so you can see the dog?'

'Oh yes,' said Mr Coleman with a smile. 'I'd like that.'

Maureen's touch on her arm was gentle.

'Bab.'

Ava called Fizz who jumped off Nev's lap and bounced to her feet.

'We've got to go,' said Ava. 'Goodbye, Mr Coleman.'

Chapter Sixty-Five

IN THE WAR ROOM, AVA chalked on the blackboard:

Mickey and Bryan were found with canine companions. Was Gary found with a canine companion too?

Black-and-yellow teddy bear with one eye missing from Banlock Farm is in Mr Coleman's room at Joseph Sheldon Hospital.

'How did it get there? Did Mr Coleman sneak out at night to walk all the way to Banlock Farm to get the bear after he'd heard on the news that it was where Mickey had been murdered?' said Ava to John.

'I would think that there'd be regular checks all night on the residents though,' said John.

'It is very important to him,' said Ava.

'But why risk it?'

'He's *not* in a *prison*, John,' said Ava.

'But he *does* have dementia,' said John. 'He'd have to be supervised.'

'Unless he's *pretending* to be senile,' said Ava.

'If he is, he'd still need to be supervised if his act is that good.' John sighed. 'Ava, it's odd, it's creepy, but that bear is *his* bear and it was found on *his* property. He could've asked for a care worker to find it for him.'

'After it had been left there in a derelict stable for years?' said Ava sceptically.

'I don't know, perhaps the murder prompted him to find it before the police took it,' said John. 'Look, I agree that Mr Coleman possibly does know more about what went on at Banlock Farm, and by extension, the Rubery murders. But if that knowledge is locked in because of senility or even fear then he'll never tell.'

'I suppose he *could* be scared,' said Ava. 'But I really need to see him again, find out more. I can't help it, John. I may never get to the bottom of it but I'm going to give it a go.'

'Let me come with you,' said John.

'No,' said Ava. 'Thank you.' When John made to complain, she added, 'I don't think Mr Coleman likes boys very much, John. He likes Fizz ...' She smiled. 'And he likes me.'

Chapter Sixty-Six

Mid-November

RON MILLWARD DROVE HOME ALONG the empty road. As he reached down to switch on the radio, a blur shot out of nowhere and into the path of his car. The car struck the blur with a sickening crunch, sending it spinning into the undergrowth at the side of the road.

The car screeched to a halt.

Ron scrambled out of the vehicle and ran to see what he'd hit.

A boy. *Fuck.*

The child whimpered as Ron lifted him into his arms. He knew he shouldn't move him, but something had to be done.

Lights flickered on in windows up and down the residential street – the impact and the scream of brakes awakening people from their slumber – and Ron felt a stab of relief as he saw hurrying figures approach, wrapping nightgowns around their forms, slippers flip-flapping.

The boy rolled his eyes towards the undergrowth on the opposite side of the road. 'Ulf-ink! Ulf-ink!' he garbled. He lifted his hand feebly, pointing to the darkness. His bloodshot eyes held the gaze of whatever it was he thought he could see, and now Ron stared too, saw the bushes move. And then a terrifying, animalistic sound. Was that a growl? There was no wind and, even if there was, the wind couldn't make that unearthly noise.

Ron squinted deeper into the undergrowth. There was something there, he felt its presence, the pressure of its regard upon him.

And then, a moment later, he heard twigs snapping like gunfire as it retreated.

Ron felt the form sag in his arms, felt the weight change and become heavier, the heart beating beneath his palm, still strong and steady. As sirens filled the world, he just hoped he hadn't killed the boy.

Chapter Sixty-Seven

D R WILLIAMS CHECKED THE DETAILS of the new patient in Intensive Care and frowned. Doctors talked to doctors, and he had been mentor and friend to Professor Angela Simmons for years.

'Get the police on the telephone for me, please,' said Williams to the nurse. 'Tell them it's urgent. I think we might have one of their boys.'

* * *

Sarah Booker, senior care manager at Beacon House care home from which Keith 'Trigger' Magaw had run away, explained the boy's background to Delahaye while they waited for more information at the hospital. 'He was born in Glasgow to an alcoholic mother and he's never known his father,' she said. 'He's been in care since he was five years old because his mother had tried to sell him for cash to buy lager. He's lived across the country in various homes, often getting into trouble for fighting, often running way to live on the streets for a week before being picked up by police and sent back. But he's such a lovely lad under that toughness, DS Delahaye. All the staff at the home thinks he's a great kid.'

'Did you find any ... expensive kinds of sweets among his possessions? Like a sugar mouse, jelly crocodile – something unusual but he never told anyone about?' asked Delahaye.

Sarah shook her head, perplexed. 'No. He shares what he has.'

'Let's hope he recovers,' said Delahaye.

'He'll recover,' said Sarah with conviction. 'He's a fighter. He'll fight this.'

Keith Magaw lay in an induced coma, surrounded by beeping machines and swathed in bandages which made him appear even slighter and smaller than he already was.

'He's emaciated and malnourished after living rough for almost six weeks,' said Dr Williams to Delahaye and Lines as they stood with Professor Simmons around the boy's hospital bed. 'His injuries are numerous. That contusion that covers the left side of his face is older than the more recent bruising on his body caused by the accident.' The doctor lifted the blanket over the boy's torso. 'You see the wound just above the umbilicus? It has been stitched in a neat, short row, in sewing cotton. There are cuts on both wrists with bracelet abrasions too – restraint marks; on the right wrist is a human bite. There is a friction rash on his neck. There are scabs on the knuckles of both hands. All his fingernails are split, some to the cuticles, and had been packed with material. There's an odd-shaped bruise on his chest, just above the sternum.'

Mr Trent and a member of his SOCO team had processed Keith's body as if he was lying dead on a mortuary slab. When they had gathered as much evidence as possible, they had left as silently as spectres. It was then a nurse took over to reopen, clean, and re-suture the stomach wound.

'The general pattern matches the marks found on the other boys,' said Professor Simmons to Delahaye and Lines as they stood around the hospital bed. 'That stomach wound was treated *before* the car accident, and it's not a bad job either. I believe Keith was held captive for a few days. All his wounds made prior to the accident are healing very well. I've asked for a fast-track on the blood test results but I'm willing to wager we'll find antibiotics in his system. There's no sign of infection. There's no evidence of sexual assault. His body shows signs of a vicious beating, but the bruises are a few days old with no other signs of any recent trauma other than the head injury.'

'His wrists have restraint marks like Bryan and Gary,' said Delahaye. 'The rash on his neck suggests a collar. I've seen these little nicks on wrists before ... '

'Have you?' Simmons's eyes gleamed. 'I was wondering what they were.'

'They're the last desperate resort of a bound person to escape their restraints. He bit into his own skin in the hope the blood greases his wrists enough to ease free of the binds,' said Delahaye.

Dr Williams held up a clear plastic bag with a damp-swollen notebook inside. 'Mrs Booker, the Beacon House manager wondered where his rucksack was as he never went anywhere without it,' said Williams. 'But only these items were found on his person.'

Lines took the bag from him. 'Poor kid.'

'Trigger survived our killer,' said Delahaye. 'He's a warrior.'

* * *

In the car, Delahaye snapped on latex gloves, lifted Trigger's notebook from the evidence bag and flipped through it. Cramped, tiny writing filled its pages: short day-to-day diary entries; lists of stores from which food could be easily shoplifted; fresh water sources; a rota of streets and house numbers from which milk could be stolen from doorsteps. Diary entries, one for every day since he'd absconded from the home six weeks ago. The last had been from four days ago. This was the date Trigger must have confronted the killer.

Delahaye flipped to the back of the notebook to reveal a series of simplistic line drawings etched by a shaky hand, perhaps in a hurry. A blobby-looking animal with lines drawn horizontally from the neck and rump, with a vertical line crossing through its abdomen. The last of the drawings was a crude map – jagged shapes and lines, and a square with 'RED HOUSE' scrawled in its centre. The word 'HERE' was written in capitals with an arrow pointing to a scribble of what looked like trees or bushes, labelled with:

Dungeon
Skinny trees
Ponies

Delahaye handed Lines the notepad. 'Does this make any sense to you?'

Lines studied each drawing. He pointed at the animal. 'That could be a ... pony?'

'Dungeon ...' read Delahaye. 'Is that where the murderer is taking the boys, do you think?' He traced the deep lines of the pencil strokes with his finger.

'But where do we start looking for a dungeon?'

'Well, one thing's for sure,' said Lines. 'The boy's not going to be able to tell us for the foreseeable.'

Delahaye flicked to the last page of the notebook. Three words were written in capital letters:

THE WOLF KING

Keith 'Trigger' Magaw's 'ulf-ink' had been him trying to say 'Wolf King' with a dislocated jaw.

Chapter Sixty-Eight

FROM THE RETIRED ESTATE AGENTS, the McIntyres, WDC Gibson had obtained Neville Coleman's property portfolios and she had perused them for any information that could assist the case. She approached Delahaye's desk, her eyes bright with victory.

She placed a series of folders before him and said, 'Skip! By 1968, Mr Coleman had acquired several residential properties, two farms and one piece of brownfield land. The majority were residential until 1971 when most of the properties had been sold, though Scullion Farm was sold cheap to a Mr Nicholas Marlowe in 1968.' She opened another folder. 'Only Banlock Farm and a strip of land in the middle of Birmingham were still owned by Coleman. All properties bar the city brownfield site were located in South Birmingham.'

Delahaye's instinct roused itself and started ringing bells. 'A brownfield site?'

Gibson nodded. 'Yes, the anomaly. It's the only land he owned in an urban area.'

An anomaly he had an inexplicable prescience about.

'Anomaly indeed,' said Delahaye. 'Thanks, Olivia. You're a star.' He stood and caught Lines's eye across the desk.

'Detective Constable Lines,' said Delahaye. 'D'you fancy a trip to Digbeth?'

'Nobody fancies a trip to Digbeth, Sarge.'

Delahaye threw him Suzi's keys.

* * *

Delahaye gazed out of the car window at the people bent like Lowry figures on the rainswept streets, at the looming buildings blurring past as they drove deeper in the city's heart.

'You look tired, Sarge,' said Lines.

Delahaye sighed. 'We all do.'

'It's been ages since you came with us for a bevy,' Lines continued.

It was true that Delahaye hadn't socialised with the squad for a while but he couldn't relax when he was in the midst of a triple homicide investigation: three dead boys and a surviving fourth victim. The killer was still out there.

'When this is over, the first round will be on me,' said Delahaye.

'All the rounds will be on you, Sarge,' Lines scoffed.

* * *

With an hour of daylight remaining they drove into Digbeth, ending up at a squalid intersection; a street bisected by a blackened railway bridge with corroded iron sidings, boarded-up arches beneath it.

Coleman's site was surrounded by a brick wall and a gate laden with padlocks. It was a tiny plot situated above a rail cutting, and a train rumbled past, shaking the earth beneath their feet.

The detectives strained to see what was behind the gates.

'Sarge?' Lines watched, incredulous, as Delahaye took a short run to the wall, jumped, hoisted and straddled atop it, his face flushed with the exertion. 'Should you be ... up ... there?'

'I'm just looking,' said Delahaye. 'Are you coming over?' Lines shook his head. Delahaye grinned at him and dropped down the other side.

He landed on his feet in what appeared to be a long-abandoned fly-tipping dump. Rusting oil drums and weathered plastic tubs were piled in one corner; scraps of eviscerated vehicles lay scattered as if the place had been bombed. A white Morris Minor was mounted on breeze blocks tucked away in the opposite corner. Perhaps the land itself was worth something, but there wasn't much of it.

Delahaye walked over to the metal drums and, for a brief moment, he thought of Béla Kiss, the Hungarian who had murdered then disposed of women in oil drums before getting killed himself in the trenches during the Great War. He shook one by the rim, but it was empty, and rust had eaten holes in the rest.

Then Delahaye spotted fresh footprints.

He tracked them back to their origin, locating their owner's landing spot by the wall. Someone had entered the same way he had. One by one, he followed the prints to a huddle of grit bins. He began opening lids: in one, ancient, crusted salt-grit and, in another, congealed cardboard.

When he came to the decrepit Morris Minor, he tripped over the remnants of a small fire. His fingers brushed the ashes: still warm. He peered through the passenger window, patchy with condensation, and saw a sleeping bag. Somebody had been camping here, very recently. The door was unlocked. Inside, he discovered a thick wad of fabric, damp to the touch. Delahaye carefully lifted the material from its dry confines: a waxed jacket. But there was something else tucked inside the garment.

'My God,' Delahaye murmured.

A rucksack, Polaroid camera, toy Comanche on a horse, and a pair of red training shoes. The missing belongings of the victims. Inside the rucksack, Delahaye found the remnants of soap, a dented metal flask and two bloated books. The inside covers revealed a name written in Biro: KEITH MAGAW.

Dusk was fast becoming full dark and, from the shadows, Delahaye heard a soft scraping noise. He straightened and peered into the corner, tried to see into the gathering night. When Lines whistled a tune behind the wall, he spotted something moving with incremental stealth, dark against darkness. The hairs rose on his nape when he stepped closer.

A growl – a deep, low rumble.

'Sarge?' Lines must have heard it too.

Delahaye stepped closer and saw it leap up and over the wall, a large, tenebrous shape that had little trouble clearing the eight-foot-high obstacle, lithe and quick as it disappeared out of sight.

'Steve! Can you see it?'

He heard Lines's shoes pound as he too gave chase. Delahaye clambered up the wall and straddled it, hoping his greater vantage point might help him see where it was going. But the dingy street was deserted except for DC Lines sprinting back towards him.

'Did you see what it was? Who it was?' Delahaye asked.

Lines shook his head. 'No, Sarge. It stayed in the shadows then disappeared in the alley behind that big van.'

'I think we can discount Bob Aster,' said Delahaye. 'No pensioner can clear a wall and run away like that.' He turned to jump down onto the street. 'And there're signs of someone living rough here like in the woods when Gary went missing.'

'Did you find anything else, Sarge?' Lines said, looking up at him.

'Oh yes,' said Delahaye. And he jumped.

Chapter Sixty-Nine

AVA WALKED HOME AGAINST THE barrage of car head-lights. As she was about to cross Park Way, headlights flashed at her from the patch of grass on the roadside, and she spied Suzi parked on it. DS Delahaye exited the car and leaned against the driver's door, the little light illuminating DC Lines in the passenger seat. The fact they were here, waiting for her in the freezing dark, was not a good sign.

With tentative steps, she approached the car. DS Delahaye opened the back door for her and she climbed in. DS Delahaye kept the interior light on – was this to be her interrogation?

'How did you find me?' Ava said. 'If I'm late home I'm deep in the sh—poo.'

'Veronica told us you were in detention,' said DC Lines. 'She said you're moving to Frankley soon – exciting times, ay?'

'Yes,' said Ava. Her gaze was fixed on DS Delahaye.

'I promise you aren't in any trouble, Ava,' DS Delahaye said. 'But I need to know for certain and I want you to tell me the truth: are you Miss Misty?'

'Yes,' she said.

Lines grinned. 'Christ, Ava.'

'And are you one of the two children who called in the discovery of Bryan Shelton's body?' DS Delahaye asked.

'Yes,' said Ava, and, without warning, burst into tears. It was as if she had been waiting for DS Delahaye to ask this question, as if he'd given her permission to finally feel. But it was only temporary relief – she was still in big trouble.

For a moment, the detectives didn't know what to do. Eventually, DS Delahaye handed Ava a clean handkerchief.

'If you don't stop crying, you'll start DC Lines off and he cries like a gargoyle.'

Ava laughed through her tears. She wiped her face and began to calm down, hiccoughing every so often, feeling strangely cleansed, and very, very tired.

'How did you know I was Miss Misty?' she murmured.

'The 999 call recording had your voice in the background. And then on the last Miss Misty telephone call, the gasp you made at the end of it was your voice, Ava. It confirmed my suspicions. And you and Luke were the only people outside of CID who knew Miss Misty was the name we gave our mystery caller.' DS Delahaye grinned, and Ava allowed that infectious dimple to win her over just this once. 'We've always known it was you and a friend who'd found Bryan's body, that it was you who saved his hand. You're just too Ava to miss, sweetheart.'

'Why didn't you say anything?' she asked.

'Because you did us all a favour,' said DC Lines. 'You did all the right things, bab. I don't know how you know what you know but thank God you do.'

'But why Miss Misty?' asked DS Delahaye.

'If I'd used my real voice, you'd have dismissed me,' said Ava. 'I have to sound grown up to get anything done.'

The men didn't respond to this admission, perhaps because they knew it was true.

'How'd you find Mickey, Ava? Why were you out in the streets at half two in the morning when you should've been in bed?' asked DS Delahaye.

Ava took a shuddering breath. 'I can't tell you. I want you to think well of me.'

DC Lines and DS Delahaye exchanged a nonplussed glance. 'Ava, we already think well of you,' said DS Delahaye. 'That can't change.'

'It might,' said Ava. 'I'm not a normal girl.'

'Normal's useless,' said DS Delahaye. 'If you were normal, we'd still be looking for Mickey Grant.'

So, Ava told them. She told them about her roadkill body farm, about her Red Book of observations. About the night she went out to observe the fox and finding Mickey's body. How on the day she and her friend (she still wouldn't say John's name) were going to the Rezza to collect frogspawn, she'd used her acute sense of smell to locate Bryan Shelton. How she recognised the importance of preserving the boy's hand from further damage. She told them about her interest in clinical lycanthropy and her obsession with bones. She told them she'd called the killer The Wolf.

But she didn't tell them about the War Room because she didn't want them to know she and John had been conducting their own investigation into the murders. She wanted to continue doing so. The detectives listened and any judgements they made of her she couldn't read from their faces. DS Delahaye looked amazed, and an awestruck DC Lines lit a cigarette, shaking his head in wonder.

'I'd love to have a look at your Red Books, Ava,' said Delahaye.

'Did Gary Clarke have a dog with him when he was found?' Ava asked.

'Yes, a stillborn puppy,' said Lines. 'But that's a secret from the public, like the others.'

'So that when people call in claiming to be the real killer, they have to tell you this secret to prove they are?' asked Ava.

'Yes,' said Lines.

'The killer hasn't killed for a while,' she said. 'And he's due new prey, you know.'

The detectives exchanged a glance then Delahaye said: 'Have you heard of Keith Magaw, Ava?

Ava frowned. 'He was in the news. Isn't he the runaway who was hit by a car?'

'Yes. He's in a coma, and we won't know for sure until he wakes up, but we believe him to be a surviving victim of The Wolf, as you call him. There's evidence to suggest that Keith was held captive for a few days, treated for his injuries, even fed. He escaped and that's when he was hit by the car. Ava, this is confidential information and it won't be in the news . . . '

'I know,' said Ava. It was apparent Delahaye trusted her as much as she trusted John, and she felt honoured. But Keith was a total shift in The Wolf's pattern. Why save this boy and not kill him?

'The same kind of concrete grit found beneath Keith's finger-nails matches that found beneath the nails of Bryan and Gary,' said Lines.

'The lair,' said Ava.

'Keith kept a diary,' said Delahaye. 'He referred to it in it as "dungeon".'

Below ground, thought Ava. 'Do you think the dungeon is on Banlock Farm?'

'We've searched around it,' said Delahaye. 'We used Ground Penetrating Radar after you found those graves, and again right across the property. We found nothing except dog bones.'

'Do you think Mr Coleman has anything to do with it?' she asked quietly.

'We feel he's connected to the murders without him being the murderer,' said Delahaye.

'You need to find the lair,' said Ava. 'And I still wonder who put the daisies and the cat skull on the graves.'

'It could be a well-meaning member of the public who found those graves before you did,' said Lines.

'I suppose so. And all of his family *are* dead . . .' said Ava.

The detectives swapped glances. 'We *did* find out that Mr Coleman has a grandson but he was adopted by a family in Staffordshire when he was a toddler,' said Delahaye. 'He'd be a teenager by now.'

Ava logged this information, surprised by it, her curiosity wanting to sniff around it and track it. She also itched to share with the detectives the black teddy bear but she couldn't – not yet. As Miss Misty, as an anonymous advisor, she was confident and sure of her words but as plain old Ava, not at all. She needed to be sure about who brought the bear to Mr Coleman and then she would immediately tell them about it if there was anything to tell. She intended to see Mr Coleman again and, in doing so, see Maureen too. It had to be early morning again – because of the cold weather and the early dark evenings, her mother didn't like her going out except to walk Fizz. The blinker lights ticked, revealing the view beyond in orange flashes.

'You won't tell my mom, will you, about my being Miss Misty and ... all the stuff about bones?'

'Only if you promise not to be Miss Misty ever again,' said Delahaye, and she nodded at him in the rear-view mirror. 'If you feel inspired to help us, just be yourself.'

'I will. I promise.'

Delahaye turned in his seat and regarded her with such pride she blushed.

'Let's get you home,' said Lines, and Suzi roared to life.

PART FIVE

Chapter Seventy

December

AVA WAS GOOD AT WRITING letters. She'd written to Maureen at the hospital since their last meeting, and Ava had sent Mr Coleman a photograph Nanny Bea wouldn't miss of her and her sister Orla as young girls on Scullion Farm. Maureen wrote back and thanked her, telling Ava that Mr Coleman had it next to his other pictures on his sideboard. Ava sent it not to be kind but to pave the way for her proposed visit. She knew it was sneaky.

Maureen had told Ava the times of visiting hours at the hospital so she and Fizz arrived at the reception. Dogs weren't allowed but the manager had listened to Maureen's glowing report on Mr Coleman's improvement of mood and cognitivity in the presence of the girl and dog, and agreed it was a kindness to let him see them.

Mr Coleman, under Maureen's watchful eye, met the pair outside. It was a very cold Saturday morning and, because it was Daddy Day, Ava couldn't stay long but she watched Mr Coleman make a fuss of Fizz. Ava relinquished the lead to the old man and he and the dog walked the length of the building exterior. Ava and Maureen walked behind them, chatting, until Ava felt secure enough to ask, 'Maureen, has that teddy bear in Mr Coleman's room always been there?'

Maureen shook her head. 'No.'

'So, how long has it been there?' Ava asked, keeping her tone completely casual.

Maureen frowned – not because she thought it was an impertinent question but because she was genuinely considering it. 'I dunno, bab. Since spring sometime, I think.' She darted a look at Ava. 'Why're you asking?'

'It's an unusual bear, that's all,' said Ava.

'It turned up in his room one day. He lived in Bromsgrove before he came here and sometimes stuff gets missed when they pack their belongings and it gets sent on later,' said Maureen. 'I just thought the manager put it there for him.'

'He seems happy with my dog.'

Maureen sighed. 'Yeah, he does, but he hasn't been well recently. He's gone back to talking to himself at the window late at night. It's usually a sign he's not right again.'

'What does he say?' Ava asked.

'He mutters so I can't work out the words. But he sounds like he's telling someone off.'

Mr Coleman had stopped walking and was dabbing a handkerchief at his eye.

'Oh dear. His blue eye is seeping again,' said Maureen.

'His blue eye?' asked Ava.

'Yeah, he's got odd eyes, bab.' Maureen strode towards him while plucking paper tissues from her tunic pocket. Ava watched as Maureen insisted he remove his sunglasses to access his eye, and her own vision blurred then sharpened when she saw that Neville Coleman had *heterchromia iridum* ... like Nathaniel Marlowe and the same kind: left eye brown and right eye blue. Mr Coleman had reminded her of someone and it wasn't a pop star – it was Nathaniel. The chances of two men who looked alike with the same eye distinction in the same area *not* being related were slim.

Ava's shock almost made her forget her facade and she quickly collected herself.

'I have to go home,' said Ava. Mr Coleman gave her Fizz's lead, and blinked at her with those incredible eyes.

'Thanks, bab,' he said as Maureen reset the sunglasses on his face. 'You take care,' he added to Ava as she pulled Fizz away.

Chapter Seventy-One

OURS LATER, AVA AND HER sisters were in Town with their dad, looking for Christmas presents, and their trek culminated at the Rag Market. Ava usually loved the Birmingham Rag Market. It was a city within the city: streets upon streets of stalls. Colour was everywhere: the wares, the produce, the language, the clothes. The smells. Voices rose to the ceiling where echoes collided.

But Ava wasn't enjoying the bustling market. She wasn't interested in anything. The noise and crowds bothered her, even scared her. If someone brushed against her by accident, she wanted to scream. She couldn't enjoy the lights and the excitement of the crowds, she was too busy thinking and worrying. Since her last visit to see Neville Coleman, she hadn't slept well and she'd lost her appetite. She couldn't escape the twin hunters of dread and denial that were stalking her at close quarters, threatening to leap on her and drag her down. She had to lock her suspicions and her fear inside while ensuring that her stress didn't show on the outside.

She needed to speak to John immediately but immediately was out of reach.

In a queue for hot dogs, Ava observed a big brother teasing his little sister, making her cry. Little kids were rarely frightening to big kids. Children were frightened by other children the most; not by creatures in nightmares, horror films or the-thing-under-the-bed. In daylight, children knew such things didn't exist. Bullies were always going to be the real monsters and children could get away with murder simply because they were children, like Mary Bell and . . .

Ava went numb. The name was the key to unlock her.

Mary Bell.

Clinical lycanthropy was, if anything, secondary to something else entirely. Having this disorder wasn't the reason the killer hadn't been caught – he'd evaded capture by donning the best disguise of all. Everyone had been looking in the wrong direction because they'd been searching for the most obvious demographic, the typecast murderer: a grown-up.

Ava stood in the queue and wondered how she'd been so stupid.

The kid killer was another kid.

And she thought she knew which kid.

* * *

During times of fear and misery, the last people on earth Ava considered running to for help were her parents. But who else could she turn to? Mrs Rose was on maternity leave, and she trusted no other teachers. Her grandparents were too hard on one side and too soft on the other. Plus, none of them would believe her. Ava had been in denial the whole time. The Wolf was another child, a teenager – one of their tribe. Nobody would suspect a child of killing children. Mary Bell was old news best forgotten. The Wolf knew every inch of the area because his job took him all over it – he knew everybody and everybody knew him. He attended the local school and he knew his peers' siblings – especially those with younger brothers. He was charming and he knew just how to inveigle his way into children's trust.

Nathaniel Marlowe.

There was a conviction that played on a loop in her head like a pop song: *Nathaniel is good. He looks out for me. It's not Nathaniel. It can't be.*

Absolutely everything made him the principal suspect. Who else could make a den on Banlock Farm other than the heir to its tragedy?

Nathaniel Marlowe *had* to be related to Neville Coleman. DS Delahaye had told her that Mr Coleman's grandson had been adopted in another county but what if he'd somehow come back? She couldn't guess how but what if?

Nathaniel Marlowe *had* to be Neville Coleman's grandson. And every time she tried to touch on what that might mean in relation to the murders, she shied away from it.

Nathaniel is good. He looks out for me. It's not Nathaniel. It can't be. Nathaniel was a *murderer*.

She balked at this revelation because it was hard to see the worst in someone who always showed her his best but . . .

The daisies placed on Tisiphone's grave and, on Zasha's, the cat skull.

Had he been responsible for the other skulls and bones found at Banlock Farm? She closed her eyes. *Yes*. Had he been the person who had returned the black teddy bear to his grandfather's possession? *Yes*.

And he shared exactly the same kind of heterochromia iridum as Mr Coleman who was the owner of Banlock Farm.

Nathaniel Marlowe was Neville Coleman's grandson.

Nathaniel Marlowe was the Wolf.

Chapter Seventy-Two

THEIR FLAT HAD BECOME A sparse chamber. Usually, in the first week of December, they had their Christmas decorations up, but they were packed too, ready for The Move. As soon as Dad had dropped them off home, Ava harnessed Fizz and left before her mother could say anything. She ran to John's granddad's house, rang the bell, and stood on the doorstep, seriously impatient.

When John opened the door, she said, 'War Room, now.'

* * *

'The Wolf is a child,' Ava declared, as Fizz sniffed about the winter garden.

'He's a *what*?' John said.

Ava rubbed out 'MARY BELL' with her sleeve and wrote down another name: 'POMEROY'.

'Between March and April 1874,' she said, 'two children went missing and were later found dead. A fourteen-year-old boy called Jesse Pomeroy was charged with their murder. Before the murders, he'd attacked young boys for years, beating and stabbing them. Like Mary Bell, he was a kid who killed kids. And the St Severs werewolf—'

'Yeah, Jean Grenier...' John interrupted.

'The St Severs werewolf,' Ava pressed on, 'was *fourteen years old* when he killed his child victims. The only reason he wasn't burned at the stake was *because* he was a child, so he was sent to a monastery for the rest of his life instead. The Wolf is a mix of Bell, Grenier and Pomeroy.' As she talked, Ava scribbled notes on the blackboard and then grabbed one of the big marker pens and started writing on the back of the poster. 'And it's Nathaniel Marlowe, John.'

John's jaw fell open. He didn't speak for a few moments, a look of shock etched on his face. 'We have to be sure, Ava.'

'I *am* sure. I don't want to be. But I feel in every part of my being Nathaniel is The Wolf,' Ava said, tearfully.

'It can't be him, because . . .'

John trailed off as the thought tumbled in his head. *Why* couldn't it be Nathaniel? Because he was *just* a teenager? Because he always seemed such a good person who was funny and clever and protective? Can a person be too nice, too good to be true?

Then he remembered. 'Ava, a few months ago, I helped Nathaniel carry a little dead dog to some bushes so it wouldn't be messed about with by kids and such. He really cared about it, the way you are with dead animals but . . . ' He groaned at his own naivety. 'Christ, it *is* Marlowe. How much do you want to bet that little dog was the one found with Bryan?'

Ava looked as ill as he was feeling. 'Why didn't you tell me this before?'

John shrugged. 'I don't know.' He'd thought it might have been jealousy that had prevented him from sharing this incident with her because Marlowe always called her *Lady A*. When she'd told him about Nathaniel showing her his den on the roof of the apartment building, he'd been so jealous that a crucial connection between events had been missed.

'He showed you the Sky Den. Do you think he had access to all the roofs of all the blocks of flats, Ava?' John had always harboured a suspicion about Marlowe, some instinct about him – the charm with a void behind it. 'Like the roof of your flats so that he could throw a tortured cat off it?'

Her eyes were so large in her small face. 'Why didn't I see it? I've been so stupid.'

'Why would you, Ava?' said John. 'He's charming, he's helpful and he's just a kid. Granted, a strong, man-sized kid but he's still a teenager. Why would anyone suspect a child killing another child especially the way he kills them? And, Ava, he likes *you*, he *protects* you. You'd miss the bad in him because he shows you only the good. It doesn't make you stupid, only human.'

Ava looked relieved when he said that. 'He had some bandages around his forearms when I last talked to him at the Sky Den. I think those wounds were caused by his victims fighting back not by playing with his dogs like he said.' She paled. 'Oh, God, John! I think I know how he makes his wolf suit!'

John felt sick.

'That bloody teddy bear! His bike,' said Ava. 'I remember seeing those trailer buckets at Banlock Farm! I should've made the connection then. That trailer is large enough to carry a child, dead or alive. I know this because he took me home in it.'

John covered his face with his hands.

'That's not all,' said Ava. 'In the news, you know Keith Magaw, the runaway boy who was knocked down by a car and is in a coma?' John nodded. 'Well, DS Delahaye told me that Keith is a victim of The Wolf who survived! The Wolf attacked him, treated the wounds he caused then Keith escaped!'

Although it was fantastically good news the boy had survived, John had to ask, 'But why did he keep Keith Magaw alive?'

Ava shook her head. 'I don't know. Maybe Keith made The Wolf like him – like the opposite of Stockholm Syndrome or something. Oh, we have to find that bloody lair!'

John straightened. 'I'll find it.'

Ava stared at him. 'What? How?'

'I deliver the Marlowes their newspapers, remember? I know their routine. They both leave for work around the same time every morning. Mr Marlowe leaves in his car and turns right towards the hills and Nathaniel leaves on War Horse minutes later and turns left towards Rubery. When they leave, I'll take a look around their back garden.'

'The news said bunkers could be anywhere . . .' Ava said.

'My granddad says that many fallout shelters were built *away* from houses so that, if the house was destroyed during the bombing, it didn't collapse on the bunker door and trap everyone inside. There was a house in Edgbaston that had a bunker built in the back garden that the new owners only discovered when it caved in. They thought it was a sinkhole at first.' John folded his arms. 'I'll find it.'

'I'll come with you, said Ava.

'No,' said John. He crossed his arms. 'Not this time. *I'm* doing this. You won't be able to sneak out with Trevor staying with your mom every night before the move. And she's become strict on where you go and when you come back. You can't risk getting into trouble, Ava, because she'll stop you going anywhere if she catches you. I know where Marlowe lives. I'll try and find the lair around the property. If I do, then I'll tell the police. If I don't, well, let's just tell the police what we've guessed anyway. There may even be a bunker somewhere under the scrapyard.'

Ava brightened. 'Yes! I hadn't thought of that!'

Because you're stressed, John thought. *The Wolf, finding dead children, Trevor, your mom, school, the move – it's a wonder you aren't screaming mad in a padded room, Ava.* He'd expected her to insist she go with him but the relief on her face told him she was pleased he'd offered to go alone. He'd always been the voice of caution and she'd always been the one taking risks. It was time he stepped up and took action rather than act like a health and safety officer. He was the bloke and it was time to act like one and he found he didn't mind at all. Was he scared? Not yet. But he was bigger and stronger now, certainly bigger than The Wolf's four victims.

'So, the plan is: tomorrow I try and find the lair at the Marlowe's property. If I do, I tell the police where it is and that The Wolf is Nathaniel. If I don't, I *still* tell them it's Nathaniel and recommend they start looking at the scrapyard for the lair,' said John.

Ava nodded, her expression worried. 'But, John, Nathaniel hasn't been at school all week because of his headaches,' she said quietly. 'What if he's home?'

'But he *isn't* home,' said John. 'Because he's left every morning this week at the same time the way he always does while wearing school uniform. He's duping his dad into thinking he's going to school when he's not. He's going somewhere but it's not school and not home.'

Ava hugged him. John was so shocked by the unexpected close contact that he was unable to react let alone reciprocate. By the time his arms stretched to wrap around her, she was gone from them. She opened the shed door and a cold blast of air invaded the small space. As they left the War Room, John saw his granddad gazing out of his kitchen window. John waved but the old man didn't seem to see them as he stared at the War Room shed, sipping a cup of tea.

Chapter Seventy-Three

11th December, 12.02 a.m.

AS MAUREEN APPROACHED THE FAR end of the hospital corridor, she heard whispering coming from Nev's room. Nev was becoming more confused and secretive lately and all the more belligerent for it. His old habit of talking to 'imaginary people' had returned, usually with him sitting muttering against the window of his room.

Maureen entered the room quietly so as not to alarm him. When her eyes adjusted to the gloom, she saw that Nev was in his usual spot at the window. He was muttering away and, curious, Maureen stepped closer.

Something was out there.

Some ancient instinct warned Maureen to hide. She crouched, and saw, in the gap lent by the chair legs, the silhouette of a massive furred animal, its head close to the old man's face with only glass barrier between them. She crept closer and she heard the strangest, most terrifying, conversation for Nev wasn't mumbling words, he was making sounds – tiny snarls, whines and huffs – and the thing at the window responded with deep, rumbling growls. It was as if the old man was trying to appease it in the language of wolves.

She knew what it was: it was the creature she'd seen the night before Bryan Shelton's body was found.

Terrified, she shuffled out of the room, and only stood when she was safely in the corridor.

Maureen padded into the staff area, rushing past her bemused colleagues to find the small automatic camera they used to photograph the residents' special occasions. She quietly opened the fire exit doors then peeped around the corner to the opposite end.

The outside lighting was inadequate, but if she squinted she could just about see its shape: an animal the size of a Great Dane, sitting close to Nev's ground-floor window. Maureen quickly raised the camera and took a picture, the burst of intense light from the flash lighting up the moment.

It immediately came running, first on two legs and then on all fours, in bounding strides, hurtling towards her. She took another picture when it was halfway close, revealing in a flash its true monstrousness and she fled to the doors, slammed them behind her and backed into the shadows. The beast didn't stall – it galloped past the building, and cleared the barbed-wire fence to be devoured by the night.

From the other end of the corridor, came a long, wretched wail.

Chapter Seventy-Four

4.35 a.m.

JOHN SNUCK OUT OF THE house and started running. It was still dark, the opal moon high above, and as he ran snowflakes flecked the air.

He sprinted through slumbering streets, and then to the wall and hedge that surrounded the Marlowe property. It was set far back from the main road down a long drive. He checked his watch – the Marlowes would be leaving the house very soon.

But today was different. John hid in the bush and, right on cue, Mr Marlowe's sleek Fiat Dino purred into view but this time, it turned *left* and drove down the hill towards Rubery. He waited for Nathaniel to appear on War Horse, as usual, but he didn't. Crouched low as John was in a hedge in the dark, he couldn't see who was in the car so he assumed that Nathaniel had gone in the car with his father or was still in the house.

John sidled from his hiding place then briskly walked along the drive. From the street no one would ever know this place existed. It was a large Edwardian house surrounded by a huge garden with imposing hedges.

War Horse leaned against the porch, its trailer empty. No lights were on in the house. No lights on didn't mean the house was vacant – Nathaniel could be ill and sleeping, and had decided not to go to work and school today as he hadn't apparently been going every day this week.

The police had visited every house in Rubery, including this street, looking for basement access. They would have come to Russet Lodge to search for a cellar as this style of house would have had one back in the day. John circled the house and couldn't see any ventilation grates or windows that would indicate a basement presence. Lack of such factors didn't mean there *wasn't* a room under the house but John suspected there wasn't. If he was honest, he didn't think there was a bunker in the garden – he believed it would be found at the scrapyard. But John needed to check, to be as thorough as Ava.

He was in dark clothing and he kept to the shadows cast by the moon and the street lights peeping over the property wall. The main part of the garden wasn't to the rear but to the fore of the house – two rows of hedges formed a corridor of plush lawn. John squinted into the darkness and saw the curve at the end of the privet avenue. He kept at an angle to the house, never turning his back on it just in case Nathaniel appeared, as he ran along the eerie hall created by the bushes. The wind made them rustle and sway as if dancing and, as John hugged the curve around to the very rear of the garden, he came upon a copse of silver birches. The trees weren't very old and weren't very well – they were spindly yet spectrally beautiful, silvered by moonlight. The moon illuminated something else that transfixed John to the spot.

Horses.

There were three carousel horses among the frail trees, painted white so that they glowed with lunar lustre, as if carved from alabaster. Impaled into the earth by their central poles, they pranced as if floating in mid-air, their forms tethered by twisting ivy skeins.

John's heart was beating hard and fast. Every hair on his body prickled in warning. He turned and couldn't see the house for the hedges, which meant he couldn't be seen from the house. Driven by his curiosity, he stepped off the lawn and into the strange grotto. It was hemmed in by the back wall, which loomed above him and the trees, the brick old and flaking.

John stared at the horses. They appeared to form a circle, the ground beneath them soft with mulch and mosses. The trees formed a rectangle frame around the bewitching tableau, in summer their leaves would interlink creating a roof over the horses, and John wondered if they had been planted that way deliberately rather than allowed to grow in a natural, less organised, formation. He still didn't think the lair was in on this property but there was something odd about how this garden was set out.

He padded towards the horses, the ground soft and bouncy as in woodland. Other than the wind through the foliage, there was no other sound so when a car zoomed down the road behind the wall, he jumped and tripped over. He'd fallen on a rock because there was something digging into his back. He rolled onto his front and, as he was about to get to his feet, his hands detected a change in the ground texture, not earth but something else – a subtle give. John rummaged around in the soil and the 'rock' he'd fallen on was a padlock.

He gently knocked on the ground. The mulch was thinner on this patch, and it sounded hollow. John stood and, as lightly as he could, jumped. There it was, a reverberation, an echo, as if he was standing on metal sheeting – or a door.

He crouched and moved dirt with his hands. He worked around the padlock until his fingertips scored the outline of a trapdoor. His heart kicked a harder, faster beat.

He'd found the lair!

Scared, excited, he scuttled back on his haunches, when his hand brushed against something else, an object. He picked it up, too dark to see it properly, and slid the thing into his pocket. He scampered along the foot of the garden, along the driveway then checked the empty road. He stood beneath a street light and pulled the item from his pocket. A flick knife. Its handle was a little rusty but the blade was still sharp.

Engraved on its side was the word: 'TRIGGER'.

Chapter Seventy-Five

5.15 p.m.

THE MURDERER WAS A TROPHY collector; as discerned from the find at the Digbeth property. They finally had fingerprint evidence, but no matches in the record, and not Bob Aster's. Lines suggested that these prints might belong to an accomplice to Aster, a younger man, and this was certainly possible because the person had scaled that wall in Digbeth like oil poured in reverse, with no effort at all. Keith Magaw's rucksack produced an interesting clue – a chunk of concrete which, when forensically analysed, matched that found under Bryan Shelton and Gary Clarke's fingernails: Keith must have taken it during his incarceration in the beast's lair.

The discovery of the objects and to whom they'd belonged was released to the media and Delahaye hoped it would harry the killer, wherever he was. There was little else they could release to the public without causing panic and riots. The tabloids would have a field day with their clinical lycanthropy theory, and Delahaye dreaded the kind of picture they'd splash on their front pages.

Dr Tremblay had sent him a book on lycanthropy, by Sabine Baring-Gould, which he'd found enlightening – and its accompanying woodcut illustrations disturbing, particularly those depicting children being attacked by two-legged werewolves.

'Sarge?'

Delahaye glanced up from evidence sifting to find WDC Gibson holding up the telephone receiver.

'It's the hospital. They tell me Keith Magaw is ready to speak to the police,' she said. 'In fact, he urgently wants to talk – as in right now.'

* * *

Delahaye and Lines found Keith Magaw in a room not on a ward, with a woman sitting at his side they recognised as his Aunty Maxine Loughlin. They had met her when she'd arrived from Scotland soon after Keith had been admitted to hospital. She was blonde, small-boned and wiry like her nephew. There were flowers in a vase and a row of Get Well Soon cards on the windowsill. Keith was sitting up, his bright grey eyes serene.

'Hello, Keith, hello, Miss Loughlin,' said Delahaye. 'I'm Detective Sergeant Delahaye and this is Detective Constable Steve Lines.'

'Hello. I've seen you on the telly news,' said Keith, sitting up and stretching his arm to shake their hands. The boy's manners impressed Delahaye. Keith would soon be going home to live with his Aunt Maxie on the Isle of Skye. Delahaye had learned that the Glaswegian authorities had sought Keith's mother and discovered her living on the streets, totally uninterested in what had happened to her child. The authorities had deemed it in the boy's interests at last to allow him to live with his aunt.

'Shall we call you Keith or Trigger?' asked Delahaye.

'Keith. Trigger died in the accident,' said Keith, his voice quiet and firm.

'How are you feeling, lad?' asked Lines.

Keith looked up at him. 'Comfortably numb, like my favourite song.' He almost smiled. 'I went for my first walkabout yesterday.'

'You did well,' said his aunt, squeezing his hand.

'Thank you for seeing us,' said Delahaye.

Keith nodded, and his face was grave. 'Aye, I want to get this done now.'

'We want to ask you a few questions—' began Delahaye but Keith cut him off.

'I need to tell you everything about the Wolf King,' said Keith. 'It's why I needed to speak to you as soon as I was well enough.'

'The Wolf King?' Delahaye repeated. He placed a cassette recorder on the bedside table. 'Do you mind us recording our conversation?' he asked, and Keith shook his head. Lines stood by the window while Delahaye sat on his left and Aunt Maxie remained on his right. She helped Keith drink water through a straw then he asked, 'Where do you want me to start?'

Delahaye pressed RECORD on the cassette player. 'From the night you encountered the Wolf King,' he said. 'Take your time.'

The boy closed his eyes as if to collect his thoughts then began.

'The first time I saw the Wolf King, it was in the dead of Wednesday night, and it was running on the park field at the back of Lo-Cost. It didn't see me, or so I thought, though I'd felt watched for a while when I went out at night. I was scared because it looked like a mix between a gorilla and a massive wolf. I thought if that thing sees me and gives chase, I'll never outrun it, but then it stood up and I saw it was almost human. I froze, even though I was hiding behind the big bins, but then it dropped onto all fours again and galloped out of the park.' Keith looked at the detectives as if checking for cynical disbelief.

'The next night was when it happened,' Keith continued after another sip of water. 'I was walking through Rednal bus terminus. And as I was passing the public bogs, I heard this humming noise from behind the building. I turned the corner and there was this lad. I'd seen him around. He's got this monster bike with a motor, with a trailer attached. I checked my watch and saw it was two o'clock in the morning. I knew why *I* was out but why was *he*? He looked like he knew I'd be there, like he'd been waiting for me.' Keith paused. 'He gave me the creeps seeing him there. He's got odd-coloured eyes, and he was wearing leather gloves. He just stood there like he was waiting for me.' Keith paused.

'Go on,' Delahaye prompted.

'He offered me a smoke but I said no thanks because it was scary suddenly seeing him there like he ... owned the night.' Keith's hands clenched against the bed sheets and Aunt Maxie gave him a reassuring squeeze. 'He knew my name. When I asked him how he knew it, he didn't answer but asked me if I'd like a chocolate bar. I said yes because I was starving and he handed me a Mars. I ate a huge chunk of it ... ' Keith's eyes widened. 'And then he hit me around the head so hard I conked out.'

'How old was this boy, Keith?' asked DC Lines.

Keith thought about it a moment. 'I'd say he was about sixteen to seventeen years old.'

'A teenager? Are you absolutely sure?'

Keith was adamant. 'I'm absolutely sure.' His eyes narrowed and he frowned. 'I can't remember his name right now . . .'

Delahaye met Lines's gaze across the room. The prospect of a name was the breakthrough they had been waiting for.

Keith took a deep breath and continued. 'I came to, I think sooner than he expected. I saw I was in a big garden with a . . . sort of corridor of hedges, and he was dragging me down it. He'd taken me there in that bike trailer. There was a big house that looked like it was built of red brick even in the dark. It was closed in by tall walls. There were little trees and strange horses . . .'

'Horses?' Delahaye repeated.

'Yes. Carousel horses painted white and stuck in the ground. I fought back. I shouted and that's when he went mental like an animal, biting and shaking me about. I knew, then, what had got me – the thing in the park, the thing that killed those boys. I managed to stab him in the shoulder with my flick knife but he swiped it out of my hand. The pain . . .' Keith gulped. 'I kicked and punched but he was so strong, he was on me like a lion or a bear.' He shuddered. 'He cuffed me really hard on the side of my head and knocked me out again.' He shuffled in the bed so he was sitting straighter, his gaze narrowing.

'I woke up in a place that had grey concrete walls, a closed door, which had a terrible smell coming from under it. It had a toilet, a sink, and I was lying on a mattress. I had a chain around my neck and leather handcuffs on my wrists. And it was underground.'

'How did you know this?' asked Delahaye.

'Because when he left me, he'd go up a flight of stairs then out of a small door in the ceiling, and I could smell cold, fresh air, which would blow in. I would hear the wind in the little trees. When I woke up, it was this boy wearing that *thing* like a cloak. He was the Wolf King. I was frightened but my belly hurt. While I was unconscious, he'd sewn the bite on my stomach, and cleaned me up a bit. When I cried, he flipped back the head-hood, and he was human again. He went to the kitchen part, got me some tablets and a glass of water then he helped me take them. He wasn't vicious at all. And then I fell asleep. Can you believe that?'

'Did he speak to you at all?' asked DC Lines.

'Barely,' said Keith. He shrugged again. 'I never begged him to let me go though. He was nice but I could feel he was really angry underneath.'

'*Nice?*' Lines asked, bemused.

Keith shrugged. 'Well, he'd stopped hurting me. That's nice in my book.' Aunt Maxie was obviously horrified by everything he was telling them, but Keith carried on. 'And he helped me wash and go to the bog, fed me bacon sandwiches and cups of tea from a flask. He never wore that thing again around me, thank God. I couldn't rewind my watch so I lost track of time, and when he left me for hours, I had no idea if it was day or night. I practised getting out of the cuffs by nipping the skin on my wrist with my teeth then the blood would grease them off me. I'd go and wash my hands in the bog while flushing it then I'd use soap to ease them back on again so he didn't know. I'd stretch them so that eventually they were easier to slip on and off. I couldn't try for the ceiling door because of the chain, and I heard him lock it from the outside. He didn't notice or if he did he might have thought I'd failed. He'd dumped my rucksack close to me so I managed to get my diary out and drew what I could remember from the garden: the trees, the horses and the house. Then I tucked it in my pocket. There were chunks of concrete on the floor from the walls so I put one in my bag, because on the news they said there'd been concrete grit found under the boys' finger-nails. I thought that if someone found the bag, they'd match the grit with the concrete, and if he killed me and my body was found, then I hoped I'd given some sort of map to help you find the place ...'

Aunt Maxie sobbed when he said this, and the boy squeezed her hand. 'The night I got away, he took my collar off and I let him lead me upstairs then out. I was so glad to be out. I didn't fight back. He was too big and strong, and I needed all my strength to escape, if I could. My eyes were everywhere, trying to find a way out, to run but there wasn't just then. One shout and I know he would've killed me to keep me quiet.'

'Did he say anything then?' asked Lines.

'Yes,' said Keith. 'He said it was time I met the pack.' He scrunched the coverlet in his fists then relaxed. 'There was a driveway and I looked down it and I recognised where I was ...'

Delahaye's eyes were bright. 'Where?'

'I can't remember the name of the street right now but it's the one with the old library on it and those maisonettes on the cliffs ...'

'Leach Green Lane,' said DC Lines.

'Yes! That's it!' said Keith. 'And then I got into the car ...'

'Car?' asked Delahaye.

'Yes, he was going to take me out in a car,' said Keith. 'I don't know the make of it, but it was very shiny, a purple or dark red, I think. I sort of hunched over, facing the window so he couldn't see me slipping the cuffs off. Then he started to drive up into the hills. He didn't say anything the whole time.'

'He trusted you,' said Delahaye, impressed.

'If he did then I don't know why,' said Keith. He was obviously tired and his words slurred a little. 'But I knew if I stayed calm and quiet, he'd be the same. When I managed to remove the cuffs, I looked out of the window to find we were approaching tall gates, and the barking of dogs.' Keith swallowed with a dry click. 'He stopped outside a scrapyard. *Marlowe & Son*, the sign said it was.'

Delahaye knew exactly the place the boy talked about. 'We know it,' he said.

Keith swallowed with a dry click so he took another sip of water. 'When I heard those dogs howling, I panicked and I opened the door as soon as the car stopped and started running. I just ran and ran. I knew he'd become the Wolf King and catch me but I had to try.' Tears fell down the boy's cheeks and Aunt Maxie swiped a tissue from a box and dabbed his face. He looked exhausted now.

'Thank you, Keith,' said Delahaye. 'You've be—'

Keith was shouting. 'I know his name! I remember his name!'

'Tell me,' said Delahaye.

'It's Nathaniel!' Keith said. 'Nathaniel Marlowe!'

Chapter Seventy-Six

6.27 p.m.

IN THE CID OFFICE, THE entire squad listened to Keith Magaw's taped interview in silence. When it had concluded, Delahaye switched the machine off, and they sat there for a moment, pondering what they had heard with a mix of shock, disbelief and a great deal of horror.

DCI Brooks sighed hard. He shook his head. 'Kids killing kids? It's like . . . *Lord of the Flies*.'

'Can we really believe that a teenager would kill little boys like that?' asked DI Perrin.

'Ava as Miss Misty gave us the clue months ago when she mentioned Mary Bell in passing. Bell was eleven,' said Delahaye. 'And Jean Grenier of St Severs was a teenager, fourteen no less, when he committed his crimes. We said it even then that although kids killing kids is rare, it does happen.'

Considering all they knew, and what they'd just learned, there were no protocols or regulations for a case like this. Right from the start, they'd been flailing around in the mire.

'It's not a coincidence. Coleman sold the farm cheap to Marlowe. And I bet you its guard dogs are Banlock Shepherds,' said Lines.

'It isn't a coincidence,' said Delahaye. 'Because I'm sure Nicholas Marlowe is the mysterious "Jip" as he was known then, the young man who had worked for Neville Coleman at Banlock Farm. Nick had fallen in love with Neville's daughter, Tiss, and Nathaniel is their son.'

'Neville Coleman's grandson,' said Lines.

'We need to bring the Marlowes in *now*,' said Delahaye. He couldn't keep the impatience out of his voice. 'Before they abscond like bloody Bob Aster.'

'All right, DS Delahaye. But no warrants ... yet,' said DCI Brooks. 'We'll make coordinated visits to the Marlowe residence and scrapyard, as well as the boy's school. We'll make it seem like routine inquiries. If the father knows what the son is doing, and is protecting him, we don't want to spook them into making a run for it, as you rightly say.'

Olivia Gibson, meanwhile, had found no references to a boy with odd eyes in witness statements or interview transcripts, but did find the distinction referenced in Delahaye's notes of his conversation with Harry Marshall concerning Neville Coleman and his daughter Tisiphone. She found the name Nathaniel in the notes of his interview with the Shelton boys when he'd asked them about the game Wolf: 'Last year, the big kids found us but he let us go,' Tom had said, and Rob had added, 'Karl and Nathaniel.' *Nathaniel.*

Right there – hidden in plain sight. Not an old paedophile or irritable ice-cream man, but another child. Surrounded by other schoolchildren, a predatory child wouldn't be noticed – a wolf in sheep's clothing.

On hearing that the CID squad were looking for a teenaged killer called Nathaniel Marlowe, a sheepish and apologetic police constable who was on the team operating the telephone lines admitted he'd taken a call from a member of the public very early that morning. 'He was a young man who insisted the murderer was a sixteen-year-old boy named Nathaniel Marlowe,' said the red-faced officer to the exasperated detectives. 'I thought it was a crank call, Sarge, you know, a lad just trying to get another lad into trouble for a prank. I didn't know! He said something about finding the lair ...'

'Fucking hell!' Delahaye snapped and the whole office fell silent. He rarely lost his temper but when he did it was a shock. '*Please* tell me you took his name?'

The PC shifted uncomfortably. 'Erm, John ... something ...'

'John *Something*?' Delahaye had to check-chain his rage before he'd do or say something he might not regret. 'Did he say where he'd found the lair?' he demanded.

'I'm so sorry, no. I told him to grow up and put the phone down on him ...'

'Shit!' Delahaye swung his coat on. 'Let's get a move on. Time's running out and we have no bloody idea if this John Something alerted the Marlowes in finding that bloody dungeon.'

Colmers Farm Secondary School was closed but WDC Gibson was blessed to find a teacher working late who helped her look through the fifth year attendance registers. Her inquiries yielded quick results: Nathaniel Marlowe had been absent for the past week. The teacher said Nathaniel's terrible head injury after his accident at the scrapyard the year before had given him regular debilitating migraines so his absences were attributed to these: 'And he always brings in a note from his father to explain why first day back,' said the teacher had added. 'He's all right, isn't he? He's such a good lad.'

It wasn't hard to find the Marlowe residence in Rubery after a vehicle check relayed that Mr Nicholas Marlowe owned a maroon Fiat Dino, and a blue Ford van. The property was known as Russet Lodge – the red house.

Delahaye and Lines drove to Marlowe & Son Breakers Yard. The tiny snowflakes that swirled in the air, too restless to settle, reminded the detectives of the pulviplume floating around Banlock Farm. It was freezing cold and dark. Houses and flats glittered with Christmas decorations, and Rubery Village sparkled with festive lights.

They could hear dogs barking in the near distance as they parked by the junkyard gates, and a man approached them. Delahaye showed him his warrant card and the man, Minty, took them into the house. When Delahaye asked to see Nicholas Marlowe, Minty shrugged.

'He hasn't been in all day,' he said. 'He's usually in before me. I've had to feed the dogs today and that's most unusual.'

'Would he ordinarily ring to let you know he wouldn't be in?' asked Lines.

'Always,' said Minty. 'Our van's not here either. Boss might've gone off to an auction or to deliver a part somewhere, but he always lets us know.'

Another man came into the house: who introduced himself as Tim. 'What's going on?'

'Just routine inquiries,' said Delahaye.

'Concerning what?' Tim asked.

'Concerning his son, Nathaniel,' said Delahaye.

'What's he done then?' asked Tim. 'He's a good lad.'

DC Lines's radio crackled at his hip and he stepped outside to answer it.

'Nathaniel hasn't been at school for a week,' said Delahaye.

'That's rubbish,' said Minty. 'He's come here every day this week with his uniform on. After school, he's here to feed the dogs and walk 'em along them back hills.'

'Has he been here today?' Delahaye asked, and Minty shook his head, confused. Delahaye tried a different tactic.

'How has Nathaniel been since his accident last year?? Since he had his head injury?' Delahaye asked. The two men exchanged a glance.

'Well, he's not the kid we used to know,' said Minty.

'His temper was really bad for a while,' said Tim. 'He'd turn very suddenly, the way the dogs can. He never used to get angry quick, did he?' Minty shook his head. 'But then it's gone as quick as it came, and he'll be all right for a while, as if nothing's wrong.'

'Was his father afraid of him?' asked Delahaye. He saw both men were fiercely loyal to the Marlowes but there was genuine concern for father and son.

Tim shuffled his feet and nodded. 'Nathaniel's attacked his dad a few times.'

'Boss has had to punch him to put him down,' said Minty. 'Lock him up until it was over. Not to be cruel, like; just to stop him.'

'But the past year, Nick said Nathaniel had calmed down, he seemed to have found a way to control his temper.' Tim suddenly stared at Delahaye with dreadful realisation, a dawning so awful the man's skin leached white.

'Do either of you know that Nathaniel isn't even supposed to be here with his father?' said Delahaye. 'That as a toddler he was adopted by a couple in Staffordshire? How did his father get him back? Do you know?'

Tim glanced at Minty who said, 'Me and Nick found out where the boy lived ...'

'How?' asked Delahaye.

'It wasn't easy and it took a while. It took a lot of money too, a hefty couple of backhanders to the right people in the know. The system was easier to corrupt then, I dunno. Anyway, after a year, we tracked the couple down and we waited in a van for days for the right opportunity, but there never seemed to be an ideal time. Then his adoptive mom took him to the park. I chatted her up while little Nathaniel was mucking about on a swing. Nick grabbed him and ran. By the time she realised what was happening, Nathaniel was already in the van with his dad. His adoptive mother couldn't identify Nick but the police questioned him about it, him being the dad and all. It was in the news as a child snatch, but they used the boy's new name in the reports. Nathaniel never answered to the new name. Nick hid him at my mom's house in Redditch for a few months until the furore died down. He was living in Alvechurch at the time and had just bought this place. He was always paranoid that Nathaniel would be taken from him again so the boy wasn't registered with a local doctor or dentist. If he needed either, Nick just booked an appointment with a practice far from where they were living. He bought Russet Lodge a year later.'

'You told me when Nick took him from the park, Nathaniel didn't make any noise,' said Tim.

'That's right. He didn't scream or cry. It was as if he knew he was back with his dad,' said Minty. 'As soon as the lad saw Nick's dogs, well, that was it. He became our lovely little boy, happy to be with us. I know it was never all right, I know it was wrong what we did, but they're father and son.'

'How did Nick get Banlock Shepherds?' asked Delahaye.

'His girlfriend Tiss, Nathaniel's mom, brought him some puppies the night she was killed,' said Minty. 'It was on the way back she had the accident. That's why he blamed himself.'

And why Neville Coleman blamed him too, Delahaye thought.

'You know, after the police raided the farm, Nick went back and buried the dogs that were killed,' said Minty. 'And he buried the old man's favourite next to Tiss and her mother. His three graces he calls them.'

'Is there any place you can think of where Nick would go if the authorities knew Nathaniel was here?' Delahaye asked.

'I'll make a list of every property Nick owns and every friend who might take them in,' said Minty.

Delahaye was about to thank him when he heard Steve Lines shout from outside. 'Sarge!'

The frightened urgency was so unlike Steve that Delahaye ran to the back door of the house to find his partner confronting a pack of giant dogs. The animals sat on old tyres, on the patio, on the roofs of the adjacent outbuildings, their hackles ridged, yet completely silent, their eyes focused on the tall detective. Delahaye counted around thirty animals, all large, feral, and dangerous. Lines wouldn't stand a chance if *one* attacked him let alone if all of them pounced.

'Banlock Shepherds,' Delahaye whispered.

'They've never done this before,' murmured Minty at the detective's shoulder. He turned to Tim. 'You know how Nathaniel does it.'

Tim stood beside the frozen Lines, cupped his hands over his mouth and made a single husky bark. The dogs immediately fled; they spilled off their perches, streamed around the corner and were gone.

Steve's face was white, his eyes frightened. Minty handed him a flask-cup of tea. Tim walked around to make sure the dogs were away from the house.

'Gibson and Perrin are at the Marlowe residence,' Lines said, his teeth chattering. 'No one's home: it's locked up and there're no vehicles in the driveway – just a bike. It looks like the Marlowes have done a runner.'

Delahaye patted his partner's shoulder and, on a whim, turned to ask Minty, 'Was Mr Marlowe known by another name . . . like a nickname?'

Tim answered: 'Yeah, he used to be known as Jip but he hated it.'

A long, drawn-out howl sounded from beyond the hulks of twisted metal and the gaunt remains of the Ferris wheel. The entire pack joined in an echoing, mournful chorus, the only honest song of farewell.

Chapter Seventy-Seven

7.30 p.m.

NOW MADE HORIZONS DISAPPEAR, SHORING up the landscape with porcelain walls tall as the sky; flawless walls to write on. Little Adam tucked his head into his scarf, and trudged towards John's house. There was twinkling tinsel in every window, and some windows even had real electric lights on their displayed Christmas trees. Even though he could've just waited until the blizzard waned, he'd wanted to go out in the dark, in the snow, by himself. He'd been grounded since his parents had found out about his stint as a vandal though he'd never tell them he'd been Harry Ca Nab. He'd just pop the Christmas card through the letter box and return home slowly, taking his time through the deserted, silent street so as to enjoy his brief new freedom.

He posted the card then plodded back to the road, his head bent; the snow smattering his cheeks with fleecy kisses. He stopped at the junction when he heard something large, fast and heavy advancing behind him. He turned to see what it could be, but it hit him so hard he was rendered unconscious before he ever got a look at it.

* * *

John picked up the card from the doormat, opened it and saw it was from Little Adam. In his slippers, he rushed to the front door to catch him before he left. The snow fell in insouciant spirals, and for a moment, John didn't know what he was witnessing.

And then he did see.

The Wolf was hunched over Little Adam. Blood had fanned across the white like thrown ink. It was big, its grubby white fur raggedy; and stained teeth gleamed in its bald skull with demon-set ears. It rested its weight on the boy's chest, looking into the closed, pale face, and John saw how its eyes reflected the snow in gold discs – because it was wearing sunglasses, the vintage ones he'd seen Nathaniel wear in the summer. Seeing them made him lose his temper and override his fear because although it was monster, it was just a boy too.

'GET OFF HIM YOU *FUCKIN'* FUCKER!' John bellowed.

The Wolf raised its ugly head as if bored. John saw the human chin then the human mouth, which ruched into a wide snarl and revealed strong sharp teeth.

'*We* know who *you* are!' John said. He was shaking with so much rage and terror he thought he might explode. '*We* know where *you* live.'

It growled; a rumble John felt through his feet, but it had been John's shout that made doors fly open and indignant people wander out to see what was going on. The beast leaped over Little Adam and, instead of attacking John, bounded off into the silent white night.

It was heading for its bunker lair. John charged after it but not for long; his wet feet were numb with the cold. His granddad had carried Little Adam into the house, and John's mother had already rung for an ambulance. John followed her into the living room where Little Adam lay, pallid but alive, the blood from his head wound already clotting. His mother tucked a blanket around him. John ran to the telephone. He dialled the number he now knew by heart: Delahaye's, waited with rising panic as it rang and rang endlessly.

His grandfather snatched the receiver from him. The old man slapped a hand-drawn map on the table, the map of Russet Lodge and where the Wolf's lair was hidden. It was the map John had intended to take to Ava before the snow came, and he'd stupidly left it in the living room. His mother ignored it because it meant nothing to her but the fact Granddad understood what it repres-ented meant he knew about War Room, and if he knew about War Room, he knew everything. The relief of sharing the burden after so long was too overwhelming to ever explain but there was apprehension too because Granddad was angry with him.

'I'll tell them what they need to know,' said Granddad. There was a voice at the other end of the line. 'Yes,' said Granddad. 'Good evening. I'm Mr Deryn Cadogan. May I please speak to Detective Sergeant Delahaye? Please tell him it's an emergency – there's been an attempted child abduction in Rubery ...'

Chapter Seventy-Eight

NO TIME TO THINK. JOHN had to reach Ava. Whilst Granddad was on the telephone and his mother with Little Adam, John pulled on his boots and was out of the house before anyone could stop him. He ran across St Chad's park, through the Village, and paused for breath, sweating and panting, at the Flyover.

He was about to resume the pace when a car drew alongside him and a voice said: 'Mate, d'you want a lift?'

John saw Paul Ballow in the driver's seat. Ava knew Paul – he was a friend. He nodded and Paul opened the passenger door.

It was warm in the car. For a moment, John shivered and didn't speak. When Paul asked where he was to drop him off, John said, 'Ava's.' When Paul asked what he was doing out in such weather, John told him everything. He might as well – the whole world would know soon anyway.

Chapter Seventy-Nine

8.12 p.m.

I N THE ROOM WHERE SHE began, almost fourteen years
ago, Ava plucked ice from the bottom of the windowpane
and popped it into her mouth. She stared out at a quilted
world which forsook sharp edges and colour. Headlights on the
A38 moved at snail's pace, the blizzard slowing the cars down to
a crawl.

The room echoed, with no carpet or furniture to absorb noise.
The carpets had been taken up and recycled for wherever they
fitted in the rooms of the new house, as the carpets had from
Trevor's flat. The furniture was already placed in the new home
just where Colleen wanted it to be. Ava had her own wardrobe
and dressing table – her own space. The Bonneys weren't officially
moving until tomorrow, so the radiators and lights were still on;
both blessings when the temperatures kept falling. She and Luke
remained to pack the very last of their belongings, and Trevor
had planned to collect them. But then the snow came. They would
have to stay another night.

From the Front room, Ava could hear Human League's album
Dare on Luke's cassette player. She thought about their first
Christmas in the new house; how she'd never look through this
very window ever again after tomorrow.

There was an urgent banging on the door. Luke opened it, John
and Paul poured in, dripping onto the bare floor.

'Granddad knows everything. Paul knows ... well, some. The
police know where the lair is ...'

'In the Marlowes' garden?' Ava asked.

'Yes, but when I rang this morning they didn't believe me,' said
John. 'My granddad found the map I'd drawn for you and he's

353

telling the police where it is right now.' He dug into his pocket and showed her the flick knife he'd discovered in the carousel copse. Ava saw the name TRIGGER carved into its handle. She returned it to his pocket.

Paul stood silently, as if in shock.

Luke's face paled. 'I can't believe this,' he said as John explained what had happened that evening, how he had seen the Wolf hunched over Little Adam, his granddad calling the police, how he knew everything. When John assured Ava that Little Adam was alive and on his way to hospital, she hugged him tightly.

'But I can't hear any sirens ... ' he said. They became still, listening. 'Perhaps the police didn't believe Granddad ...'

Ava opened the front door and freezing wind slapped her face as she stepped onto the communal gallery. The snow had eased but the opaque sky promised more. The boys assembled around her, listening for sirens. She remembered she hadn't heard any sirens the night she'd found Mickey – perhaps Delahaye had arrived stealthy and silent: when the hunter doesn't know he's being hunted he becomes the prey.

'What's that?' whispered Luke.

'I still can't hear sirens,' said Paul.

'No, not them ... *that*.'

They all heard it then – a single plangent bark. Ava instinctively dropped into a crouch, tucked behind the exterior cladding, her eye peeping through the gap between. John, Paul and Luke crouched too.

No cars, no people, only an immense hush. And then the beast came. It was huge, its fur camouflaged against the white, its long strides swiftly carried it along the road. It switched direction, leaped the wall, and plunged into deep powder, surfing sugary spray, its ugly magnificence a Boschian nightmare. John was the only one who'd seen it close up but its skull face still made him shake. Paul was stock-still with terror.

Ava felt Luke tremble against her. Poor Luke: he'd never recovered from Banlock Farm, and she'd selfishly never asked him about it. She'd readily absorbed its horror and she'd automatically thought he had too, but Luke wasn't her, he was Normal; he couldn't unsee what he'd seen: the bloodstains, the bones. Luke's fear was palpable, almost as visible as their pluming breath. Ava placed her hand over his and squeezed, and Luke looked through her.

'What the mc-fuck is that thing?' he whispered. Ava didn't answer because not only could you not unsee what was seen, you couldn't unsay what you said.

They watched the Wolf plough through drifts that would make a human stumble. The Wolf had left a scar in the virgin snow; it had popped silence back into place in its wake, and it was fleeing. It ascended the hill and it knew where it was going. Ava was sure she knew too.

Chapter Eighty

8.32 p.m.

A S OFFICERS ATTENDED MR CADOGAN with Adam Booth, other uniformed police breached Russet Lodge's front door with CID. Delahaye and Lines sprinted after Gibson as she led them through the garden to a silver birch copse with a bizarre display of white carousel horses and, as they crowded into the space, they saw the trapdoor. It was clear of earth, its padlocks thrown aside, and light glowed from within. The detectives unclipped their truncheons and, at Delahaye's nod, Lines opened the hatch.

Tepid electric light glimmered from light bulbs attached to caged fixtures on the walls, and the stink that arose had the force of a punch. A set of concrete steps led twenty feet down into a squalid oubliette. Delahaye silently descended, Lines and Perrin close behind, into a space that had been vacated in a hurry: lights still on, door left unlocked, and items of clothing littering the floor. It was a mundane yet wretched place, separate from the main house – no wonder they'd not discovered it. The walls had peeling paint, exposing the degrading concrete beneath. A bare bulb hung from the low ceiling. There was a camp bed with crumpled sleeping bags, a bare mattress, a small electric heater, a coiled garden hose, and a makeshift kitchen area with worktop, sink, and a kettle. There were no personal possessions. A musky odour hummed in harmony with the light bulb's buzz. This was where Keith Magaw was held captive, and exactly how he'd described the place.

There was another door: closed, battered, exuding spent Molochian malevolence. A reeking wolf suit of petrol-and-platinum fur and a despicable skull-like mask with leathered pointed ears hung from a hook on the door. There was no lock or latch. From the gap at the bottom spread a broad, dark stain. As Gibson, and uniformed officers, paused halfway down the steps, waiting, Delahaye knocked. No response. He stepped to the side so that anyone armed couldn't use him as a direct target. At his nod, Lines pulled on the handle and swung it open.

The miasma that pervaded couldn't compare to the slaughterhouse stench that barged forth to greet them. Delahaye covered his mouth and nose with a handkerchief, and entered a gore-splashed chamber with screams etched into the walls with the scratch marks. His torch revealed its confined hell as every known behaviour of blood loss splashed the interior: spots, streaks, gobs, spatters, drips and congealed, hardened pools stained the walls and bare floor. Lines's torch illumined chunks of dried meat in the corner, and he wretched when he saw they were the skeletal remains of Bryan's fingers.

This was the kill room.

'Sarge?' It was PC Daryl Morgan. Delahaye and Lines swiftly vacated the ghastly pit and slammed the door before the young man could see it. 'We've found bloodstains back at the house,' said Morgan, his eyes on the door.

Chapter Eighty-One

8.38 p.m.

I N THE HALL, ON THE coat pegs, among their jackets as well as Ava's new maroon duffle was her old coat she'd worn on the night she'd found Mickey. She'd stopped wearing it when the warm weather came and then she grew out of it but it still hung there. As the boys tried to comprehend what they'd seen and argued about what to do next, she rummaged in the old coat's pockets to find Nathaniel's mittens that she'd repaired then forgotten to return, and an old blue pencil, blunt at both ends. She took the silver sharpener she'd begun to carry with her for this very purpose, and tapered the old pencil's tips to lethal points. She then tucked it and the gloves deep into her new coat pockets.

She needed the men out of the way. She went into the Front and said, in a loud voice that was as close to Miss Misty as she'd allow, 'I'll stay here and keep the door locked. Paul will take John home and he'll give Luke a lift to the Marlowes' house to tell the police what we've seen – and where it's going.'

They stared at her, aghast. 'Where's it going?' asked Paul, not really wanting but having to know.

'Dowry House – the last block on the Lane,' she said. 'To the roof.'

Chapter Eighty-Two

8.50 p.m.

A VA KNEW WHAT SHE HAD to do: lead the Wolf down the mountain. She must do it soon, before the police brought guns. Last time police brought guns to Rubery it hadn't gone well.

Once upon a time, there had been Nathaniel. He'd been warm, funny, expressive, kind. Now, Nathaniel lived in the skin of the Wolf and whatever was left of Nathaniel wasn't strong enough to throw it off. Ava suspected it was because he didn't want to; he'd not so much given in to his savage side as acquiesced. The world of the Wolf was the world he preferred, and returning from it was an option cast aside. Despite this, or because of it, he still liked Ava.

There was a cordial respect; a connective understanding with Ava because he believed her to be kith or kin . . . but she wasn't either. She certainly didn't feel chosen: she couldn't imagine what he wanted from her, and he probably didn't know why either. It wasn't her *understanding* because she figured he'd resist being understood. He'd developed a taste for losing control with violence, savagery was his high, and he wouldn't want her interrupting him. There was nothing else because she'd nothing to give him. She was just a highly strung weirdo; and all the other things bullies said about her. Being female, however, was an inexplicable advantage: she had power because the Wolf didn't kill girls. The Wolf had just attacked a boy in the open. It was desperate. It meant Nathaniel was losing his good Nathaniel-ness. She doubted she'd be able to reach into the Wolf and bring Nathaniel back, but she might. A caveat in her courage: because it wouldn't harm her didn't mean she wouldn't harm it, if she had to – and she might have to. She wouldn't consider that she might want to.

* * *

Ava pulled on boots, hat, and Nathaniel's sheepskin gloves. She waited until Paul's car was rumbling slowly down Cock Hill Lane then she was out.

No people about: too cold, too dark; too thick with snow. The few cars moved so slowly along the road she wondered if the occupants would be faster walking. Ava ran up the hill as the fresh powder lent her traction, and her breath steamed. When she slid to a halt outside Dowry House foyer, it was snowing again; fat flakes tumbled in lattice patterns. She eschewed the elevator – the Wolf might hear it. She took the stairs, noting the melting paw prints every fourth step until she reached the top floor.

The turret door was wedged open, and she pushed through the gap onto the roof. As her eyes adjusted, she stepped onto a frozen realm of daggered drifts swept either side along the roof ridge, leaving the centre free as a path in a Narnia stage-set; the snow emanating an ethereal cyanic phosphorescence. The gale screamed as she braced against it in defiance, the ground crackling beneath her boots. Her heart sank as she looked down: bones again: the feathers blown into the ether. She pulled her hood further over her forehead and she peered out through streaming eyes at the jagged plane.

One of the drifts created a tall corner around which she was careful to sidle. The Wolf had cleared the roof edge of snow, and was staring into the black void beyond. Its fur ruffled and its tail billowed in the bullying wind, but it was still as still. Adrenaline coursed through Ava at what felt like a thousand miles per hour, making her fingertips tingle and her pulse throb like a bass drum in her throat. Time was a hand pressing on her back, urging her forwards: she lifted her nose to the sky and howled.

Chapter Eighty-Three

THEY WERE SILENT AS PAUL drove down the road. It was slow progress, and there were a couple of vehicles that had obviously been unable to ascend the hill and were parked haphazardly on the kerbs.

'Stop,' said John.

Paul glanced at the boy in his rear-view mirror. 'John?'

'Stop. Now. Please.'

Paul braked and the car slid to a halt. John was out and running back up the Lane before Luke and Paul realised what the slammed door meant. They stared at each other. Paul mentally shook himself and said, 'You go and tell Sergeant Delahaye that thing is at Dowry House.'

Luke was obviously afraid but he nodded. Paul parked the car with the other forsaken vehicles. The orange motorway lights turned the sky to a brown sheet above them, but over the top of Leach Green Lane, they could see flashes of blue light bouncing off the low cloud. Luke would follow the blue light like a nativity star.

After watching Luke sprint under the Flyover towards Russet Lodge, Paul ran after John.

* * *

The Wolf howled in harmony with Ava. The wind snatched the song, and broadcast it wide to the surrounding lacuna so that dogs by firesides, by radiators, on laps or on beds joined in the chorus, communicating a rise-and-fall melody that was aeons old in the dominion between earth and stars.

There was no point in being frightened. She was here now. Turning her back on the Wolf would delay its capture or it might

363

just as well kill her despite Nathaniel still inside it. She withdrew her gloved hands from her pockets then barked once. It trotted towards her, its stride graceful, as if it didn't have long fixed clavicles or a central magnum foramen or flat feet or wing-set scapulae.

It paused a few feet away and tried to catch her scent but the wind stole it with each swooping pass. This close, it was big, its bony head at her waist level, and she could see the patchwork of its pelt. There had been endeavours to taxidermy – the ears were leathered and stiff with amateur attempts to preserve. The underbelly was dark clothing and the whole was strapped on somehow. The wrists were bound by thick leather bands to support and protect the tendons beneath from strain. Her heart sank: *malice aforethought*. If it had modified a costume to better aid and abet its hunting, it wasn't only madness that governed it – it was a will to destroy on purpose, with desire. Pain and madness often mongrels cruelty but sometimes cruelty is born pedigree.

She could see Nathaniel's lower face framed by the jutting mandible that formed a chin strap. She couldn't see his eyes but the weight of his gaze was like a concrete slab. The sockets were full of the reflective gold lenses of vintage goggles she'd seen him wear in all weathers and she guessed they made the world even in colour and depth, be it night with or without snow. He sat on his haunches then, slowly, he removed the glasses and threw them aside. The wind brought her the new stink of the Wolf's rotting hide but also his heat for he was generating warmth like a fever. He wasn't well and, when he stood back to look at her, she saw, with a sadness she barely understood, that all the good in Nathaniel was truly gone. His black eyes glowered beneath the ledge of bone, the distinction of his heterochromia iridum lost in blown pupils rife with agony, lunacy ... and glee.

Ava kept calm. She and the Wolf faced each other whilst the snow flurried, the wind screamed, and the world spun. She extended a hand, and it padded to sniff the proffered glove, recognising it. The Wolf dipped its scabrous head and she touched the bald pate, its stink greater when closer, and she huffed in return. She had listened all her life to animals' words without words – and mimicked. She realised that this ability might save her life.

In stories, films and TV programmes, the villain, when faced with his trapped enemy, would reveal his plans to take over the world; explain why he had to kill and spread his evil then reinforce his reasons with an evil Vincent Price-style laugh. Not this villain: Ava was not a Marguerite Poirier to this Jean Grenier – the time for boasting and explaining had long departed. Ava, facing her villain, expected no reasons or excuses because there never are for murdering children.

She remembered Bryan in his wolf suit, leaning his warm weight against her as she read to him in silly voices: she touched Tom's scar on her lip, her letter to Kelly – their absence from her life because of the Wolf. She thought of Little Adam and how he always expected her to know the answers to his questions about animals. Such memories were cushioned in anger. She turned her back on the Wolf, and walked away.

The Wolf followed for how could it not? Ava knew it had lost its pack, its territory, its prey, and it was alone except for her. She felt as well as heard its rank breath gush in and out of it, as its feet crackled on the bone-strewn floor: dead creatures whose only crime was to cross the Wolf's path between big kills. The Wolf had stolen its fur coat from the very dogs he professed to love. Whatever Nathaniel had been was finished.

At the crux of the roof, John appeared in the doorway of the turret. The shock of seeing him there – unexpected, unpredicted – forced her to stop in her tracks, fear sweeping her calm away in a brutal current. The Wolf rose slowly onto its hind legs, and towered behind her.

Chapter Eighty-Four

THERE IS A STORY ABOUT a man who clung to the top ledge of a skyscraper and was so tired of being terrified of the fall that he let go just to end it. Paul had never understood why a person would kill themselves this way for that reason. He supposed it was similar to President Kennedy's adage: Nothing to fear but fear itself. What he saw in John's face was the fear of fear and the exhaustion it tolled until he made a rash decision to let go.

He'd followed John through the creamy, desolate streets, slipping and sliding in ice and snow, to Dowry House: up the flights of stairs to the top floor instead of the lift because there was no way of telling which method was faster. John was first through the maintenance door with Paul just behind him. He'd time to register John's expression before the boy charged at the monster rearing behind Ava.

The Wolf swept Ava into a snow bank as if she were a rag doll. The force of the hit winded her so she floundered for air. The Wolf leaped at John and Paul tried to shout, but the wind swiped it from his lips. The Wolf was caught in mid-air by Paul in a clumsy rugby tackle that sent them both sprawling in the charnel detritus. It shook itself and slowly turned to face the two youths backing away from it on their haunches. There was no escape now except to jump off the roof and that wasn't much of a choice.

Paul staggered to his feet and the thing charged, its bounding strides preternaturally powerful, and it launched at his throat. John threw Trigger's flick knife open and, as the Wolf sailed over him, he thrust the blade upwards with all his might. The strength taken to hold the weapon aloft as it cut through fabric and flesh almost broke his wrist bones. The Wolf cried out in pain and surprise, its hot blood rained on the churned snow, injured but not fatally. It swung into a loping jog then sprung at the prone John who instinctively held his arms up as a flimsy shield. Paul witnessed, in the Wolf's attack, how the boys had died.

Its strong jaws snatched John's arm and shook him, trying to break the barrier so it could bite into his face and neck. John's thick coat and scarf protected him from the savaging but the powerful jaws crushed his fingers through his woolly gloves, and he cried out in agony. He kicked at the Wolf's slashed underbelly and it roared; its bleeding turned the snow beneath them into gory slush, the boy's screams challenging the wind to a contest that it couldn't win. Paul grabbed the thing by its hindquarters – by the *legs* – then swung it as hard as he could to let it crash into a drift, the impact exploding the brittle ridge into icy shards.

Ava stumbled over to John and lay across him, her arms on Paul's legs, her body shielding them from the bloodied jaws of the Wolf, who snarled and snapped, its growls and rumbles inhuman and loud in their ears, closer and closer, larger and larger. They could smell its breath: of raw meat, and fresh saliva. It crept onto her chest and the boys beneath her felt the weight of it as well. Paul went to kick it but Ava held his legs down. John lay very still.

Chapter Eighty-Five

I T PEERED INTO AVA'S FACE, its eyes bright with insane light. Blood caked its chin and stained its teeth, its breath pluming thick whorls into her face. She was terrified yet she still knew, right in the core of her being, that it wouldn't harm her.

Ava did not flinch from its gaze. She murmured, 'Trigger.'

It stopped panting. It cocked its head to one side then the other. It whined so uncannily like a real dog's puzzled plaintive that their nape hairs spiked. For a fleeting moment, humanity returned to its eyes, the name a spell to calm it. It stepped off her and they all breathed deeply, straightening their squashed bodies. It turned its face into the freezing wind and sniffed. Paul eased out from under then Ava saw him slowly, quietly, take the flick knife from John's undamaged hand. When its gaze returned to their sprawled heap and saw the weapon, it snarled and plunged its teeth into Paul's flesh exposed just above his boots then it bit into his wrist above the hand that held the knife. The crunch of bone was despicable. It was then the Wolf was kicked in the head.

Chapter Eighty-Six

DELAHAYE'S CLEATED BOOT FLASHED ABOVE their heads and kicked the side of the Wolf's head so brutally that splinters from the obliterated skull-helmet pierced the scarred flesh beneath. It lunged at its new pursuer but Delahaye was a grown man, physically fitter, bigger and denser than little boys, so his weight pushed against the Wolf's, pound for pound, leaving track marks in the bloodied slush. His revulsion for this thing with its horror-garb and stink lent him extra strength to administer a solid roundhouse punch to its human face with the other. The Wolf collapsed, but its madness awarded swift recovery. It bit into a drift to clean its teeth and reset its jaw, leaving a bloody smear on the flawless white. It shook itself. Paul had dragged John to the turret and propped him against the door. Delahaye confronted the Wolf with Ava crouched between them.

Despite being there, in the moment, facing the thing he'd been hunting for almost a year, Delahaye still couldn't quite believe that what he saw, touched, smelled and heard, was real. His knuckles bled from impacting bone during the punch but the cold was so cold he barely felt the sting. The Wolf regarded him with a peculiar sardonic interest, recognising him and amused by it. It cocked its head all the better to see him and its paws flexed all the better to claw him. The policeman drew out the truncheon from his waist clip, and the Wolf growled.

It reverted to bipedal stance and its paws snatched Ava by the shoulder, dragging her away. Each time Delahaye tried to pounce on it or sidle around it or raised the truncheon to hit it, the Wolf grabbed Ava by the throat and drew her face closer to its teeth, its message clear: Ava was barter, and if it was harmed then it would harm her. Its bare head was Nathaniel's face but there was no Nathaniel in it.

Chapter Eighty-Seven

AVA'S THICK COAT SAVED HER from the pain but not from the power of the Wolf as it pulled her away from her three graces towards the Sky Den. She didn't fight back. Instead, she sagged, so her dead weight had to be dragged in fits and starts, for dead weight is unhelpful weight as both knew from experience. Inside, she beheld a totally unexpected but welcome calm, warm as sun and bright as day. She knew what she had to do way before this second, in this place, at this time. If the Wolf was threatened, it would forget it protected her and kill her instead. With every drag, she relaxed as if into an eidolon trance. Her clothes were wet through but the cold barely touched her. The Wolf pulled her beyond the bottle-window den and deposited her close to the edge.

Ava beheld a startling flicker of clarity: she knew what she was to the Wolf. The Wolf killed the boys and then placed dead dogs with each of them, to make the dogs feel loved and safe, not the murdered boys accompanying them. She was to be the dead child to the Wolf's dead canine, to keep him company in whatever afterlife deluded, insane murderers believed they had a right to despite the carnage they caused in life. The Wolf wanted to be in nevermore and she was going with it.

Only she wasn't. She wasn't going anywhere except into her own future – miseries, battles and all. Her plan was no plan and she might've run out of time to plan anyway – it was an opportunistic course of action she must instantly recognise and take. Delahaye was following them, she could see him panicking on her behalf, asking the Wolf questions about Nathaniel's dad, where was his dad, where'd he put him, what he'd done to him ... Ava could've told Delahaye where she knew Nathaniel's father was: at Banlock Farm with Nathaniel's mother and grandmother.

The Wolf clearly thought Ava was compliant with terror as it turned its full attention to the encroaching, annoying man. Ava quietly sat on her haunches behind the billowing tail of the Wolf who did not hear her shift because of the bellowing wind. As Delahaye moved forward in jerky incremental inch-long steps like stop-motion animation, the Wolf hunched over, its head level with its jutting shoulders, and prepared to spring.

Ava patted it on the rump.

Surprised, it turned to regard her with Nathaniel's face wrinkled into a vicious snarl. When it lunged to bite her, neck extended, Ava calmly plunged her blue pencil into its brown eye, reversed it then plunged it with all her strength into its throat, into the jugular. The Wolf screamed but it wasn't an animal scream, it was all human, of terror and rage and pain. Blood spurted in rhythmic bursts from Nathaniel's throat as his hands tried to stem the double geysers but to no avail.

'Lady A,' Nathaniel garbled. Delahaye stopped in his tracks, as if knowing any move made would lose his prime suspect forever though the suspect was already lost. Ava suspected Nathaniel had made up his mind since Trigger: he stood at the prow of his sky galleon, beyond which writhed an ocean of darkness. The Wolf took over for the last time, and he leaped into the feathering white, tumbling down and down ... then gone.

Aftermath

EVERYBODY ONLY HAD GOOD THINGS to say about Nathaniel Marlowe. Despite the shock and disbelief throughout the community, however, it was apparent that nobody really knew him at all. As charming and kind as he'd appeared to be, over the past year he'd maintained no close friendships and his classmates couldn't recall talking to him about anything. He'd become a shade in their midst.

The only anchor in his unravelling existence had been his dogs. The pack at Marlowes' scrapyard was partially disbanded – some were rehomed with Mr Harry Marshall, and the rest remained yard guards under the care of Tim and Minty.

Experts discussed and disagreed on what had possibly created a monster out of one so young while the police kept quiet about what they'd learned about Nathaniel from the evidence he'd abandoned in the bunker and the Sky Den.

The news told the world that sixteen-year-old Nathaniel Marlowe, the main suspect in the ongoing police investigation into the recent spate of South Birmingham child murders, had committed suicide after being cornered during a police pursuit. Nathaniel had stabbed and strangled his young victims during uncontrollable rages that had manifested after his traumatic head injury. The families of the murdered boys were unhappy that the cause of their grief had escaped proper justice but were glad he was dead so he'd never hurt anyone ever again.

All this was mostly true.

There was no mention of children present at the time and place of the 'pursuit', and no mention of wolf suits and werewolves.

Children killing children *was* rare ... but not unheard of.

* * *

At Marlowe & Son Breakers Yard, Mr Trent and his SOCO team discovered in one of the old charabanc buses evidence of unsuccessful attempts at amateur taxidermy, and the fails before the successful wolf suits. There was no evidence of flesh and bone but the cruor stains told their own tale – the remains of the flayed dogs were buried at Banlock Farm.

The blood smears at Russet Lodge were outside a room that had clearly been a cell – a cooler, with one mattress, a toilet bucket and locks on the outside. It was clean and carried a faint smell of bleach. It hadn't been used for months until the early hours of that dark day when a terrified, despairing Nick Marlowe had tried to drag his furious, struggling, biting son to the place he usually let him rage off steam – the scratch marks around the door and its frame were an inch deep. This time, however, Nathaniel, fully grown and as big as his father, had completely metamorphosed into his monster and wouldn't calm down, refused to be incarcerated, and had fought to be free. As the Wolf, he'd attacked his father.

Nicholas Marlowe remained in critical condition in hospital. He'd experienced severe concussion, and hypothermia from when his son had driven him to Banlock Farm and laid him across graves in sub-zero temperatures where he remained unconscious for hours. Both the van and car were found with Mr Marlowe at the property. Still in a coma, he'd yet to be told of his son's death, and his crimes, for it seems he was unaware of his son's activities, or even of the garden bunker's existence as Nathaniel had discovered it when he'd put the carousel horses there a year before his accident, and liked having a secret den. In the ambulance, Marlowe had come around long enough to tell the paramedics to look for his boy, 'as he's all I have left of her'.

After Nathaniel's accident, when Nick witnessed his son's psychological meltdown and lived under siege because of its unpredictable outrages, he'd been so concerned for, and afraid of, his son that he'd never once made the connection between Nathaniel and the Rubery child killings. And why would he? His son was a good boy.

The antibiotics Nathaniel had used to treat his own as well as Keith Magaw's injuries were taken from his father's prescription for recurring ear infections.

* * *

Neville Coleman wasn't directly informed of his grandson's death because it was considered to be a kindness to allow him to slip into ignorance as well as dementia.

And Delahaye had been prepared to accept this, resigned to never knowing the full story of why Nathaniel became the Wolf, until Maureen turned up at reception with a photograph of total horror to show him: the Wolf running full pelt towards the camera in its macabre regalia.

'Nev's pretended to be worse than he is for years,' said Maureen. 'I know when he's lying about his dementia but I couldn't tell anyone because I'd get the sack for doubting a patient's diagnosis. He's always known what that thing was. I think he knew right from the off when the first lad was killed, and that's why he hid behind his illness and said nothing. He's lucid, Detective Sergeant, and he has been since that night. I think you should talk to him.'

* * *

Delahaye's footsteps were sharp intrusion in the suspended quiet of the hospital late at night. As he approached Neville Coleman's room, he could hear music faintly playing and recognised Billie Holiday's dulcet tones. In his satchel, Delahaye carried copies of the social service reports of the day Nathaniel Marlowe was forcibly removed from his grandfather's care. Dementia sufferers had difficulty focusing on large amounts of text but if what Maureen had said was right, then Neville Coleman wouldn't have any difficulty.

He stood on the threshold of the old man's room. It was dingy, illuminated only by the muted lights of the corridor. Coleman sat in his armchair in the corner by the window, gazing out at the night. He clutched a tatty teddy bear in his lap.

'Mr Coleman?'

The old man turned to regard Delahaye without surprise. 'Hullo, Detective Sergeant.'

'Good evening, Mr Coleman. Do you know why I'm here?'

Coleman's odd-coloured eyes were evenly black in the dim light, and they narrowed into pitchy slits. 'To tell me who killed that babby on my property.'

More than one 'babby' had been killed in the area since then but it was impossible to tell if Coleman really knew it. Delahaye sat in the opposite armchair and couldn't gauge how authentic the man's dementia was, if at all. If Maureen was right, this old man had fooled people into thinking he was mad for years to protect a grandson who'd grown madder.

It was true Coleman wasn't responsible for Nathaniel's catastrophic head injury, which had detonated such destructive behaviour, but his treatment of the child at Banlock Farm had contributed to Nathaniel's feral violence. Dr Tremblay had said there was often a dormant psychological condition that could be awakened by trauma, and Delahaye suspected that Nathaniel's underlying malady had been roused not by the accident but by what happened during that terrible day when he was taken from Zasha, the pack, and his home.

Delahaye removed the files from the bag and placed them on his lap. Coleman didn't look at them, patient and waiting.

'You had a visitor the other night,' said Delahaye, not a question but Coleman answered as if it was.

'I did,' said Coleman.

'Nathaniel Marlowe,' said Delahaye. 'Your grandson.'

Coleman's slow blink was affirmation.

'How long had been visiting you?' asked Delahaye.

'Since he found out I was here. About two or three years ago,' said Coleman. 'Not regular visits, mind, every so often and always at night.'

'Why didn't you tell anyone about these visits?' Delahaye asked.

'Because I couldn't believe he was real, at first, after being away for so long,' said Coleman. 'And he made me promise not to tell anyone in case he was ... taken away ... again.'

Maureen had told Delahaye that Neville only watched TV for the news so he must know about the spate of child murders in the area over the past year. Delahaye wondered if he'd connected his grandson to those dreadful killings. The old man's flinty gaze was inscrutable.

'He was ... himself ... at first,' Coleman added. 'A fine pup; good bones, good lines.'

Delahaye remembered the little speech Coleman had relayed at the end of their very first meeting, when he'd said, '*Good pups become bad dogs if you're cruel to them, Detective. I should know. Punish 'em too much, too hard, and they turn rogue, they do.*' He'd been talking about Nathaniel, had hinted that his visitor had become a darker presence, had even warned the detectives in a vague way that this was what they should be looking for. There was no way the police could have guessed who Nathaniel was, and what he'd become. As with all tragedies, it was too late now.

'When did Nathaniel stop being ... Nathaniel?' asked Delahaye.

'Late last year. I could tell he'd hurt himself, and he wasn't the same.' Coleman looked blindly out of the window at the freezing night.

'He was the rogue pup you referred to when we first met,' said Delahaye evenly.

Coleman frowned as if he struggled to recall then he nodded. They settled into silence. The wind groaned through the skeletal trees without while Lady Day crooned within.

'The very last time he was here, that night, he frightened me,' said Coleman.

'The very last time?' Delahaye repeated.

'Well, he isn't coming back is he, Detective Sergeant?' said Coleman without a trace of emotion in his voice. 'Maureen tried to hide the news from me but I hear things.'

So, Neville Coleman knew his grandson was the murderer, and that he was dead. Delahaye couldn't find grief in that proud, lined face but then the man had experienced so much loss perhaps he couldn't show more. It was strange he didn't ask questions about how Nathaniel had died because those details hadn't been released to the media.

'He frightened you?' Delahaye prompted.

'The animal had completely taken over,' said Coleman. 'It's harsh to admit it but he's out of his misery now and he can't hurt others because of it.' The clock on the bedside table ticked in time with the pulse point visible at Coleman's throat above his pyjama collar.

'Tell me about the day he was taken from you,' said Delahaye.

Coleman shifted in his chair, the scowl heavy along his brow. 'Why? It's all in that little file there, isn't it?'

'I want to hear about it from you,' said Delahaye.

Colman sighed. 'My mind plays hide-and-seek with memories but I can remember how bad I'd become, I don't need a little report to tell me that. I lived it.' He blinked slowly at Delahaye. 'It was Jip Marlowe who grassed on me, wasn't it?'

Delahaye nodded. 'Nick had tried to take his son from the farm. He'd seen the appalling state of the place and yourself, and you'd threatened him with both the dogs and a shotgun. He'd no choice but to call social services, hoping that they'd give him his son, but with no birth certificate to verify his claim, he couldn't prove he was Nathaniel's father.'

'All of it's my doing. I did so many things wrong thinking I was doing right.' Coleman shook his head.

'Because of the dogs, social services entered your property with armed police,' said Delahaye.

'The dogs that attacked them were shot,' said Coleman. 'They had to hold me back because I was raving. They kicked in the stable door and they found my boy with Zasha ...' Coleman's gaze fell to the floor as if ashamed to continue but Delahaye knew what the police found: a chained-up, muzzled, starving toddler cowering on a makeshift bed with Zasha. Zasha, protecting her human pup, had attacked the police and been shot dead in front of the terrified boy. The police had released Nathaniel from his chain, and, blood-spattered, he had escaped long enough to run to his grandfather only for them to have been violently separated by police and social workers.

'It was a fucking bad day,' said Coleman. His take on events married with the version in the file but there were vital details missing. Neville Coleman blamed himself but there was an underlying defiance that irritated Delahaye.

'Why was Nathaniel chained up?' Delahaye asked. '*Muzzled*, for God's sake? Why was he starving and locked in the dark for days at a time?' It was the detail Delahaye couldn't understand, couldn't forgive, because no matter how deep into grief and depression a man could fall, how could he have done that to his own little grandson? Delahaye wouldn't ask the latter as it smacked too much of sentimental pleading, and sentiment was something Coleman clearly eschewed.

Coleman's gaze was sharp. 'Boys need a stricter hand than girls, Detective Sergeant. Boys are just like dogs – they need to know who the pack leader is, and in the world of wolves correction is harsh. Even so young, Nathaniel was becoming unruly, belligerent. I hated him and I loved him too, and he paid no attention to me, only the dogs. It was when he bit me that I lost my temper because he meant to hurt me even though he lost some of his baby teeth doing it. I know I shouldn't have, but I threw him in the stable, and left Zasha with him to keep an eye on him, seeing how she'd become so much of a mother to the boy.' He rubbed the faint oval scar on his wrist then shrugged. 'Other than his eyes, there wasn't much of my daughter in him.'

'And you forgot to feed him?' asked Delahaye.

The pupils in Coleman's eyes were huge, as dark as the night beyond, his mouth a grim line, the face expressionless, and the hairs rose on Delahaye's nape as he saw in the old man all of Nathaniel. 'I didn't ... *forget*,' said Coleman in gentle correction. 'I just ... *didn't* ... feed *him*.'

There it was: the confession. Nathaniel had become a monster before his father or his foster parents had had time to rectify the damage inflicted. Nothing helped, nothing could bring his victims back, but at least Delahaye had answers as useless as they were now. Shaken by the old man's nonchalance after admitting such a terrible thing, Delahaye stood to leave, but Coleman's hand grabbed his wrist with strength unfettered by age.

'You want to blame me and you can if you want,' said Coleman, releasing Delahaye, and sinking back in the armchair. 'But it weren't me who killed those babbies.'

Epilogue

23rd December, 1981

JUST WHEN YOU THINK YOU can't cope, just when you think
that life can't get any worse and does, just when you think
you'll never get over the shock, the misery, the grief – the
mind folds over and you're still alive, still functioning. You take
whatever lessons you can learn from horror and you move forward.
There is no choice. It's how the strongest humans survive.

In five days, Ava would become fourteen years old: a nonde-
script age about which no songs were written. It was the same
age that Neville Coleman had been when he'd signed up to fight
in the trenches. It was the same age that Mickey had been when
he'd fought then was killed by the Wolf. War and murder, then,
but not songs.

Delahaye vacated the Range Rover and squished through slush
to where Ava waited, leaning against the street sign proclaiming
her new neighbourhood. Ava clocked the red-haired, Sophia
Loren lookalike in the driver's seat, and the telltale glow in
Delahaye's cheeks.

He had a heavy carrier bag dangling from his wrist. He smiled
at her. 'Ava.'

'Delahaye,' she said. He studied her face for breakdown,
insomnia – but he knew he'd find only Ava. They'd corresponded
via telephone and letter but this was the first time they'd met in
person since the Night of the Wolf.

'How's your new room?' he asked.

'Mine!' she said, and he laughed.

He glanced around at the tidy cul-de-sac with its neat houses.
'How's Mr Bax?' he asked.

Ava shrugged. 'Behaving.'

'If that changes, you call me, yes?'

Ava nodded. He handed her the carrier bag and she saw a manila file, a few envelopes, and a small wrapped gift. He also handed her a folded piece of paper. 'It was found in the Sky Den,' said Delahaye.

She opened it and saw it was a list. There were over a hundred boys' names written into sections, local areas, and beside each name was written a confectionary: *Jacob Knott – chewy nuts; Lee Smith – jelly babies* ... It was a list of potential victims, and the bait to tempt them. He saw her tremble as she recognised some of those names but the look of relief told him she couldn't find John Eades' name because he wasn't on it. She refolded it, handed it back to Delahaye and wiped her hand on her coat.

'It's a horrible thing,' she said. Delahaye knew she'd have to carry for the rest of her life the secret knowledge that some of the boys she knew had been a hunter's target ... but not John. 'Why show it to me?'

'You needed to see that John's name wasn't on it,' said Delahaye. 'You'd want to know and if I'd said he wasn't on it you'd never have believed me.'

'This is true,' she said.

'The more important the victim, the more expensive the sweets Nathaniel gave them,' said Delahaye.

'The sugar mouse for Bryan,' said Ava.

'Yes,' said Delahaye. 'Nathaniel got his friend Karl to steal certain sweets from Hardy's Gifts then Nathaniel gave them to certain children. They had to keep his generosity secret, which they did.'

He knew she didn't like Karl so he said, 'I believe Karl when he said he didn't know, Ava. He told me he stole them as a favour to Nathaniel. They were friends. I don't think he'll ever get over it.'

She nodded, scuffed her boot in the slush then said mischievously, 'I saw Dr Tremblay on telly last night,' and Delahaye grinned. Dr Tremblay wanted to interview Ava but Delahaye had made excuses because the joke was, after one session with Ava, Tremblay would probably be the one needing therapy.

'There are scrapbooks of Nathaniel's drawings I'd like you to look at, and a couple of copies of his autopsy X-rays,' he said. It didn't cross his mind not to trust her or that speaking to a child about such things was abnormal.

'X-rays,' she said, honoured.

'We are our bones,' Delahaye murmured.

'We are,' said Ava. She nodded towards the woman waiting in the car. 'Lady friend?'

'Fingers crossed,' Delahaye said. 'She's Professor Angela Simmons, the forensic pathologist who took care of our boys.' *And Nathaniel.*

Ava brightened, and waved at the woman who waved back.

'Little Adam's asking to see you,' said Delahaye. 'Have you seen John recently?'

'He visited yesterday,' said Ava. 'His hand was bandaged. He's given everyone the excuse of tripping over on the ice and falling on it. His granddad had studied the War Room every time we'd left it, and he'd known we'd been conducting our own investigation into the murders.'

But only Ava and Delahaye knew the exact role Ava played in Nathaniel's death. Delahaye had explained Nathaniel's eye and head injuries as those sustained by his defending himself with the only weapon he had.

Paul Ballow and Luke Bax would never speak of that night. It was because they were loyal to Ava and it was because the death of a child-killer pardoned the visceral appeal of eye-for-an-eye justice. There was also the possibility that nobody would have believed them if they'd said anything.

Her mother and sisters would never know, and Delahaye would never tell them even though he really ought to. Ava might have been killed, after all, but she hadn't been. Delahaye was sure that night would catch up with her, and that she would feel it all to relive it in bad dreams and waking nightmares, but not yet. Past trauma was like a predator in that it waited for when you were at your most vulnerable or your most happy then it pounced.

From under her coat, Ava presented Delahaye with all of her Red Books. He accepted them with surprise, obviously pleased that she'd remembered him saying he'd like to see them. 'Are you sure, Ava?'

'I don't need them anymore,' she said, tapping her temple. 'I have it all in here.' She had a new interest to test her anyway.

Delahaye extended his hand and she shook it. 'Thank you always, Ava.'

* * *

In the wonderful privacy of her own room, Ava pulled out the varied contents of the manila file. She studied the X-ray copies of Nathaniel's head and neck.

The human skull, the most identifiable of any species, and heavily laden with symbolism in every culture, is a symmetrical 3-D jigsaw, composed of twenty-two bones – fourteen facial and eight cranial – and thirty-two teeth. Much can be made of cephalic indexes and cranial capacities, but the skull's main functions were to house and protect the oversized, incredible human brain and scaffold the muscles that control the expressive human face. Professor Simmons had highlighted in red pen the odd little notch in Nathaniel's magnum foramen that had developed due to his holding his head up while on all fours since childhood but this subtle anomaly paled into insignificance to the impact trauma caused from falling from a great height, and the older injuries caused by his accident the year before. The right side of his face was smashed, but the left side was intact, and Ava experienced a wave of sorrow as she traced with her fingertip the spectral shadow behind his beautiful mask.

She tucked the X-ray back into the folder and retrieved the scrapbooks. In them were drawings, childlike yet obviously already proficient with proportion and perspective, and all signed by Nathaniel at various ages from five to ten years old. The subject of each picture was the same: a small happy boy surrounded by a pack of happier dogs. Like Ava, Nathaniel had preferred to render more detail on the animals rather than the human figures and, when she looked closely, the dogs had human eyes and the boy had dog's eyes – he hadn't replicated his heterochromia iridum in any sketch.

Nathaniel had once been happy. His true happiness had been running wild with his grandfather's dogs, and Zasha, as surrogate mother. He'd loved his grandfather dearly despite the old man's neglect but the boy hadn't felt neglected in the embrace of the pack; he'd been safe, secure; free. When Nathaniel was stolen twice, it had frightened him, he had become mistrustful when he'd been forced to learn that two-legs were the only good and four-legs were bad. The accident might have made him mad but not exclusively – some seed of awful had grown quickly thick after his near-death experience. His grievance about being thrust from happy and into unhappy, his envy for the boys he saw around him, who were loved and knew their place in that love, had spawned pulsing rages. A lost temper was its own freedom, an exaltation that rivalled that on the run in the hills. Killing was the reward for withholding for so long before unleashing. Like all hunters, his desire to hurt was nothing personal – it was just easier to kill the small ones with the soft throats and softer underbellies, be they feather, fur or human flesh. Killing reset a balance long since neglected. The dogs he'd loved whether or not they were his own: the lost and missing were given the gift of a boy to love them into the afterlife. He'd come to this ritual when he'd found the fox at the mouth of the den in which he'd laid Mickey.

The more recent drawings were the designs for the wolf suits, ugly in their macabre magnificence – further proof he'd deliberately fed the beast within and starved the saint without. He'd chosen evil and learned to enjoy it.

As ill as Nathaniel was, he'd become a man, and the reason why bad men do bad things is because they want to – and sod the consequences. No excuses or reasons would convince her otherwise because such soft comprehension led to sentiment, which had no place, for it allowed evil to thrive unchecked, and mocked the bereaved. For Ava, it would have to be Mercy, for Mercy unlocked ignorance and ushered empathy through its heavy doors just once.

Ava suspected the Wolf kept Trigger alive because there had been something about the Scottish boy that had reminded Nathaniel of Mickey. Mickey had been his one regret, his mistake, and he hadn't wanted to make the same terrible decision, the same horrible choice. Mickey's murder had been the catalyst for the Wolf to take over Nathaniel because it meant his rage could be truly free to rampage, but he hadn't *wanted* to kill his friend – and he hadn't wanted to kill Trigger. The boy's escape had caused the Wolf's mask to slip until the urge became too strong to deny.

Because murder cleansed the anger for a while, he'd believed himself cured and happy – but he was neither and it had become his nature.

Monsters born and monsters made. Monsters would be her new hobby: the study of the rogue hunters of humans. She retrieved all her father's *Crime & Punishment* magazine folders from the War Room, and she had obtained the very few books of the subject from the library. She had new *purple* notebooks to fill with her observations. She had already begun with her collection of 'vampires' from Germany during the first decades of the twentieth century: Peter Kurten had been the first she'd learned about but there were others: like Fritz Haarmann, Karl Denke, Carl Grossmann ...

Ava tucked the scrapbook and folder under a box beneath her bed then rummaged in the carrier bag for the other items. She opened a Christmas card signed by the whole of the investigation team, and another from Steve Lines. She opened the note from Delahaye attached to the gift and it simply said, *You never know.* She unwrapped the present and found a slender silver box. Inside was a set of beautiful, new blue pencils sharpened at both ends.

Ava smiled.

Acknowledgments

There are many people I will thank for their faith and support.

A massive thank you goes to my agent, Luigi Bonomi. You have been my rock throughout this process, and had confidence in my writing right from those first 1000 words for the Daily Mail's First Novel competition.

A huge thank you to my publisher, Ben Willis, and the lovely team at Bonnier Books for seeing something special in this dark tale of a strange girl with macabre interests. Thank you for keeping me on track and for your guidance in helping me to create a better book.

Thanks to Peter James for the coolest early review!

To the Rubery Past Facebook page, to its administrators and members whose photographs, information and reminiscences of The Village have been crucial to corroborating my own history and memories while writing the book.

Thank you to retired DCI Carl Flynn for answering my often random questions.

Many thanks to David Carson for your friendship, and your recollections of our shared time at the same school and area have been invaluable.

Special thanks goes to my three graces, my dearest friends: Jackie Harvey for always knowing that this would happen and whose faith and friendship I couldn't do without; to Shelagh Brady, my first and constant reader, who loved Ava and DS Delahaye right from the start; and to Sally – my champion and guardian angel. You are all beloved and appreciated.

Thanks to my sister, Claire – always.

And the most exuberant thanks goes to my husband Steve and my son Joe for giving me the patience, time and space to write and just get on with it. With your love and support, these are the best gifts.